ECHOES

ERIN GRADY

BERKLEY SENSATION, NEW YORK

THE BERKLEY PUBLISHING GROUP
Published by the Penguin Group
Penguin Group (USA) Inc.
375 Hudson Street, New York, New York 10014, USA
Penguin Group (Canada), 10 Alcorn Avenue, Toronto, Ontario M4V 3B2, Canada
(a division of Pearson Penguin Canada Inc.)
Penguin Books Ltd., 80 Strand, London WC2R 0RL, England
Penguin Group Ireland, 25 St. Stephen's Green, Dublin 2, Ireland (a division of Penguin Books Ltd.)
Penguin Group (Australia), 250 Camberwell Road, Camberwell, Victoria 3124, Australia
(a division of Pearson Australia Group Pty. Ltd.)
Penguin Books India Pvt. Ltd., 11 Community Centre, Panchsheel Park, New Delhi—110 017, India
Penguin Group (NZ), Cnr. Airborne and Rosedale Roads, Albany, Auckland 1310, New Zealand
(a division of Pearson New Zealand Ltd.)
Penguin Books (South Africa) (Pty.) Ltd., 24 Sturdee Avenue, Rosebank, Johannesburg 2196, South
Africa

Penguin Books Ltd., Registered Offices: 80 Strand, London WC2R 0RL, England

This is a work of fiction. Names, characters, places, and incidents either are the product of the author's imagination or are used fictitiously, and any resemblance to actual persons, living or dead, business establishments, events, or locales is entirely coincidental.

ECHOES

A Berkley Sensation Book / published by arrangement with the author

PRINTING HISTORY
Berkley Sensation edition / December 2004

Copyright © 2004 by Erin Grady.
Cover photo of woman by Alexa Garbarino/Photonica.
Cover photo of woods by Getty One.
Cover design by George Long.
Interior text design by Kristin del Rosario.

ISBN: 0-425-20073-6

BERKLEY® SENSATION
Berkley Sensation Books are published by The Berkley Publishing Group,
a division of Penguin Group (USA) Inc.,
375 Hudson Street, New York, New York 10014.
BERKLEY SENSATION and the "B" design are trademarks belonging to Penguin Group (USA) Inc.

PRINTED IN THE UNITED STATES OF AMERICA

10   9   8   7   6   5   4   3   2   1

"OH MY GOD . . ."

Tess couldn't take her eyes off the covered wagon as it stopped on the far shore of the river. Two women and a small boy sat on the bench.

Tess stared at them while in her head a frantic voice whispered, *Not real, not real, not real*. She clenched her eyes tight, praying that when she opened them again she would be gone from here. Back in her car . . . back in a world that made sense.

In the space of a moment, the man on horseback arrived at the wagon, and the rest of the world became a diaphanous fabric of colors and shapes that blended without meaning. But none of it was real. It couldn't be—

The younger woman on the wagon bench turned and caught Tess in a penetrating stare, pulling Tess forward as the sound of the river and pounding rain faded beneath the hammering of her heart. Tess wanted to scream.

Not real, not real, not real, not real!

Suddenly, the shout of confusion in Tess's head was silenced as the moment unfurled and snapped like a banner in the wind. Tess recoiled at the rush of strange, overwhelming emotions that entwined with her own. She felt her identity slipping away and reached out, desperate to hold on to herself. But she couldn't break free. She couldn't pull her gaze from the woman's pale face, or the anguish in her eyes.

The rider called the woman's name, his voice deep and compelling.

As one, Tess and the woman faced him . . .

continued . . .

ACKNOWLEDGMENTS

I have been very fortunate to have champions of my writing, without whom this book would never have found its way to the shelves. My sincerest thanks go to Alicka Pistek, of the Alicka Pistek Literary Agency, and Susan McCarty, of Berkley, for their insight, editing, and support.

For their technical expertise and willingness to read early versions, I thank: Sharon and King Ackermann, Scott Adair, Sue Adams, Judi Barker, Patti Clavier, Rebecca Goude, Karen Griffith, Ross Kasminoff, Mary Rose Rhodus, John Scott, Val Swanson, and James Wick. Special thanks to the Thomas family for letting me borrow the wonderful name "Rancho Almosta," and to Hailey and Taylor Alcaraz for their patience, understanding, and love.

And of course, my most heartfelt thanks to fellow author Lynn Coulter, for her talent, dedication to the craft, and honest feedback. Words cannot express my gratitude.

chapter one

"*WE shouldn't be here, Mommy.*"

Caitlin had spoken the words the minute the tiny town of Mountain Bend came into view through the windshield of their '83 Datsun. But Tori had refused to listen to the solemn warning in her seven-year-old daughter's voice with the same single-minded determination she used to deny late-payment notices and speeding tickets.

In the three months that had passed since then, Tori had finally grasped what Caitlin knew all along. Unpaid fines and fiercely worded credit statements couldn't kill them.

Staying in Mountain Bend could.

Gravel sprayed as she skidded into her drive, shifting into park before the car even came to a stop. She jumped out and rushed up the steps to her front door, fumbling with her keys as she glanced back the way she'd come. No telltale clouds of dust trailing up the dirt road. Yet.

She slammed the door behind her and locked it. A moment to catch her breath, and then she took the stairs up two at a time. Her sweater stuck to her back where perspiration had pooled between her shoulder blades. The sour smell of fear clung tight to her skin.

At first sight, Mountain Bend had seemed a tranquil paradise to Tori. Nestled low in a basin between the rugged peaks of the Sierra Nevadas and a shocking blue sky, it looked like heaven. She'd rolled down her window, taking a deep breath of air scented with eternal Christmas. What possible wrong could be hidden in the quaint little haven?

We shouldn't be here, Mommy . . .

She'd been irritated with Caitlin for saying something so negative before they'd given the place a chance. Before they'd even stopped the car.

"Of course we should be here," she'd said sharply. "Maybe now we can finally settle down."

Victoria France, Tori to anyone who knew her, had believed it, too.

She should have listened, she thought now as she glanced at the clock on the wall. She should have turned tail and run. But Tori had been running her entire life and she'd ended up here all the same.

She took her overnight bag from the hall closet and darted into Caitlin's room. A pink-and-white lace comforter covered her daughter's bed. Caitlin made it each and every morning. Not because Tori asked her to. Tori never even made her own bed. Her room was knee deep in clothes, shoes, and boxes she didn't pretend she planned to unpack. Not Caitlin. Her bedroom was her private sanctuary. Order in a chaotic world she had no way of understanding or controlling.

In this way, as in so many others, Caitlin reminded Tori of her sister. Caitlin should have been her sister's daughter. Lord knows, her life would have been better, easier . . . saner.

Tears of frustration burned Tori's eyes as she grabbed a few necessities for Caitlin and stuffed them into the bag. To have come all this way . . . To have met the one man who could stop the madness that had always directed her life . . . And then to realize that nothing she could do would change anything that was to come. . . . She wanted to shout her rage.

Instead she hurried to her own room and grabbed a change of clothes from the pile on the floor. She couldn't risk taking the time to pack more. Her breath came in harsh gasps and her throat was raw from it. She caught sight of herself in the mirror as she passed it. Wild-eyed and scared, she looked as if she'd seen the resurrection of the devil himself. Perhaps she had.

"It'll be okay," she said aloud.

They'd find someplace new to live, she continued silently this time. Someplace where dreams didn't become nightmares.

Where nightmares didn't step from the dark and draw breath in the light of day.

As if called by her thoughts, the wall in front of her shimmied, shimmered like oil on water and terrifying images streamed across its surface.

"Go away," she breathed.

But by coming here, Tori had unwittingly crossed more than a border into a new town. Now she was trapped in an echo that went on and on until she couldn't distinguish her own screams from those that had been waiting for her to take that final, fatal step.

She couldn't stop it. She couldn't understand it. She couldn't tell anymore what was real, what was not . . .

She had to stay focused. She would grab the money, pick up Caitlin from school, and they'd head for New York. God knew it wouldn't be the first time she'd shown up homeless at her sister's door.

Overnight bag in hand, she hurried back downstairs. All she had to do was get away from this place. Get away now. But even as the words resounded in her head, a noise reached her, one that mocked the futility of her efforts and stopped her mad race. The lock on the front door jiggled and the deadbolt slid back with a final click. Tori hesitated, not wanting to accept what she saw, but then the doorknob turned.

chapter two

THE phone hadn't stopped ringing since Tess Carson walked in the door at eight that morning. Complaints, questions, orders, misorders, reorders. One after another the lines on her phone lit up. She'd been there a full hour before she escaped her desk long enough to pour herself a cup of coffee, which she immediately spilled. Lunch came and went, leaving her unsatisfied with her vending machine fare of Fritos and Diet Pepsi, but too busy to do anything about it. The rest of the afternoon passed in a blur and it was almost four when she finally looked up and realized the day was nearly over. Across the hall, she saw her friend Sara packing up to leave.

"I've had it. I can't take any more," Sara said.

Tess stretched her stiff muscles and groaned. "I didn't realize it was so late."

"I know. This felt like a really bad Monday."

Tess had joined NYC Supply and Sales a few years ago and quickly learned that the pace was never predictable. There were crazy days like this and then there were incredibly dull days when she trolled the Internet and wrote e-mails to everyone she knew for lack of anything better to do.

Sara came over and perched on the gray counter in Tess's cubby. "What'd you do on your date last night?" she asked. "Dinner, movie, wild sex?"

"Not quite," Tess said. "We did have dinner, though. The Rainbow Room."

"Rockefeller Center. Very nice." Sara waited, brows raised. "And . . . ?"

"*And* I spilled a giant glass of water all over his leather coat. *And then* he took me home."

"Was he mad?"

Tess sighed. "No, actually he was really nice about it. He acted like I had a defective glass or something."

Sara rolled her eyes. "What a jerk. So he was too nice. What else was wrong with him?"

"I don't know, Sara. There was nothing wrong with him . . . there just wasn't anything *right* with him either. He kept pausing in the middle of these long, drawn-out stories and I never knew if it was my turn to talk, so I kept interrupting him and then we'd have these awful silences while we waited for the other to finish. It was just awkward the whole night."

"I hate when that happens."

"Do you think it happens to me a lot? I mean, lately I've been thinking that maybe I'm too picky. My sister falls in love every time she's gets close enough to smell a man's cologne. I can't even make it to a second date."

"Maybe they're not wearing the right cologne."

Maybe. But after she got home last night, she couldn't stop thinking about it. It wasn't like she was desperate for a man—far from it. She was so busy most of the time, she didn't know how she'd fit a man into her life. But she was frustrated by the feeling that she was missing something. Something or someone.

She was coasting, never really liking anything she did, but never disliking it enough to change it. This morning she'd had to force herself to come to work and tonight she'd have to force herself to go home. She sighed, looking around her colorless cubicle with distaste. She was twenty-eight years old. Shouldn't she at least have an idea about what she wanted?

The phone started ringing again.

"Ignore it," Sara said. "It's time to go home."

"I know, but I've got a couple of things I need to finish up anyway." She waved bye to Sara with her free hand and pinned the receiver between her shoulder and ear with the other. "NYC Supply and Sales, Tess Carson," she answered.

"Ms. Carson? This is Craig Weston speaking."

"Hello, how can I help you, Mr. Weston?"

"I'm the principal of Mountain Bend Elementary—calling you from California."

California wasn't exactly the other side of the world, but he said it like it should mean something to her. She flipped through her mental Rolodex trying to place the account. T-shirts for a fund-raiser? Literacy folders? "Mountain Bend Elementary?" she repeated softly.

And then it came to her. She sat back and covered her face with her hand. Mountain Bend, California. Tori. What kind of trouble was her sister in now?

"I'm calling because you're listed on Caitlin France's school records as the person to contact in case of an emergency."

"Has something happened?"

Across the walkway, Sara was just stepping out of her cubicle, coat and purse in hand. She paused at the sharp tone of Tess's voice.

"Caitlin's mother didn't pick her up from school today and no one's heard from her."

"What do you mean, no one's heard from her? Where is Caitlin now?"

"She's here and she's fine. However, our attempts to reach Caitlin's mother have been unsuccessful."

"You tried her cell phone?"

Sara set her purse on Tess's counter and watched her with concern.

"Yes, no answer. Not that cell phones work all that well out here. We're a bit isolated."

"What time was she supposed to be there?"

"A couple of hours ago—we had early dismissal today for parent-teacher meetings. Ms. France missed her appointment for that as well."

Frowning, Tess looked at the pictures tacked to her gray cubby walls. She'd vacationed with her sister and niece last fall. They'd gone to Disneyland, worn mouse ears, and had their picture taken with the chief mouse himself. Tori smiled back from the photos, dark as a gypsy and as predictable as the wind.

"I put off calling right away, hoping of course that she'd make an appearance," he continued. "Honestly, Ms. France is not known for her punctuality, but we did expect to see her by now."

It didn't take much to read between the lines of that one. Tess knew firsthand how unreliable her sister was. If they'd been talking about anyone else, Tess's first reaction would have been worry, but where her sister was concerned . . .

"Our records don't show a number for Mr. France. Perhaps you know how to reach him?"

"There is no Mr. France. I mean, there was at one time, but he's not involved with Caitlin at all. I don't think he's ever even seen her."

"I see." Mr. Weston's pause felt weighted. "The problem is, school has been out for some time and there's no place for Caitlin to go. I realize you're in New York, but you are the only person she has listed to contact for emergencies. Normally I would be calling someone local who could just swing over and pick her up after school." His statement trailed into a question.

"And that's why you're calling? You want me to come get her?" A mixture of resignation and disbelief washed over her—although how she could be surprised by anything that came with a call concerning her sister was a mystery. Beside her, Sara mouthed, "To California?" Tess nodded.

"Well, yes, I was calling to have her picked up," Mr. Weston said, answering her blunt question. "I mean, that's usually what happens in situations like this. But if it's not possible for you to come, I can contact the sheriff's department and they'll take her into custody until—"

"Sheriff's department?"

"They'll bus her up to Piney River and put her in the shelter—"

"Shelter? Why there? Isn't there some kind of after-school program or daycare center?"

"I wish there was. But we're just a little community and we depend on Piney River for help in these areas. It's not as bad as you're thinking it is, I'm sure."

"I doubt Caitlin would agree with you there." Tess raked

her fingers through her short hair. The thought of her niece being sent to a shelter made her stomach clench. Dammit, what was Tori thinking, not being there when school was out? Didn't she remember how it felt to stand on the curb after everyone else had been picked up and worry about what happened next? How could she put Caitlin in the same situation?

"I wish I had another option," Mr. Weston was saying, "but I don't have anyone else to call—"

"Sure. I understand." Tess looked at the picture of her smiling niece and let out a deep breath. There *was* no one else to call. There never was, just as there was never a choice as to whether or not Tess would drop everything and come to the rescue. It was a pattern that had repeated many times in their lives. But what if this time something really had happened? Tori was unreliable, but not when it came to Caitlin.

"Okay," Tess said. "I'm on my way. I mean, as soon as I can book a flight. Can you at least keep her until I get there?"

Without a word, Sara went back to her cubby and picked up the phone. Tess caught the word "reservations" before Mr. Weston spoke again.

"Keep her? Well, that's not—"

"I know, not what's usually done in cases like this, but please. I can fax you written permission if that would help."

He gave a soft chuckle. "Fortunately there are *some* advantages to being a small town. The bureaucrats don't look our way too often. I think we can bend the rules a little. What time can you be here?"

Good question. She'd gain three hours going west, but . . . "I need to check into flights, tie up a few loose ends." Still on the phone, Sara gave her a thumbs-up signal. "Why don't you give me your number? I'll call you back as soon as I've booked my ticket."

"That sounds fine." He gave her his office and home numbers. "I'll have to pull some strings, but I'll work out some arrangements for her until you arrive."

"Thank you, Mr. Weston. There's one more thing. Where *is* Mountain Bend exactly?"

"We're a couple hours east of Sacramento or several hours west of Salt Lake. More or less in the middle of nowhere."

The middle of nowhere. How appropriate.

"I know it's crazy," Tess said, yanking shirts from her closet and tossing them on her bed. "But what choice do I have?"

Sara pulled them off the hangers and began folding. "I know. Poor little kid. I'm sure she's scared and worried. Have you called the police yet?"

"Tori hasn't been missing that long. Believe me, I know from experience they won't start looking for her yet."

Sara frowned. "You know from experience?"

"Oh yes," Tess said, moving to the bathroom for her toiletries. "Tori's a pro at the disappearing act."

"You never told me that."

"It's not my favorite topic. And since Caitlin was born, she's been more, I don't know, more stable. At least I thought so, but maybe I was just fooling myself. Mr. Weston made it clear that he's fed up with her always being late. Why else would he have been so quick to ship a little kid off to a shelter?"

Sara shook her head. "Maybe he's some crotchety old fart who lives to enforce rules."

"Maybe." Tess stepped in her closet and quickly changed her clothes. "When we were kids, Tori was always running away. She loved to piss off the Colonel."

"The Colonel?"

"Daddy Dearest."

"You called him the Colonel? Did you salute him too?"

"Only when he came in the room."

"Wow. How about you?" Sara asked, trying to organize the items Tess had thrown in the bag.

"How about me what?"

"Did you like to piss off the Colonel?"

Tess shook her head emphatically. "No way. He was a man of God—a chaplain—but he wasn't a man to cross. It wasn't pretty when he'd catch her."

"Where was your mom during all this? In the mess hall?"

"Not exactly. She was locked away in a funny farm." Tess tried to keep it light, but her voice betrayed her.

Sara looked embarrassed. "I didn't know. I'm sorry, Tess."

"What can I say? We're a colorful family."

A picture of Tess and Tori sat on Tess's dresser. Sara lifted it and stared at the smiling sisters. "Are you sure you weren't adopted? You don't look anything like her."

Tess paused, holding a handful of underwear, and looked over Sara's shoulder at the picture. Tori was a mixture of darkness and vivid color. Beside her sister, Tess had always felt transparent.

"She looks like my mom. I got the honor of looking like the Colonel." Tess crammed her underclothes into the suitcase and shut it. "I keep thinking of the last time Tori did this. I got a call from the cops at three A.M. Tori was gone, her boyfriend's place was trashed, and the guy's brother was sure they were both dead. I spent three days in a panic, a fourth convinced she'd been murdered, and then, lo and behold, who should come strolling up on the fifth. Tanned, rested, and stunned that anyone might have been *worried* about them."

"Where were they?"

"They'd had a fight and then took off to make up someplace romantic. It's the way she is."

"So why are you running around like a maniac to get there now?"

As Tess pulled her bag off the bed, she looked at her friend, answers coming at her in images that would take too long to explain. Finally she said, "Because she's my sister. We grew up with the Colonel preaching do unto others while he acted like God himself. We moved every five minutes, so neither one of us had any friends. And after my mom checked into La La Land—well, it wasn't exactly the nurturing environment you might imagine. We were there for each other, though. She and Caitlin are the only family I have left. I love them. And besides, Caitlin's just a little girl. She shouldn't have to pay for Tori's mistakes."

chapter three

WHEN the call came in that afternoon, Deputy Hector Ochoa didn't think much of it. Mountain Bend had its drunks and troublemakers like everyplace else, but they rarely got going before nine or ten at night. A call before suppertime was as likely a wrong number as anything serious. He didn't even bother to put down the sports page as he answered the phone.

The voice on the other end, however, got his attention. Hector listened for a moment, his mouth going dry before he assured the caller they'd be right there. His excitement made him speak overly loud and he banged down the receiver.

Sheriff Smith looked up from the business section with a frown. He'd been gone most of the day and had only just plopped down in his chair to grumble over the stock market.

"That was Grant Weston," Hector said.

"The actor?"

Hector nodded. "He said he needs us out at his ranch right away."

"What happened? His hair get messed up?"

"Sounded like he'd had the crap scared out of him."

"He didn't tell you what the problem was?"

Hector faltered. "Well, no."

"And you didn't bother to ask?" Smith demanded. "For Christ's sake, Ochoa, didn't they teach you anything at the academy?" With a muttered curse, he flung down his paper and stood. Every day of Smith's thirty years in the Chicago PD showed on his face and in the hard eyes he pinned Hector with. "You always ask. You don't know if he's got a gun to his head or his cat's stuck in a tree, do you? Do you?"

Knowing he'd just shot himself in the foot—*again*—Hector shook his head.

"No," Smith said.

To his credit, he left it at that. He didn't need to say more. From his first day Sheriff Eugene Smith had made two things clear: One—he'd come to Mountain Bend this year to escape the grind of big-city crime, not to work with amateurs and idiots. And two—never, under any circumstances, call him Eugene.

Silently Hector followed the sheriff to the car and got in. Smith eased himself into the driver's seat, his paunch making a tight fit beneath the wheel. He claimed to have given up the bottle the same time that he'd tossed his last pack of Marlboros in the trash, but he still looked like a man who'd spent too many years drinking whiskey straight and inhaling smoke. Fine red capillaries made a map across his nose before branching into tributaries of abuse over the rest of his face. The skin beneath was ruddy and puffy. But Smith's eyes were a sharp, cold blue that missed nothing.

They made the short drive to the Weston Ranch in silence while Hector tried to clear his head and focus on the possibilities of what might await them instead of dwelling on what a dumb rookie he was. He hadn't been exaggerating when he'd said Grant Weston sounded scared. Scared of what? That was the question Hector should have asked.

Angry with himself, he stared out the window as the ranch came into view. Once it had looked like something out of the movies. The pastures had been the lush color of money and the fences bright and unending. The kind of place where bad things never happened.

Now the fences were broken down and the paint worn to the dull gray of neglect. The paddocks were still green, and a scattering of horses grazed on the waving grasses, though the stables beyond looked like they could be toppled by a determined breeze. The house itself had a hard time appearing anything but impressive, though. The sprawling porch and overhanging verandahs gave the illusion of success and prosperity. Even the granite basin of mountainsides surrounding it seemed to hold the acreage in a protective embrace.

Smith brought the cruiser to a stop in front of the house and gave him a warning look. "Can I trust you not to get excited and shoot someone, or do I need to take your gun away?"

"I can handle myself," Hector mumbled.

Smith snorted. "Well, at least try not to shoot me, all right?"

Grant Weston was waiting for them on the porch steps. The last time Hector had seen him was a few years ago in his last movie—an action flick where Grant had kicked ass and slept with both a beautiful blonde and a gorgeous redhead. Grant wasn't one of those pansy actors who looked like they might moonlight as a woman. He was bred from mountain ranchers and he was built to handle the load. He was a man's man. The kind who always beat the bad guy and *always* got the girl.

Hector didn't know how or why he'd given up all that and moved back to Mountain Bend. No one really knew why he'd left Hollywood behind. But like the ranch, he'd changed.

As Hector and the sheriff approached, Grant kept his eyes fixed on the small herd of horses grazing in the meadow. He sat with his forearms resting on his knees, hands hanging between. No gun to his head, Hector was relieved to see. He wore a Harley-Davidson T-shirt, faded blue jeans, and work boots caked with mud. Even sitting, there was no mistaking the size and power of him, but he looked diminished somehow. And his skin was the gray color of river rock. High on his right cheek there was a dark smudge of black. Two other black prints smeared the front of his shirt. A slight tremor shook his dangling hands.

Sheriff Smith strode to the porch and put one shiny boot on the step next to where Weston sat. He waited for Grant to say something, letting the silence ask the questions. Hector had seen the sheriff reduce a belligerent drunk driver to a babbling baby once, without saying a word.

Grant just sat staring at his horses.

A cold bead of unease slipped down Hector's spine at his vacant expression. He scanned the area around them, frowning at the strong singed odor that hung in the air.

"What's going on, Grant?" Smith asked at last.

Grant finally looked at them. His eyes were swollen and red rimmed, dark with shock. He opened his mouth and closed it again, as if searching for an appropriate response to the question. At last he simply said, "Out back." He jerked his head in the direction of the front door. Hector supposed that meant he and the sheriff should cut through the house rather than take the long way around.

"What's out back?" Smith asked.

Mute, Grant shook his head as tears filled his eyes and his shoulders began to shake. Finally he covered his face with both hands and sobbed.

Smith waited a moment, obviously hoping Grant would pull himself together and offer an explanation. All Grant managed was to choke out something that sounded like "Dad," and nothing else.

Cursing under his breath, Smith drew his weapon and climbed up to the porch with Hector a step behind. He glanced back over his shoulder as Hector pulled out his own gun, silently repeating the warning that had been given in jest in the car. Flushing, Hector nodded.

Their boots made hollow *thunk* sounds in the velvet quiet. The shadows inside stretched down a long, narrow hallway that led from the front door into the cavern-like house. Heavily framed portraits dating back to the 1800s lined the walls from floor to ceiling alongside pictures of Westons taken with Calvin Coolidge, Babe Ruth, John Wayne. Westons had settled Mountain Bend, and in the old days, they'd been high society and prominent leaders. Even newcomers like Smith knew who they were.

Hector had never been inside the house, but kitchens seemed to occupy the same place no matter where you went and back doors invariably opened off them. The Weston place was no exception. Hector tapped Smith's shoulder and indicated the way. Carefully checking everything in between, the two men rounded the corner to the kitchen and approached the open back door.

A small stoop and two steps led down to mud, dormant grass, and beds that might have once held blooming flowers.

The stable, in its state of unsightly disrepair, hunkered to the left of a paddock where a brown horse with a white star on its face grazed beside a sleek honey-colored palomino. Beyond, a corral with a broken-down fence waited for the next rider up. Deep tread marks scarred the earth from the opening of the stable to a point outside the gate of the corral. Hector and Smith followed the tracks with their eyes to the tractor.

It was an old one, probably a survivor of the glory years when the Westons had money. In its prime, it had been a fine machine. Now the paint was chipped, the hull rusted out, and the John Deere logo missing. And it was overturned. Blackened wheel rims poked up at the sky, yet there were no tires, no mud caked tread on them. The freshly turned earth smelled rich and fecund beneath the sharp and acrid scent of burnt rubber.

Frowning, Smith began to pick his way through the mud. Hector almost smiled at the attempt to save his shiny new cowboy boots from the muck, but he knew better than to get caught smirking at the sheriff. Then a dank and pungent odor caught in the breeze and obliterated his trace of amusement. Whatever they found on the other side of that tractor wouldn't be a laughing matter.

On the sheriff's heels, Hector made his way across the yard and rounded the overturned tractor. He was looking down and didn't see Smith stop until he plowed into his back, nearly knocking him on top of Frank Weston's body, face up on the ground.

Frank was dead, trapped from the waist down by the heavy machinery which had apparently toppled on him. Worse, what was left of Frank was as badly burned as the smoldering, hissing tractor. The steering wheel, the knobs on the dash, the gear shift handle, and the tires had all melted in what must have been an inferno.

"God," Hector said, falling back a step. To his shame, he felt his stomach pitch and roll. He stumbled a few steps away, praying that he wouldn't disgrace himself further by losing his lunch. Sweat made his gun slippery. He put it back in the holster, fighting not to breathe in the stench of charred flesh, burnt rubber, and death.

He wiped his face with his sleeve and forced himself to speak calmly in the hope that the sheriff hadn't noticed his reaction. "Looks like the gas tank ignited," he said. "Must have flipped when it blew."

"I don't think so," Smith said as he studied the tractor. "It's a rollover."

He pointed to the chain hitched at the back of the tractor and the tree stump a few feet away. The front end of the tractor faced the stump, lying over the chain attached to the drawbar in the back. "He hitched it too high and when the stump didn't give, it flipped. It rolled over on him."

Hector nodded, wondering how a city boy like Smith knew about rollovers. Hector should have recognized it himself. He'd known a kid in school whose brother had killed himself the same way fifteen years ago. New tractors came with rollover protection. This tractor was too old for that.

Smith squatted down close to the crisped husk that had once been Frank Weston. Hector took a few more steps in the opposite direction, trying to look at anything and everything but the body. The tractor's gas cap had been blown off and it lay in the mud of the corral. Hector carefully made his way to it.

Although dirty and covered in soot, the embossed letters across the surface were legible. DIESEL. He looked from the cap to Frank and back.

"We better call out to Piney River. Tell them to send a wagon and get this cleaned up," Smith said, standing.

The stench of death was so overpowering that Hector didn't think he could take it much longer. But he couldn't stop looking at the fuel cap on the ground. "That tractor ran on diesel," he said.

"So?"

"Well, it's just that it shouldn't have exploded. I mean, diesel's not like gasoline. It's more stable. It usually doesn't just blow up."

"Tell *him* that," Smith said, pointing at Frank Weston.

Wishing he'd kept his trap shut, Hector nodded and started back to the cruiser to make the call. He was careful about giving the scene a wide berth. Smith, however, squatted right beside

Frank Weston's remains. He didn't look the least bit nauseated by the sight or smell. Obviously this wasn't *his* first dead body.

Once Hector had cleared the area, he breathed deep, but the scent lingered in the air and there was no escaping it. At the cruiser, he radioed the Piney River SO to send assistance and notify the coroner. Mountain Bend didn't even have its own morgue. They relied on their neighbor for those services. After he signed off, he popped a piece of chewing gum in his mouth and, bracing himself, took his Polaroid camera back to the corral.

The tractor had trapped Frank from the waist down and he was twisted and mangled. From what Hector could see, the part of him beneath the heavy machine hadn't been burned. Hector took several pictures of his arms and the steering wheel. It looked as if they had somehow become entwined in the spokes of the wheel and now they were skewed at unnatural angles. He thought about pointing it out, and then decided to keep it to himself. The coroner was on his way. If there was something strange about the position of the body, he would see it too.

When the two returned to the porch, Grant was still sitting on the steps, staring out at the open land, the stables, the trees, as if they could explain the horror behind his house. Hector had expected Grant to come back and see what they were doing for the long time they were photographing, but he hadn't. He didn't know what, if anything, to make of that. His experience was limited, but everything he'd been taught about survivors of trauma showed them to be clingy. They wanted witnesses to their pain. They wanted confirmation that they were alive and grieving.

Not Grant Weston.

"I called you as soon as I got home," Grant said, not looking up. "I was only gone a few hours."

"You found him like that?" Smith asked.

Grant nodded, reaching in his shirt pocket for a roll of Life-Savers. He thumbed one off the roll and put it in his mouth. The action seemed to bring him composure. When he spoke, his voice was steadier. "It must have happened right after I left."

Smith frowned. "Why?"

"The fire was burned out when I got home."

Hector took that down in his notebook.

"You got black stuff all over your face. How'd it get there?" Smith asked.

"I touched him. I thought he was alive."

Hector didn't know how anyone could have made that mistake. He gave Grant the benefit of the doubt, though. It was his father, after all.

"Did you move him?" Smith asked.

"I—I tried, but I couldn't. He's caught." Grant's voice hitched and broke. He took a deep breath and nodded. "He's caught."

"Was anyone else in the house when you got here?"

"No . . ." Grant trailed off.

"No?" Smith repeated. Hector could hear his own impatience mirrored in the sheriff's tone.

"Tori France should be here. She's been working for us, trying to straighten out our bookkeeping. She was out running errands when I left. I thought she'd be back by now."

Hector glanced up to find Smith staring at Grant, eyes narrowed, forehead creased in a frown.

"Is anything missing from the house? Anything disturbed? Signs of a struggle?"

That question seemed to pierce the fog around Grant's eyes. He looked at Smith. "No. At least nothing I noticed. Why? He had an accident on the tractor. What does that have to do with the house?"

Smith shrugged, leveling a cool look at Grant. "Probably nothing, except there's a dead body in your backyard and possibly a person missing from your house. Or didn't you put that together?"

chapter four

MAP spread on the seat of her blue rental car, Tess turned down yet another one of the dark, winding roads that littered the California mountainside. She still couldn't believe she'd made it. The race from office to home to airport felt like some impossible blur. Sara had driven ninety to get her there and had a rental car waiting at the other end. Tess didn't know what she'd have done without her help.

Now that she was here, more or less in the middle of nowhere as Craig Weston had phrased it, every mile she put between herself and home came with a deepening disquiet. It felt like she'd been spiraling around pine and granite for days. And it was probably all for nothing. She'd get there, find Tori was back, wondering what all the fuss was about, and Tess would be left feeling angry and foolish for all she'd put herself through to get there.

A few miles later her headlights picked out a sign that stated in no uncertain terms—MOUNTAIN BEND, NEXT RIGHT—and then the thick woods along the road opened up. Ahead Tess glimpsed the twinkling lights of a picturesque town sheltered by the rugged mountains surrounding it, vivid in the bright moonlight. Snow still clung to the higher peaks, neon against the purple shadows of the ravines and boulders scattered beneath. Towering pines and aspens cast shivering silhouettes into the night and brushed an explosion of stars in the sky.

Even in the dark, the community at the center of the basin looked like something Walt Disney might have fabricated to house dwarves or fairy princesses. Old-style street lamps illuminated vacant roads and deserted walkways. Lights glowed from graceful front porches and peeked from behind closed curtains.

She turned down the street where Principal Weston lived and parked, grimacing at her wrinkled slacks and blouse as she stepped from the car. She'd eaten on the road and managed to get ketchup on her sleeve and smear it on her pants before she'd noticed. At least she'd taken her blazer off before starting the drive—it was still crisp even if everything else about her looked as if it had made the drive in the trunk with the spare tire.

She followed the walk to an impressive two-story house with white shutters and pale blue paint. The night air had a bite to it and she shivered in the silent chill. Like most of the other houses, the front porch was wide and inviting. Her footsteps echoed against the wood.

As she rang the bell and waited, she smoothed at the wrinkles in her pants and tried to adjust the blazer to hide the ketchup stain. After a moment, footsteps sounded and the spotless white door swung back. Tess pasted a smile on her face and looked up to greet Craig Weston. Standing there instead was a very large woman with jet-black hair and unearthly violet eyes.

"Hi, I'm Tess Carson."

"Come in, Tess. We've been waiting for you," she said and moved aside. Tess had expected to be met by a bleary-eyed, balding principal. Not only was this woman not that, she looked like she'd just come from a day of beauty at the spa. She wore a silky pantsuit the exact shade of her unusual eyes—Elizabeth Taylor eyes, Tess thought. Her makeup was salon perfect, like her hair and nails. With the exception of the fact that she was a hundred pounds overweight, she might have been a model. Tess felt like a frumpy, smelly bag lady as she entered.

"I'm Lydia Hughes," the woman said in a soft, sweet voice. "Craig asked me to meet you here. I'm afraid he's been called away unexpectedly."

A moment of panic gripped her. "Is Caitlin still here?"

"Oh yes, she's here. Still awake, in fact." Lydia's smile was warm and understanding. If she'd been wearing sweatpants or a housedress, Tess might have hugged her.

"And my sister?"

"I'm sorry. No word."

No word. Dammit, where was she?

"Craig felt badly that he couldn't be here. He's had a family emergency, I'm afraid. His father was in an accident."

"I'm sorry. I hope everything is all right."

"It doesn't sound good." Lydia inhaled and softly let her breath out. "It's been quite a day all around. First little Caitlin's mother and then Craig's father . . ."

Tess didn't like her sister being grouped into the family tragedy category like that. It shook her conviction that Tori not showing up today was nothing more than Tori just being Tori.

Lydia led Tess down the hall of Craig Weston's immaculate home, moving with the grace of a woman half her size. The chic silk pantsuit billowed around her, distracting from her broad, fleshy shoulders and the bulk beneath. A whiff of her perfume drifted back at Tess. It smelled light and expensive—unlike the eau de McDonald's and rent-a-car fragrance that Tess was currently sporting.

"Caitlin, your Aunt Tess is here," Lydia said as she stepped into the kitchen.

Tess smiled brightly, hoping Caitlin wouldn't see the worry that she couldn't justify away anymore. Hand poised over a puzzle piece, Caitlin looked up from the kitchen table and regarded Tess solemnly.

She had huge baby blues and a small, elfin face framed comically by two uneven, blond pigtails. Like Tess, Caitlin bore no resemblance to her mother. Where Tori was dark and exotic, Tess and Caitlin were fair and ordinary. At least Tess was. Caitlin had inherited that imp of mystery from Tori. She wore a "Puppy Love" T-shirt and blue jeans, and she had marker smudges on her chin and both hands. Her scuffed sneakers swung anxiously above the floor.

"Hey there, girlfriend. Got a hug for your Aunt Tess?"

Caitlin stared for a moment and Tess felt as if she were

looking through the lighthearted tone to the weight that had settled around Tess's heart. Finally, she scooted off the chair and stepped into Tess's open arms. Tess hugged her tightly, trying to reassure the girl by touch. Her hair smelled of strawberries.

"Do you know where my mom is?" she asked, holding tight to Tess.

"I don't, honey, but I'm sure she'll be home soon." Groaning, Tess lifted Caitlin and settled her on a hip. "You grew a foot since September, do you know that? And good grief, what has your mother been feeding you? Rocks?" Caitlin still looked uncertain, but she managed a grin, revealing two gaps where teeth had once been. "You lost teeth, too?"

"And I can read," she added.

Tess staggered over to a chair and sat down with Caitlin on her lap. "I thought I told you to stay little."

Caitlin shook her head, the small grin wavering. She gave Tess another tight hug and then said seriously, "Are you sure Mommy didn't call you?"

"I'm sure, Caity, I haven't heard from her. I wish I had. But I'll tell you what. When I do"—Tess made a monster face—"when I do I'm going to grab her, and tickle her until she promises never to be late again."

This seemed to suit Caitlin fine. She gave Tess a real smile and hugged her again.

"We're all hoping we'll hear from her soon," Lydia said. Her voice was childlike and musical. "Cell phones don't work for beans out here, so she probably just hasn't been able to call."

"You hear that?" Tess said to Caitlin. "I'll bet Ms. Hughes knows what she's talking about." Over Caitlin's head, she gave Lydia a grateful smile.

"Are you hungry?" Lydia asked. "We had pizza earlier, but there's some left in the fridge."

"I snarfed a Big Mac on the way, but thanks for the offer. We should get out of your hair now. I can't thank you enough for watching Caitlin until I could get here."

"Oh, she's a little angel. It was no trouble." She waved off Tess's thanks, but she looked pleased by the appreciation and sincere as she said, "I'm glad to help. What will you do now?"

Good question. Between racing to get here and expecting to find Tori waiting when she arrived, Tess hadn't thought much further. Now she looked blankly between Lydia and Caitlin.

"Are we going to your house or mine?" Caitlin asked.

"Well, my house is in New York and I don't know where yours is."

Lydia said, "It's not far from here. I can give you directions."

It really hit her then. Tori wasn't home yet. Whether or not she would stroll up tomorrow remained to be seen, but right now, tonight, Tori was missing. Outside, dark pressed against the windows and seeped into the corners of the room. It had been easy to rehash her anger at past escapades when deep down she'd been certain Tori would be home before Tess's airplane even landed. But now . . .

"Or if you'd feel more comfortable staying somewhere else," Lydia went on, "I own a bed and breakfast in town. This time of year the coffee shop is the only part of it that I keep open, so I have plenty of room." She made a bitter sound. "Honestly, any time of the year I have more vacancies than I care to claim. I swear, the only thing keeping this town from shriveling up and blowing away are the rocks."

"Why can't we just go to my house?" Caitlin interrupted. "If Mommy comes home and I'm not there, she'll be worried."

Tess swallowed thickly, trying not to think about how worried she and Caitlin would be waiting for Tori to walk through the door.

"I know, Caitlin, but for one we don't have keys and for two—"

Caitlin jumped off Tess's lap, reached a hand into the pocket of her jeans, and pulled out a key. She set it on the table. It made a hollow, clicking sound against the wood.

"Oh, you have a key," Tess said, strangely uneasy.

Caitlin nodded. "Mommy gave it to me. She said I should give it to you when you got here. She said if something happened, you would come."

chapter five

TORI'S house was just around the corner from Craig
Weston's. their backyards shared a fence, or so Lydia had told
Tess, though several acres of open pasture divided the two
homes from sight of one another. Clouds had blotted out the
moonlight and stars, leaving the night beyond her headlights
basement-black and alive with unseen movement. She'd been
driving awhile and still she hadn't seen the side street Lydia
described.

Tess took her eyes from the road for a moment to glance at
her niece. Since she'd pulled the key from her pocket, Caitlin
had been quiet and withdrawn. Reaching over, Tess patted her
leg.

"Caity?" she said, choosing her words with utmost care.
"When your mom gave you the key, did she think something
was going to happen? Was she worried that you'd need me to
come?"

"I don't know. She didn't say."

"Did she mention that she might go someplace today?"

Caitlin shook her head. Tears filled her eyes. "She said
she'd see me after school."

"Did she give you the key this morning?"

"No, a while ago. I don't remember when."

"Did she say why I would be coming?"

She looked down at her swinging feet. "She said just in
case."

Her words settled in the stillness of the car. "In case what?"

She lifted her shoulders in a small shrug. Tess licked her
lips and tried not to look tense, but it didn't work. Caitlin

pulled her knees up and wrapped her arms around them. She tucked her chin against her chest and withdrew.

Tess caught sight of what looked like a porch light gleaming in the distance and a moment later she came to a road that branched off toward it. The light winked between the trees, looking at once deceptively close and suspiciously far away. Tess followed it all the same, turning onto a narrow dirt road which passed beneath sentries of ancient trees standing guard on either side. A little while later she saw a shadowy grouping of buildings ahead.

"Is that where you live?"

Caitlin looked up and shook her head. "No."

Tess cursed silently. The road wasn't wide enough to swing a U-ey. She'd have to keep going until it opened up. Gravel crunched loudly beneath her wheels and the darkness seemed to layer in thick folds just outside the beam of her lights. At last she pulled in front of a large house with unlit windows that looked creepy as hell. She almost had the car turned back the way they'd come when she saw a silhouette move away from the other shades of darkness and step forward.

She slowed to a stop as the shadow became a man in a heavy jacket wearing a cowboy hat pulled down low on his head. She couldn't make out his features as he stopped a few feet from her car, but there was something familiar about him. How that could be, especially when she could hardly see him, she didn't know. The feeling was undeniable, though.

She rolled down her window partway and said, "Excuse me, I think I'm lost. I'm looking for Old Post Road?"

The man stood still for such a long moment that she began to feel uneasy, thinking that a city girl like herself should have had more sense than to stop in the first place. Then he took a step closer to the car and that overpowering sense of familiarity monopolized her thoughts. How did she, how *could* she, know this man? The brim of his hat concealed his face, giving her only the vaguest impression of glittering light eyes. He was very tall and lean, yet powerfully built. Not like a bodybuilder. More a man who worked in a physically demanding job. Well, duh. He was a cowboy if the attire and locale were anything to go by.

She wished he'd step closer nearly as much as she hoped he wouldn't. She felt anxious and strangely excited with him as near as he was. "Next turn down," he said. His voice was low and even more familiar than his silhouette. Deep and rich, it reached across the distance dividing them and brushed against her senses. He pointed back the way she'd come. "Go right at the end of the drive. It's about a quarter mile more."

"Thank you."

She started to roll up the window and then paused. He was staring at her. Watching her with an intensity she could feel, even if she couldn't see it. Maybe he was trying to place her as well?

She nearly laughed at her own thought. Yeah, right. If she'd really ever met this man before, she knew she'd never have forgotten him.

"Drive careful," he said.

As she pulled away, she glanced in the rearview mirror. The night quickly cloaked him, but she felt as if he still stood watching her.

"It sure gets dark here," she mumbled as she peered back over the steering wheel at the road.

"I know. I hate the dark."

Tess gave Caitlin a quick look. The little girl sat huddled against the door. "Well, scooch on over here next to me and we can hate it together."

Caitlin didn't need to be asked twice. With one hand, Tess raised the console that divided the front seat and Caitlin settled in as close as she could get.

"We'll be to your house soon. Do you know who that man was?"

"I couldn't see him good," she said. "Maybe Mr. Weston."

"Your principal?" Tess asked, surprised.

"Or the other ones." Before Tess could ask what she meant by "other ones," Caitlin exclaimed, "Turn there. That's our street."

It began to rain as they bumped up the pitted drive to Tori's house. Apparently Tori had expected to be back before sunset because, like everything around them, the house was dark.

Tess turned off the ignition and stared at the place where her sister lived. It was small, two-storied, with a tiny front porch and a big picture window in the front. The glass reflected her headlights back like eerie, vacant eyes.

Shadowy bushes and trees shivered in the chilled spring air while the drizzle coated them in a damp, glossy sheen that gave life to their barren limbs. A haunted graveyard would have fit right in with the scenery.

"Mommy's not home," Caitlin said in a small voice.

"No, it doesn't look like she is, does it?"

In her mind, she watched Caitlin pull out her key and say, *Just in case.* Just in case what? What had Tori told her daughter after that *just in case*?

She squeezed Caitlin's hand. "Honey, everything's going to be okay. Your mommy will come home soon and she'll have a perfectly good explanation for why she was gone. You'll see."

Just then, the inside of their car lit up and another vehicle pulled in behind them. Surprised, they both turned and peered out the back window. Dark though it was, they could easily make out the blue and red bubble lights on the roof and the two uniformed men in the front seat.

Tess's stomach plunged at the same moment her heart contracted and a surge of adrenaline shot through her. There was only one reason the police would be there.

Tori.

chapter six

IT seemed the weather waited for just the right moment to let loose. As Tess and Caitlin stepped from the car, a huge gust of icy wet wind tried to push them back in. The officer who had been driving motioned for them to make a run to the house. Without hesitating, they did.

The key turned easily and the front door opened without a sound. Tess reached inside the house and flipped the light switch. She ushered Caitlin in first. The two officers followed. She called out for Tori, even though she knew she wouldn't get an answer. Caitlin raced up the stairs, shouting for her mommy. She came back slowly, her expression revealing all the hurt and confusion she felt.

Tess didn't give the officers a chance to shrug out of their wet coats before she asked, "What happened? Has there been word from Tori?"

"No," the older of the two men said. "I'm Sheriff Smith, this is Deputy Ochoa. We're here to ask you some questions."

Sheriff Smith stood square and purposeful, but his uniform hung on his bulky frame with a negligence that echoed the disillusionment on his face. A dark spot, which she knew from experience could only be ketchup, marred the beige shirt at the slope of his belly. His skin was pasty pale, his expression weary.

In contrast, the younger man behind him was tall and fit. His uniform was pressed and creased with an attention to detail that Tess's military father would have appreciated. Unlike her father, he had warm brown eyes and a compassionate face.

Caitlin stood at her elbow, tense and frightened. Tess squatted down and took the girl's shoulders in her hands. "They haven't heard from your mom, honey. Do you understand?"

Caitlin nodded.

"Okay, I want you to go change into some dry clothes and then come back." When Caitlin didn't move, she added, "I promise I'll tell you if they say anything about your mom."

"I want you to come with me."

Tess glanced up at the sheriff. He frowned with impatience.

"Go on and help her," the young deputy said. "We'll wait in the kitchen."

Caitlin led the way up a narrow flight of stairs and Tess followed, turning on every light they passed. Her niece's room was neat and pretty, filled with stuffed animals and frilly pillows. Caitlin went straight to a small, stuffed kitty that lay in the center of the bed and cuddled it close.

"A friend of yours?" Tess asked.

"Purcy. He's my best friend."

With the kitty under one arm, Caitlin went to her drawers and pulled out a soft fleecy pair of pants and an oversized T-shirt that said COWGIRLS RULE in bright pink letters across the chest.

"Okay?" Tess asked.

Caitlin nodded solemnly. "I'll come down when I'm changed."

Tess smiled, gently touching her silky head. "I'll see you in a minute."

"Ms. Carson," the sheriff said as soon as she stepped into the kitchen. "You are Tess Carson? Ms. France's sister?"

"That's correct."

"I understand her husband is estranged?"

"Ex-husband. They haven't spoken since before Caitlin was born. The last time I asked, she didn't even know where he was."

"Any reason to believe he might have resurfaced?"

"No," Tess answered. "I mean, I don't think he's ever shown the slightest interest in either one of them."

"When was the last time you saw your sister?"

Tess decided she should sit down before answering.

Deputy Ochoa took a seat in the chair opposite her at the small dinette and pulled out a tablet and pen. Smith remained standing with his hands on his hips and his eyes narrowed. He made Tess feel like he was just waiting for an opportunity to whip out his weapon and take aim.

"I saw Tori in September. We went to Disneyland. She was still living in Los Angeles then."

"Have you spoken to her since she moved to Mountain Bend?"

"No. We played telephone tag last week, but we never hooked up."

"Why did she leave L.A.?"

Tess stared at him, not liking his tone any more than the random vein of his pointed questions.

"Why are you asking?"

"These are standard questions, ma'am," Deputy Ochoa interjected. "Your sister is still missing."

Missing. Not lost or late. Missing.

"Wait a minute. Who reported it to you?" Tess asked.

The deputy looked up in surprise and the sheriff stared at her blankly.

"As I understand it, Tori hasn't been missing twelve, let alone twenty-four hours. Why were you notified?"

Apparently the sheriff was not accustomed to being questioned himself. He frowned before finally answering. "We're investigating an accident. Your sister's employer was killed this afternoon."

"Oh God."

Caitlin stepped into the kitchen at that moment. "What happened?" she asked, her tension a live thing that drew Tess out of her chair. Tess took her hand and led her to the front room.

"They weren't talking about your mom, honey."

"Why are they here then?"

"Something happened to the person your mommy works for."

"Not Mommy?"

Tess glanced over her shoulder at the sheriff. He gave a sharp shake of his head.

"No, not your mommy."

Caitlin peered into Tess's face for a long moment. Although her eyes still looked older and wiser than they should, the expression on her baby soft face was young, naïve, and desperately vulnerable. Tess was swamped with the need to reassure her.

"Not your mommy, little one. I promise."

Caitlin let out her breath and nodded with acceptance.

Inside, Tess sighed with relief. "How about you watch some TV while I finish talking to the sheriff? Would that be okay?"

In answer, Caitlin settled herself on the couch and Tess turned on the TV, scanning through a few stations until Caitlin said "Okay" to *Scooby-Doo*.

When she returned to the kitchen, the sheriff picked up with his last question. "Why did your sister leave Los Angeles?"

As far as Tess knew, Tori left because she couldn't commit to anything for longer than a few minutes. Not even a place to live. But she'd be damned if she was going to tell that to this flaccid-faced small-town sheriff.

"Tori enjoys traveling. Her job gives her the flexibility to do it. She moves a lot."

Deputy Ochoa scribbled something on his notepad. Smith cast him a disparaging glance.

"What about her current position?" Smith asked. "Do you know how she set that up?"

Tess shook her head. "I'm sorry. I don't even know where Tori works, just that she's keeping the books for someone here. I think she said a farmer or a rancher. But she gets most of her jobs by referral. She's very good at what she does."

In fact, numbers were the only thing Tori ever trusted enough to keep as a constant. They fascinated her, she'd said on more than one occasion, and they'd never betray her. Tori was consumed with the thought of betrayal. Ironically, she never managed to apply her talent with numbers to her personal records. Tess couldn't count the times Tori had had her phone shut off for not paying the bill.

"You don't know where your sister works?" the sheriff

asked with patent disbelief. He exchanged glances with the deputy.

Feeling as if she were being both interrogated and excluded, Tess stiffened her back defensively.

Smith said, "Ms. Carson, your sister works at the Weston Ranch."

"Weston? As in Caitlin's principal at the elementary school?"

"His father was killed today," the deputy said.

Dawning comprehension joined the murky undercurrent in the room. "I didn't realize—Lydia Hughes met us at Mr. Weston's house this evening. She mentioned that he'd had a family emergency. I just didn't put it together with Tori."

"Do you know why Tori tried to reach you last week?" Smith asked.

Tess shook her head, looking uncertainly from the deputy to the sheriff. "She didn't say there was a reason on her messages."

"You talk on a regular basis?"

"Yes. Every few weeks or so. No schedule. Just when we think about it. Sheriff Smith, I don't really understand how these questions relate to Mr. Weston's accident or Tori."

"We believe your sister was there when it happened."

"You think she witnessed it?"

"Possibly. We haven't determined what her role was yet."

It took a long, quiet moment for that one to sink in. "What does that mean?"

"Just that we want to speak to her. If she did witness the accident, she left the scene without calling it in. I'd like to know why."

"And if she didn't witness it?"

"Then she left suddenly and unexpectedly and hasn't been heard from since. Again, I'd like to know why."

"What *kind* of accident are we talking about here, Sheriff Smith?"

"The kind that ends with someone being dead. That's all I can tell you right now."

But that wasn't all he was saying, was it? Did he think Tori had caused this "accident"?

Smith adjusted his holster and leaned forward. "How are your sister's finances?" he asked.

"I'm not her banker."

"But she lives in rentals, moves around a lot. She's had her phone shut off in three different states. Not a great record for a highly recommended bookkeeper."

Smith had obviously done his homework this afternoon. Tess said, "Apparently she doesn't like to bring her work home with her."

"Apparently not. Frank Weston had a good deal of cash in his house before he died. It's gone now."

"Is that why you're asking me these questions? Because you think she robbed a dying man?"

"I'm just trying to piece together what might have happened, Ms. Carson."

"Tori wasn't hurting for money. If she'd been in need, she would have called me."

"But you said she did call you. You just never had the chance to speak."

Frustrated, Tess rubbed a point between her eyes. "Yes, that's true. But if she'd had an urgent situation, she would have made that clear. Perhaps I'd be better able to answer your questions, Sheriff, if you would shed some light on this accident for me."

"Sorry, ma'am, at this time that's not possible."

She wanted to demand that Smith tell her everything he knew, but he didn't look like the kind of man who would be swayed by demands. Tess smoothed her hair away from her face and tried for calm. She'd thought finding Tori here, untroubled by the turmoil she'd caused, was the worst thing that could happen. Clearly, she'd been wrong.

Even so, chances were Tori would show up before morning. Maybe she'd seen this accident and freaked out. Tori didn't deal well with the unexpected. She never had. Squaring her shoulders, Tess stood. "Is that all, Sheriff?"

Smith rocked on his heels, looking for a moment as if he might say more. She raised her brows and gave him what she hoped was a haughty, "I'm in control of the situation" glare. It was hard to pull off when she was wrinkled from head to toe, had ketchup on her clothes, and was more tired than she'd ever been, but somehow she managed. Frowning, he put on his hat.

Standing, the deputy asked, "Do you have a recent picture of your sister?"

Tess took one from her purse. "This was taken in the fall," she said, handing it over. The deputy stared at it for a moment, as if committing Tori's vibrant features to memory. Carefully he put the picture in his pocket with his notebook.

"We'll be in touch, Ms. Carson," Smith said. "And if we find your sister, we'll let you know immediately."

"Thank you." The tone of her voice could have frozen the balls off a polar bear, but she didn't care. Tess knew her sister was a flake, a pain in the ass, and at times downright disagreeable, but she didn't deserve the sheriff's unspoken suspicions. She was glad to hear the front door close behind him.

chapter seven

AFTER their mother left—or more accurately, after she'd been institutionalized—their father had instigated a regiment of rules. Tori and Tess were to rise early, work diligently and productively throughout the day, and give thanks to the Lord for the privilege of being alive. When his young daughters had rebelled, the Colonel had resorted to discipline without hesitation. Work detail was among his favorite methods of punishment, second only to solitary confinement. Tess still feared basements in the same way others feared heights.

To this day, Tess could not sleep past 6 A.M., and on the rare occasion that her internal clock malfunctioned, she awoke in a panic. The morning after Tori disappeared was no exception. Her eyes opened as the digital display on the clock switched from five fifty-nine to six and she was awake, even though it had been after two before she'd finally managed to jam the receptor between her worry and exhaustion. When she did drift off, it was only to be haunted by strange dreams and terrifying nightmares. This morning she couldn't remember what the dreams had been about, only that they'd chased her relentlessly through the night.

She rolled over and looked at Caitlin, who was curled into a ball beside her, stuffed kitty clutched tight even in slumber. Sleep had smoothed the anxiety from her face and revealed the baby softness of her features. Tess pressed a light kiss to her forehead and climbed out of bed.

Still wearing her gray flannel pajama pants and an oversized Dixie Chicks T-shirt, Tess went downstairs. She glanced in at Tori's room on the way, knowing it would be empty but hoping all the same that her sister might have slipped in during the night. Only the shadows of filtered sunlight moved about the room. Downstairs was equally still.

A small television sat in the corner on the kitchen counter and she switched it on while she searched for coffee and a coffee maker. Neither was where any logical person would keep them. Frustrated, she riffled through the few cupboards in the small kitchen and then forced herself to slow down and make a more determined search. Without coffee in the morning, Tess was useless and even this small task was overwhelming. Finally she spotted a jar with a green lid and promising brown contents tucked in the back with the spices. She pulled it out. Taster's Choice. Instant. Decaffeinated. But coffee.

She filled a mug with water and turned in circles looking for the microwave, feeling somehow betrayed when she realized there wasn't one of those either. At last she set a pot of water to boil. The local news was on the little TV and she listened to the tail end of a story on trash pickup in Mountain Bend while she waited. Apparently Mountain Bend not only depended on Piney River for child care facilities, but also relied on them to dispose of their waste—a fact that Piney River resented.

She decided the water was hot enough and scooped a healthy spoonful of the instant decaf into her cup.

"I can't believe you're related to me, Tori," she muttered as she stirred.

On the news, a blond reporter segued from trash to the latest controversy on a proposed expansion project which could give Mountain Bend some much-needed financial independence. Operating on four hours of sleep and decaf coffee, Tess couldn't grasp what the point of contention was before the blonde moved on to the traffic report.

She was about to switch the television off and take a shower when the anchorwoman launched into a segment about a tragic accident that had claimed the life of Frank Weston.

At last Tess learned that the fatal accident had involved his tractor exploding. Somehow that made her feel better—not that he had died so horribly, but that at least it hadn't been from the "accidental discharge of a gun" or something equally suspicious. The program turned to national news and Tess switched it off.

As she stood staring at the blank screen, a light tapping sounded on the front door. Startled, she spun around, thinking of Tori. She raced to the door, only pausing at the last minute to peek out the window. Disappointment and trepidation hit her at once. Instead of Tori, a man in a conservative blue suit stood on the porch.

"Who is it?" she asked through the closed door.

"Ms. Carson? It's Craig Weston—from the elementary school."

Surprised, she opened the door. When she'd spoken to him on the phone, she'd unconsciously formed an image of an older, spectacled man with a balding head and a bulging waist-line. That's what all principals looked like, wasn't it? But this man was in his mid-thirties, tall and fit, with thick, black hair and eyes so blue they seemed to glow. He had an easy smile that crinkled his eyes at the corners and brought out a small dimple in his cheek. He was handsome enough to make her forget for a moment that she still wore her pajamas, but his quick glance down reminded her and brought a rush of embarrassed heat to her face. A whiff of cologne came in with the crisp morning air as he reached out to shake her hand.

"I'm sorry to drop in like this," he said as she closed the door behind him, "but I felt badly for not meeting you yesterday. How are you doing?"

"Okay, I guess," she mumbled. "How are you? The sheriff came over last night and told me about your father. I'm very sorry."

His smile faded and he looked away. "It's starting to sink in, that he's gone. Yesterday it didn't seem real, I guess."

Tess searched for something more to say, but his father's death and Tori's disappearance seemed too closely entwined for the usual sympathies.

"How is Caitlin doing?" he asked.

"She's still sleeping. The poor kid was exhausted by the time we got to bed."

"I'd hoped you'd find her mother waiting for you last night."

"Yeah. Me, too." Tess led him into the kitchen. "Can I offer you some truly awful instant coffee, Mr. Weston?"

The smile came back. "Thanks, but I've already had a double dose of caffeine this morning. And please, call me Craig." He hesitated, looking around as if for inspiration. An awkward moment passed and then he said, "I guess it was a good thing you came."

If she hadn't, Caitlin would have spent the night in a shelter and Tess would never have forgiven herself.

"Your sheriff seems to think Tori was involved somehow in what happened to your father." It sounded like a question, though she hadn't intended it to.

"He's not *my* sheriff," Craig said immediately. "But he mentioned that he thought Tori was there when it happened. It makes no sense, though. If she was there, she would have called for help." He looked up at Tess. "Wouldn't she?"

Tess nodded quickly. "Of course. I'm as confused as you are. I don't understand what happened to her. She can't have just vanished into thin air."

Couldn't she? Hadn't she done it before?

His pause felt sad and contemplative. He followed it with a soft sigh. "Listen, there's another reason I stopped by this morning. I spoke with our school counselor. She'd like to see Caitlin today, if possible. I told her I doubted Caitlin would be at school, so she wanted me to get in touch with you and see if you could bring her out this afternoon for a meeting."

"A meeting?"

"She's concerned about how Caitlin will be dealing with this."

"Don't you think that's jumping the gun a bit? I haven't given up hope that Tori simply had some difficulty that delayed her. She could walk through the door in the next minute. I don't want Caitlin more upset than she already is, especially when we don't even know what happened. I mean, don't you think we should at least *know* what Caitlin is going to be dealing with before we try to help her?"

"Apparently Caitlin has been expressing fears of abandonment almost from her first day of school here."

Tess crossed her arms in an automatic and protective way. "Expressing her fears in what manner?"

Craig cleared his throat. "I know this must be painful for you."

"I can handle it."

"She's verbalized them."

"I don't mean to sound so skeptical, Craig, but I know how these wannabe psychiatrists can mess with a kid's mind. I'd like to know to whom she's *verbalized* this fear of abandonment and in what context her words were taken." She sounded defensive. Hell, she felt defensive.

When he spoke, his voice was gentle. "She talked to me, for one. And her words were pretty straightforward. I'm sorry, Tess. I know you have a lot on your plate right now."

Tess waited, knowing that he had more to say and knowing that she wasn't going to like it. "Spit it out, Craig. Whatever else, just tell me."

He glanced away and then back. "Over the past week, Caitlin's mother has been acting very strange."

"Strange? Compared to what? My sister is not your average person, Craig, and you've only known her what, a couple of months? What may seem strange to you could be perfectly normal for her."

"You're right, of course. It's just that—God, I don't know how to say this." He raked his fingers through his hair then leveled a serious look at her. "The truth is, she's been acting extremely paranoid. Is paranoia standard for your sister?"

Tess jerked and knocked her coffee cup over. Brown liquid spread across the table like a stain. They both jumped to their feet as it spilled over the edges onto the floor.

"Shit," she said, reaching for the paper towels.

Craig grabbed a handful of napkins and began blotting the spill up. Keeping her face down, Tess tried to regain control. Paranoia. He'd said paranoia. Her thoughts rebelled against that word and all the implications it brought.

Craig tossed the handful of soggy napkins into the trash and glanced at her with sympathy. "Listen, Tess, why don't you bring Caitlin in to see Mrs. Sanders. She's a wonderful counselor and she wants to help. Afterward, maybe you and I can talk some more."

She took a deep breath. Slowly, she let it out. "All right. Sure, I guess it can't hurt."

Wondering if that was entirely true, Tess agreed to a time. As Craig stepped out into the bright morning sun, she said, "Craig? I—you've done so much. Thank you. Please give my condolences to your family."

He gave her hand a light squeeze and then left.

chapter eight

AFTER Craig had driven away, Tess stood in the yard, filled with helpless anger and fear. What in the hell was going on here?

She faced Tori's house, as if for the answer. A retro set of pink-and-white metal chairs graced the small porch, looking old and weathered, but comfortable all the same. The overgrown yard sprouted in chaotic clusters of greens, reds, and yellows that defied landscaping, reminding Tess of its irrepressible tenant. The rain had given everything a fresh, scrubbed appearance. Under normal circumstances it was the kind of morning that would lift her spirits and renew her faith. But today it only served to contrast with the tumultuous emotions inside her.

Tori was a survivor, Tess reminded herself for the umpteenth time. She was tough and self-centered and she could take care of herself. But what if Craig was right? Paranoid behavior wasn't normal for Tori. It had been, however, the defining trait of their mother's dementia.

She squinted at the sun, forcing that thought to the back. Maybe Craig didn't have a clue what he was talking about. He was a principal, not a psychiatrist. He probably couldn't tell paranoia from hypochondria. She clung to that rationale with an unshakable single-mindedness.

In the house, stillness settled around the stiff-backed sofa and matching chair in front of the fireplace. The wooden floors stretched from wall to wall, broken by a few scattered throw rugs. It was cozy, but reflected nothing of Tori's vibrant personality. Above the mantel an unremarkable painting tried for ambiance but failed, and on the opposing wall a dime-store replica of Jesus, in all his glory, gazed back with sorrow.

You definitely came with the house, she thought, looking at it. It was amazing that Tori hadn't yanked the picture of Jesus down and stuffed it under a bed as soon as she'd moved in. The Colonel had crammed religion down their throats to the extent that neither girl knew how to believe anymore.

The only personal items in the room were a framed photograph that sat on an ancient coffee table and a big wooden sunflower standing on the floor next to it that Tess had made during an arts-and-crafts phase. The photo was of Tess and Tori, taken in front of a shrine in Japan. They were Air Force brats, the two of them, and had traveled the world with the Colonel. In the photo, Tess was nine or ten years old, pale as creamed butter with her summer-blond hair cut boy-short. Beside her stood Tori, probably fourteen, tall and big-boned, already showing the beginnings of what was to become a voluptuous figure. She wore her dark hair long and loose. Her eyes held the glint of a dare, a gleam of mirth. She'd always been on the prowl for trouble.

Tess swallowed thickly, hoping to God she hadn't found it in Mountain Bend.

As Tess set the picture back on the table, Caitlin stumbled downstairs in her kitty-cat PJs with Purcy tucked under one arm.

"Did Mommy come home?" she asked.

"No, honey. She didn't."

There was nothing more she could say and they both knew it. Tess fixed Caitlin breakfast then settled her back on the couch with a blanket to watch cartoons. Dark circles framed her blue eyes. The child looked as if she hadn't slept in a week.

Wishing she didn't have to ask, Tess knelt down beside the sofa and said, "Caitlin, have you been worried about your mom—I mean, before yesterday?"

Caitlin looked at her, not answering.

"Has she been acting strangely—stranger than usual?"

Caitlin ducked her chin in a tiny nod. "Sometimes. She said things were going on here that weren't right."

"What kind of things?"

"Crazy ones."

Tess felt cold, chilled to the bone. "Crazy?"

Caitlin shrugged, anxious and pale.

"And you were worried about her?"

"Sometimes," she whispered. "I was afraid she'd go crazy like Grandma and leave me."

The hushed words stole Tess's breath away and brought tears to her eyes. Tess had been eight years old when they'd strapped her mother down and wheeled her out of the family house, yet she remembered it clearly. Even now, it hurt. Trying hard to keep it together, Tess smoothed Caitlin's hair back. She couldn't lie; she couldn't tell Caitlin that Tori going nuts was impossible. For all she knew it had already happened.

"We don't know where your mommy is. I don't—all I do know is that I'm here now, and as long as I've got breath in my body, you will never be alone. Do you understand?"

Caitlin's eyes had grown huge and wet, but Tess's words seemed to register somewhere in their depths. She nodded.

"Okay, let's get you snuggled up here on the couch."

Tess tucked Caitlin's blanket in around her and kissed her again. With the babble of the TV to chase back the silence, Tess washed the breakfast dishes and wiped the counters. She felt numb, overwhelmed by the unguarded terror she'd heard in her niece's voice. She was swamped by her own fear of losing another person she loved to the black void of insanity.

On edge, she went upstairs. Caitlin's room looked even more cheerful in the daylight. The bed was made, the stuffed animals neatly arranged. The sight of it reminded her of when she and Tori were kids and shared a room. Tess's side was always precisely kept—just like Caitlin's. The Colonel could find no fault in her tightly pulled bedspread and organized drawers. Tori's side was always piled with books, magazines, shoes, hair ties, fingernail polish, and a million other things she'd gathered along the way. She didn't believe in hanging up clothes she'd only be taking down to wear again or putting away an item she'd finished using. What was the point when sooner or later she would need it once more?

Last night after the sheriff and his well-behaved deputy left, she'd toured Tori's small house and discovered that some things never changed. Tori's bedroom still looked as if it had been ripped apart by a tornado. She'd been too tired to face it then, but now she crossed the hall and waded into the chaos.

Small towers of taped-up boxes skulked in the corners, and a cluttered mess littered the dresser top. The matching mirror leaned against the wall, propped between the dresser and the floor. It cut off her reflection at the neck. A shiver slid down her spine as she stared at it. Quickly, she faced the other way.

Tori was acting strangely this last week. Is paranoia normal for your sister?

"No."

She hadn't meant to say the word out loud, but there it was. Denial at its finest.

Could Tori have crossed over the edge? Raced into the night to escape her own personal demons? Before her mother was committed, she, too, had vanished. A week passed before they found her, naked and starved, living in a broken-down shack off old Highway 40. They'd put her away for good after that and then the Colonel had accepted an assignment overseas. The three of them had left Mom behind. She'd died within the year.

Tori's closet door was open, but few of her clothes actually hung inside. Behind the door, a baseball bat leaned against the wall. She lifted it, knowing that Tori never used it to hit a home run. Did she sleep with it beside the bed?

A tiny bathroom opened off the bedroom and Tess stepped in. The countertops were an ancient beige with an ugly gold streak woven in. A mirrored medicine cabinet hung on the wall by the door. She stared at herself for a moment. Her eyes were still blue, skin still fair, hair still short, but she wasn't a kid anymore. The apprehension showing on her face was all grown up.

She opened the cabinet and her reflection slid off the glass. Inside was toothpaste and a toothbrush. Hair gel. She took out a prescription bottle and studied the label. Prozac, prescribed three years ago, still three quarters full. She lifted Tori's perfume, *Obsession*—what else?—and sniffed. Then a box on the top shelf caught her eye. She reached for it and something fell out as she brought it down.

For a moment she stared at the small, white, wand-shaped object that had clattered into the sink. She knew what it was, but why would Tori have it?

Duh, Tess. Why does anyone have a pregnancy test kit?

Okay, stupid question. She picked it up and made realization number two.

Tori had taken the test already. A bright blue plus sign showed in the little window. Tori was pregnant? When? And by whom? How old was the test? Days? Weeks? Or, like the Prozac, years?

Tori, why does everything have to be so complicated where you are concerned?

Frustrated by so many unanswered questions, she shoved the test back into the box and replaced it on the shelf. Back in the bedroom, she moved to the big window overlooking the yard and the pastures beyond the fence. A ponderosa pine grew to the left of it, partially blocking the view, but also offering privacy from the frontage road. She stepped closer and peered out.

Directly below was a man on horseback. He was looking right at her.

She jumped back. Who was that? How long had he been out there? Why was he staring at Tori's bedroom window? She thought of the man last night—the cowboy with the piercing stare. Quickly she moved around the window to the other side, where she could see without being seen. She looked again in time to see his horse disappear into the woods across the road.

She grabbed the bat and raced down the stairs, pausing only long enough to say to Caitlin, "I'm going outside for a minute. Will you be okay?"

"Uh-huh. I'm watchin' TV."

She glanced at the bat in Tess's hand and away without comment. Maybe it was commonplace for the bat to accompany her mother on brief excursions to the front yard. Maybe she was too tired to wonder why her Aunt Tess had it in her hands. She looked as if she might nod off at any moment.

Closing the front door behind her, Tess stepped off the porch and rounded the corner. The pine towered up to the shock of cobalt sky and brushed the wispy clouds with its blue-tinged crown. Warm sunshine beat down on the thick blanket of dried needles surrounding its base and danced across the riot of flowers and long, waving grass that stretched from the yard to the road and into the fields beyond. The air smelled of thick woods, fallen leaves, and rich, sun-baked earth.

Her grip tightened on the bat and her muscles tensed in anticipation as she moved to the spot where she'd seen the horse and rider. Overhead, an enormous black bird soared, its harsh caw jarring the uncanny silence.

Shielding her eyes, she tilted her head back and looked up at the window where she'd just stood. The sun glared against the glass, turning it into a mirror filled with bright light. She moved a couple of steps forward, back, to the sides with the same result. Even if the man had been looking at the window, he wouldn't have been able to see in. At least partially reassured by that, she turned away and stared in the direction he'd ridden.

Who was he? The father of Tori's baby maybe?

Traces of an ancient trail wove between the clumps of wild grass. The dirt was soft beneath, yet there were no hoofprints. Where she had walked, the tread of her shoes was clearly embedded in the soil, but a horse and rider had passed over the same terrain without a trace. Frowning, she widened her search, moving out on either side of the trail, but still, she could not find a single print.

What the hell?

As she turned, an icy wind blustered against her back, spinning her around again. An eerie silence leeched all other movement from the air. The branches on the pine were suddenly still, the long grass and tall flowers, frozen.

Everything was unnaturally static.

Above her, the sun flickered then dimmed, as if by a

switch. Frowning, she stared up at a festering gray sky that only moments ago had been a perfect blue. Shivering in the sudden cold, she looked over her shoulder at the trail without tracks that seemed to lead to nowhere.

Then imperceptibly, something else in the air changed. Something visceral but invisible raised all the hairs on her body and triggered the ancient fight-or-flight instinct within. She took a step backward as the feeling grew, amplified like an echo by the granite mountainsides surrounding her. Apprehension pulled at the pit of her stomach and she fought the urge to bolt for the house.

In an instant thick and unyielding clouds overtook the sky. Her breath plumed in the suddenly frosty air. Goosebumps shivered beneath her light shirt and her teeth began to chatter.

No storm could move this fast. It wasn't possible.

"Mooollllly?"

The echoing name pierced her like the cold, turning her in place as she grappled with fear. Through the trees across the road, the man on horseback came into view. He wore his hat pulled low on his head and the collar of his long black wool coat turned up against the vicious cold. A rifle jutted from his saddle holster.

A shaky, unstable sound parted her lips as he moved out of the woods, his harness jingling. He looked familiar, like the cowboy last night, yet he was not the same man.

"Molly?" The rider looked right through her.

Shaking her head, Tess followed his seeking stare with her own. Wisps of last night's tormenting dreams surfaced and merged with the image in front of her. With them came the same gripping terror that had chased her from nightmare to nightmare. What the hell was happening here? She peered over her shoulder, her mind rebelling against what she saw.

Tori's front yard had vanished and in its place was a massive, roiling river that couldn't possibly exist. Rumbling like an avalanche, it surged from its banks and thundered madly through the spot where seconds before the house had stood. The wind howled and whipped the foamy current into a frenzy.

Huge branches that looked as if they'd been ripped from trees churned in its wake.

No. Even in her head, the word sounded puny. She was hallucinating. She had to be hallucinating.

Overhead, lightning snaked beneath the turbulent clouds, rending a hole that let loose a deluge of icy rain. It sheeted the skyline in a metallic hue. Then, out of nowhere, a covered wagon pulled by a team of oxen appeared on the other side of the river. It lumbered toward her at a quick pace.

"Oh my God." Tess's step backward sank her shoes deep into a hole filled with freezing water. Still, she couldn't take her eyes off the wagon as it came to a stop on the eastern shore of the river. Two women sat on the bench, a small boy sandwiched in between them.

Tess stared at them while somewhere in her head a frantic voice whispered, *Not real, not real, not real.* She clenched her eyes tight, praying that when she opened them again she would be gone from here. Back in her car, maybe. Back in New York, in a world that made sense.

In the space of a moment, the man on the horse had arrived at the wagon and the rest of the world became a diaphanous fabric of colors and shapes that blended without meaning. Everything beyond the covered wagon seemed unreal and out of focus. But none of it was real. It couldn't be—

The younger woman on the wagon bench turned and caught Tess in a penetrating stare. She wasn't looking through Tess as the man had. Her steady gaze pulled Tess forward as the sound of the river and pounding rain faded beneath the hammering of her heart. Tess wanted to scream, tried to scream, but her voice was sealed inside her.

Not real, not real, not real, not real!

Suddenly even the shout of confusion in Tess's head silenced as the moment unfurled like a banner that snapped in the wind. Tess recoiled at the rush of strange, overwhelming emotions that entwined with her own. She felt her identity slipping away and reached through the onslaught, desperate to hold on to herself. But no matter how she tried, she couldn't break free from the spell. She couldn't pull her gaze from the pale face or look away from the anguish in the other woman's eyes.

The rider called the woman's name again, his voice deep and compelling.

As one, Tess and the woman faced him.

chapter nine

GRANT Weston was thinking of his father when the woman bolted into the road. His truck was old, the brakes worn and his reflexes shaky. He swerved, skidding across damp mud and gravel and into the ditch. He had the indistinct impression of her body rolling to the other side of the road before he smacked his forehead on the steering wheel. Instantly, black-and-red patterns exploded behind his eyes.

"Goddammit." Pain followed the colors in a riot that convinced him his skull was split in two. He touched his head, expecting blood, relieved to find only a lump that promised to swell. He stumbled out of the truck, praying he hadn't hit her, whoever she was. He still couldn't figure out where she'd come from.

He saw her on the side of the road about twenty feet back from the truck. She was sprawled in the gravel, as still as his father had been when he'd found him beneath the tractor. A feeling akin to vertigo stopped him. Christ almighty, was she dead?

What sanity remained in his head reasoned that he hadn't felt an impact, so he hadn't hit her. But she'd appeared from nowhere and it all happened so fast . . .

From where he stood, he shouted, "Hey? Are you okay?" His voice echoed in his pounding head. But the woman didn't move.

"Hey, lady? Are you okay?" Reluctantly he forced himself forward. At her side, he knelt and touched her. "Hey . . . Are you hurt?"

She moved and Grant nearly passed out with relief. The whole scene had been playing out too much like yesterday.

She made a soft moaning sound as she eased herself to a sitting position and stared past him. She was small, fine-boned, with short blond hair that curled around her ears. Her face was smudged and dirty, her expression frightened. She looked lost and vulnerable and a protective instinct he'd thought long dead awoke inside him and responded.

Gently he touched her shoulder. "Are you hurt? Can you move everything?"

She didn't seem to understand that he was asking her questions, or that he was waiting for answers. She was shaking. That was a sign of shock, wasn't it? Or was that just how actors portrayed it in the movies? Hell, he didn't even know.

"Wait here," he told her. A light drizzle chased him back to the truck, where he grabbed a blanket from behind his seat, and then he returned to wrap it around her shoulders. When he touched her, she jerked away. Her sudden movement scared the crap out of him and nearly knocked him on his ass.

"It's okay," he said, holding his hands up, palms out. "I'm not going to hurt you. Are you injured? Did I hit you?"

She stared at him as if he'd just dropped from the sky. "You hit me?"

"No. I don't think so. You ran out in front of my truck."

Her big blue eyes shifted, looking past him to his truck. A freezing wind howled across the road and sprayed them with rain. The woman shivered violently. Who was she?

"Should I take you to the hospital?"

"No. I want to—" A look of alarm crossed her face. "Oh my God. I've got to—What time is it? I've got to get back." She was on her feet in an instant. "What time is it?" she repeated urgently.

"About ten."

"Ten? You're sure?"

He glanced at his watch and nodded. She shook her head, looking so unconvinced that he checked again. She murmured something that sounded like "thank God" and her eyes fluttered closed.

"I have to get back to the house. My niece is there. I have to go now."

"I think you should—"

"I'm fine. I just want to get back."

"Okay," he said, hands up again. "I'll take you."

She hustled to the passenger side of his truck and scrambled into the seat before he'd finished speaking. He followed, feeling like he was missing some major piece of a puzzle.

"I'm Grant Weston." He started the engine. "Where to?"

"The house is . . . *Grant Weston*?"

She turned her head and stared at him. For a moment it seemed that she didn't believe her eyes, that he was some bizarre, post-shock hallucination. It had been a long time since anyone had looked at him like that. He'd almost forgotten what it felt like.

"Grant Weston? *The* Grant Weston?"

He gave her a sardonic grin. "Yeah, famous person to the rescue. So which way am I going?"

She continued to stare at him with a stricken expression. "Are you . . . Is that Weston as in the Weston ranch?"

It was his turn to stare. "Yes."

She lowered her lashes, concealing her thoughts. "Go to the gray house off Old Post Road," she said in a husky voice. "I can't remember the street number."

"You mean Tori France's house?"

"Yes. I'm her sister."

Her sister. Of course. And the lost woman from last night as well. Smith had mentioned that she'd come to take care of the kid. Christ, and he'd almost run her over. He patted his pocket for the roll of LifeSavers and thumbed a green one into his mouth. He offered the roll to Tori's sister but she didn't even glance his way.

An awkward silence followed and Grant searched for a way to fill it. At last, he asked, "Have you heard anything?"

She shook her head. "Have you?"

"No." It seemed appropriate to offer some kind of reassurance with that, but he didn't. The mere mention of Tori France had left a bad taste in his mouth.

It began to rain in earnest as they bumped down the pitted dirt road. Beside him, Tori's sister gripped the edge of her seat and stared out of her window. The gray outside made a mirror of the glass. In the reflection he could see dirt on her face and mascara rings around her eyes. Above the black smudges, her blue eyes glowed like polished stones. She looked scared, lost. Alone. He touched her hand briefly with his own and she jumped, turning those wide eyes on him in confusion.

"You okay?" he asked, thinking that her hand was cold, wondering if the rest of her was, too.

She nodded quickly and looked away. Turning his attention back to the road, he scratched the stubble on his chin and indulged himself in his weekly—*daily*—craving for a drink. If ever he'd been tempted to climb back into the bottle and stay there, it was this week. Each minute he held out was a small victory.

Lightning split the sky as he pulled into Tori's driveway. The storm had moved in fast, even for the mountains. "You have a key?" he asked over the quaking thunder that followed.

"Key . . ." She looked at him, as if for assistance.

"Don't worry about it. The back door doesn't latch. I'll go around and open up the front."

"No, it's not locked. Caitlin's home."

"Then you can get in okay?" He posed the statement as a question, hoping for a reassuring answer, but her vacant nod didn't do it.

He couldn't just drop her off when she looked like she'd been to hell and back. Not when he'd nearly made road rash out of her. For all he knew, she was in shock or had a concussion—or both.

Pulling his collar up, he jumped out into the pouring rain and escorted her to the door. As soon as she was inside, her gaze went immediately to the child sleeping on the couch.

"Oh, thank God," she whispered, sagging against the wall.

Grant stood awkwardly by the door. Somewhere a fire was burning and the smell of wood smoke hung heavy in the air. His stomach rolled with thoughts of his dad and the sickening stench that had lingered in the corral long after the coroner had taken his body away. He took deep breaths, fighting nausea.

"What's wrong?" she asked. Her voice sounded raw yet

soft, unbearably gentle. She moved closer and he caught the scent of her perfume, fleeting but enough to pull him back from the horrible memories. He had the sudden desire to take her in his arms, bury his face against her skin, and breathe in her sweet fragrance.

Quickly he stepped away. "Are you sure you're not hurt?" he asked, hand on the doorknob. His voice sounded gruff.

"I'm fine." She crossed her arms defensively. "Thank you. And . . . and I'm sorry about your father."

He nodded. Would he ever be able to think about it without feeling like his guts were on fire? He pulled the door open and stepped out. The splash of rain felt good on his hot face.

"Mr. Weston?" she said.

The tone of her voice, her formal address, the fact that she was Tori France's sister and therefore trouble in the flesh, or maybe nothing more than his desire to touch her, made him hesitate while a feeling like ants parading beneath his skin urged him to bolt.

She looked like an orphan, small and defenseless, framed between the door and the cold gray world. "Yeah?" he said more sharply than he'd intended.

"My name is Tess. Tess Carson."

She said it forcefully, as if she expected he might argue. He searched his dwindling stock for a suitable response. An inadequate "okay" was all he found.

Her nod was firm and decisive. The gesture more like the seal on a bargain than a casual acknowledgment. He felt like he'd been slipped the wrong script in the middle of a shoot. She stepped back and firmly shut the door.

Soaked right down to his boxers, Grant climbed into the truck and began the ritual of reminding himself of all the reasons why he'd given up drinking.

chapter ten

TESS waited until she heard the truck drive away before collapsing against the wall.

Grant Weston.

As if things weren't bizarre enough, she'd just been picked up on the side of a road by a movie star. She brushed a shaking hand over her face. Outside, the world looked wintry and bleak, as alien as the stupefaction she felt inside. Wasn't it just a few hours ago that she'd thought it a day to lift spirits and renew faith? Now, it looked more like the end of the world.

At the far corner of the yard, the pine tree bent and shook in the pounding rain. Off to the left, the pale wood of the baseball bat gleamed in the sodden pine needles. Her thoughts slammed up against a wall of memory and stuck. When had she dropped the bat? She'd gone outside to look for the man riding the horse . . . That much she remembered. And she'd had the bat.

Her vision blurred and the tree became an unfocused mass of shivering green. What then? What happened then? She'd gone to the tree and looked at Tori's window . . . She pushed open the front door and stepped onto the porch. She was freezing in her damp clothes but she didn't turn back to change. The rain pounded against the roof like gunfire. Mentally she tried to retrace her steps from the tree to Grant Weston's truck, but the last thing she remembered was . . . was . . . the man. The man on the horse.

Goose bumps raced over her skin as Tess chased the fleeting memory of him through the dark corridors of her mind. But he vanished in a confusing flash of fragmented images.

"Dammit."

The bat mocked her from the thick bed of pine needles. Why couldn't she remember dropping it? Why didn't she remember anything after she'd seen the horse and rider disappear into the woods? How could that be? And why did she feel like she'd been gone for hours after that, not minutes? Equally important, where had she gone *to*?

Spooked, she went back inside and closed the door on the storm. Somehow she'd ended up nearly a mile away before she'd run out in front of Grant Weston's truck. But she didn't remember that either.

Grant Weston.

He'd barely responded when she told him that she was Tori's sister, but she sensed his reaction just under the surface. He didn't like her sister, which in itself was strange. Usually men liked her too much. Damn, but she wished she'd tried harder to reach Tori last week. For all she knew, he was the sperm donor responsible for the positive pregnancy test upstairs.

She brushed back her hair and pulled out a piece of grass. Her hands still shook, her muscles ached, and the skin on her arms felt as tender and raw as her emotions. She must have scraped herself when she'd fallen. She needed some dry clothes and some semblance of order, and she needed them now.

Taking a deep, calming breath, she turned down the television. Caitlin made a soft, mewing sound and snuggled into her blanket. Some terrific guardian Tess was turning out to be. Thank God Caitlin hadn't awakened while she was gone.

There it is again. Gone where, Tess? Gone where?

Checking that the front door was locked, Tess went upstairs to the bathroom. Without a window, the beige room seemed dingy and bare. After a glimpse of herself in the mirror, she wished it was dark, too. No wonder Grant Weston had looked at her like she'd crawled out of a cave.

Blocking everything from her mind but the mechanics of changing into dry clothes, Tess shrugged out of her drenched sweatshirt and dropped it on the tile. Wincing, she did the same with her T-shirt. Shoes and pants joined the pile. She was freezing and her mind felt numb.

As she reached for her dry shirt, the bathroom mirror caught her reflection and bounced it back. She stared at herself in stunned disbelief.

Dark purple and green bruises made a terrifying psychedelic madness out of her shoulders, ribs, and thighs. She twisted around to see the splotches on her back as well. Her right arm had an abrasion from elbow to shoulder, adding texture to the color. She was lucky she hadn't broken anything when Grant Weston's truck hit her. Except . . . he'd said that he didn't hit her.

She stared at herself in the mirror as something shifted deep in her memory. She tried to grasp it but it sifted through her fingers like dust.

What in the hell had happened to her today?

chapter eleven

CRAIG Weston was directing traffic in the rain when Tess and Caitlin arrived at Mountain Bend Elementary School. He wore a bright yellow raincoat and held an umbrella with a downpour of colorful ABCs on its dome. By ones and twos he escorted children from the overhang by the school's front door to the waiting cars in the circular drive.

Tess saw him look their way as she and Caitlin parked in the lot and raced for the door under their own umbrella—blue, no alphabetical adornments. She waved but didn't stop.

A plump secretary with Doris Day hair and buckteeth smiled sweetly at Caitlin and told Tess to wait in the chairs outside Mr. Weston's office. The school was small. Tess would have been surprised if it had more than two hundred students. Crayon artwork offered some relief to the beige and brown color scheme, but not much. The hall smelled of pine, green beans, and wet wool.

After a few thinly veiled glances, Doris asked, "Have you heard anything from your mother, hon?" in a voice filled with long Southern vowels and soft twangy consonants.

Caitlin shook her head, clutching Purcy, who she'd brought along.

"Aw, don't you worry, sweetie. She'll be home soon. She won't be able to stay away from you for long."

The implication that Tori was gone by choice was not lost on Tess. She glanced at Caitlin from the corner of her eye, but her niece didn't seem to have caught the double meaning in the words. Caitlin nodded and continued to watch her swinging toes. For the first time, Tess wondered what Caitlin thought of her mother. Was she aware that others perceived Tori in a less than flattering way? Or was she as oblivious to any negativity directed at her mother as she appeared to be now?

A moment later, Craig pulled opened the door and blew in with a gush of rain. "Damn, where did this storm come from?" he muttered, shaking off the ABC umbrella. He pulled back the hood of his raincoat and shrugged it off. Beneath it he wore navy blue trousers, blackened to the knee by water, and a white button-down shirt. This morning, his formal suit coat had hid his tie. Now the jacket was gone and Tess could see there were frolicking Mickey Mouse characters down the length of it. He'd loosened the knot and rolled his sleeves back to the elbows. He looked tired. She wondered why he'd come to work at all. Surely the school would have understood if he'd stayed at home.

"Tess," he said, smoothing back his wet hair. "And Miss Caitlin. I wasn't sure if you'd brave the storm after all."

"It didn't seem so bad when we left, but then it was like the sky just opened up," Tess said.

He nodded in agreement and squatted down to Caitlin's level with a look of concern on his face. "How are you doing, Caitlin?"

Caitlin gave him a tiny smile and a shrug.

"Yeah. Me, too. But we've got to hang in there and hope for the best, don't we?" He ruffled her hair and stood straight again. "How about you, Tess? How are you holding up?"

"I'm fine." She brushed her hair back from her face and looked away.

"You don't look fine. I mean—of course you look fine, but . . ." He stopped. A faint blush crept up his face, and an awkward silence fell between them. Doris Day watched them with unbridled curiosity.

"I suppose Mrs. Sanders is waiting for us," Tess said.

"I'll show you where her office is. Will you stop by after you see her so we can talk?"

Looking forward to that with the same enthusiasm she had for dental work, Tess agreed and fell in step beside him. Silently Caitlin moved around to slip her hand into Tess's.

* * *

MRS. Sanders had iron gray hair, black glasses, and no chin. One of her hands was curled into a permanent claw by arthritis, and Caitlin blatantly stared at it. But she gave them a kindly smile and extended her other hand for Tess to shake. For the first few minutes she spoke cheerfully, explaining that she was a counselor, a music teacher, and occasionally, a cafeteria worker.

"We don't get the luxury of one job here."

She had legitimate credentials, though, and an easy manner that inspired trust. She instructed Tess to wait while she and Caitlin went into her office.

Tess glimpsed panic in Caitlin's eyes as the door closed, and it was all she could do not to jump up and insist on going in with them. The minutes felt like hours while she waited, wondering if she *should* have insisted, wondering what Tori would have done. She shifted in her seat, remembering how the Colonel had taken her and Tori for regular psychiatric evaluations after he'd had their mother committed. Tori was convinced he was looking for the merest excuse to have the girls put away, too. She warned Tess not to trust the kindly doctors. She'd told her not to talk to them—never to tell them anything they could use against her. If it meant crying for the whole hour to make them back off, do it.

"Miss Carson?" Tess started, looking up to find that Mrs. Sanders's door had opened again and Caitlin stood at her side. "Miss Carson?"

"Yes. All finished?" Her voice sounded shrill, but Mrs. Sanders didn't seem to notice. Caitlin had loosened her hold on Purcy, and he dangled by a paw at her side. She had a sticker on her shirt and a lollipop in her mouth, which she slurped loudly.

"No, we're just going down the hall to get Caitlin a soda from the machine in the faculty office. With your permission?"

"Yes, of course." She reached out to Caitlin. "Everything okay, Caity?"

"Uh-huh. I'm thirsty, though."

"Do you want me to come with you?"

"You can wait for us here," Mrs. Sanders said with a friendly, but decisive smile.

After they left, Tess wandered the small room. Ghosts from her childhood made uneasy company, but she was grateful for anything that kept her from thinking about where her sister was or what had happened this morning.

Several framed black-and-white photos hung on the walls, and Tess wandered from one to another. They were of the town in its early years of development. A picture of a tiny church with a boxy one-room structure beside it had an engraved metal tag proclaiming it the first Mountain Bend school. The present-day one was bigger, but not by much.

Another picture showed the front steps of the school, where a group of twelve or fifteen children gathered. They all wore solemn expressions and dark colors. Behind them a dour woman in a long black dress stood, holding a bell. The sky was dark with rain clouds, the ground muddy as the banks of a river . . .

A gust of cold air washed across the room. Tess spun around to face the still silence behind her. She didn't expect to find an open window, but hope died all the same as she stared at the four solid, windowless walls. The cold pressed in from everywhere. Her breath plumed in front of her face.

No. Not again.

She pulled open the office door and stared out at the still hallway and deserted classrooms. Not a whisper in between. Slowly she shut the door, afraid to turn, afraid to find her worst nightmare waiting between the pictures and corners. She clenched her fists tight and faced the room.

The walls had vanished.

Around her everything seemed to pull in tight and suddenly it seemed that she was staring out of a small window in a darkened shelter. The word "carriage" formed in her resistant mind. Through the window she saw a man who stood in front of a small building that looked like a studio set from an old western. His face was in shadows, but she knew him . . . she knew him . . .

She covered her eyes in a desperate attempt to hide, but

gloves, white with a dirty tinge, cloaked her icy hands. Between her spread fingers she saw the full skirt of a dress that hung from her shoulders to the floor. The toes of black boots poked out from under the hem. Where were her jeans, her sweater, her sneakers?

In an instant of exploding sensation, stays poked and pinched her ribs beneath a corset as alien as the dress. Pins jabbed her tender scalp, holding hair suddenly long enough to wear in a tight twist. Woolen socks rubbed where anklets had comforted, and scratchy underwear chafed in place of the soft cotton panties she'd donned after her shower. And the cold. The cold damp air swirled around her . . .

"Oh God," she breathed hoarsely.

Terrified, she looked back at the man knowing he was why she'd come, knowing he wouldn't welcome her, knowing there was no turning back. Of their own volition, her lips formed his name.

chapter twelve

ADAM. There he was, waiting when at last the carriage came to a stop in Oak Tree, Ohio. She'd feared he wouldn't be there. Nervous, Molly glanced down at the dust coating her skirts and skin. She could taste the grit and dirt that was as much a part of the tedious journey as the rutted paths that masqueraded as roads. But she was here. Finally, she was here.

From the dark shelter of the coach, she peered out again at her sister's husband waiting in front of the tiny mercantile. Cool afternoon shadows played beneath the brim of his hat, keeping his expression hidden, but she knew Adam Weston was less than pleased by her arrival. No surprise there. He had promptly responded to her intentions of coming with a frank, though polite, insistence that she not bother. Perhaps under other circumstances she might have heeded his wishes.

He leaned against the hitching post, idly whipping his heavy work gloves on his thigh. They made a small snapping sound against the thick fabric of his weathered denim britches. The sleeves of his faded shirt were rolled to the elbows, revealing sun-browned forearms that flexed with the movements of his wrists. A small black-and-white dog sat obediently at his feet.

Even without two six-shooters holstered to his hips, he looked like the frontier men Molly secretly read about in the penny novels. He had the long stare of a man whose aim never wavered, even as he pulled the trigger. Molly could not imagine those cool gray eyes filled with warmth or emotion. She doubted that they had ever gazed lovingly at her sister or that even her death had managed to bring grief to their bleak and unwavering depths.

Reluctantly, she opened the carriage door and stepped out. She held her skirts as high above the squelching mud as propriety allowed, while carefully placing her booted feet on the rare patches of solid ground. The team of tired horses that had drawn the carriage across rough, rocky trails shuffled their hooves in the thick mud and snorted at the damp air.

Molly had traveled by train from New York to Columbus. There she'd transferred her person and belongings to this unwieldy coach and continued on to Oak Tree. Had she blinked at the town's border, she could have missed it entirely. Her bottom was sore from the constant bumping against the planked bench and every joint, from jaw to ankle, felt rattled. But it was nothing compared to the pain in her heart. Her sister was dead.

"Who's fer the bags?" the driver shouted from atop the carriage. A swarm of flies buzzed madly above him.

"You may hand me my baggage," she said, holding her arms up for the first.

The vile driver had the look of a man kicked in the head not just once, but one time too many. His left eye wandered disconcertingly under a protruding ridge lined with wild and wooly brows, and a giant mole crouched on his lip like a bug on a bruised and lumpy peach. He had watched Molly at every junction of the journey as if she were a wounded hare that could be caught with a well-planned pounce.

"I said, you may hand down my baggage," she repeated patiently.

Open-mouthed, the uncomely man glanced between Molly and Mr. Weston, who had at last abandoned his position and moved to the carriage. The driver's blackened teeth looked like ancient tombstones marking dark, desecrated graves.

"Toss 'em on down, Dewey," Mr. Weston said.

Dewey brightened with comprehension. Apparently Molly had not been speaking a language with which he was familiar. Or perhaps he'd merely been too enthralled with his detailed assessment of her bosom to respond to something as dull as her voice.

"Well, all right then," Dewey called back. He nodded

furiously as he grabbed the handle of the largest. "I'll just toss 'em on down."

The weight of the first bag caught Mr. Weston by surprise, and he gave Molly a cool look before dropping it to catch the next two.

"Thank you, Mr. Weston," she said when he'd finished loading her belongings and they had seated themselves in his wagon. He did not spare her even the curtest of answers. Instead, he gave a low whistle for his dog and gently snapped the reins. The dog leaped into the back as the horses started and the wagon lurched forward. Moving up to put her front paws on the bench between Molly and her master, the dog let her mouth hang open in a moist and noisy pant.

"You have not brought the baby," Molly said, when it appeared that Adam Weston would be content riding in silence.

"Ma's got him."

"Him? It . . . he is a boy?"

Mr. Weston nodded.

"Is he . . . well?"

"Well as can be expected."

How very enlightening.

Irritated, she held on to the bench, endeavoring to stay on her own side and not let the swaying and eternal bouncing inch her closer to him. Her gloves made her grip on the seat less secure. Did she dare remove them? She very much doubted the society of Oak Tree would notice and the gloves no longer resembled the delicate white apparel they'd been when she left New York anyway. Like the letter, she thought, quickly pulling the gloves off and stuffing them in her pocket next to the battered envelope that she had carried with her the entire journey.

Torn and grease-stained, bearing both the grubby smear of fingerprints and the beveled indent of a horseshoe, the letter had taken more than two months to arrive from the time of its posting. When at last it had been delivered, she'd stared at the thick, slanting words written with a hand unaccustomed to holding a pen, and a deep foreboding had settled on her. It was addressed to the Reverend Thomas Marshall, brick house on

Columbus Avenue, west side, middle of the block, New York City. Apparently in this part of the country they did not bother with such things as house numbers. In the upper corner of the envelope the initials "AW" and "Oak Tree, Ohio" identified its origin. AW, Adam Weston. Her sister's husband.

Only two weeks had passed since she'd waited through the long day and well into the evening for her father's return home before the envelope could be opened. During the endless hours she had held hope against the dread that settled inside her. She reasoned that a message with urgent news would have arrived by telegram, but she could not stop pacing until the Reverend walked through the door. Silently he took the letter from her hand, opened it, and read it. Silently he passed it back.

Her fingers felt strangely numb as she held the sheet of paper. "Dear Reverend Marshall," the letter began. "I am sorry to tell you that Vanessa has died. We gave her a good Christian burial on Sunday. The baby is alive and doing fine. Regretfully, Adam Weston."

The wagon bumped over the bridge and back onto the muddy road, painfully wrenching Molly from the past. Vanessa was three months buried, but to Molly she had only just lived and laughed, only just died.

"We did not know that Vanessa was with child," she said to Mr. Weston. She paused and an anguished laugh tittered out. "She had not mentioned it in her letters, though since last winter those were few indeed. Was it the baby that . . . Did she die . . ." Molly took a deep breath, willing her tears back. Her grief was still too raw, too private to share with anyone. Especially Adam Weston. "Our mother died in childbirth, when I was born. I suppose the malady was handed down to Vanessa and to myself, most likely."

It took so long for Mr. Weston to respond that she thought he might intend not to speak at all.

"No," he said at last. "She didn't die bringing Arlie into the world."

Molly frowned at his cryptic tone and the immediate, thick silence that followed. Turning to face him, she asked, "How then? Was she ill?"

"No. She wasn't sick. There was an accident."

"What accident?"

Her question met with another of his pauses, but in this silence she could see that he searched for the words to explain. She waited, a part of her wishing that he might never find them.

"She fell," he said at last. "She fell from the loft. No one was home but her and the baby." He swallowed and the muscles in his jaw knotted. "She was bad off by the time I got there. We did what we could for her, but she never woke up. Never spoke, never even opened her eyes. She held on for a few days, but after that she didn't have the fight left."

This time there was no stopping the tears that brimmed in Molly's eyes and burned down her cold cheeks.

"I'm sorry, Molly."

Molly fumbled in her pocket for a handkerchief but somewhere on the journey it had been lost. She found only her gloves instead. She wiped her eyes with one and blew her nose with the other.

"I wrote you as soon as I got your letter saying you were coming," he continued, as if answering a question.

Molly sniffed and shook her head as if she did not know to what he referred.

"When I got your telegram yesterday, I figured you must not have gotten the other."

"Was it important, the second letter?"

"It said for you not to come."

The wagon hit a rut and Molly bounced against his arm, which was as tight and knotted as a seasoned oak. Quickly she pulled back and scooted to her side of the bench.

"Why would you tell me not to come?" she said. "You must know that nothing would have prevented my journey."

"I figured that too. I just didn't see the point in it. She's gone and buried. There's nothing you can do about that now. We could've used your help before she went, but we've managed to get along without you so far."

That his words closely echoed those the Reverend had used to dissuade her from going did nothing to make them easier to bear. If she had not intercepted Adam's second message, she would never have gotten away. Even thinking that she was welcomed, her father had tried to forbid it.

Molly turned her face away, hiding her discomfiture. It was not as though she had anticipated open arms and a warm reception, but she *had* prayed that by the time she arrived, Adam Weston would have been grateful for her appearance. After all, there was the baby to tend to.

Perhaps once he saw how good she was with children, he would have a change of heart. She peered at him from the corner of her eye, noting his stiff back and stern expression. Perhaps not. For the first time since making the decision to come, Molly began to doubt the wisdom of it. Never before had she dared to defy the Reverend and to do so only to be sent back . . .

No. She wouldn't go.

For her entire life she had lived with the chains of the Reverend's rules, his strict dictations of worship, his rigid religion, his lack of the spirituality that took the charity out of faith. Molly had watched from her obedient shell as her sister fought his rules, losing with painful repercussions time and time again. Through Vanessa, Molly had come to accept that their own wall of Jericho would not be tumbled down.

But then Vanessa *had* escaped. Adam Weston had rescued her from their holy purgatory, and though the Reverend never acknowledged it, he had been devastated by her defection. In retaliation, he had tightened his iron control over his remaining daughter. When Molly had insisted that she was needed in Ohio, that it was her duty to come and care for Vanessa's child, the wrath of the Reverend blazed like the fires of hell.

And yet, she had defied him.

Clenching her fists into tight balls, she said, "I've just spent nearly a week getting here, Mr. Weston."

He looked at her and then quickly away. "That didn't come out quite the way I meant. You're welcome here. I just meant to save you the trouble of coming."

"It would trouble me more to not see where my sister rests. It would trouble me greatly not to reassure myself of her baby's well-being."

Moments later, Mr. Weston pulled back on the reins and brought the wagon to an abrupt halt in front of a stunted wooden house perched behind a tiny wooden porch. Molly stared at it, trying to picture her sister living here. Dying here. She bit her lip to stop it from trembling.

"This is it," Mr. Weston said, as if it needed clarifying.

A window on either side of the front door gave a sense of balance to the structure, but compared to the home she and Vanessa had shared with their father, it might as well have been made of sod. Where theirs was a brownstone with white pillars, this had rough planks with knotted wood. In New York City, they had neighbors just a few steps away. Friends would stroll down the avenue and stop to take tea in the afternoon or share prayer with the Reverend and his pious daughter.

And yet Molly had never felt at one with the people or the life. She was—and might forever have been—nothing more than the Reverend's devout pawn. How she had envied Vanessa when she had left. Afterward, there were many long nights when Molly pretended that it was she who had unexpectedly wed the handsome Adam Weston and moved to the wilderness.

The front door opened and a small, gnome-like woman stepped out onto the porch. She wore an apron so white it defied existence in this mud and dirt country. Beneath it, a faded red dress swayed in the crisp breeze. Her gray hair was pulled back into a neat bun and the pink of her scalp showed through. She bounced in a gentle rocking motion and against her shoulder she held a bundle wrapped in a blue knit blanket. The baby . . .

Mr. Weston grabbed Molly's bags. Molly followed him to the porch, staring, mesmerized at the bundle in the old woman's arms.

"Guess you'll be the sister," the old woman said in an accusing voice. Before Molly could answer, the woman sniffed and trailed Mr. Weston inside the house. A gust of wind captured the door and slammed it shut with a loud clap, leaving Molly outside.

She stared at the closed door. In all her life, she had never crossed a strange threshold without first having been invited to enter. Neither had she ever been left to wonder if the invitation was assumed or if the door was closed against her.

Holding up her head, she reached for the door and let herself in.

"Wondered if you was going to stand out there all day," the old woman said. She no longer held the blanket-wrapped bundle. Instead she had a big blue coffeepot in her hand.

"Where is the baby?" Molly asked.

"He's been cutting teeth and squalling 'bout it since the sun come up. Finally gave him some sugar teet and nip o' whiskey. He'll be out for an hour, I hope. I forgot what a handful a baby can be."

She made a raspy laughing sound high in her throat. Molly noticed that she had only four front teeth both upper and lower. They were small and white, and perched as they were in the front, she looked like a peculiar bunny.

"Maybe I'll get to supper with him asleep."

Molly looked around the small house, wondering where the baby slept and where Mr. Weston had managed to vanish. Vanessa's letters had indicated that her new family was one of carpenters and that her husband was an extraordinary craftsman who had made all their furnishings. She ran a hand over the back of an elegant rocker that swayed from her slight touch on soundless runners. A smooth table and carved chairs nestled on a braided rug near the kitchen stove. Around the cooking area, crockery lined the shelves above a butcher board, and heavy pots and iron skillets dangled from hooks beneath. The strong scent of bacon grease hung in the air.

"Ain't nothing grand like I suppose you is used to. Your sister didn't think much of it neither," the woman said.

"On the contrary, Vanessa wrote to me of the fine workmanship in Mr. Weston's house."

The woman snorted. "You talk just as fancy as she did. We don't go much on that here. It's going to be tiresome if you insist on calling us Mr. and Mrs. and such. I already done that with your sister and I'm not going to have it with you. He's Adam, I'm Rosie."

Embarrassed, Molly nodded. "And I am Molly."

"I know. She talked about you." Rosie turned and reached into a tin filled with flour. "You could grab me some pork chops from the smoke house if you was a mind to."

Molly stared at her blankly.

"Oh, you *are* just like the sister."

"I'll get the chops," Mr.—*Adam*—said, coming from another room. Molly allowed herself a small, internal smile at her use of his given name, even if it was silent. The Reverend would be appalled by such informality.

"You might as well get the thickest of 'em," Rosie called after him. "I don't reckon we can take all of 'em with us." She clicked her tongue a couple of times and turned to Molly. "Can you snap the beans, then, or don't you know how to do that neither?"

"Have you a spare apron?"

Rosie made the bunny laugh and plucked another white apron from a hook. "This was your sister's. Not that she had much use for it."

Molly reached for the apron. "Rosie, I loved my sister very much. Her faults were no more, or less, than my own. And since she is no longer here to defend herself, I must take offense for her if you insist on making disparaging remarks about her character."

Rosie rested her upper teeth on her lip and stared at Molly. She had the same silver gray eyes as her son. "You got more gumption than she did, don't ya?"

"I doubt that."

"I don't. It's good that a person stands up for their family. Ain't nothin' more important than that."

Rosie handed Molly a bowl and a colander filled with green beans. Taking them, Molly said, "You did not care for my sister."

"Ain't true. I cared for her when she was heavy with that baby and I cared for her through the night she birthed him. After, too. And I cared for her when she was dying."

"Then I owe you a debt of gratitude. Thank you."

Rosie gave a half nod and Molly noted with surprise that her eyes looked misty. "It weren't easy for her having that baby. Thought for a while she might not make it at all. She was such a small thing, just like you. And Arlie was such a big cuss to carry, bigger to deliver." The bunny laugh accompanied her words. "Just like Adam and Brodie. Big as horses they was."

"When was Arlie born?"

"March. He'll be a year come shortly."

Molly frowned. Vanessa had met Adam Weston in New York in September and wed him in November of the year before last. During the two months between their introduction and marriage, he had returned home to Ohio. Silently, Molly counted nine months back from March to June. That did not make sense, though. Vanessa had not yet met her husband in June.

"Was the baby born early?"

"A bit."

A bit? Even assuming that Vanessa had become with child on the eve of their wedding in November, it hardly gave the baby enough time to grow.

"Certainly more than a bit," she answered.

The front door shut behind Mr. Weston—*Adam*—she reminded herself again, and suddenly Rosie became a whirlwind of activity. She did not speak again until her son left to chop wood.

"Rosie?" Molly said.

"The baby weren't more than a bit early."

Molly shook her head. Rosie did not strike her as one capable of deception, but if Arlie had not been born dreadfully early, then that meant—

"It were September," Rosie said. "Couldn't have been no other time."

"But Adam was only in New York for a few days."

Rosie sucked her front teeth and widened her eyes. "Don't take more'n a few minutes."

Molly flushed hot from head to toe, remembering the first time she and her sister had met Mr. Adam Weston. They had gone to visit members of the Reverend's congregation and bring baskets of sweets and breads. Adam had been at the McCartys' home, delivering a custom dining table and sideboard that Mr. McCarty had ordered for his wife as a gift. While the

Reverend blessed the new furnishings, Adam exchanged pleasantries with the women.

Molly had offered him her gloved hand in introduction and watched as it was swallowed by his own. He'd seemed somehow larger than life, this man from the West with his drawl and quicksilver eyes. She'd been excited by the sound of his voice and the flash of his smile. For a moment, it seemed that he, too, had found something fascinating in her and the very idea had sent her heart pounding.

Then Vanessa had moved forward, laughing and teasing her way through their introduction, flashing him her flirtatious eyes and pouty smile. Of course he had been hopelessly entranced by her wit and beauty. Who could blame him? Vanessa was a gust of fresh air in a closed and stuffy room. Before they had left for home, he had asked the Reverend for permission to call, and reluctantly, the Reverend had granted it.

Adam visited one evening and then another day joined them for church and Sunday supper. Afterward, when he had returned to Ohio, Vanessa had written many letters to him, and he had written back, though none so frequent or wordy as Vanessa's. Then suddenly in November he had arrived at their door and asked to marry Vanessa.

But when had they . . . *How* had they managed a secret meeting? Vanessa had never mentioned it, never chosen to confide in Molly.

"Arlie's the sweetest babe I ever knowed," Rosie said. "You'll see when he wakes up. He's a joy."

Adam came back in with an armload of firewood and the conversation stopped. Molly wished her thoughts could be stopped as easily. She understood why Vanessa had not mentioned the coming birth of her son. A child conceived in sin would never be accepted by the Reverend. For all his talk of forgiveness, he himself had none to give to his daughters, and this crime against the church could not be overlooked. How long had Vanessa intended to keep Arlie a secret? Had she intended to lie about the time of his birth once he reached an age where it would not be obvious? Why had she not confided in Molly? Had she feared her own sister would betray her?

The questions circled relentlessly through her mind while Molly finished snapping the beans and put them on to boil.

"Put a wallop of fat in there," Rosie told her as she set the pot on the fire. Molly did as she was told.

Rose dropped breaded pork chops into a skillet of sizzling grease and soon the scent of frying pork filled the house. Molly had peeled potatoes and sliced them into wafers that Rosie added to the sizzling grease. She could not remember food ever smelling so good.

"May I set the table?" Molly asked.

Somewhere between snapping beans and slicing potatoes, Rosie had softened in her demeanor and Molly found that her bunny laugh had a contagious quality to it. She discovered a smile on her own lips whenever the old woman let loose the raspy titter, which was often. Rosie found humor in everything.

"Why don't you check on the baby and I'll put out the plates." She laughed at Molly's surprised glance. "Was you thinking I'd keep him hidden from you all night?"

"No, of course not. I just long to hold him."

Rosie's smile was gentle. "He done stole your heart already and you ain't even laid eyes on him yet."

Rosie led her into a bedchamber that was obviously her son's. In the corner, Adam's shirt was draped over the chair, and on the chest of the drawers, his black-handled comb and brush sat near a small mirror.

Molly's eyes circled around, bouncing lightly over the quilted bed to the crib pushed against the wall.

"He is awake," she breathed, moving forward.

Arlie lay on his back, arms and feet kicking in the air. He had a wide grin and as many teeth as Rosie.

"Hello, there," she murmured and reached in for him.

His diaper was soaked through and he smelled strongly of urine, but there was also a sweet scent to him, one of innocence and love and a bit of maple syrup. With a triumphant hoot, he wrapped his chubby arms around her neck and tried to free her hair from its twist.

"He's got nappies over there. You're lucky. That one's just wet."

The sound of Rosie's laugh drifted away as she left the room. Molly carried the drooling, babbling bundle of motion to a low table with diapers stacked on a shelf beneath. She found herself laughing as she worked his squirming body free of his wet diaper. Once naked, he squealed with joy.

Getting Arlie's clean diaper and dry clothes on was like trying to dress an octopus, but what Molly lacked in skill in other areas, she made up for with babies. While her father cared for the eternal souls of his congregation, Molly cared for the children.

As Rosie finished preparing their meal, Molly sat in the rocker and gave Arlie his bottle. Looking down on him as he sucked and slurped his milk, Molly's heart contracted into a tight knot. He resembled his father very little, but he looked so much like Vanessa it hurt.

As if beckoned by the thought, the front door opened and Adam came in with a gust of chilly evening air. Behind him was an adolescent boy of about sixteen who bore an uncanny likeness to Adam.

As he hung his coat on the wooden pegs beside the door, Adam caught sight of Molly rocking his son in the warm glow of the fire. For a moment he stared with a look that bordered on astonishment. Before she could wonder at his surprise, he stepped closer and gazed down at Arlie's chubby face, pressed close to Molly's breast as he suckled. Arlie smiled, but couldn't be bothered to let loose the bottle.

Molly looked up just as Adam bent down to touch the downy soft hair of Arlie's head. The fire, the contented babe, the blissful rocking, the virile, gentle father all joined with Molly in an instant that seemed both out of place and time but completely at peace with the moment. A deep feeling of belonging moved within her, and the temptation to cover Adam's hand with her own nearly brought her to the action.

"He's awake," Adam murmured. "And not fussing for a change." Arlie turned his head at the sound of his father's deep voice and cooed. "Hey there, fella. Did you find a pretty woman to take care of you?"

Molly's face felt as hot as the fire that kept the winter cold away. Adam's brother moved to the stove, where he sneaked a potato out of the skillet. Rosie rapped his knuckles with her wooden spoon and shooed him out. He came to join Adam in front of the fire and the oddly tender moment ended as quickly as it had begun.

"You must be Molly," he said, licking the grease off his fingers.

"Yes, I am."

"I'm Brodie." He cocked his head at Adam. "Adam's brother."

"It is a pleasure to make your acquaintance."

Brodie grinned. "You talk just as fancy as Vanessa." The smile vanished, leaving him open mouthed and flushed. "I mean, as she did. Before . . . uh . . ." He stared at his shuffling feet and backed away with a mumbled apology.

They settled Arlie on a blanket on the floor and gave him some smooth painted blocks and beads that were strung with twine. Adam's dog flopped down on the floor beside the baby's blanket and watched with sleepy eyes.

At supper, Brodie asked, "So what'd she say about California?"

"Didn't say nothin'," Rosie scolded, " 'cuz no one but you brung it up."

Molly had just taken a bite of the most succulent pork chop she'd ever eaten. Mouth full, she watched the conversation jump from one Weston to another.

"Doesn't matter," Adam said. "She's got to know sometime."

"Know what?" Molly asked, finally swallowing. Rosie skewered a piece of pork and popped it in her mouth, where she daintily chewed it with her front teeth.

"We're not staying on here," Adam answered.

"You are not staying on? What do you mean?"

"Me, Brodie, Ma, and Arlie. We plan on pulling up stakes in a few weeks. That's why I sent the letter."

She frowned, certain she would have remembered mention of an intended move—but she could not very well argue the point over a letter she had pretended not to receive. She took a drink of water, giving herself a moment to gather her wits.

"Have you found a new property?" she asked at last, pleased to hear the note of calm curiosity in her voice.

"Not exactly. Like Brodie said, we're going west. To California."

Brodie let out a yee-haw at that. Rosie shushed him.

Fork poised halfway to her mouth, Molly finally registered exactly what was being said. Going west . . . A few weeks . . . California . . .

The Reverend's voice resounded through her thoughts. *"If you go to that house of heathens, Margaret Louise Marshall, this house of the Lord will not welcome you back."*

"Why would you move to California?" she asked in a stunned voice. "I've heard that nothing has been settled there yet. It's only wilderness and savages that will kill you."

It was Adam's turn to look uncomfortable. Using her ploy, he lifted his glass and took a long drink of water. However, he was not forced to illicit a calm response.

Before Adam's glass had returned to the table, Brodie exclaimed, "Sure it's wilderness but that's not all it is. Hell, there's gold laying around in chunks just waiting for some lucky son of a bitch—pardon, ma'am—just waiting for someone to scoop 'em up. And land. There's so much land, all for the taking. Families are pulling out all over for California."

Molly had only heard horror stories about the West. Stories of savagery and hardship and starvation . . . her father had told her how the heathens would as soon scalp a man as look at him and he wouldn't even say what they did to women. Not that she took everything the Reverend said as gospel.

Still . . . She looked at her nephew playing on the floor. It was one thing for the adults to test fate, but to drag an innocent child into the unknown seemed unconscionable. And if they went to California, what was she to do?

The anger came on her so quickly she had no chance to consider or contain it. It was just there, suddenly, irrevocably, burning hot and furious. After all she'd risked in coming, now this?

Brodie jammed a huge bite into his mouth and waved his fork in the air. "Once we hit Independence, we'll hitch up with all the others heading out. Ain't that right, Adam?"

She faced Adam. "And what of Vanessa?"

He looked at her as if she'd sprouted horns and a pitchfork tail. "Vanessa is dead."

"I know she is dead, but you've buried her here and now you intend to just leave her?"

"It's not like she's going to know," Brodie said, a look of genuine confusion on his face.

"But *I* know," she answered, looking right into Adam's cold gray eyes. "I know that you took advantage of my sister and compromised her so that she would have no choice but to marry you and go away from her friends and family. And now she is dead and you will just leave her behind like your garbage."

"Vanessa never went anywhere she didn't want to go," he said in a soft, steely voice.

"Had she stayed, her life would not have been worth living. Nothing she could have done would have made up for the sin of conceiving out of wedlock. But she would not have suffered alone. The Reverend would have hunted you down, Adam Weston, and he would have killed you even if it meant spending eternity in hell for it."

Her words struck like a whip, and Molly was instantly horrified by the sting they left behind. Adam's face turned the color of paste while her own flamed. But deep inside, a part of her felt vindicated by what she'd said. She wanted to wound this man who had turned her world upside down when he'd taken her sister as his wife and then not protected her from the world to which he'd brought her.

Still, to think it was one thing, but to say it, to speak so to him when she was a guest in his house, was inconceivable, unbelievable, and most of all, unforgivable. In her entire life, she had never behaved in such an appalling manner. Mortified, she cleared her throat.

"I, I must apologize," she said hoarsely. "The journey has obviously exhausted me to the point of incoherence. Please forgive me my unwarranted disrespect."

He made a harsh sound that held neither anger nor forgiveness and shook his head.

Rosie cut a neat bite of pork chop and said, "Losing Vanessa has been hard on all of us, Molly. Now you ain't had as long to deal with it as we have, so we'll just let this pass. You remember this, though, don't none of us know how it was when Adam went back to New York City. Ask me, all you people living so close to each other are crazy. But I do know that I raised my son to know right from wrong." She popped the bite in her mouth and chewed vigorously with her front teeth.

"I can handle this, Ma."

"I know you can."

Adam took a deep breath and slowly blew it out, but the tension remained in his face. Molly closed her eyes tightly and desperately searched for something to say.

"What of Arlie?" she asked, picking him up from the blanket. He gripped a bright yellow block in his chubby fist. Victoriously he waved it in Molly's face.

"What about him? He goes with me."

"I could take him back with me as well. I could give him a good Christian upbringing."

"Yeah, well, as I understand it, Vanessa had one of those. It didn't do her much good."

His words felt like a slap in the face, but she knew she deserved it. And it was true, as much as she wished it were not. Vanessa most certainly had been a willing participant in their tryst.

"You can stay on until we're ready to pull out," he went on. "I expect by then you'll be ready to go back to your way of things in the city anyhow."

Molly felt cornered, ambushed by her own cruel tongue, trapped by her circumstances. Why had she let loose her temper? How could she tell these people that going back to New York was not an option? She would rather join Vanessa in the cold, foreign dirt of Ohio than face the condemned life that would be hers if she tried to go back to the Reverend's house.

Molly said, "What if I wish to go to California, too?"

Not even Arlie made a sound at that. They all stared at her

like she'd grown another head. Had she not been the one to make the brash declaration, she would have been staring as well. What was she thinking? Go to California with them after what she'd just said?

As she braced herself for Adam's jeering laughter, Arlie laid his little head down on her shoulder and found his thumb. The sound of sucking filled the quiet room. Adam stared from his son to Molly; however, he did not laugh.

"You're crazier than Vanessa," he said finally.

Insane was more like it. "You will need someone to watch the baby."

"Ma will do it."

Molly turned to Rosie. "Tell me you could not use another pair of woman's hands."

Now Adam did laugh, though Rosie remained silent as she watched the exchange with bright, curious eyes.

"You won't be any help," he said. "Vanessa couldn't have found a skillet with a map."

Molly knew that it was true. But she also knew something else, something Adam Weston had not yet come to realize. Shifting Arlie to her other hip, Molly raised her chin and stared him in the eye.

"I am not Vanessa."

chapter thirteen

TESS heard Caitlin's voice as if from a great distance. It echoed down the cavernous hallway and pulled her to the surface. She blinked and suddenly she was back.

Back . . .

She was still standing by the door, still staring at the corners of the small waiting area outside the school counselor's office. But her heart was hammering and her knees shook. She glanced at the clock, numb to the realization that only minutes had passed since Caitlin and Mrs. Sanders had gone to get Caitlin a soda. Only minutes . . . But it felt like days, weeks . . . centuries. She recoiled from the feelings of bewilderment and displacement that lingered.

"Here we are," Mrs. Sanders said a moment before the door opened and she and Caitlin walked inside. She smiled kindly at Tess, and Caitlin gave her a tiny wave, more at ease than she'd been earlier.

"Why don't you sit down and relax, Ms. Carson. We may be a while," the counselor said as she ushered Caitlin into her office and closed the door.

MOUNTAIN Bend Elementary was quiet by 4 P.M., tomb-like by 4:30. Sitting alone in his office, Craig Weston tried to concentrate on the paperwork stacked on his desk, but he knew that no one really expected him to accomplish anything this week. They were all surprised he'd even shown up for work when his father had died just the day before. But he hadn't wanted to stay home. There he'd be alone with nothing to do but rehash everything that had happened.

He looked at the few items on his desk. A coffee cup with pens his secretary had given him, a brass bell engraved with the date he'd become principal here, a lucky five-dollar chip from the casino in Piney River, and a picture of himself para-sailing in Mexico. There was nothing else personal on the desktop. What did that say about him? Nothing he wanted to address at the moment; of that was certain.

He riffled through the stack of pink messages Donna had left for him by the phone. Most were sympathy calls. Parents, friends, and neighbors, all wanting to offer him their condolences. Lydia had called three times. She was concerned, he knew. He should have stopped in this morning for coffee and talked to her. But he couldn't deal with Lydia any more than he could deal with himself, alone at home. He needed the quasi-anonymity that came from doing a job in a building full of kids that didn't even know he had a first name.

Craig tossed the messages back onto his desk and let out a pent-up breath. His thoughts played hot potato in his mind, bouncing from one sensitive hold to another, leaving behind a dull burn and the promise of a revisit.

During the past few years, his father had become more a burden than anything else. They loved each other in their own way. But the quality of their relationship had spiraled from the occasional perfunctory dinner to confrontations about Frank's future. He was too old to maintain the ranch and too stubborn to give it up. With Grant off living the Hollywood dream, the weight of responsibility had fallen on Craig's shoulders and he'd managed to carry the load. Then Grant had returned like the hero in one of his own movies and everything had gone completely to pieces.

Craig rubbed his hands over the rough stubble on his cheeks. He was tired of thinking about it, about Grant, about Tori, about Dad, about the entire mess preceding and following his horrible death. Death by fire, just like his wife, their mother. Craig didn't know how he would make it to the funeral.

He looked at the clock, wondering how much longer

Mrs. Sanders would keep Caitlin and Tess. He wondered what Mrs. Sanders was harvesting from Caitlin's ripe, young mind. Before she'd disappeared, had Tori given her any hints? Or was Caitlin as confused as everyone else by her mother's disappearance?

He heard their footsteps echoing in the hall seconds before their voices. Quickly he grabbed his raincoat and umbrella. He pulled his office door shut behind him and stepped out to wait.

When he saw Tess, Craig was startled by her appearance. This morning she'd been disheveled and embarrassed to be caught in her pajamas, but she'd recovered quickly and with grace. Without makeup, a hairbrush, or even coffee, she'd been beautiful and alluring. The moment he set eyes on her, he'd wanted to abandon his agenda and focus on nothing more than getting her into bed. But Tess Carson wasn't a woman who'd be easily manipulated or seduced. She was different. She struck him as a woman who had it all together, and she would expect the same of any man.

Later, when she'd arrived at the school, she seemed preoccupied. That was understandable. But something had changed since he'd left her in Mrs. Sanders's office. Something had darkened those confident blue eyes, given them a panicked glow and a gleaming frailty that they hadn't had before. What had Mrs. Sanders told her?

"How did everything go?" he asked, trying to sound more cheerful than he felt.

She looked beyond him, silent for a long moment. "It's still raining," she said, her voice sounding oddly flat.

An eerie sensation crept down Craig's spine. *Someone's walking on your grave,* his grandmother would have said.

"Hasn't let up at all," he answered slowly.

"Like the wrath of God," she murmured, staring at the gray-streaked world outside the glass doors of the school.

This time her edgy tone sent a shudder through him. "No, just a spring storm," he said, rethinking his assessment that she had it all together. Right now, she seemed to be completely out of it. "It might rain through the night. They're socking in for a flood up in Piney River. Of course the weather guy is only right about half the time, so it probably won't be all that bad." He squatted down next to Caitlin. "Did you have a good talk with Mrs. Sanders?"

"She let me have two suckers."

Her bright pink lips and tongue added testimony to that statement. Craig smiled at her. "Do you feel better?"

"I should talk more," Caitlin said solemnly.

"About what?"

"Things I think about. Sometimes I don't talk about them."

"Yeah, sometimes I do that too."

His knees popped when he stood, adding to the feeling that he was much too old for any of this. Ancient before forty. It didn't seem fair. Tess didn't say anything, but her silence was unnerving. Something must have happened in Mrs. Sanders's office, but what? What had she learned?

"I was thinking maybe we could grab a bite to eat," he said. "Talk over dinner." She was shaking her head before he finished, but he rushed on. "Come on. You gotta eat."

"Aren't you . . . I mean, I'm sure you have family matters to deal with right now that are more pressing than our problems."

"Well, we Westons are an unusual family and our family matters usually turn into brawls. My brother and me—well, put us in the same room and there's bound to be trouble."

She still looked confused, though now she seemed a little less disoriented. Like she'd been in a haze that had suddenly cleared, but left her wondering how she'd gotten there in the first place. Whatever she'd learned about Tori in Mrs. Sanders's office, it was major.

She said, "I met your brother today."

He couldn't help the knee-jerk reaction that caused. When had she met Grant? He checked his emotions and forced a teasing grin. "Is that why you're not jumping at the opportunity to have dinner with me tonight? Forget all the movie star stuff. I am the *principal* of the elementary school. I'm the most famous person in town. Come on. Have dinner with me."

She made a nervous sound that he supposed might pass for a laugh. "Thank you, Craig. But I don't think either one of us feels up to being in public." She looked down at Caitlin, who was watching her aunt with wide, curious eyes.

"In this weather, we'll probably be the only fools out," he said. "In *any* weather we wouldn't have to worry about a crowd. This isn't exactly a thriving metropolis we live in."

"I'd noticed it's a bit . . . quiet here."

His laugh was genuine. "Please, say yes. I really don't want to go home to a dark house and another zapped lasagna." She hesitated and he pressed on. "There's a restaurant right around the corner—the Steak Your Claim. Home of the ultimate twenty-ounce porterhouse."

She gestured at her faded blue jeans and sneakers. "I'm not dressed for anything nice."

"Who said it was nice? You're in Mountain Bend. We think getting dressed up is washing both sides of our hands."

She touched the silky golden hair on her niece's head. "What do you want to do, Caitlin? Do you want to go?"

Caitlin shrugged. "I guess. They have fish there."

"You like fish?"

"Not to eat. To watch. I like to watch them."

STEAK Your Claim was a small restaurant squatting in a stamp-sized parking lot between Benson's Grocery and a Mobile station. Tess followed Craig's dark blue Lexus from the school and pulled in beside him. She saw Grant's truck parked by the door and, next to it, a sheriff's cruiser. Strange that they would all meet up here tonight, but then again Mountain Bend was a very small town and most likely had little to offer to the dining connoisseur. Still, she couldn't help feeling that she'd been set up for an ambush.

If she hadn't been so disoriented and mixed up earlier, she would have been firmer with Craig. She wasn't up to small talk across a table, but his plea to be saved from a dark house had echoed her own desperation. She didn't want to return to Tori's home and part the shadows with the stifling fear building inside of her.

Craig was already out of his car and waiting at her door. Wishing she could just throw it into reverse and peel out, she shut off the engine and joined him. The three of them raced through the downpour. As they reached the front door, it swung open unexpectedly and Grant nearly knocked her over on his way out.

Craig caught her arm and held her steady. "Watch where you're going," he snapped at his brother.

Grant didn't answer and the look he gave Tess was filled with censure. What she'd done to deserve it, she couldn't begin to guess. Without a word, he turned up his collar and sprinted to his truck.

"He's never had any manners," Craig muttered.

The restaurant had an Old West theme with wagon wheel railings and horseshoe coatracks. Dark red leather booths lined the walls, and a scattering of walnut tables and matching chairs took up the limited floor space in between. A crowd of thirty would start a waiting list. But this evening, most of the tables were empty.

Smith and Ochoa sat in a booth against the far wall. Each had a section of the paper open beside his plate. They glanced up as Tess, Craig, and Caitlin came in. Smith's eyes narrowed on them. Ochoa gave Tess a concerned smile and a small salute.

A white-haired foursome had a table in the middle of the room and they watched with unconcealed curiosity as a waitress led Craig's group to their table. Tess heard them whispering behind her.

The only other customer sat tucked behind a half-wall. Tess realized it was Lydia. She was staring at them, or at least staring in their direction with a look of stunned disbelief. Tess didn't understand why she looked so shocked at the sight of them . . . unless it was something else, someone else, in the restaurant that had upset her. Perhaps someone who'd just left?

Tess paused at her table and said, "Hello, Lydia."

Lydia quickly masked her feelings with a shy smile and said hello.

"Lydia, how are you?" Craig said as if he'd just realized

she was there. "I didn't think anyone else would be nuts enough to brave this storm for a steak and potato."

Tess could tell that he hadn't intended to insult her, but Lydia most certainly interpreted the remark that way. Her fleshy face flushed deep red and she lowered humiliated eyes to her plate, where a sprout of parsley perched on the edge, the sole survivor of a feast among the crumbs and a cleaned T-bone. A second plate, partially cleaned, was on the other side of the table. Tess wondered who had dined with her? Grant? Possibly. Possibly the plate had been Lydia's as well.

"It looks like we're too late to ask you to join us for dinner," Craig continued, unaware of the embarrassment he caused her. "But how about a cup of coffee and dessert?"

She shook her head, glancing at Tess from the corner of her eye. Craig had obviously hurt her feelings, and Tess felt bad for her.

"Please join us," Tess said immediately.

"I'm all through," Lydia answered in that soft, breathy voice. "I want to get home before the storm gets any worse." She snapped open her purse and pulled out some money. She set it on the table and stood, forcing Tess to take a step back. Lydia wore an elegant coral silk skirt and a matching top, but the rain had riddled both with water spots and a large grease stain lay like a gaudy brooch between her ample breasts.

"Why don't you go ahead to the table," Craig said to Tess. He waited for her nod before trailing Lydia to the door, where she was struggling with the sleeve of her tan trench coat.

Caitlin and Tess followed the waitress, who had stood there patiently through the exchange. She wore a name tag that said CECE.

"I know where *you* want to sit," she said to Caitlin as she stopped at a booth beside an aquarium that bulged, globelike, from a partial divider wall. Caitlin scooted up to it and stared in at the brightly colored fish, holding Purcy so the stuffed Kitty could see as well.

"Can I get you something to drink?" Cece asked Tess.

"Yes. White wine, please. No—make that a rum and Coke. Easy on the Coke."

Cece winked. "How about you, honeybunch. You want your usual?"

Caitlin nodded without turning away from the fish. Craig and Lydia had stepped out of sight, and in the quiet Tess leaned back against the soft leather of the booth and took a deep breath. Like a movie, her memory flashed to scenes of Molly and Adam, Rosie and Brodie Weston . . .

We Westons are an unusual family . . .

The blackout this morning still hovered like a dense fog in her mind, but she could recall every detail of the *episode* she'd had in Mrs. Sanders's office. And now she'd made a connection—the man on horseback, the man she'd seen from Tori's bedroom window—he was Adam. She was sure of it. So what was he doing here and now?

Tess covered her face with her hands. She had to have dreamed it all up, for God's sake. Clearly she'd incorporated her stress and worry into some dream world where her subconscious had cast the Westons into strange roles. She nodded to herself. It was the only thing that made sense. She'd hardly slept the night before and her exhausted mind was playing tricks on her.

It had to be, because the alternative was that she was delusional.

Cece returned with a tall glass filled with pink liquid and ten cherries for Caitlin and a short glass with cola-colored rum for Tess. Tess thanked her and then forced herself not to gulp the drink down. Her hands were shaking.

"Cece seems to know exactly what you like," Tess said to Caitlin when the waitress had left. "Do you and your mom come here a lot?"

"Sometimes."

"Alone?"

"Sometimes. Sometimes with Mr. Weston."

"Which Mr. Wes—"

"Sorry about that," Craig said, suddenly appearing at the table. He smoothed his hair, and slid into the other side of the booth. "I didn't mean to keep you waiting so long."

"No problem."

"Lydia called me several times today to offer her condolences, but I didn't call her back. Her feelings were hurt."

"You don't have to explain."

"I'm not. She's a sweet woman, and I wanted her to know I appreciated her concern."

"I'm glad you saw her then."

Wishing he'd have stayed out another minute until Caitlin answered her question, Tess opened the menu. In silence, they both studied it. Caitlin, it seemed, had a regular dinner choice as well as drink and she told Tess what it was before returning her attention to the fish.

After they'd ordered dinner, another rum and Coke for Tess, and a beer for Craig, he leaned forward and asked, "How did it go with Mrs. Sanders today?"

It was the second time he'd asked, and something made Tess wonder if it was more than courtesy or curiosity that made him do it.

"Caitlin says it went fine."

Caitlin scooted out of the booth and circled around to the other side of the aquarium. They could see her face, distorted by the water, through the bowl.

"Mrs. Sanders spoke to Caitlin alone, so I don't know what was said. You were hoping that Caitlin told her something about Tori."

"Weren't you?"

Tess shrugged. "If she knew something about her mother, she would have mentioned it by now. It seems more likely she'd tell me than a stranger."

"Why? For all practical purposes, you are a stranger, aren't you?"

"What do you mean?"

"You only see her a couple times a year."

"How do you know that?"

Craig took a drink, looking away. "Caitlin told me. Honestly, Tess, I think Caitlin does know something. Maybe she just doesn't think it's something important."

"Like what?"

"Well, Lydia told me about Caitlin pulling that key out and

saying Tori had given it to her. Don't tell me that's not strange."

The restaurant suddenly seemed very warm, and the smell of roasting meat was sickening. She took a drink before answering. "I'm her only living relative. Who else would she have given a key to?"

"You have a point. But Sheriff Smith said Tori's car is still missing. He thinks she must have seen the accident and ran."

"Everyone seems very willing to believe that of her. My sister is not the kind of person who'd just take off and leave an injured man to die."

"I wasn't saying she would. But what about the money, Tess? It didn't just walk away on its own."

"Did you invite me here to interrogate me? Was that charming principal routine an act to get me out here?" Her voice rose in the quiet and she struggled to bring it back down. "I don't know what happened. I don't know where Tori is. I spent the afternoon calling hospitals as far away as Los Angeles and she's not at any of them. It's as if she's just disappeared and I'm the only one who doesn't think it's because she wanted to."

Craig was shaking his head. "Tess—I'm sorry. The last thing I meant was to upset you."

Tess glanced at Caitlin. Her niece seemed absorbed with the fish, but Tess sensed she was listening. She took another drink, letting the cool rum slide down her throat.

"I swear, Tess, all I wanted was to take both of our minds off all this. I guess that's just not possible, though. Not with all the uncertainties."

"I just don't know why everyone is so quick to think she'd just up and leave her daughter. She loves Caitlin."

"Of course she does. No one is questioning that, Tess." Craig took a long drink of his beer. "It's the small-town gossip—there's no getting away from it. My dad dying and Tori . . . vanishing are the most exciting things to happen here since the church burned down years ago. Everyone has an opinion. My brother thinks the sheriff is blowing it all out of proportion just to add some spice to his life."

"Could that be true?"

"No. Grant's just looking out for his own interests. He doesn't want the ranch tied up in probate by a lengthy investigation." He paused and took another drink of his beer. "Or maybe he doesn't want the investigation for other reasons."

Tess frowned. "What other reasons?"

"Hard to tell with Grant. Could be anything." Bitterness etched lines in his face. "He has a lot at stake."

"You're talking in circles, Craig."

"Grant gets the ranch. That's all he's ever wanted."

Tess stared at him, as bewildered by his words as she was stunned by the intensity behind them.

"There I go again. I'm sorry. I really am. Grant is like a hot button with me. He hasn't been back that long and . . . we're having to learn how to live together—in the same town anyway—all over again."

Cece appeared at their table with a smile and hands full of plates. "Hope you're hungry."

They ate in silence. At least Craig and Caitlin ate. Tess suddenly felt sick to her stomach. The rum had begun to burn and she just wanted out. She wanted to feel the cold rain on her face. She wanted to breathe air that hadn't steamed with the scent of beef.

"Has anyone thought to call friends Tori might have contacted in . . . where was it she was living before?" Craig asked between bites.

"Los Angeles. She wasn't there long enough to make friends. I've called everyone else I can think of, but they haven't heard from her. Before that she was in Salt Lake. And before that, Ohio."

Ohio. Tess took a drink of water.

"Mommy doesn't like to stay in one place too long," Caitlin said, swirling a french fry in ketchup.

"Why not?" Craig asked.

Caitlin shrugged, stuffing the french fry in her mouth. She held up another for the fish to see. Watching her, one would never guess that she was dealing with such incredible uncertainties. Mrs. Sanders had been right on when she'd said Caitlin was repressing it all.

Tess sighed. The ability to block out everything must be a family trait. Wasn't Tess doing the same thing? Carrying on a conversation while inside she felt like her whole world had been turned upside down and shaken? She wanted to ask Craig why he'd accused Tori of acting paranoid this morning. What had she been doing that made him think she was paranoid? Was she delusional? Did she see people waltz off the pages of history books? Did she feel like she should know who they were and why they'd appeared like the sudden storm buffeting the restaurant outside? But Tess didn't ask. She didn't think she could handle the answers.

Gently, Craig touched her hand. "It'll be okay," he said. "We'll find Tori and get to the bottom of this."

"Do you know her very well?" she asked.

"No better than I know most of my students' parents. Not very well at all."

Caitlin yawned loudly. "It's getting late," Tess said.

She reached for her purse to pay for dinner, but Craig insisted that he buy. She didn't want to feel beholden to him, but it would have been ridiculous to argue over a dinner check.

"I can follow you home and make sure you get there safely," he offered as they moved to the door.

"Thanks, but we'll be okay."

As she started her car and pointed it in the direction of Tori's house, Tess hoped that was true.

chapter fourteen

THE storm had gathered steam while Tess and Caitlin were inside the restaurant, making the drive home a harrowing test of man against nature. The rain came in thick, powerful sheets that pelted the roof and slammed the windows. Thunder exploded in the pitch-black sky, and just ahead of them a bolt snapped down and cracked open a huge oak. Caitlin screamed. White-knuckled, Tess swerved around the branch that crashed to the ground.

Her tires churned over the rough, flooded roads, defying the slippery, sucking mud as they inched closer to their destination. At last the driveway leading to Tori's house appeared, and she turned onto it with a deep sigh of relief. She brought the car to a gentle stop in front of the house, but her clutch on the wheel was much harder to disengage.

She and Caitlin raced to the porch, knowing they'd be soaked no matter how fast they ran, but trying to beat the torrential rain all the same. They were both shivering as Tess shut the front door behind them. The dark stillness dispelled any hope Tori might be there, but they both called out for her all the same. No one answered.

Tess's despair nearly overwhelmed her as she reached for the switch to turn on the lights and said, "Let's get into some dry clothes and I'll make us something hot to drink."

The click of the switch followed her words, but no illuminating comfort came with it. Tess switched it on and off again and then tried the lamp with the same result. The darkness of the house folded back like a layered swathing, tight enough to suffocate.

"What's wrong with the lights, Aunt Tess?"

"I don't know. I guess the power is out."

Caitlin made a small hurt sound and clutched her stuffed kitty. "I don't like the dark. I don't like the way it smells."

Tess had never thought of the dark as having an odor, but as she gave Caitlin a reassuring smile, she realized it did. It had a definite scent. And she didn't like it either.

Headlights sliced across the yard and through the open living room curtains as they hovered there, unsure of what to do next. Tess let her eyes flutter down in relief. Craig. He must have known about the power and followed them home. She'd never been so happy to have a man disregard her wishes.

But as the headlights stopped behind her car, she realized that they couldn't belong to Craig's Lexus. They were too high. Too far apart. The vehicle's door opened and the interior light bathed Grant Weston and his rundown truck in a buttery glow.

Famous person to the rescue . . .

Tess reached up to smooth her hair in an action that was at once automatic and ridiculous. Rain had plastered it to her head and probably streaked her makeup down to her chin. Why was it she looked like hell every time this man appeared?

"Who cares," she mumbled to herself, moving to the front door.

Turning on a high-beam flashlight, Grant made a dash for the porch. She opened the door as soon as he reached it and stepped back to let him inside. Caitlin took Tess's hand and moved with her like a shadow.

He shook off his coat on the porch and came in. "Power's out, could be for the night. I thought I'd make sure everything was all right over here."

He spoke with cool detachment, but those light eyes scanned her face with a glimmer of concern and something else. Something she could no more identify than she could deny. A warmth that belied her shivers spread up to her face.

Tess quickly looked away and tried to match his tones. "When did it go out?"

"I heard something hit about ten minutes ago. Sounded

like a cannon went off. The lights went at the same time. Do you have candles and a flashlight?"

"I don't know. We just got home. I haven't even looked."

His flashlight beam cut across the dark living room as he went into the kitchen. Tess followed with Caitlin close behind, watching as the light bathed barren counters, faded cupboards, and deep corners. He opened doors and searched drawers before coming back empty-handed.

"Is he going to make the lights come on?" Caitlin whispered. Shadows played across her face, and her eyes looked huge above her pale cheeks.

"No, honey, but don't worry. We'll be okay."

"I don't wanna be in the dark."

The fear and anguish in Caitlin's eyes were nearly Tess's undoing. Not only were the two of them here, alone and frightened, but Tori was out there somewhere and all they could do was pray she was safe. Tess smoothed Caitlin's hair back from her face and pressed a kiss to the top of her head. She caught Grant staring at her and had the eerie feeling that he'd read her mind.

"I saw some wood outside," he said. "I'll start a fire for you."

"It's okay. Don't trouble yourself, Mr.—"

"Grant. Just Grant."

His voice was deep and smooth, just like in the movies. She caught herself staring at his mouth, watching his sensuous lips form words.

"Grant," she said. His name felt strange rolling off her tongue, strange and somehow intimate. His eyes darkened and Tess felt awareness heat her chilled skin. "I've already inconvenienced you enough for one day. I can get the wood myself."

"Good. Glad we got that out in the open." As he handed her the flashlight, his fingers brushed against hers and the warmth of his touch registered on a thousand different levels. He hesitated, or maybe she just wished that he would let the touch linger. But then he turned up the collar of his jacket and went outside. A moment later she heard an engine start and his lights switched on.

Disappointment washed through her. So much for him being a real-life hero. He'd just left the damsel in distress to drown in the dark. His headlights danced up the wall as the truck backed up and then they swung away from the window. Holding Caitlin's hand, she peered out in time to see Grant moving past the corner of the house toward the woodpile. The headlights illuminated the way.

Surprised, Tess gave Caitlin's shoulders a reassuring squeeze. "See. He seems like a nice man."

Caitlin didn't say anything.

"Come on. Let's find out if the stove is working."

A bright blue flame *whumpfed* up to the burner when Tess turned the knob. Trying not to look as relieved as she felt, Tess pulled out a box of hot chocolate she'd found earlier, filled a small saucepan with water, and set it over the fire. What she really wanted was coffee, but she couldn't stomach another cup of the instant stuff. She still couldn't believe Tori didn't have a coffee maker—not that it would do her any good with the power out, but it would have been at least comforting to know that one existed on the off chance that the electricity would be restored by morning.

"While we wait for that, why don't we change into something dry?" she said to Caitlin. "Then we'll snuggle up in some blankets in front of the fire. It'll be fun. Just like a campout, only inside."

By flashlight they went upstairs. Caitlin brought her pajamas into Tori's room so they could share the light while they changed.

Tess draped Caitlin's discarded clothes over the bathtub before undressing herself. Taking a deep breath, she faced the bathroom mirror. The glow of the flashlight turned her reflection into a ghost that floated in the gloom. She looked for the bruises she'd gotten during her afternoon of insanity. But her skin was clear and unmarred. The bruises were gone. All of them.

"Aunt Tess?"

If they had existed at all.

"Do you think there are lights where Mommy is?"

Tess gripped the sink. "What did you say?"

"Do you think there are lights? Where Mommy is? Does she have lights?"

Tess thought hard, trying to find an answer in the chaos of her thoughts. *The bruises were gone, gone . . . where did they go . . . had she imagined them? Dreamed them up like she had those people today?*

"I hope there are lights where she is," Tess managed at last. Quickly she changed into a dry sweatshirt and soft gray sweatpants. She forced the uncertain hysteria back. "I'm sure there are lots of lights."

Tess stepped out of the bathroom. Caitlin had scrambled up on the bed and sat cross-legged atop the bright red comforter, dressed in lavender pajamas with black-and-white kittens parading over them.

"Mommy hates the dark, too."

The front door slammed and footsteps thumped the wooden floors. Caitlin jumped off the bed and hurried to the top of the steps.

"It's *him*," she whispered and started down.

They found Grant bent over a stack of wood by the fireplace. He reached for some paper in a bin next to the wall and began to crumple it up and shove it beneath the grate. After arranging some logs on top, he lit it. The paper burned bright and fast, but the wet wood hissed and smoked in protest before finally giving in to the flames.

Looking up, he said, "I put a stack of wood right outside the door there. Should be enough to get you through the night." He stood and set his matchbook on the mantel instead of returning it to his pocket. On the front of the pack, Tess could see two silver teacups and teal and pink embossed writing.

"I'm making hot chocolate," she said. "Would you like some?"

He paused and then shrugged. "Sure."

Tess filled three mugs with powder and boiling water and added a big splash of milk to Caitlin's so she wouldn't burn her mouth. In silence they took their cocoa and sat in front of the fire. Grant seemed too big for the small room, or maybe it was simply her awareness of him that made her think so. He sat on the chair, forearms resting on his spread thighs and the cup cradled in his big hands.

He looked around, his eyes lighting on the life-sized sun-flower that had taken Tess weeks to make.

"Huh," he said, reaching out to touch the seeds that she'd painstakingly glued, one by one, in the flower's center. "That's a lot of sunflower seeds."

"Only about a billion." She could feel her face grow hot. "That's how bored I was."

"You made it?" He raised his brows and looked at the flower again.

"Believe it or not. I don't know why Tori kept it."

"We love that flower," Caitlin said in an injured voice. "It's beautiful."

Tess smiled at the adoration on Caitlin's face. She gave her small shoulders a squeeze. "I love you, Caity."

The warmth had already begun to spread through the room, but the booming thunder and cracking lightning kept them at the edge of their seats. Caitlin drank her hot chocolate quickly, then lay down on the couch with her head on Tess's lap. Absently, Tess stroked her silky, damp hair, overly conscious of Grant sitting so close that their knees nearly touched.

"This is twice today you've come to my rescue," she said in the gaping quiet that followed the thunder.

He looked up and his eyes crinkled at the corners with a smile. "Well, seeing how I almost ran you over earlier, I thought it was the least I could do."

Tess grinned, briefly overcoming the nagging anxiety that stuck in her head like a high-pitched hum. "I guess you were indebted to me for not having a broken neck."

"You've got that right. The way my luck has been lately, I wouldn't have been surprised to have a lawsuit waiting for me by the time I got home."

There was just enough bitterness in his voice to make his smile transparent. Tess thought of the paparazzi and the pulp newspapers that had used his name like toilet paper in the last few years. She hadn't noticed until just then, but his face, either bloated by booze, or disfigured by recent alien abductions, had been noticeably missing in the checkout aisle at the grocery store lately. Looking at him now, he didn't even resemble the man they'd exploited. Apparently he'd managed to elude their prying and lies long enough to vanish and clean up his act. Or had he become old news and been allowed to pass on the lime-light to the next victim of fame?

It seemed he followed her train of thought to its unpleasant conclusion because he stood suddenly and took his cup into the kitchen. She heard water in the sink as he rinsed it. Caitlin had fallen asleep and Tess gently eased her up so she could scoot out from under her. She settled a cushion beneath Caitlin's head without waking her. In the kitchen she leaned against the counter behind Grant, watching as he carefully set his cup in the drying rack.

He faced her and leaned against the opposite counter. "The wood is right outside on the porch," he repeated.

"Thank you."

The narrow kitchen was dim and his face was shadowed, but she felt his gaze, felt the light touch of it as it traveled over her face. "I'm just next door if you need anything else. I'll give you my phone number and you—"

"You're next door? You mean you're a neighbor?"

Grant Weston was Tori's neighbor, too?

Westons, Westons, everywhere . . .

"Well, our properties share a border, if that's what you mean. The ranch is the only thing between here and Piney River. It's a fair hike to my front door, but if you give me a call, I can be here in five minutes."

She frowned. "You and Craig *both* have property border-ing this one?"

"This place is part of the ranch. The foreman used to live here."

"Who owns this house now?"

"I do."

The ranch means everything to Grant.

A shiver stood her hair on end and ran down her spine. "Tori pays you rent?"

"Not yet."

What did that mean?

"She had something worked out with my father."

"Is that who hired Tori? Your father?"

"No. She did some accounting for a producer I know. He recommended her when he heard I was going into business."

"What *is* your business?"

"Horses. I started in Hollywood as a stunt rider."

"And then you were discovered?"

He shrugged. "Something like that."

"So Tori is managing your accounts now? Is your business doing so well that you need a full-time accountant?"

Grant half laughed and shook his head. "No. I can't afford her, but I can't afford not to have it done. She's just trying to get me to ground zero. Dad hasn't—Dad didn't keep track of things. I can't tell where the money's gone. I sent enough home when I was making it—but who knows where it is now." He let out a breath. "I think she's close to finishing up."

The frustration in his tone was clear. The two people who might have given him answers were gone.

"Tori's been working out of your house for several weeks. You've probably gotten to know her fairly well . . ."

He drew back, his expression wary. "We say good morning and good-bye."

"Did you see her yesterday?"

"Just for a minute when she came in. We were both busy."

"Did she seem different to you?"

He grinned sardonically. "Tori always seems different to me. But no, she didn't seem more different than usual. It was just another day. She was working on the books, I was cleaning out the stables. Dad was . . ." His voice trailed off.

What? Dad was what?

He took a breath and continued. "I'd pulled out the tractor to work on it. I didn't know he was going to try to clear out that stump."

"I'm sorry."

"Yeah. It's a mess, isn't it? Dad's dead, Tori's gone. Who knows what the hell happened yesterday."

"Sheriff Smith told me that money is missing from your house."

"That's right."

"He thinks Tori took it and ran."

"He thinks a lot of things."

"How about you, Grant? What do you think happened?"

He stared at her for a long moment, his expression inscrutable, and then he lifted his hand and brushed a stray lock of hair away from her face. "You seem like a nice person, Tess. Don't go looking for answers here."

She thought of Craig, leaning across the table at dinner, saying in an anxious voice, "He doesn't want the ranch tied up in probate by a lengthy investigation."

She looked quizzically at Grant. "That's a strange thing to say."

"You think so? You think you're going to like what you find? You think you're going to feel better if you know that Tori took off and left her kid and a dying man for five grand?"

Tess stiffened. "I don't think that's what I'm going to find at all. Tori wouldn't do that."

His expression made her want to look away. She fought the urge.

Finally he answered, "Like I said, I don't know her that well."

A clap of thunder followed his words and bright white light shot their features into stark relief.

"The storm isn't letting up at all." He frowned and reached past her to the phone, picked up the receiver, and listened for a dial tone. "Damn it. The phones are out, too." He looked at Tess with indecision while outside rain pounded against the roof and windows.

"Listen," he said slowly. His voice was pitched low and it rubbed against her heightened senses. "Why don't you two come back to the ranch with me? There's plenty of room and . . ."

And? And they'd be safe there? Was that what he'd been about to say? Safe from what? From whom?

"And what?" she asked.

Grant leaned forward as if to catch her words, and the narrow corridor of the kitchen brought him close enough to touch. Close enough to breathe in the clean smell of him, the faint mysterious scent of his cologne, the warmth of his skin. She studied his face, trying to see what he thought, what he felt. He shook his head, as if to deny her access, but when he spoke, his voice was gentle. "And I won't have to spend the night thinking about you," he said.

What she saw in his eyes told her that his statement was less about concern and more about the electricity that seemed to spark and flow between them. Lightning lit the room in almost the same instant as earth-shaking thunder rattled the house. In the other room, Caitlin cried out in fear, breaking the spell Grant had cast on Tess. Quickly she rushed to her niece's reaching arms.

"Shhh, honey, it's okay. Just the storm," Tess soothed, holding her trembling niece. Over Caitlin's head, Tess met Grant's eyes. "It's just a storm. Nothing to be frightened of."

He met her stare, looking for a moment like he would press the matter. Did he want them to go with him because he wanted to be with her? Or was he worried about them being here alone? Was he thinking of Tori? Did he know something about her disappearance? Something that made him fear they wouldn't be safe in a storm?

He exhaled and rubbed a hand over the light bristle on his cheeks. "You're sure you won't come? The roads were flooding when I got here. It might be hard to get out later."

"It's just a storm," she repeated, though her voice lacked the conviction she'd hoped for.

Awkwardly they stared from one to another, each waiting for a sign.

"I'll leave you my flashlight."

Caitlin buried her face in Tess's shoulder and held tight when Grant walked through the door. In silence they watched again as his headlights climbed the wall and then slid away.

"Hey," Tess said, catching Caitlin's chin between her finger and thumb. "What's that long face for? We're not afraid of a little rain, are we?"

But as Tess looked around her, it felt as if Grant's departure had released the clustered shadows from corners. Now they danced and writhed in the flickering firelight, waiting for her to let down her guard so they could close in. If the fire should die, they would take control, growing like a stain from the far reaches to the center of the room where she and Caitlin sat, defenseless.

Knock it off, Tess . . .

But like it or not, silly or not, she was afraid.

chapter fifteen

LYDIA wiped away her tears as she stepped through her front door. She'd spent the day wallowing in her despair, crying, eating, stalking. She felt both naïve and stupid, horrified by the magnitude of her gullibility. She'd even toyed with the idea of taking Highway 53 and never coming back. If Tori France could disappear into thin air, why couldn't Lydia Hughes? But she knew Tori hadn't performed her vanishing routine willingly, and becoming her follow-up act would be a mistake of untold magnitude. Worse, if Lydia disappeared, there'd be no sister or daughter to care. All Lydia had was her pathetic little coffee shop and the largest dress size in town.

She hung up her wet coat and reached for the light switch, wanting to cry when the lights didn't come on. With a deep sigh, she made her way through the dark to the kitchen cupboard, where she kept candles and matches. Always prepared, that was Lydia.

When she'd opened the bed-and-breakfast, she'd had big dreams of success, power, and respect. But instead of growing and thriving like their neighbor Piney River, Mountain Bend had dwindled, taking with it her hopes. Now the town was just a potty stop on the way to somewhere else. That could change, though—would change—had to change. She was mortgaged to her dyed roots. She'd lose everything if it didn't.

She sighed, looking around the shadowed back rooms that made up her home, a place that usually brought her peace. But tonight she hated every prissy doily and velvet chair. She hated the dainty parlor lamps and provincial tables. She even hated her prized Precious Moments collectibles. Mostly, though, she hated herself.

He'd played her for a fool and she had let him.

In her bedroom, she undressed, fighting to control the unbearable ache of betrayal as she did. She faced her closet, and the full-length mirror hanging inside trapped her in its glass. Her reflection caught her unaware and brought her to her knees.

She reached past her favorite white sweats to the aqua lounger he'd bought her for her birthday. Betrayed or not, she had to be prepared. He might show up at her door. He was worried about her cracking under pressure, after all. It would serve him right if she did.

But even as she hated him, she felt a thrill at the thought of seeing him. She wanted him the same way she wanted cheesecake and pizza even when she wasn't hungry. She couldn't deny herself, even when the consumption brought sickness and self-loathing.

Numbly, she brushed her teeth, repaired her face by candlelight, and then arranged herself on the sofa with a fresh pot of Earl Grey. An hour later, she'd worn a path from the couch to the window. The tea was gone. So were the dozen brownies she'd made that afternoon. She felt panicked, alone. What if he didn't come?

But then she heard his knock and it silenced the screech of fear in her head. The brush of his knuckles against her door was soft and intimate. It coaxed her to her feet and drew her forward a step before she even realized it.

I'm here, the knock whispered, *Let me in . . .*

He didn't have a key of his own. Why would he need one when she was always there waiting for him? Any other night she would have been standing at the opened door before the sound of his engine died.

But now everything was changed; everything was wrong. She pressed her damp palm against the cool wood of the door and called, "Who is it?" when she couldn't bring herself to say, "Go away."

She felt the pause on the other side of the door, she felt the shift in the night air, and she knew he'd heard her thoughts. Thunder rumbled and lightning illuminated the windows.

"Baby, open the door," he said when it faded. His voice was gentle and persuasive.

She shook her head, unable to force the word "no" past her lips.

"Come on, Lydia, I know what you're thinking, but it's not like that. Open the door, let me explain."

A part of her grasped at the hope that he *could* explain. That he might have the words to make it right. But transposed on to the vision of that hope was the reflection of herself. Obese and unlovable. She'd been fooling herself with him, and it was time to face that.

"Lydia." His tone was firm, not yet angry. This was his "reasonable man" voice. She was no stranger to it. "Open the door."

She swallowed around the dryness in her mouth, wondering at the insanity that had possessed her. He wouldn't tolerate this defiance. Her expectations and doubts fell outside the margins of their relationship. He made the rules; she followed them. Why else would he keep a woman like her?

The silence on the other side screamed as she stepped back, staring at the door with dread and indecision. What should she do? If she opened it now after delaying, he would be angry with her. *Very* angry. But if she didn't open the door . . . The pounding of rain on the roof grated against her raw nerves.

Her hands were sweaty. They shook violently as she reached for the deadbolt and checked that it was still secure. She needn't be frightened, she told herself.

But the small oblong knob shivered for a moment as a key slid in to the lock.

She was frozen in disbelief as he threw the door open and rushed at her in a dripping blur of dark clothes and rage, clamping a wet hand over her mouth before her scream became sound. He pushed her back, unmindful of the table in the entry and the wall behind it. She heard the door slam, then her treasured Precious Moments figurines shatter against the tiled floor and the crack of her antique mahogany table as it splintered. He plowed her backward until she hit the wall with a *whump* that rattled the light fixtures and knocked the air out of her lungs. For one crazy split second she thanked God that there were no guests to hear them, then he slammed her head into the unyielding plaster and black patterns exploded behind her eyes.

He was taller than she, but nowhere near her mass. Still, his wrath kept her trapped against the wall. He pressed his hand tight over her mouth and nose, so tight she couldn't breathe. In contrast, he took deep ragged breaths. He leaned in close, letting her see the full scale of his uncontrolled fury.

"I don't like games, do I, Lydia?"

She tried to shake her head but couldn't move. He was smothering her and she was letting him.

"When I say open the door, you better—open—the—door."

He accented each word with a shake that snapped her head back against the wall. Eyes clenched tight, she tried to hold on to consciousness, but weakness spread through her veins in place of oxygen. Her knees buckled and she began to slide down the wall. Still he kept her mouth and nose covered. She opened her eyes and looked deeply into his until her vision blurred to darkness.

When she came to, she was sprawled on the floor. Her mouth was dry, but no longer covered with his hand. She didn't know how long she'd been unconscious, but her lungs burned as she gulped in breaths of air. Her feet stung from the glass she'd stepped on. Her head hurt. The silky fabric around her legs was wet and the smell of urine hung strong in the air. All that tea . . .

Humiliation crowded in between the fear and pain. From the corner of her eye she saw him move away from the wall and come at her again.

"I'm sorry," she whimpered before he kicked her hard in the gut. She screamed and curled up into a ball, trying to protect herself from the anger that was far from spent. He circled, kicking her in the legs and arms and fleshy expanses in between. "You didn't know I had a key, did you?" he asked in a voice so soft she barely heard. "Did you really think you could lock me out?"

He reached down and grabbed two handfuls of her aqua gown, squeezing her flesh in his punishing grip as well. He hauled her to her feet and slammed her back against the wall.

"I'm sorry," she said again, sobbing now. "I'm sorry."

He slapped her face so hard with the back of his hand that it felt like her cheek had exploded, and then he shoved her away. As much as anything, the slap stunned her. He was usually careful to avoid the face, where evidence of his abuse could not be concealed. She fell to her knees in the broken pieces of her figurines, crying and begging for him to stop, to forgive her. He kicked her hard in the rump and knocked her flat, belly down in the broken glass.

"Clean up this mess, you pig," he said, striding angrily into the kitchen.

She lumbered to her feet, weeping silently as she picked up the fragments of her collection. She was covered in blood from her hands, feet, and knees, but she swept up the glass like a robot who felt no pain. Outside the storm raged on.

Knowing there was no way to avoid it, she limped into the kitchen to wait for whatever came next. Keeping her eyes downcast, she paused in front of him, soaked in her own urine and bleeding from a hundred different places. He was standing at the island, a drink in his hand and a bottle of Crown Royal on the counter beside him. When he drank, it was always ugly.

He watched her with dispassion as she went to the sink and ran water over her bloody hands. She was shaking too hard to remove the pieces of glass that stuck out of the fleshy pads of her palm. His stillness behind her was as frightening as his fury had been. Muttering a curse, he moved suddenly to the sink and reached for her. She yelped like a beaten dog and scooted away, but his touch was gentle now and his voice soft as a lover's.

"It's okay. Let me help."

Carefully he bent to extract the slivers and let them rinse down the drain. When he was satisfied that he'd gotten all of them, he went to the cupboard where she kept her first aid kit. The candle cast shifting shadows that played devil with his features.

"Wait here," he told her, getting a clean towel and some ice for her face. She couldn't stop crying, but she did as he said. He took a candle and disappeared for a moment. When he returned, he brought her white sweats and a pair of underwear. The sight of the enormous undergarment in his hand filled her with mortification. Powerless, she let him pull off her wet clothes, like she was a baby. Making her stand naked except for her industrial-strength bra, every roll and bulge of her milky flesh exposed, he bandaged her hands, told her to sit, and then washed the glass off her feet and knees. Only after he'd wrapped both up with clean gauze and tape did he allow her to dress.

When she'd finished, he swung a chair around and sat in front of her. "What were you thinking, Lydia?"

She gulped deep draughts of air, fighting the tears that clogged her throat. "I—I saw you at her house."

"You were spying on me?"

Cringing, she nodded. He took a pensive drink from his glass, closed his eyes, and smiled. "You're full of surprises, aren't you?"

Wary, she sniffed and brushed at the tears on her face. "I got scared and I thought—I thought . . ." She couldn't finish. "I got scared."

"I know," he murmured. He put his arms around her and rocked her as she sobbed all over his shirt. The side of her face where he'd hit her felt like it was on fire, and her hands and feet throbbed. Gently he cupped her cheeks and kissed her.

"Are you okay?"

There was forgiveness in his tone and the tender look he gave her. Forgiveness and blessed mercy. Grateful, she nodded. Her smile felt as weak as her will, but he answered it with a grin of his own.

She sniffed and took in a shaky breath. "She's beautiful. Like her sister."

"Yes, she is."

His acknowledgment brought more tears. Futilely, she blinked them back. "Do you want—do you want to be with her?"

"You see where I am now? This is where I want to be. I want you, baby. You belong to me."

Yes, she did. If she had ever doubted that, she wouldn't anymore.

He looked deeply into her eyes. "Trust me, honey. Everything's going to be okay. We'll get through all this and then everything will be just like I said. You're going to be rich and famous, a household name. Didn't I promise you that?"

She nodded. "But what about—"

"Don't worry about it. I told you I'd take care of everything, and I will. Right? I will."

She nodded again, but inside doubt mingled with her fear and shame.

"Hey? You trust me, don't you?"

She swallowed thickly. "Yes. I trust you."

chapter sixteen

AFTER Grant left, a part of Tess wished she had chased after him and begged him to come back, keep them company, make her feel safe. But security was arbitrary. It could be snatched away at any moment. In New York City. In Mountain Bend. Anywhere. It was best not to rely on anyone.

Knowing every worry showed on her face, she rubbed her hands against her arms and faced Caitlin, who looked tiny and lost. Tess felt as if she were looking into a reflection of her own past as she knelt down beside her. She wished she could tell Caitlin that everything would be okay. This morning she'd managed to pull it off, but tonight she wouldn't fool anyone.

Her sister was missing. In the worst scenario she was dead; in the best she'd bailed out on her kid and possibly a dying man. Since arriving, Tess had been hallucinating, nearly run over, watched by a mysterious horseback rider who didn't leave tracks, and beaten up by who knew what and who knew when. Outside, the storm sounded like a herald for the end of the world. Oh yes, and the power was out.

She was about as far from okay as she could get.

"I know you're worried about your mom," Tess said gently. "I'm worried about her too. All we can do is pray that she's safe."

"I don't know how to pray."

Tess bit her lip, knowing that Tori had left God behind with the Colonel. Tess herself had abandoned the rituals of religion at the first opportunity. But it didn't seem right that this little lost child before her did not even know how to pray.

Feeling as if the eyes of the Jesus painting were burning

into her back, she said, "I know how. I'm a bit rusty at it, but I can show you."

Caitlin's face gleamed like bleached bone in the firelight. It seemed that Tess could see right through the translucent covering to the fear and stress beneath. Caitlin clutched Purcy tight against her chest, dampening his fur with her moist palms.

"Aunt Tess . . . Do bad guys know we don't have any lights?" she whispered, as if hushing the words would take away any power they might have to be real.

"Bad guys? What bad guys, Caitlin?"

"The bad guys that scare my dreams. Do they know that it's dark here?"

"Oh, sweetheart," Tess said, taking her niece's shoulders in her hands. "I'm sure they don't. And even if they do, I'll be right here to scare *them* away."

"Even the ones with the horses?" she whispered, softer still.

The question instantly brought the image of the man on horseback to Tess's mind and a feeling of deathly stillness to the air. The hair on her arms stood on end and her mouth went dry. She couldn't help the glance over her shoulder any more than she could the shudder that went through her.

"What do you mean? You dream of men on horses?" she asked.

"Mommy says I do. I don't remember them usually. I just wake up scared and she says I cry about the horses."

Mooolllly.

Tess straightened suddenly, dragging her clammy palms down the sides of her sweats. "Dreams can't hurt you, honey. No matter how bad or scary they are, they have to go away as soon as you wake up."

"Sometimes they follow me."

The room felt tight, closed in. Tess wanted to open the door and let the cold revive her. She wanted to run.

"How do they follow you?"

"I don't know. My mommy's scared of them, too. She said the horse ones were after us."

"After you? Caitlin, nobody's after you. Dreams are just your imagination working overtime."

Caitlin stared at her, unblinking. Unconvinced.

"Don't worry," Tess said, stronger now. "I promise I won't let the bad guys get you."

"I'm glad Mr. Weston came," Caitlin said, moving closer to the light of the fire. The flashlight remained on the mantel, the light switched off to conserve the batteries. Caitlin stared at it with a look of longing.

"You know your mommy works for him."

"Mommy works for *old* Mr. Weston. He got killed, didn't he?"

"Yes."

"Mommy was afraid for him."

"Afraid . . . You mean she thought something might happen to him? Caitlin, why didn't you mention that before?"

"Because I knew you'd ask me why she said it or what she meant." Caitlin lifted her shoulders and shook her head. "I never know what she means. She just says stuff like that. I don't know why."

Anyone else might not have understood what Caitlin meant. But Tess knew. She knew exactly.

"Honey, you remember at the restaurant tonight, when you said you'd been there before?"

Caitlin nodded, watching Tess with wary eyes.

"Who do you go there with? Which Mr. Weston?"

"All of them."

"All of them? You mean, together?"

Caitlin almost smiled. "Usually just alone with Mommy. Once we all went, but . . . They don't really like each other."

Tess struggled for a neutral expression, as she absorbed this. *All of them . . .* Usually alone, not together, because they didn't really like one another. Couldn't Tori have foreseen trouble in that situation? And if she was dining with all three Weston men, what else was she doing with them? That speculation made Tess sick and uneasy.

All of them.

And yet the two surviving Weston men had claimed no

more than passing knowledge of Tori. Neither knew her well. She presumed that went for the bright blue plus sign on the pregnancy test upstairs as well. They wouldn't know anything about that either.

"Caitlin? Can I ask you another question?"

The girl nodded, but the lines of stress deepened on her face. Tess could see the anxiety bunching in her shoulders, in the tight grip she had on the stuffed animal. "Does your mommy have a boyfriend?"

"You mean a real one?"

The question should have made them both laugh. What other kind could there be, but the real kind? But neither cracked a smile. "Yes, a real one."

"She used to, but then we moved."

"There's no boyfriend here?"

Caitlin clutched Purcy a little tighter and shook her head.

"You can tell me if there is. Your mommy trusts me."

"She never said she liked someone here," Caitlin said.

"Was this other boyfriend in Los Angeles or Salt Lake?"

"Los Angeles. I didn't know him, though. She said he was a secret."

A secret. Married, maybe? His wouldn't be the first vows Tori had trampled on. "Do you know why she kept him a secret?"

"You know how Mommy talks, Aunt Tess." She gave a deep sigh and stared down at her shoes. "She talks like she's crazy." She looked up and in her round blue eyes Tess saw all of her own fears hovering there. "Is she?"

Tess didn't know the answer to her question, but she knew how it hurt to ask. Right or wrong, Tess couldn't let her bear that pain right now. "No, Caitlin. She might be confused sometimes. Or maybe she knows something we don't. But I don't think she's crazy."

Caitlin's tension held tight to the breath she released, making it wheeze as it escaped. This poor kid was going through hell and there was nothing Tess could do about it.

Reluctantly, Tess searched for a way to ask her next question, trying to pose it in a manner that wouldn't sound threatening. "Caity, does your mommy ever see people who . . . who you don't see?"

She'd worded it awkwardly, but Caitlin didn't look confused as she shrugged, only weighted with anxiety. "Sometimes I guess."

"Do you think maybe she started seeing them when she came here?" Tess asked.

Another shrug, this one smaller, defenseless. Her silence was hurt and frightened, her psyche overloaded by everything that had happened.

"Okay, sweetheart, no more questions. I'm going to bring in some more wood from outside, then we'll just relax, okay?"

Caitlin held the flashlight at the door while Tess hurried outside to grab an armload of wood. After she'd added some to the fire, they snuggled into a blanket bed Tess had made on the floor. Together they clasped their hands and prayed.

Now I lay me down to sleep . . .

Surprisingly, they both seemed to feel better as they said Amen and closed their eyes.

It must have been hours later that Tess awoke with a start. The rain had stopped and the wind was quiet. Caitlin had kicked off her covers, but still she slept peacefully beside her.

Only the glowing ash in the banked fire lit the room and Tess thought about adding more wood, but without the storm howling outside, it didn't seem an urgent need. It would be morning soon, anyway. She settled back into her pillow in the thick quiet, wondering as she began to drift off again, what had woken her up. It must have been a dream or the—

She sat bolt upright. What was that?

She strained, listening to the dark until her ears rang. There was no rain, no wind. No movement in the thick silence.

She stood, reaching for the flashlight but leaving the beam off as she tiptoed to the front window and moved the edge of the curtains aside. Staring out at blackness so deep it absorbed all sound, and movement, she frowned. What had she heard? A branch thumping the house? But there was no wind.

Behind her, a floorboard creaked. She spun to face the gloom. The house seemed to take a breath and hold it. She peered from left to right, trying to see everything at once. The eyes on the portrait of Jesus seemed to glow.

She was being ridiculous. Of course she was. And who could blame her? Alone with a child, in the middle of nowhere? It was dark and spooky and—

Another sound from the back of the house. Footsteps? Was someone on the back porch? In the kitchen?

Do you have the key? Doesn't matter, back door doesn't latch. The memory of Grant Weston's words traveled on the nonexistent wind.

She looked around for something she could use as a weapon. The fireplace tools had a lethal look to them and she knew there were knives in the kitchen. But the thought of using either one was almost as frightening as what she might use it against. She grabbed the poker from the set on the hearth. Quietly, she tiptoed to the kitchen.

The wall blocked off the dim light from the fireplace, yet when she turned the corner, the kitchen seemed to glow. She inched forward, poker thrust out in front of her. Her head swiveled from side to side, her body braced for an attack. Frantic thoughts babbled in her head.

The shadows in the kitchen flickered and shifted. Patterns danced on the ceiling and cupboards. She stared at the back door. She'd tried to lock it earlier, but Grant was right. It wouldn't latch all the way. Who else in town knew that? Everyone? What about Tori? It could be her out there.

I swear to God, Tori, if it's you, I'm going to clobber you for doing this to me . . .

The yellow curtains covering the window in the back door had worn to paper-thin sheers. They ruffled slightly in the draft from the warped frame. And they glowed.

Sidestepping, she tightened her grip on the poker and crept forward. Her hand shook as she reached for the curtains and pulled them aside.

What she saw numbed her. She wasn't aware that she'd opened the door until the cold air rushed against her over-heated skin and her bare feet moved across the rough planks of the porch.

She'd seen the black kettle grill earlier when she'd arrived. Then, it had been pushed to the side of the house like forgotten junk. Now it stood on the porch, the lid off and to the side. Inside, wood smoked and sputtered. Hot flames leaped up toward the rafters of the porch roof. They licked at the crisp air and hissed at the black night. In the midst of the blaze, something gold and shiny glowed.

Tess held the poker poised for attack and inched forward. In her head, a voice screamed, *"Get back in the house! Close the door!"*

But the door didn't lock. And she'd been brought up never to show fear.

She took a step closer, looked behind, ahead, to the side. Another step. She realized she was holding her breath. She let it out all at once. The fire heated her icy skin, but what lay nestled in its hot arms froze her to the core.

It was the photograph of Tess and Tori. The last time she'd seen it, it was sitting on the coffee table, not three feet from where she'd been sleeping soundly beside Caitlin.

She stared, gripping the poker with fingers that had turned white from the pressure. The flames slithered beneath the glass and curled the edges of the picture into black ash. The glass cracked with a pop that made her cry out. Now the flames moved greedily, eating away her smile, Tori's eyes, poking up between them and devouring everything they were.

As she watched their faces vanish, she felt as if the world zeroed in to the tiny point she made in the universe. Nothing else mattered but Tess and the fire and the inconceivable realization that whoever had stolen this picture had stood over her and Caitlin while they slept.

This was personal. This was not Tori running off on a whim. This was not Tori broken-down, hitchhiking home. This was a message. A threat. A warning.

Tess turned in place, searching the darkness around her for the gleam of watching eyes. Every cell in her body sensed that whoever had left this message was still out there, making sure it was received.

Oh I get it, Tess thought. *You bet I get it.*

Slowly she lifted the lid of the grill and placed it over the flames. The metal clanged then sealed. She switched on the flashlight and aimed it out, sweeping the penetrating light across the pines and oleander. A rustle came from high in the tree branches, a scuttle low from the brush. A bat screeched in protest and took flight. The beam slashed back and forth, searching for the source of each whisper, finding nothing but shivering leaves and quivering treetops.

She was shaking. Every inch of her trembled. Someone had plucked that picture from the table while she and Caitlin slept a few feet away . . . unaware. The vivid image of it filled her head like the smoke that streamed from the vents in the grill lid.

She tried to deny it. Someone could have taken the picture earlier—she couldn't remember seeing it on the table when they'd returned from dinner. And then Grant Weston had come over. He'd been downstairs alone while she and Caitlin were changing . . .

She poked the light defiantly into the shadows. "You'll have to do better than that!" she shouted. Or tried to shout. The words came out choked and husky, trailing off into a whisper.

As if in answer, the rumble of an engine gunned in the distance. In an instant the sound flared and then began to retreat. Tess scanned east to west and back for headlights, taillights, anything—but nothing glimmered beyond the black.

Tori would have been able to tell the make of the vehicle by the rumble it made, but Tess couldn't distinguish a VW from a Mercedes.

She eased her grip on the poker and the flashlight. The crippling terror eased, too, but in its place a wild rage rose up. She stared at the smoking grill, angrier than she'd ever been in her life. Furious. Spitting mad, her mother would have called it.

How dare they, whoever *they* were.

She strode into the house and slammed the door behind her, forgetting for a moment that Caitlin still slept in the other room. The girl rolled over and continued to sleep, but the echo of the slamming door took life, reverberating in Tess's head, becoming a sharp, cracking sound that split open reality.

A plunging sensation followed the plunge in temperature. She felt it coming on like a tidal wave that built as it moved, gaining speed and power until it crashed down and obliterated everything in its wake. She braced herself, resisting with every instinct. She heard another crack, recognized that it wasn't coming from here, from the house, from Mountain Bend.

She turned her head and watched the room blur into sepia-hued shadows. The hole her flashlight beam made in the gloom felt like the center of her being. She couldn't look away from it. It became a white moon in a starless sky, and like the tide, it pulled her forward.

No, she shouted silently. *No, not again . . .* But it was already too late, and she knew it.

chapter seventeen

MOLLY awoke in the dark to the unfamiliar sounds of the others sleeping. She'd been dreaming about rivers . . . terrifying, engorged, rampant rivers. There'd be many to cross between Ohio and California. She shuddered at the thought.

Beside her, Rosie mumbled and rolled over in her sleep. Next to her, Arlie slept with the wild abandon to which only young children succumb. Two other indistinct lumps marked the bedrolls of Adam and Brodie. With the furniture gone, it had seemed logical that they all pile their blankets in the front room for their last night in the house. The mood had been quite festive as they'd blown out the candles in their communal bedchamber.

Had he known, the Reverend would have been scandalized by such arrangements. But of course he didn't know, would *never* know anything else about his daughter. That chapter had been closed and a new one opened.

Sighing, she kicked at the hot weight of her blanket. There were still hours before the Weston family would all be awake and eager to set off. Off to see the elephant, as the travelers before them referred to the arduous journey westward. And Molly would go with them.

No wonder she'd had nightmares.

Wide awake now even though exhaustion had shut her eyes at sundown, Molly quietly got to her feet in the dark. Her white shift stuck to her damp skin in the most inappropriate ways, but the thought of pulling her dress on over it was decidedly unappealing. With a last glance at the sleeping Weston clan, she silently opened the door and slipped outside to the velvet cold of early spring.

The brisk air rushed at her hot skin, frosting her sweat into a clammy chill. She shivered, but at least, for the moment, the cold felt good.

"Can't sleep?" Adam's deep voice came from the edge of the porch.

Molly whirled around in surprise. He sat on the steps, casually lounging against the railing as if it were noon instead of the middle of the night. One hand hung loosely between his knees; the other idly stroked the fur on top of the dog's head. The little pooch actually belonged to Brodie, who'd found it stray, but she seemed to prefer the company of Adam and was rarely far from his side. No one had given her a name yet, which Molly discovered was not an uncommon oversight that afflicted the Westons' animals. Molly called the dog Lady. So far, Lady hadn't objected.

"Something must have woken me," she murmured. "You?"

He shrugged, picking up a small object and a thin-bladed knife that flashed silver in the dark. "Too much on my mind to sleep."

She nodded, excessively conscious of her inadequate attire. As if to add to her discomfort, her bare arms puckered with gooseflesh and her nipples peaked into hard little knots that no doubt showed prominently through the lightweight shift.

"Sit down," Adam offered, gesturing to the step beside him.

The last thing she wanted was to plop down in her underclothes beside Adam Weston. However, the alternative was to be rude, and after her horrific outburst on that first night, she'd been extremely careful to mind her manners.

"What are you making?" she asked, perching awkwardly on the step beside him.

He held up the small chunk of wood for her to see. Although a work in progress, he'd already managed to capture the fey essence of a spirited horse in the knots and grain of wood.

"Arlie will be delighted."

"Thought I'd make him a herd."

"Tonight?"

He grinned at that, and she found herself smiling back. Overhead the budding branches of an oak rustled as a fierce gust of wind whipped through them. The cold blustered up the porch and under her shift with a vicious bite that made her shiver violently.

"You're cold," he said, shrugging out of his jacket. He slung it over her shoulders before she could protest, not that she wanted to once the warmth settled on her. Gratefully, she slipped her arms in the long sleeves and pulled her knees up to wrap inside with the lingering heat of his body. She turned her face into the collar and breathed in the warmth and spice, piney winter winds and fresh spring breezes that mingled with a scent that was Adam's own.

"Better?" he asked.

"Yes, thank you, but won't you be cold?" The corner of his mouth twitched up and he shook his head. She raised her brows. "You are impervious to cold?"

"Just wound so tight I feel like my blood's on fire."

"You're excited for the journey to begin."

The sound he made was not quite mirth, not quite misery. "Begin, end. I'm sitting out here wondering what kind of fool I am for even thinking about hauling my family across the country."

His confession surprised her. Adam struck her as the epitome of self-assurance. Through all the planning and preparations, he'd never expressed a word of doubt.

"Why are you then?" she asked.

"Gold," he said.

"I don't believe you."

"Why not? Half the men in this country are counting themselves rich before they even get there."

Adam Weston was not half of the men in the country. That much she did not need to be told. "You'd go alone if gold was your only goal."

He grinned. "You're pretty smart, for a city girl."

Flushing, she ducked her chin and tried to pretend that his teasing praise hadn't pleased her.

"See this land?" he asked, gesturing with a wide sweep of his arm. "All of it, as far as you can see, used to be Weston land. My grandfather bought it, worked it, and when he died, he left it to my father."

"Why do you not work it now?"

"Doesn't belong to us anymore. My father sold it or lost it, piece by piece. All that's left is the plot where the house sits." He stared past her, seeing something more than the endless vista. "Sometimes things don't work out the way you plan."

"Is that what is keeping you awake, Adam?"

She felt the intensity of his gaze on her even before she looked up to meet it. His eyes gleamed like pewter between the long, sooty lashes.

"Everything I hold dear is going with me in that wagon," he said simply. "I'd be a bigger fool than my father if I didn't lose some sleep over it."

She huddled deeper into his coat, trying to picture Adam's imprudent father. It was difficult matching such a character to the Westons she knew.

"Why did he choose to sell the property? Was farming not prosperous for him?"

Adam gave a humorless laugh. "It's hard to plow a field when you're living in a whiskey bottle. Between the drink and the gambling, he lost everything that wasn't nailed down. The house would have gone, too, if he hadn't died first."

He grew silent and Molly searched for something appropriate to say. An expression of sympathy for the loss of his father seemed no more fitting than an exclamation of good riddance.

"Land, that's why I'm going. I want so much land that you won't be able to see the end of it. I want my son to know how that feels, to own something that you can work and build."

"It's important," she said.

"Yeah. It's important. You know when we get to California, we'll be settling land that's never known a plow? Never had a shoe print? Maybe never even been *seen* by anyone but the Indians."

"What about all the other eager emigrants? Where will they be in this untended land?"

"In the hills, blasting for gold. Far away, I hope."

"You don't like other people?"

"Some. Some I like a good deal."

Her face grew hot again under his steady scrutiny. Refusing the urge to squirm, she stared into eyes so silver they became twin mirrors, reflecting her pale, uncertain shape. The burnt glow of moonlight turned his face white and ghostly and gilded the dark browns and deep golds in his hair.

"Land," he said softly. "But I wouldn't turn down a nugget or two of gold either."

"No, indeed."

"How about you, Molly? What are you hoping to find?"

"Gold," she said.

He chuckled, pulling his carving closer to work a detail with the tip of his blade. His knife made a soft, raspy sound as it stroked away fine curls. A silky cloud of sawdust drifted to the porch step between his feet and settled.

Molly watched as he worked the knife over the emerging horse. His hands were big and wide, yet his long fingers moved with the grace of an artist as he carved out the minute details of mane and tail, the wildness in its eyes and the prance of its hooves. She relaxed a bit, listening to the sounds of the night and enjoying the tentative, yet peaceful companionship.

"When you first came," Adam said, glancing at her and then quickly away. His voice rang deep and serious and the night beyond seemed to add resonance to its timbre. "I wasn't too happy about it."

The mammoth understatement made her want to guffaw, but for once common sense subdued the urge. Instead she said, "I understood your reluctance to welcome me."

"I'm sorry if I was rude."

"No, it was I who was rude. Unforgivably so."

"Yeah, well. Things were rough."

He looked up then, surprising her in the act of burying her nose in his coat and inhaling his scent like a perfume. She felt as if he'd caught her stripping down for a bath or fumbling with drawstrings in the privy. A warm flush spread from the top of her head down.

"Yes," she mumbled. "Things were very rough."

"I thought you were going to be trouble. I figured you came to stir things up and cause as much havoc as you could. But I figured you wouldn't last long enough to do too much damage. I gave you a week, two at the most, before you'd be ready to go home."

"Why?"

Now *he* appeared taken aback. He brushed the sawdust off his leg, looking everywhere but at her. She shifted so she could see him better. What he didn't say was there in the tightness around his mouth and the narrowness of his eyes. He was looking backward, into the past, and he didn't like what he saw.

They had not spoken of her sister since the night Molly arrived, but Vanessa had been there at every meal, every dawn, and every dusk. She hovered like a ghostly entity that had not found its way to the world beyond.

Staring at the tips of her fingers poking from the sleeves of Adam's coat, Molly said softly, "When she was alive, I was so very jealous of her. It was awful of me and I knew it was sinful, but I felt it all the same. She was like a bright light. Beside her, everything else was drab and colorless."

He nodded, not needing to ask of whom she spoke. Molly was swamped by a fresh and unexpected wave of envy followed immediately by a wash of loss. Even from the grave, Vanessa would shine.

"Sometimes a bright light will blind a man," he said softly. "Make him forget what's right."

"Vanessa was everything I longed to be. Her daring, her *courage* . . . She was the only person I have ever seen defy the Reverend." Pausing, she searched carefully for her next words. "When I . . . when I accused you, Adam, of compromising her . . . I . . . I . . ." She took a deep breath and exhaled. Silently he waited, not a flicker of emotion showing on the shadowed planes of his face. "I know that it was not so. Vanessa was not a woman *to* be compromised. She made the rules that would govern her and then she broke them. It was her way."

His jaw tightened and his face became a mask of bitterness.

"I've offended you," she whispered. "I am sorry, I meant it as an apol—"

"No." He shook his head. "No, I'm not offended. Apology accepted. I guess we both made some errors in judgment. It's over and done with."

She swallowed, drawing herself deeper into the shelter of his coat. "There's more . . ."

His hands tightened on the carving and the cynical lines deepened. She exhaled, forcing herself to continue. "I did get your second letter, Adam."

Whatever he had expected her to say, apparently it had been far removed from the words she actually spoke. In an almost comical sequence, his mouth dropped opened and his brows drew together in confusion.

"The one that told me not to come. I intercepted it before the Reverend could see it and then I destroyed it. I knew you did not want me here, and I came anyway."

He let out a harsh breath and laughed. "Well, I'll be damned," he said.

"You have every right to be angry. What I did was wrong and I have no excuse for it. If you want me to stay behind tomorrow, I will not cause a scene." She looked at him, raising her chin. "But I will not go back to New York."

Adam leaned forward, placing his elbows on his knees, and rubbed his face with his hands. "You took a big risk," he said at last.

"I take one now."

"I guess you had your reasons for doing what you did," he said. "One way or another, we all have our reasons."

She waited for his next words, sickened by the mixed-up feelings inside her. Shame, for lying but not for coming. Fear, that he would now cast her out. Sadness, for the tentative connection both begun and ended on the porch step this night.

"We should turn in," he said at last. "Dawn's not too far away and tomorrow's going to be a long day."

"Is it?" she asked.

He stood and turned to look at her. She sat dwarfed by his big coat, like a child playing dress-up in her father's clothes.

His smile was slow and she watched with a sort of fascination as it moved across his face, curving his full lips before spreading to a dimple that appeared like an unexpected ray of sun on a cloudy day. He reached down and engulfed her icy fingers in his large, warm hand. "Yes, city girl. It's going to be a long day. Nobody takes a shortcut to see the elephant."

DAWN came in the middle of the night. At least that's how it felt when Adam gently shook her awake.

"Come on." His voice held a smile. "Rise and shine."

"Tell that to the sun," she grumbled, pushing herself up under the heavy blanket. "It's still dark."

Adam hunkered down beside her and grinned. "You better get used to it, city girl. There's a hundred and twenty dark dawns waiting for you down the road."

Too tired to protest, she sat glowering at him with bleary eyes. Still grinning and looking far too rested for a man who'd been up in the middle of the night, Adam handed Molly the clothes she'd laid out at the end of her blanket.

She felt self-conscious pulling on her dress in a room with so many other people, but they all were engrossed in their own preparations. As she reached for her shoes, however, she caught Brodie staring at her with an intensity that was unnerving. He turned the color of red wine when he found her returning his fixed look with her brows raised and her hands on her hips. He proceeded to stumble over his discarded boots and tumble to the floor, taking Adam with him.

She was careful not to look his way again for fear she would burst into laughter and make the situation that much more embarrassing for all. Brodie had the sweet baby face of a boy, but in other areas he was obviously approaching manhood.

By the time they'd packed away their bedrolls and had a cold breakfast with blissfully hot coffee, she felt more like herself. Dawn crested the skyline and frosted the low mist of clouds with dusky violet and vivid ruby hues. Today was April first. The day of fools. What better day to begin a two-thousand-mile expedition?

She helped Rosie clean their small mess from breakfast and then carried the last of their things out to the men. Arlie wobbled around the wagon, babbling happily. He was now a year old and he'd begun walking just the week before. Already he was trying to run. Brodie claimed they'd have him riding a horse before they reached California. Molly shuddered at the thought.

When she returned to the house, she found Rosie still in the kitchen, wiping down the empty shelf that had once held her pots and pans. The old woman looked up when she entered. "Now just what are you smirking about?" she asked crossly.

"You, still cleaning."

"I know it's just going to sit empty and get dust and dirt. Probably spiders. But I can't go off and leave it dirty."

"It was not a criticism, Rosie. Cleanliness *is* next to godliness."

Rosie made her bunny laugh at that. "So they keep preaching. Reckon I oughta be sainted someday soon." She folded her towel and gently hung it on the rack to dry. "I was just a young woman when we came here. Younger than you are now. I delivered four children and lost two under this very roof. Bet you didn't know that, did you?"

Molly shook her head.

"The others were boys too. Now they're dead and buried out yonder with Frank—that was my husband." She sighed and dabbed at her eyes. "I can't believe I'm leaving."

Molly put her arm around the woman's strong, thin shoulders. "I'm a bit frightened myself."

"I sure hope the Indians don't get my hair," Rosie said seriously. "I ain't got much left, but I don't care for the idea of it leaving my head."

"Yes, I would prefer to keep mine as well."

Rosie caught her bottom lip with her two front teeth and stared at Molly's thick, brown hair as if its removal were tragically unavoidable.

"Rosie, you are going to scare me right back to New York."

Rosie's faded gray eyes twinkled. "I know better than that,

Miss Molly Louise Marshall." She tittered again. "I sure know better than that."

Smiling, Molly said, "If I am honest, it's not the Indians I fear. It's the rivers."

"Why's that?"

"Because we must cross them."

Still arm in arm, the women looked around the empty house, both filled with a mild sense of shock. It had all happened so quickly, it didn't seem real. Yet she could feel the weeks spent in frantic preparation in the aching muscles and knotted ligaments of her back. They had potted meat, jarred fruits and vegetables alike, stored and salted, diced, and boiled nearly everything in sight. Molly's hands were raw testimony to their labors.

From outside, they heard Adam calling their names with unmistakable impatience. Rosie heaved a sigh and nodded in a gesture that implied closure and resolve. "You ready?"

Molly handed Rosie her bonnet and tied her own beneath her chin. "I am ready."

The covered wagon was packed and yoked to a massive team of oxen. From the cover of her bonnet, she watched the Weston brothers check lines and wheels, halters, and harnesses. Adam rechecked Brodie's lines, but never so that his brother would know. Molly admired the way he looked after his younger brother and shouldered the burden of responsibility for the entire family. He was a man who took his duties seriously and it eased her concerns, knowing his competence was behind every step they would take.

"Come on, you two. Let's go!" Brodie shouted, squirming in his excitement. He motioned them forward with animated impatience.

Molly scooped up Arlie into her arms and moved to the wagon, where Adam and Brodie waited. Smiling that fine, broad smile that Molly had grown to expect from him, Adam relieved her of the pudgy, squirmy baby and hefted him onto the bench. He pointed a stern finger at Arlie and said, "You stay put."

Arlie bounced his bottom on the seat with an overjoyed

squeal that broadened Adam's grin. He looked at Molly, shaking his head. "We're in for it," he said.

"I am aware of that. Your son is perpetual motion."

She tipped her head back to look at him. Adam stood well over six feet tall with the broad shoulders and the muscular build of a man who worked with his hands. Where Brodie had an infectious charm, with his bright blue eyes and uninhibited enthusiasm, Adam's allure was more deeply male. It ran through him like the powerful current of a great river, so far below the surface it appeared not to flow at all. Until, that is, one found herself caught in the stream and propelled in a new direction because of its force.

"Having second thoughts, city girl?" Adam asked, his voice soft and deep, lowered for her ears only.

"Most certainly not," she said. "It will take more than the jitters to be rid of me, Adam Weston."

Grinning, he wrapped his large hands around her waist and swung her up on the bench beside his bouncing son. Her stomach made an excited plunge as he lifted. For an instant her face was very close to his, so close she could smell the heat of his skin, breathe in the pulse of life that flowed through him.

Brodie was watching her when she finally managed to pull her gaze from Adam and turn around. His fixed stare reminded her of earlier when she'd caught him watching her dress, but now there was something new, something brooding about him, that made her uneasy. He was flushed, whether from embarrassment, exertion, or something else, Molly couldn't tell. Before she could ask if there was a problem, he spun away and grabbed his mother by the waist, startling her. Rosie swatted at his shoulders as he gave her a twirl and a kiss on the cheek before helping her up to the seat.

"Get on now," Rosie exclaimed, wiping her cheek.

Laughing, he gazed across the bench at Molly. The brooding look in his eyes had vanished so completely, that she was certain she'd imagined it.

"You know what I'm going to do when I strike it rich?" he said to Molly. "I'm going to buy you a dress the same color as your eyes. A silk one with all the"—he waved his hands over his chest—"all the little frilly things all over it. I swear I am."

"I fear that once we reach California, shoes will be what I'm wanting."

"I'll buy you matching ones. And a big old house the same color."

"A house to match my gown and shoes?" Molly grinned, picturing a grand house painted the same shade of her eyes. Certainly it would look like the kind of place the Reverend had accused her of inhabiting.

"And I'm going to buy you a necklace with a big fat . . ." He hesitated, pointing to a spot just below his breastbone while he searched for the word.

"Emerald," Molly offered helpfully.

"Emerald," he shouted. "That's right. The biggest goddamned—pardon me—gosh-darned emerald to wear on your pretty little neck."

Rosie tittered and elbowed Molly. "Maybe I can pitch a tent in your front yard."

Brodie flushed. "Well, of course I'll buy you one, too, Ma," he said reproachfully.

Mounted on his prancing gray gelding, Adam said, "By the time you get done talking about how you're going to spend it, all the gold's going to be gone. Mount up and move out."

Brodie's blush deepened and he glanced down at his feet, looking once again like the adolescent he was. With a sympathetic smile, Molly watched him climb into his saddle before she took the wagon's cool leather reins in her hands.

A moment later Brodie's whip cracked the air above the oxen's ears and his "yah" echoed in the crisp morning. The wagon groaned as the wheels reluctantly turned and the oxen started forward. Jingling harnesses chimed with the banging pots and kettles and creaking wood. Rosie let out a second "yah" that drew the smiles of all of them. Their laughter beckoned the sun from the clouds to light their way.

If ever there had been a time for her to turn away from this journey, Molly thought, it was now gone forever. She bent her head and whispered a quick prayer. Placing her life and the lives of her sister's family—her family now—in the Heavenly

Father's care, she asked Him to guide them with His loving hands.

And taking a deep breath, she held on.

AT the edge of the town's borders, the vile coach driver who had brought Molly to Oak Tree met them on horseback. Two mules trailed him on a tether. Both were loaded down with bundles and satchels.

"Adam," Dewey said, smiling broadly. His wild and wooly brows rose up in query and his blackened teeth gleamed between his fleshy lips. "Heard you was heading on out to get rich. Can I join up? I brought my own." He half turned in his saddle and nodded back at the pack mules.

Molly pulled her gaze away from the monstrous mole on his face, scolding herself for the unchristian thoughts running rampant in her head. A man should not be judged by his appearance. Countless scriptures had been written about sinners who condemned God's messengers on the basis of their humble guise. But already she could feel the oily sheen of his lecherous gaze coating her skin.

While Adam and Brodie exchanged a few quiet words, Dewey sat open mouthed, looking from one to another like a dog waiting for a bone to appear. She wanted to shout, *No, do not let him join!*

After a moment Adam clicked his tongue at his horse and drew even with Dewey.

"You got to pull your own weight," he said. "It's not going to be an easy ride."

"Oh, I know, Adam. Sure I know that. And you ain't got to worry about me pulling my weight."

He closed a fist and raised his arm. Molly was unimpressed with the sagging bulge he proudly displayed. His odor was stronger by far than his physical strength.

"I'm strong as an ox," Dewey declared. "Strong as a *team* of ox."

And twice as fragrant. She could reprimand herself all she liked, but it did not change the fact that Dewey was the most repulsive being she had ever met. Grinning like an idiot, Dewey turned his horse in step with Brodie's and the group moved on. Molly snapped the reins over the oxen and followed.

In moments, the town became a smudge on the horizon behind them. Though Rosie chattered with cheerfulness and laughter kept them company most of the morning, Molly's attempts to ignore Dewey Yokum were thwarted. He would not stop staring at her in a manner that left little doubt as to what deplorable thoughts filled that bulbous head of his.

She tried silent recital of verse in penance and asked the Lord to give her strength of character to see the goodness beneath Dewey's foul visage. But it did no good. Dewey was like weevils in the flour, ants in the sugar, curdles in the milk.

With her thoughts unpleasantly preoccupied, it seemed that time crept by as they moved ever forward, across fields strewn with waving grasses and wildflowers. Tiny pink spring beauty mingled with blue and white hepatica turned their faces in search of the wanting sunshine. Had Dewey—Dew as Adam and Brodie were wont to call him—not been there offering a stream of pointless commentary, Molly would have enjoyed each moment.

Months, he would be with them now. Months.

Arlie kept himself busy crawling over the seat into the wagon and then back again, but by midmorning, the tired little boy curled up on the seat with his head on her lap and went to sleep. He looked so small, so defenseless. The need to protect him rose fierce and strong inside her. He was not her son by birth, but she was his mother now and she embraced the duty wholeheartedly. At twenty-eight years of age—by most standards an old maid—she'd nearly come to accept the dismal reality that she would never be a mother. Never be a wife.

Her gaze strayed to Adam's lithe figure, moving as one with his powerful horse. Flushing at her own thoughts, she looked away.

It was well after noon before they stopped to rest and eat near a small creek that gurgled across the meadow. A thick grove of oak and maple trees stretched high to the south and

brushed the low wispy clouds with their peaks. Brown squir-
rels chattered noisily from within the thicket, occasionally
dodging out to scold the travelers for their intrusion.

She looked longingly at the cool stream glinting in the sunshine and wanted nothing more than to strip off her boots and
stockings and soak her feet in the cold depths. Better yet, she
longed to soak her aching behind. Now that would turn the
Reverend and his entire congregation blue, wouldn't it? Lady
trotted up and sat at her feet, looking at her expectantly.

"What do you think, Lady? Does a bath sound good?"

Lady gave a low yip that Molly interpreted as yes. Sighing,
she hiked Arlie up on her hip and moved to help Rosie with
the heavy crates stored in the back of the wagon. Then, bal-
ancing Arlie on one side, Molly poured the four of them coffee
that was as cold as it was strong. She hoped the potent brew
would chase back her dread of returning to the wooden bench
of torture, as she was beginning to think of the wagon seat.

"Where's your cup, Dew?" Rosie asked when Molly did not.

Grinning, Dewey pulled a cup out of a deep pocket in his
oversized jacket and held it out for coffee. Reluctantly Molly
moved to fill it. As she turned away to set the heavy pot down,
she caught Adam watching her with a curious frown. No
doubt he wondered at her rudeness. A trifle ashamed of her
stingy, unpleasant behavior, Molly made an effort to redeem
herself by offering Dewey some of their lunch.

"Why, I thank you, Molly," he said, spraying her with spit
in the process. "But I brung some of my own." He reached in
his other pocket and pulled out a bundle wrapped in a dingy
red-and-white napkin. Proudly he opened it to reveal a hunk
of bread and a piece of cheese that looked like they had traveled in his pocket much farther than a half-day's ride. Gra-
ciously he offered some of his lunch to all of them.

"It's tempting, Dewey," Rosie declared, looking as if she
meant it. "But you go on. A man needs to eat a good meal."

Arlie drank milk ineptly from a cup, managing to splash
most of it down the neck of Molly's dress, while she doled out
healthy portions of biscuits and bacon from that morning.
Lady sat nearby, watching with interest.

She finished by placing a portion on Dewey's spread napkin, ignoring his protest. "We have more than enough . . . Dew."

He stopped chewing long enough to capture her wrist as she moved away. His hands were blackened and coarse and his offensive odor was stronger than the stringent stench of the pig that followed the wagon with the cow. Stronger even than the oxen and their offings. How foul would it become before they reached the borders of California?

She tried to tug her hand away but he didn't release his hold. Unbelievably, he began to tow her in like a leashed dog. Horrified she twisted her hand left and right. From the corner of her eye she saw a sudden motion as Brodie lunged to his feet. He took one step toward them before Dewey also noticed and released her.

"I saw that," Brodie said. His boyish face darkened, making his light brows stand out in stark relief. "I said I saw that."

Adam stood as well, coming to his brother's side. "What did you see?"

"He had his hands on her," Brodie said, pointing at Dewey like a two-year-old tattling on a bully.

Dewey shook his head from side to side, his mouth partly open, food clustered in gooey clumps at the corners. His eyes made hard black points in his lumpy face and they gleamed with meanness and, deeper down, fear.

"Did not."

"Did so. I saw you. I saw you."

Adam looked back and forth from Dewey to Molly to Brodie. Molly moved to Brodie's side and set her hand on his arm. "It's fine, Brodie. I thank you for your concern, but everything is all right. Sit, finish your meal. You need to eat to keep strong."

Brodie looked at Molly with the bewildered outrage of a child whose toy had been snatched away. He had not yet matured enough to hide his injured pride, but it was the possessiveness in his eyes that worried her.

Adam touched her elbow, drawing her attention away. He raised his brows and tilted his head to the side, looking concerned and curious at once.

"Finish your meal, Adam," she said softly. Without looking at Dewey, she joined Rosie at the back of the wagon.

"What was that about?" Rosie asked.

"A misunderstanding, I think. Will you watch Arlie?" she asked, reaching for the soap.

"Sure. Where you off to?"

"I want to wash up before I eat."

Rosie looked a bit guilty as she glanced at her own hands. She made a soft *hurmph* sound and called to Arlie.

With relief, Molly hurried down to the creek and splashed water on her face before she scrubbed her hands. It didn't matter. She could still feel Dewey's filthy touch. He'd held her hand as if he had every right to touch her. And if he was so bold as to do so in front of the others, what might he attempt if he were to capture her alone?

When she returned to camp, the men and Rosie had finished eating. Silently, Molly helped Rosie pack away their things.

"I see you brung a rocker, Adam," Dewey said after he'd licked the crumbs from his napkin with noisy slurping sounds. He nodded at the rocking chair strapped in at the back of the wagon.

Adam pulled Arlie onto his lap and said, "It's Ma's. Couldn't leave it behind."

"I left everything else," Rosie exclaimed indignantly.

"Shoot, no, can't leave a rocker like that behind," Dewey agreed. "Shoot, no. That's a beaut."

"Just a chair," Brodie mumbled.

"It's a fine rocker," Rosie said back.

Dewey sat forward as if suddenly struck by a thought. "Remember, Brodie? Remember that rocker *you* made?" His face split in a gleeful smile. "Remember?"

"I made lots of rockers."

"Not like Adam, you ain't. Remember how you sat in that one and it just split right out from under you?" Dewey let loose a honk of laughter.

Rosie said, "I remember. He wanted me to sit in it first but I said, no, you go ahead and give it a try." She laughed. "Hoo, he was mad."

Adam stood and dumped the dregs of his coffee in the dirt, shifting Arlie to his hip in the same motion. Arlie grabbed for Adam's hat and tried to get the rim in his mouth. "Gimme that," Adam said, tugging it away. Arlie lunged for it again and Adam swung him to the side so that the child hung parallel to the ground with Adam's arm around his waist. Delighted, the boy kicked his feet, looking like a frog caught midair in a leap.

Grinning at his son, Adam said, "We should be moving. Daylight's wasting."

Not to be distracted from his original subject, Dewey jumped to his feet and said, "You remember, Adam? You remember that rocker? Just *crack* it went and down came Brodie like a sack o' taters."

Rosie joined in with her bunny laugh as Dewey wiped the tears from his eyes.

"It wasn't that funny," Brodie said, standing as well.

"Sure it was. I near bust a gut laughing."

Dew hooted some more but Brodie obviously found nothing of humor in the story. He strode off to his horse and began tightening the cinch and adjusting his gear. At last Dewey's laughter dwindled and then died altogether. "Just went *crack*," he muttered as he carefully folded his handkerchief and put it back in his pocket. "Just like that. *Crack.*"

Molly packed their dishes in the crate at the back of the wagon as Rosie took Arlie to wash. Adam appeared at her side and moved to help her with the heavy lid to the crate. "What was going on with Dewey earlier?" he asked. "Did he do something?"

She shook her head, but Dewey stepped into her line of sight at the same moment and her expression gave her away.

"You don't need to worry about him. When it's said and done, he's ugly, but he's harmless."

"Perhaps if I were a man, I would agree with you. Men seem to have much less to fear than women."

He reached up and tweaked an errant strand of hair that insisted on escaping the tight bun at the back of her head. "Going soft on me already, city girl?"

She sighed, brushing the stray hairs back. "Maybe."

"Liar. I don't think there's much that really scares you, sweet Molly. Not even Dewey Yokum."

"Well, for once you are wrong. Quite a few things frighten me."

"Like what?"

Like growing old and never knowing what it feels like to be loved by a man . . .

He bent his knees slightly and leaned back to bring himself eye level with her. Still she didn't look up until he reached out and tilted her chin.

She tried to think of him as her sister's widower, but when he looked at her that way, she could only think of him as a man. For the hundredth, thousandth time she wondered what his relationship with Vanessa had been? Were they wildly in love? Or had they shared a moment of passion that left them trapped in wedlock?

"Molly," he said, his voice as soft as the light of his eyes. "You don't need to be afraid of anything as long as I'm around."

Not even of him? Not even of the way she was beginning to feel about him?

It seemed he heard her silent questions, because he leaned closer, so close that she needed only to raise herself to tiptoes to press her mouth to his, felt herself, in fact, shifting her weight forward without conscious decision.

"Are we going to stand around here all day?" Brodie demanded, his voice like a gunshot.

Molly started backward and Adam quickly stepped away. He looked flushed as he hefted the last crate into the wagon.

"Let's move out," he said.

chapter eighteen

THE power came back on at 4:12 A.M. and the phone lines followed shortly after. Tess knew because she'd been waiting, plug in hand, for their restoration. Her bones ached from the hours spent sleeping on the hard floor and her head hurt from the deafening confusion of her thoughts. Yesterday morning she'd begun with instant coffee and a visit from Craig. This morning, before the sun had even considered rising, she started with the Worldwide Web.

She spent the next two hours batting down her irritation as the painfully slow connection fed her pages minute by infuriating minute. Accustomed to LAN lines and instant gratification, Tess found the delays torture. Her initial search branched into another until at last she hit the jackpot. "Delusional" captured an astounding list of sites.

"Well, if that's my problem, at least I'm not alone," she murmured, adding "talks to self" to her list of symptoms. She read a few paragraphs filled with dry text and medical jargon.

The first page downloaded with surprising speed. Words like "severe psychotic disorder" and "schizophrenia" jumped off the screen and any humor she might have found in her ridiculous quest vanished. She scanned through indicators of alcohol and drug abuse to a section titled "Typical Delusional Tendencies."

Well, if that wasn't an oxymoron . . .

Delusions of God-given purpose and delusions of persecution tied for most common. Command hallucinations followed just behind. That one included hearing voices and committing acts of self-mutilation. Thinking of the bruises on her skin and the mad dash in front of Grant Weston's truck, she scrolled down. Delusions of grandeur came next. Tess felt ill as she read, "In some cases, involves the belief that the patient is a historical personality of great importance."

Tess stared at the screen, as if her absolute concentration might scramble the words and make them different. She scanned the rest of the paragraph, trying to be objective. Did it apply? Tess didn't think she was a historical person—at least not now she didn't, but Molly was someone from the past even if she wasn't an important someone. Was that simply a technicality? For all Tess knew, when these . . . *spells* came on, she could be walking around lifting her skirts over nonexistent puddles and talking to all the colorful characters in her make-believe world. She didn't *know* what happened to her *here* when she was *there*.

But what she read only managed to confuse her more. What had she expected? A checklist? Eight out of ten and you're certifiable? Seven or less and you're just a bit tweaked? In the end, it was frustration that decided what common sense should have insisted on long before. She couldn't diagnose her problem via the information highway. If she wanted a prognosis, she would have to seek professional help.

That settled like a healthy swig of sour milk.

Behind her the sun peeped from the clouds and speared the sky with a sharp golden ray. She glared at it even though inside she was glad to see it chase back the night. It was ridiculous to imagine the sunrise would bring safety—murderers preyed on their victims in the cold light of day as easily as they did the dead of night. She shifted, not liking where her thoughts had traveled. From threats to death.

The tap of the keys sounded extraordinarily loud as she logged off. Once the line disconnected, she picked up the phone and tried calling the sheriff's office again. Earlier attempts to get through had been thwarted by the canned voice of an electronic operator telling her that her call could not be placed. She'd spent hours flinching at every creak and groan an old house could make. Finally, she'd come to accept that even though her hands still shook and fear had taken her heart hostage, whoever had left the nasty threat had gone.

After a few rings, Deputy Ochoa answered the phone. She managed to keep her emotions in check as she reported last night's intruder and vandalism. In a tone that defied the disbelief she felt, Tess told the deputy about the sound that woke her up, the grill fire, and the picture that could have gone missing at any time, but quite possibly had been lifted while she and Caitlin slept. "I don't know when it was taken," she finished, relenting to the burn of tears in her eyes. She was afraid. Afraid for Caitlin, for Tori, for herself.

Ochoa's assurance that he and the sheriff would be right out did little to reassure her. Someone had taken her sense of security as easily as they'd lifted the picture from the table.

She hung up the phone and wiped her eyes with the shredded tissue clutched in her hand. Never in her life had she felt so ill equipped to deal with her circumstances. She didn't know if she should turn tail and run or dig in and fight. She didn't know what she'd be running from. What she'd be standing up to.

With a deep breath, she turned around and nearly jumped out of her skin at the sight of Caitlin poised silently behind her. Sometime after the grill incident, Tess had passed out on the kitchen floor and later Caitlin must have crept in from the living room and joined her there. When she'd woken up at 3 A.M., Tess found the little girl asleep on a jumble of blankets between her aunt and the battered dinette table.

"I never slept in the kitchen before," Caitlin said with shy smile. "Can we do it again tonight?"

Her eyes were still wet with tears, but in spite of everything, Tess laughed. Sure, they could. As long as there was a wheelchair and a straitjacket waiting for good old Aunt Tess in the morning. Caitlin didn't ask why they'd slept on the kitchen floor or why Tess had been blubbering into the telephone when she'd woken up. Tess didn't enlighten her.

"Am I going to school today, Aunt Tess?"

"Do you think you're up to it?"

"I guess. We have art today and . . . and maybe if I go, Mommy will be waiting to pick me up when it's over."

From your mouth to God's ears, Tess thought.

After they'd had breakfast and dressed, there was still time before school. While Tess washed their dishes, Caitlin got out some paper and crayons and began to color.

"Mommy came to see me last night when I was asleep," she said. Her voice was soft and serious. "She had to talk to me."

A dream. Just a dream. She took a sip of her awful instant coffee and asked, "What did she have to say?"

"She said we'd be together soon."

"Does that mean she's coming back?"

"I don't know." Caitlin pulled a yellow crayon from her box and made a sun on her drawing.

On the surface the dream wasn't so strange. Why wouldn't Caitlin be dreaming about her mother? Why wouldn't those dreams involve Tori coming to get Caitlin and taking her away? But it felt wrong. It felt as threatening as a premonition. Caitlin was old enough and bright enough to differentiate between dreams and reality. But if Tori's nocturnal visit was anything like the episodes Tess experienced in Molly's world, then Caitlin might not be able to tell the difference. But why would Caitlin have visions like that about her mother?

"How come you keep looking at that wall, Aunt Tess?"

She hadn't realized she was staring until Caitlin's voice interrupted her. She blinked, trying to grasp the trailing wisp of her thoughts. Where had she been going with that? If Caitlin was having visions like that about her mother . . . did that mean that Tori was trying to get a message to her daughter? She'd told Caitlin they'd be together soon. What did she mean? That she was coming back, or that something was going to happen to Caitlin? God, no.

Tess felt sickened by the conclusions she'd drawn. She didn't understand what was happening here, but one thing she did know. Whatever else took place, Tess was not going to let anything happen to Caitlin.

"How come you keep looking at that wall?" Caitlin asked again, frowning as she glanced over her shoulder and then back at Tess. "Is there a bug on it? Is that why you keep looking over there, cuz you see a bug?"

Tess forced a smile that felt plastic. "No, honey, I was just thinking."

Caitlin nodded, turning her attention back to her artwork. "Sometimes *I* see things on the walls," she said, choosing a green crayon from her box. The tip of her tongue darted out as she colored in the grass. "You 'member when you asked if Mommy saw people that I didn't? She doesn't, because I see them sometimes, too."

Tess's mouth was dry. She took another sip of her coffee before asking, "What kind of people? People that you know?"

Caitlin shrugged. "Sorta. I guess so. I hear them, too, but I don't talk back to them or anything. I know they're strangers."

Tess's heart hammered against her chest. What was going on here?

Caitlin frowned, looking at Tess with sudden apprehension. "I don't try to see them, Aunt Tess. I can't help it—"

"It's okay, honey. I'm not upset with you. I know you don't try to see them."

Caitlin's brow smoothed. She put down her green crayon and picked up a blue.

"These people . . . do they dress funny?" Tess asked.

The question caught Caitlin off guard. Her voice revealed her surprise. "Yeah. They wear hats and the mommies wear long dresses. Do you see them, too?"

"Sometimes." Tess sounded calm, as if they were talking about the weather. But a thousand disturbing questions bounced inside her head in a chaos of images and unfinished thoughts. How could she make sense of this?

"Is it eight-thirty yet? That's what time Mommy takes me to school."

Caitlin began gathering up her crayons and putting them away. Learning that solid, stable Aunt Tess saw people on the walls, too, had somehow relegated the experience to normalcy for the little girl and she smiled as she cleared the table. Learning that Caitlin shared her hallucinations had the opposite effect on Tess.

Caitlin took her finished picture to the refrigerator and secured it with a magnet before she picked up her backpack and headed for the door. As Tess reached for her keys, she glanced at Caitlin's drawing. Every hair on her body stood on end as she moved closer.

The drawing was of a child, a baby boy dressed in small brown trousers and a white button-down shirt. He was smiling. Behind him was a wagon; beside him stood a woman in a long skirt and apron. At his feet was a black-and-white dog. Caitlin had written "Lady" beneath it.

"Come on, Aunt Tess," Caitlin said from the door.

Numb, Tess followed.

chapter nineteen

SHERIFF Smith and Deputy Ochoa pulled in just as Tess returned from dropping off Caitlin at school. Fortunately she'd managed to get in and out without running into Craig. She didn't want to explain to him why she looked like she'd slept on the kitchen floor.

The two officers followed Tess inside and listened incredulously as she began the painful task of explaining what had happened the night before. When retold in the sunny kitchen, the events seemed melodramatic and anticlimatic. But in the dark of night, they had been excruciatingly real.

"Well, that doesn't make a goddamned bit of sense," Smith said.

At Tess's uncomprehending look, Ochoa said, "We had a break this morning. Your sister's car was found outside Piney River. There's no sign of her, but it was near enough to the bus station that a couple of officers started asking some questions and showing her picture around. One of the women working the ticket counter remembers seeing her."

Tess was glad she was sitting down. "Did she buy a ticket?"

"She did, but she paid cash and the woman didn't remember where she was going. She must have used another name, though. There's no record of a transaction for Tori France."

"What about her car?"

"Parked legally. No signs of a struggle."

Smith was watching her closely, gauging her reactions. She could read in his eyes that as far as he was concerned, finding Tori's car only confirmed what he already knew. She'd

robbed Frank Weston and taken the first ride out of town. But
Tess didn't believe it for a minute.

"Spoke to Lydia Hughes this morning," Smith said. "Seems
she recalls your sister using the pay phone outside the coffee
shop yesterday morning. She says after your sister hung
up, she seemed agitated."

"And she's just mentioning it now?"

"It was a busy morning and with Frank Weston dying that
afternoon—she said it slipped her mind."

"Even when Tori came up missing? I don't believe it."

"I don't see that Lydia would benefit from lying about it,
Ms. Carson."

Tess didn't know how to respond to that, but it didn't seem
possible that Lydia could forget Tori being upset that morning
when, by the afternoon, she'd disappeared. But why would
she lie? As the sheriff said, what possible benefit would there
be? Unless she was somehow involved . . . Involved in what?
Abducting her sister? She pictured Lydia—soft spoken,
rounded, kind to a fault . . .

"We're going to take a look outside, see what your prowler
was up to."

Tess stayed at the kitchen table and stared at Caitlin's
drawing, thinking of Tori on some outbound bus to who knew
where, imagining Lydia Hughes wrestling Tori into a dark
room in a secret keep.

She couldn't have said how long the two men were outside
before the back door opened and the young deputy came in.

Still standing on the stoop, Smith said, "There's not much
of anything left after the storm." His voice was hard and gravelly, his eyes bloodshot and flat. "You didn't see anything
else?"

"Just what I told you. I didn't even see the shadow of whoever was here. I heard a car start, but it was far away. It could
have been a truck for all I know."

Smith cursed under his breath and let the door slam shut
again. Tess scowled at the place he'd stood.

Ochoa said, "I know you must be sick, worrying about your
sister and all. But we're going to figure out what's going on

here. Finding her car was the first break we've had. Now we have a starting place to work from."

"A starting place? As far as Sheriff Bullet Balls is concerned, that starting place is my sister hitting the high road with a dead man's stolen money."

Ochoa's lips twitched at her derogatory nickname for Smith, but when he spoke, his tone was serious. "The sheriff's not happy about having so little to go on. He's used to a big city where there's a team of specialists just standing around to help other teams of specialists. As far as he's concerned, we're in the stone ages here. He's frustrated. But he's got a lot of years in law enforcement under his belt, Ms. Carson. He'll figure things out."

Tess nodded, wishing she could share his confidence. "I made a flyer this morning with Tori's picture on it. Could I e-mail it to you to print out?"

"Yes, ma'am." He pulled his pen and tablet from his pocket and gave her his e-mail address. "I'll make sure it gets distributed and posted."

She took the paper from his hand and prayed it wouldn't be too late.

chapter twenty

AFTER the sheriff and the deputy left, Tess paced, too keyed up to dwell on the turmoil of her thoughts, too exhausted to rest. She had to do something, and the idea of paying a friendly thank-you visit—complete with an egg and sausage casserole—to Grant Weston had seemed like a stroke of genius. Much better than Plan A, which had been cold-calling on him and stammering out questions on his doorstep like some amateur private investigator.

She found the road that branched off to the Westons' ranch without difficulty. The entrance was well marked and easy to see in the daylight, but it wasn't until she turned onto the gravel drive leading to the house that she realized where she was. That first night, when she'd been lost . . .

She passed beneath an iron arch that had weathered and rusted, but hanging from it was a shiny plaque, obviously a recent addition, with the words "Rancho Almosta" fashioned out of scrolling wrought iron. Rancho Almosta. Almost a ranch.

That night it had been too dark to see the details of her surroundings, but she remembered the house and outbuildings, and the stranger who'd seemed so familiar. Undoubtedly he was Grant Weston. Had some part of her recognized him from the movies? Was that why she'd felt like she knew him? It was the logical explanation, but the feeling had been deeper than mere recognition, and she knew it.

The rain had washed the lush spring growth on the trees to a glossy green and the leaves whispered merrily, dappling the sunshine as she drove beneath. Her perceptions were at odds with the fear inside her, a fear that seemed to have nothing to do with this cheerful, pleasant scene.

Between the massive trunks, Tess glimpsed the waving grasses of an enclosed paddock embraced by distant rolling hills and thick piney woods. She'd expected pristine grounds and an immaculate, if not opulent, manor. Grant Weston was rich and famous, after all. Instead, an aged white fence picked up where the oaks left off and curved with the road. The chipped and peeling paint had been altogether stripped in places; in others broken boards hung in disrepair. On the other side of the fence a dozen horses grazed contently on the waving grasses. A big pinto looked up and tracked her progress up the drive.

The house itself sprawled impressively, yet a closer look revealed despair seeping from the nooks and crannies like lichen from damp crevices. She was glad it wasn't night. Even in daylight her imagination was working overtime.

For God's sake, Tess, keep it together.

But how could she when it felt like a countdown was ticking away inside her? She parked her car next to Grant's truck and got out. Ignoring the trepidation that dogged her steps, she tucked Grant's flashlight under her arm and stepped up to the wide railed porch that sagged around the entire ground floor. Sprouting at its foundation, a riot of bougainvillea sashayed in the light breeze and scattered bright petals across the wooden planks. Overhead, verandas opened from the second-floor rooms to provide unmarred views of the desolate kingdom. It looked like something out of a ghost town in a Western movie. She wouldn't have been surprised to see John Wayne step out, adjust his holster, and mount up.

Grant yanked open the front door before she could knock and almost collided with her on the stoop. She gasped and jumped back, nearly launching her casserole into orbit.

"Oh, hell," she said, fumbling to save the dish, his flashlight, and her precarious balance all at the same time.

Grant expressed his surprise in much more colorful words. Steadying her with one hand, he rescued the dish before she dropped it. The heavy flashlight succumbed to gravity and crashed down hard on her foot.

"Dammit."

It hurt bad enough to make her eyes water. Refusing to indulge in the howl of pain that she deserved, she bent to pick up the flashlight. She didn't see Grant going for it at the same time and she cracked heads with him so hard that she saw stars. The flashlight rolled between his feet and bumped to a stop at the doorway.

Where was it written that she had to make a fool of herself every time she saw this man? Feeling like a complete ass, she rubbed the sore spot on her forehead, watching Grant do the same. She pointed at the casserole dish and said, "I came by to thank you for your help last night."

Under other circumstances, his expression might have been funny.

He said, "Come in," but didn't look as if he meant it.

"No, I should . . . You were on your way out, weren't you? I can come back another time. Or not at all. I'll just, um—"

"Tess, come in."

He was shaking his head as he stood aside for her to enter. Thinking the best thing she could do was cut her losses and get the hell out of there, she scooped up the flashlight and stepped inside Grant Weston's home. He waited for her to move a safe distance ahead then reached down for the cowboy boots he'd been carrying before he'd had to intercede on behalf of her casserole. He dropped the boots just inside the door and closed it.

From the foyer, she could see the dark wood paneling lining the hallway on the lower half of the wall and heavy, ornate portraits hung precisely above it. A room opened to the left, but heavy drapes blocked out the sun, giving it a look of perpetual dreariness. All it needed was Boris Karloff playing a pipe organ in the background. She set the flashlight on a small entryway table and tried not to look at the red spot on Grant's forehead.

"This smells good," Grant said, eyeing the casserole with suspicion.

"It's still warm. Are you hungry?"

The question seemed to catch him unaware. "I'm starved," he said, and a sudden smile spread across his face. Tess tipped her head back to stare with fascination as it transformed his features like sunlight on a pond. In that instant he changed from man to movie star.

She found herself blushing and reaching to take back the casserole. "Why don't you sit down and I'll make you a plate? Just point me to the kitchen."

Inside, she gawked at the cockeyed Suzy Homemaker who'd taken over her mouth but she couldn't seem to stop it. Last night she'd been tuned in to every glance, every chance touch of his hand, but by this morning she'd convinced herself that her reactions had more to do with being frightened of the storm than attracted to the man. Now there was no denying or pretending.

On the big screen, Grant Weston stood tall and muscular—stronger, smarter, sexier than any ordinary man. In real life . . . he wasn't much different. The rough-hewn features of his face, crooked nose and square jaw, the light gleam of his eyes, the thick black lashes, so long they should be feminine, but weren't . . . the chemistry that was so devastatingly male taunted her senses like a familiar song. It all hit at once and, deep within her, an inexplicable need awoke.

Thinking maybe she needed to take that flashlight and give her head another whack, she followed him down the somber hallway to the kitchen.

Here the theme of dark and gloomy crossed the line to dismal and depressing. Who could cook in a room like this? She glanced at the round table in the nook by the window. Not even the bright sun and fresh breeze could make eating there a pleasant experience. A scented candle sputtered on the table, as if in puny defiance of the overpowering task of brightening the room. She sniffed the air, noting it hadn't done much to improve the smell here either.

"I can't get rid of it," Grant said. He crossed to the back door and looked out at the corral. The muscles in his broad back tensed as he lifted an arm and rested it on the doorframe.

He made a fist and softly drummed it against the wood. "The tractor was right over there. Smoke must have poured in through the window and settled . . ."

She set the casserole dish on the counter and moved to his side. The corral outside looked benign, but the black spot near the fence fanned out like a malignant growth. She glanced at Grant from the corner of her eyes as he stared at it, his jaw tight and his gaze set far off.

This close, she couldn't help but be aware of his height, of the breadth of his shoulders, the length of his legs. His faded blue jeans hugged his hips and thighs below an untucked, soft gray flannel shirt that echoed the shade of his eyes. It seemed ridiculously intimate to be standing so near, her head barely reaching his chin even though he wore only socks on his feet.

"It's the craziest damn thing, isn't it?" he murmured, still looking out the window. He cleared his throat, nodding toward the corral. "I came back to see if I could be a better son . . ." The words trailed off, filled with irony.

"You probably weren't such a bad one to start with."

He turned suddenly and stared deeply into her eyes, as if he was searching for something specific that he knew would not be waiting on the surface. She didn't look away, although every protective instinct she possessed screamed for her to hide. The grays of his eyes swirled like smoke and she felt drawn into the illusion they created. Had she moved closer, or did everything else fade back? She didn't know.

"Your eyes are blue," he murmured.

And his were like falling rain, clear and opaque all at once.

His gaze shifted and she felt the heat of it on her face, her lips, her throat. She swallowed and he watched the flexing of her muscles with minute attention.

"Why are you here, Blue Eyes?"

Gruff, yet gentle, his voice caressed her like velvet. "I came to thank you," she said.

A slow grin crinkled the corners of his eyes. "You're an even worse liar than your sister," he said. The sensual pitch of his voice gave the words a feel of innuendo and absolved them of insult.

"I wonder how you'd know," she answered, her own husky response rising through the veil of his erotic spell. "You're hardly more than her acquaintance after all."

His soft laugh started a ripple that traveled up and throughout her entire body. He was definitely closer now, though she couldn't have said which of them had moved. He brushed her cheek with his fingers, his skin rough but the touch exquisite in its tenderness. She caught the warm scent of him and thought back to her conversation with Sara. Grant Weston definitely wore the right cologne.

"Want something to drink?" he asked.

Without waiting for her answer, he stepped back, leaving her swaying in place. He pulled a liter of soda from the fridge and a pair of glasses from the cupboard. She took a deep breath and quietly let it out. So much for taking charge. She felt exposed, defenseless, and completely at the mercy of the hot pulse he'd ignited within her.

Moving to the counter where she'd set the casserole, she said, "Where is your silverware?" She was relieved to hear that her voice no longer sounded like it belonged to a phone sex operator.

He nodded at a drawer to her left. She found a serving spoon and opened the lid on the dish. A delicious aroma drifted out. "Plates?" she asked.

Grant set her glass down beside her and reached over her head to open another cupboard. The movement brought him so close she could feel the heat of his body, imagine the touch of his skin. If she turned, she would be in his arms. He handed her two plates and leaned back against the counter. She felt like she had six thumbs as she scooped out servings of casserole.

In silent agreement, they left the gloom of the kitchen and went outside with their plates to the chairs on the sprawling porch. The fresh air felt like a gift from God after the stale confines of the dungeon where Grant lived. He ate as if his last meal had been days ago. From the looks of the inside of his refrigerator, that might have been true. Tess surprised herself by cleaning her plate too.

Appetites appeased, they sat in wary silence. She'd come to play hardball with Grant. As far as she could tell, he was the last person to have seen Tori. She couldn't believe that he didn't know something, *anything*. She'd planned to lull him into a false sense of security with the food then hit him hard with the questions. But somehow one long look and a brush of his fingers had skewed her agenda and now she didn't know how to begin. Worse, a weak-kneed part of her didn't *want* to ask questions. His presence had chased back the fear that clung to her like the smell of death in Grant's kitchen. She wanted to lose herself in his spell again and never resurface.

But on the heels of that thought came an outraged scolding from the realist in her. Whatever was happening here, she couldn't escape it. She had to find out where her sister was.

"You're thinking pretty hard over there, Blue Eyes."

He was watching her with a look so intense that she felt everything inside her fine-tune to respond. Was he doing that on purpose? Did he know the effect he had on her? Was it all practiced and polished or could it be as natural and forthright as it seemed? She forced herself to look away and breathe. Breathing had become quite difficult.

He stood suddenly, reached in the house for his boots, and pulled them on. "Let's go look at the horses," he said.

Tess followed him down to the stables, trying to deny the way his closeness made her feel. At the fenced corral, he stopped. He leaned his forearms on the top railing. Tess stood hesitantly beside him.

He pointed to the pinto who'd been watching her when she drove up. "That's Superman. He's been in more movies than I have." He made a thumb and finger gun at the horse. Superman looked up, pricking his ears. "Bang," Grant said.

The horse reacted immediately. He took two staggering steps to the side, then another, and then he collapsed with a grunt. He closed his eyes and froze. Not even an ear twitched.

"That's incredible," Tess said, smiling in spite of herself.

Grant whistled a strange, off-pitch note. Superman's ears twitched again and he clambered to his feet and ambled over for a reward, which Grant pulled from his shirt pocket.

"He likes LifeSavers?" Tess said with another laugh.

The horse slurped on the candy, working the small thing around its big mouth with determination. Grant grinned.

"Superman's the best dead horse in Hollywood. Too bad he's got no gas pedal. Slower than a mule, that one. Now, Midnight over there—" He pointed to a raven horse with one white sock. "She's like the wind." Midnight knew her name and came over to see what they were talking about. "Watch her hooves. See how they almost touch there—she's built to run. Only problem, she doesn't have brakes."

Midnight got a LifeSaver for her effort as well. Tess rubbed a hand down her silky neck and Superman bumped it away. Laughing, Tess scratched him behind the ear.

Grant pointed out the other horses in the corral, telling her about each one's area of expertise. His eyes glittered in the bright sunlight and his smile had a contagious quality. Occasionally his arm would brush against hers and a thrill would follow it. She had to force herself to focus on his words and not just the lips that formed them.

"Why do you have so many horses?" she asked.

"Midnight's mine. The others I'm working with to get them ready for their next movie. They're going to learn to joust."

"Is that what you do now? Train horses for the movies?"

"It's what I'm hoping to do. I've still got a few friends in the business, not many, but a few. Ever heard of Brandon Forsythe?"

"The producer?"

Grant nodded. "He's agreed to use the ranch for his next shoot. And if I can get these animals in shape, there'll be more to work with down the road. I'm hoping there will be anyway. Right now I'm hocked to my eyeballs trying to get things rolling. Dad let the place come down around his ears."

"The ranch is important to you."

"It's all I have," he said simply.

They turned and headed back up to the porch in silence. Tess couldn't stop thinking of Craig and his claim that the ranch was everything to Grant. Apparently, he was right.

"You're doing it again," Grant said when they reached the

porch. "Why don't you just come clean and tell me what's on your mind."

Tess felt another hot flush creep up her neck. "I was thinking about Tori. I mean, I'm always thinking about Tori. She's been gone for over forty-eight hours now."

"I know." He pulled the roll of LifeSavers from his pocket again and offered it to her before popping one in his mouth.

She sucked on the candy, peering at him from the corners of her eyes as she chose her next words. "I'm pretty sure she's pregnant."

His eyes widened for a moment and his nostrils flared with the quick breath he took in. His surprise looked too real to be faked. But then again, there was that whole actor thing. Taking his reactions at face value would be foolish.

He leaned against the porch railing and asked calmly, "Who's the father?"

"I thought you might know." In her head, the words hadn't sounded condemning. Spoken out loud, they were heavy with accusation.

"Why would you think that?"

"Because . . . well, I . . ." She what? She was shooting in the dark, hoping she didn't hit her target? She was looking for answers in the places her sister usually left them—with men that she couldn't resist? He stared at her, waiting for an explanation she didn't have. She moved to the railing beside him, carefully fixing her gaze on the grazing horses.

"It's just that Caitlin told me that you'd had dinner with her." *All of you Westons . . .*

"And that makes me the father of her child?"

"No. Of course not. But she's more than an acquaintance, isn't she? Why else would you be taking her out to dinner?"

"I suppose something as banal as welcoming her to town would be too simple an answer."

Her face was hot again. "All I meant is that—well, face it. Tori is a knockout. And to be perfectly honest, men don't ask Tori to dinner just to be polite. They ask her because they can't resist her. She's got that—that whatever-it-is that drives men crazy, that makes them run into walls because their heads are turned to watch her. I've yet to meet a man who isn't—who doesn't—who's not attracted to her." Somehow her voice had risen until each word tumbled out in a loud rush. Embarrassed, she looked away and tried to finish more calmly. "You can't tell me she didn't make an impression on you."

His narrowed gaze made a sweep over her, noting the flush heating her face and the quick, shallow rise and fall of her chest. "That upsets you, doesn't it?"

"What upsets me is that I don't know where the hell she is."

"But deep down, you know she's going to show up. She always does. That's how she lives, isn't it?"

"You tell me. You seem to know a lot about her."

"Not her, only every other woman like her. I spent twenty-five years running with that pack. I had an insider's view, you might say. Kind of embittered me to the experience."

"Well, you're wrong. Tori isn't like *any* other woman."

"You sound a little jealous."

"Jealous? Why would I be jealous? She's my sister."

"Your gorgeous, sexy sister. Like you said, she walks in a room and every man stops to stare. That's a tough act to follow."

"No, it's not. I mean, yes, she's all that. But I'm not jealous."

"Or angry? I'll bet this isn't the first time you've come to bail her out of trouble, is it?"

"We help each other," Tess said, watching warily as Grant moved closer. Too close. He'd invaded her space and she felt trapped by the weakness his proximity caused.

"Yeah, what's she done for you lately?"

Tess swallowed hard, searching her mind. "I don't need as much help. I don't have a kid I'm trying to raise. Life hasn't been all that terrific for Tori, you know. Just because she's beautiful doesn't mean everything comes easy to her."

"And it's a bed of roses for you?"

"Me?"

"Yes, you. Has life been easy for you? Has it been great having a beauty queen for a sister? Don't you ever wish she'd learn to take care of herself so you could you have a life, too?"

"I have a life. I have a great life. I have a job and friends and—"

"And you can pick up at a moment's notice and fly across the country to bail your sister out of her latest mess."

His tone had a soothing, coaxing quality that set off her internal radar. She realized too late that she'd painted herself into a corner, and any attempt to escape would be marked by her own messy footprints. It felt as if he'd climbed into her head and pried the lid off the box of emotions she kept sealed so tight. As he spoke the words, she couldn't deny the painful truth of them. Her life had been on hold for twenty-eight years. No decision was ever made without first thinking of Tori.

"Tori's just going through a rough time," she said, but her voice wavered, exposing the turmoil she felt inside. "When we were kids, she was there for me. Now I'm there for her."

"Is that a life sentence?"

"Stop it."

"All right. I'm sorry. It's none of my business."

Tess stared at him, filled with frustration and doubt. "I love my sister," she said. "She's the only family I have."

"I know, Blue Eyes," he murmured, cupping her face in his large hands. "I know."

And she felt as if he did know. Everything—every thought, every feeling. His thumb brushed against her lips, setting her senses on fire as he forced her to look up and meet his probing stare. She was hurt, betrayed by the reality of her own selfish feelings. He'd held a mirror to her and she didn't like what she saw in the reflection.

"You asked if your sister made an impression on me," he said softly. "She did. But not the kind she was hoping to make. And not half the impression you have, Tess. Not half."

Tess watched his mouth form each word, felt the caress of his velvet voice as he spoke, but she seemed incapable of understanding their meaning. He stared into her face, his expression serious, imploring.

He said, "With everything that's happened in the past forty-eight hours, the last thing I should be thinking of is a woman, but I can't seem to get you out of my head."

"But Tori—"

"I know you love her, but your sister is trouble. Trouble I don't need. Trouble I don't want."

His declaration felt open ended, as if the implication of what he *did* want should be apparent. But Tess was having a hard time concentrating on anything beyond the heat of his body, so close to hers. She kept her gaze fixed on the broad strength of his chest, aware all the while of the flat, hard muscles of his belly and thighs, just inches away. She raised her hands, intending to push him away so she could think, but the soft flannel of his shirt was warm against her palms and her hands lingered of their own volition.

"What fool would choose your sister over you?" he said, his lips at her temple, his breath soft and warm against her skin. He held her face between his hands with exquisite gentleness as his thumbs made hypnotic circles over her sensitive skin. Finally she could resist no more. With a quick breath, Tess looked into the warm glowing light of his eyes.

He's choosing me, she thought incredulously. *How could that be?*

And then his mouth was on hers and she couldn't think anymore, couldn't feel beyond his touch. Her arms came up and around his neck and she pressed herself tight against him, letting all her confusion and self-doubt pour from her. He gathered her closer, absorbing her pain with a heat that burned into her heart. His scent was intoxicating, clean and mysterious, and she breathed him in, wanting to make him a part of her. He tugged at her shirt, pulling it from the waist of her jeans, and the current in his touch spread up her ribs.

Her own hands roamed over his chest, his arms, down to the flat of his belly. She wanted to touch him everywhere, all at once. Everything she needed was there, on the surface, binding her to him with immediate intensity. She'd been made to fit with this man and all she wanted was more—more contact, more feeling. She wanted to give him all of her, whether it was right or wrong.

It was the completeness of her surrender that brought with it an unwelcome wave of realization. Was she so crazed that

nothing else mattered but the touch of him? Tess made a small
sound of refusal and tried to ignore the voice of reason speaking in her head, but it would not be silenced. What was she
thinking? What was she *doing*? No matter how he made her
feel, she didn't know this man. How could she trust the confused tangle of emotions inside her?

Reluctantly she pulled away, breathing heavily as she
fought her own desire to hold on to him. She felt his resistance
as he let her go, and staring into his eyes, she saw the fire burning there, knew the same longing was in her own. She shook
her head, denying them both.

Since he'd opened the door, everything had gone exactly
the opposite of what she'd planned. Her sensory perception
had been jammed by his nearness, destroyed by her reactions
to him. Now she felt like she'd stumbled into a bog that pulled
her deeper and deeper with every effort she made to escape.

She felt vulnerable and weak and angry with herself. Angry that he'd revealed her innermost feelings, angry that he'd
peeled back her protective shell and left her exposed. Angry
that all she wanted was to step back into his arms and forget
everything but the thrill of his lips against hers.

"I'd better go," she said, her voice as tight and thin as her
control.

Grant stared at her, his light eyes watching her agitated
movements. She straightened her clothes, feeling foolish and
gauche under his steady assessment. What was he thinking?
The moments in his arms already felt like a dream, yet another
hallucination that couldn't possibly be real. What would a
man like Grant Weston see in Tess Carson?

The answer to that question opened the door to another.
She thought back, remembering the conversation that had led
her into his arms. She'd asked about Tori, about the baby's father, and rather than answer her, he'd turned the tables. He'd
begun to pry, searching for tender spots to probe. Why? Because he didn't like the questions she'd asked? Because he
didn't want to answer them? Had he launched this seduction
simply to divert her?

No. She didn't want to believe that. She'd felt his heart

hammering beneath her hands. He'd been as excited by her as she was by him. He couldn't have faked it. But even as the thought formed, she knew it was very possible that it could have been just a performance given by a talented actor.

"You never answered my question," she said with a small, bitter laugh. "I almost forgot I'd asked it."

Grant still said nothing. All warmth had vanished from his face, leaving his expression inscrutable.

"You know who the father of Tori's baby is, don't you? Is it you?"

He remained silent as anger replaced the enigmatic look in his eyes. Finally he took a menacing step closer and said in a tight, low voice, "Your sister gets around. You're going to have to make a lot more casseroles if you're going to track down everyone she's screwed."

He placed a hand on the post above her head and leaned in. Looking into his taut and angry face, she felt threatened to her soul. If he wanted to hurt her, he could. He very well could.

All at once, the isolation of the ranch seemed to expand until she and Grant were the only two people in the world. Unsettling realizations, all of which she should have considered from the start, filled her head. Her sister was missing, and for all Tess knew, this man could have something to do with it. Why else would he be so evasive if he didn't have something to hide? Why else would her questions make him so enraged?

"If you're not the father, just say so." The slight waver in her voice revealed her fear and fueled the resentment that emanated from his entire body. Red hot, it hissed and sizzled.

"You just don't know when to quit, do you? You've got to dig through the garbage until you get what you came for. Is that it? Doesn't matter that it's rotten. Doesn't matter whose life you fuck up, does it?" He pushed away and paced a few steps before spinning around again. "Your dear misunderstood sister was banging my dad, Tess. You got that? My sixty-eight-year-old dad. Is he the father of her kid? I don't know. Could it be me? Not in a million years. Happy now?"

Tess stared at him in shock. His dad? Tori was with his *dad*?

"Nothing to say?" He gave a low laugh, but there was no

amusement in the sound. "This land has been in my family for over a hundred and fifty years. My great-great-grandfather founded the goddamn town, for Chrissake. I came back to get it running again. I've got a stable full of Hollywood horses and plans to expand this place. My dad was all for it until your sister waltzed in, screwed him for a couple of weeks, and all of a sudden the sun rose and set on her. There was nothing he had that she couldn't take. Not one goddamn thing. Including this."

His hand swept out to the paddock, the corral, the meadows and hills beyond, but like a skipping record, her mind couldn't get past, *"Your dear misunderstood sister was banging my dad."*

"You want to know what I think? I think she used him. I think she was here when that tractor flipped and she did nothing to help him. I think she took what she could and hit the road."

Tess shook her head, fighting to block out his angry, cruel words. But they stuck, thick with allegation and horrifying possibilities. She wanted to shout for him to stop, but just then a car came up the drive. Both she and Grant turned toward the Mountain Bend sheriff's cruiser that pulled in next to Tess's rented Honda.

"Aw shit," Grant said. "That's just what the day needs."

Tess watched with disbelief as Smith and Ochoa got out and came up the porch steps. Ochoa tipped his hat at Tess. Smith ignored her.

"Grant," Smith said. "Like you to come to the station with us. Answer a few questions."

He wasn't asking, and they all knew it.

With a frustrated glance at Tess, Grant gave a nod. "Let me lock up," he said.

A few moments later, he was in the backseat of the cruiser. Tess watched as they drove away, wondering what it was she saw in his eyes just before he closed the door. Regret? Fear? She didn't know. Equally important, what did the sheriff want to ask him?

chapter twenty-one

LYDIA watched the sunlight inch its way over the chocolate smears and grease splotches on the tablecloth. Outside, the storm had managed to scrub the world clean, leaving behind only the residue of its task in the leaves that choked the drains and the slain branches still blocking the roads into town. But inside her home, another kind of storm was settling.

She filled her coffee cup to the brim with swiss mocha café and a heavy dollop of cream, ignoring the destruction in her kitchen with a dispassion that bordered on numbness. The freezer in the pantry had long ago ceased to taunt her. She hardly felt the cuts and lacerations beneath the bandages on her hands and feet. She hardly felt anything anymore.

In the black hours before dawn, she'd begun dulling the pain with her drug of choice—three chocolate éclairs, chased with a warm bagel and half-pint of cream cheese. She hadn't bothered with a plate. Next came the simple but effective bread with butter.

She'd cut the first slice carefully and toasted it until it was crunchy and honey brown. The second and third pieces she'd sawed with urgency. Finally she'd given up on the slicing and simply slathered the butter over the exposed end of the loaf and eaten it down until all that was left was the crusty heel and a pile of crumbs that spread like sawdust across her lace tablecloth.

But she still felt the hollow, gaping void inside her and the need to fill it.

She slapped a dozen bacon strips into a skillet, impatiently devouring a piece of cold pizza while she waited for the grease to pop and the meat to crisp. In the end, her patience fell short of cooking time and she ate them still rubbery, already reaching for the cheesecake, then chips, followed by peanut butter by the spoonful, cold mashed potatoes, and pasta that hadn't even tasted good. She crammed one in after another, desperate to be released from her agony.

But the hurt only increased and with it came the loathing. Waves of self-disgust crashed against her weakened defenses and washed away any remaining self-respect.

Her white sweatpants were smeared with chocolate and butter and bits of green-flecked chips. Her face felt like one of the glazed donuts she'd managed to polish off somewhere between the milk jug and the fridge. But the barren caverns inside her bellowed for fulfillment.

She bit her lip, blinking back tears. The sun flared against the windows, turning them into mirrors that shot back the indistinct, yet nonetheless awful, image of her body.

How can that be me? How?

She dropped her face into her sticky hands, blotting out the image. She didn't have time for self-pity. She had to shower. She had to fix her hair, hide her face behind a layer of makeup, camouflage her rolls with bright patterns and an aura of self-confidence she never felt. She had to open her doors and smile at her neighbors. She had to hold on. Hold on.

She kept her mind purposefully blank, refusing to revisit the night before as she peeled off the bandages and showered. She dressed methodically, looking in the mirror only when necessary, adding layers, sheathing her self-destructive thoughts behind a mask of rouge and an armor of silk. When she finally flipped the sign on the door of the coffee shop to OPEN, she looked like the Lydia her customers expected. Poised and perfumed, smiling and chatty, cheerful and kind. A pillar of society.

She was cleaning up the mess in the kitchen when the phone rang. She answered, knowing who it would be.

"Did you talk to the sheriff?"

"Yes," she said.

"You told him you saw her?"

"Yes."

"Good girl."

And then he hung up. Lydia stared at the phone before carefully replacing it.

She didn't feel like a good girl, but then he didn't know where she'd been last night after he left. "It's not too late," she whispered. "It's not . . ." But of course, she knew it was.

chapter twenty-two

LONG after the dust had settled behind the sheriff's cruiser, Tess remained on Grant's porch, trying to isolate her thoughts from her emotions, and her emotions from the rest of the manic jumble in her head. The taste of Grant's kisses still lingered on her lips and in her mind. No one had ever touched her like that.

He'd held a spotlight on her darkest feelings. How had he seen inside her like that? He'd made her mad, but only because he'd blinded her with his accuracy. And then, before she could regain her balance, he'd floored her with the news that Tori had had an affair with his father, a man twice her age.

He'd said that Frank Weston would have given it all to Tori, land that had been in the family for generations. That placed her sister smack in the middle, standing between what Grant wanted and what was hers to take. Now Tori was missing and Grant was on his way to the sheriff's office.

The frustration of not knowing made her want to scream. Smith refused to tell her anything as he'd shut Grant into the backseat. Grant's grim expression through it all revealed absolutely nothing of his thoughts. So where did she go next?

She drove into town on autopilot as she tried to sort through what little she did know and draw some conclusions. Ahead was the Mountain Bend Library. A stop there had been on the "proactive ways to take charge and get answers" list Tess had made this morning. First, see Grant. Second, go to the library. Third, come to grips . . . But now it seemed as feeble a plan as storming Grant's door with a casserole had been.

Across the street from the library was an ancient-looking

building painted a serene pale teal. Its historical lines rose grace-
fully to a second floor, where bright shutters framed the windows. At street level, pastel pink awnings with silver coffee
cups painted on them flapped in the light wind. Last night
Grant had left a matchbook on the mantel with the same image.
As she pulled closer, she saw scrolling white letters on the windows. *The Sugar Cube Bed & Breakfast.* And below, in finer
print, *Gourmet Coffees and Fine Pastries Seven Days a Week.*

Lydia Hughes owned a bed and breakfast. How many could
there be in a small town like this? Tess parked in front of the library and crossed the street, noting the phone booth out front,
the one Lydia claimed Tori had used two mornings ago. A bell
tinkled when Tess opened the door. Inside, the Sugar Cube had
a quaint look, filled with a half-dozen French provincial tables
and matching chairs. Lacy linens covered all the surfaces. A
table spread with large silver urns promised a variety of caf-
feinated delights and a glass counter with sliding panes displayed an assortment of pastries. A tiny dish on the top of the
counter held bite-sized samples arranged on a paper doily.

The light scent of Lydia's perfume mingled with the fragrant pastries and cool morning air. But it was the aroma of
coffee that caught Tess's attention. It seemed like a year since
she'd had a real cup.

Lydia stepped from a back room as Tess gravitated toward
the coffee table. As usual, she looked prepared to greet the
President. Her hair was perfect, her outfit stunning, her smile
warm and welcoming. But there was an ugly bruise on her
face and her cheek was swollen and puffy.

Tess caught herself an instant before she exclaimed, *What
happened to your face?* Lydia read the question in her expression anyway. She raised her hand self-consciously and said,
"I'm such a klutz. Last night I ran right into the door frame."

"Ouch," Tess said. "Have you had it checked? It looks
pretty ba—painful."

"I'm fine," she said, but her voice wavered and a flush traveled up her neck. "Just embarrassed." Lydia moved forward
and took a china cup and saucer from the artful arrangement
on the coffee table. "Try the House Blend."

Tess didn't need to be asked twice. She added a huge splash of cream and took a sip. It was probably the best cup of coffee she'd ever had. Her eyes fluttered in appreciation and Lydia beamed with pride.

"One day I'm going to give Starbucks a run for their money."

"You just let me know when your stock goes public." Tess took another sip before saying, "Lydia, the sheriff was by my house this morning. He told me—"

"Oh, Tess, I am sorry. I feel like such a fool. I can't believe I didn't remember that she'd been here. I was so busy and she came in just as everyone and their brother seemed to want something. And of course at the time I had no reason to take notice."

"I understand."

"It was stupid of me to forget. If Craig's father hadn't— well, there was so much going on afterward. You would think that something would have jarred my memory, but . . ."

"What did finally make you remember?" Tess asked.

Lydia looked at her blankly for a moment and in her eyes a strange sort of panic seemed to glow. "Well, it was this morning, when I was brewing the coffee. It just came to me. I called Sheriff Smith right away. He nearly bit my head off for not remembering sooner."

Tess gave her a sympathetic look. "That sounds like him. He told me you said Tori seemed agitated when she got off the phone. Did you speak to her?"

Lydia shook her head. "I'm sorry, she just grabbed her usual and went."

"Tori's a regular?"

"House Blend every morning. But she's not much for conversation." Lydia shrugged. "I wish I could tell you more."

Tess figured her next question was pointless, but she tried anyway. "Lydia, do you know anything about her relationship with the Westons?"

"Are you asking if she had a *personal* relationship with any of them?" Lydia said, surprised.

Tess nodded. That really wasn't what she asked but Tess thought it interesting that Lydia drew that conclusion.

Lydia lowered her eyes. "Not that I know of."

Distracted, maybe even troubled, Lydia began fiddling nervously with a ring on her hand. Tess looked closer. It was the only ring she wore and it was on the third finger of her left hand. Curious, Tess said, "Is that an engagement ring, Lydia?"

Lydia looked as if she'd sucked a lemon. "Uh . . . well. It's not official. I mean, there's been no announcement or anything."

"Well, congratulations all the same. Who's the lucky guy?"

If possible, her expression soured even more. "We promised each other not to say anything until we're both ready. With Frank dying and everything that's going on, we felt it was best."

Had she meant to reveal so much with that comment? Looking into her anxious face, Tess didn't think so, but Lydia had basically admitted to being engaged to a Weston. The muscles in Tess's stomach clenched as she remembered last night at the restaurant. Grant had left just as they arrived and Lydia was upset about something. Had there been a lover's quarrel? Grant certainly seemed angry when he'd walked out the door. Or was it the sight of Craig escorting another woman to dinner that had put that look in her eyes? Her heart made a desperate plea for the second scenario as images of this morning on Grant's porch filled her head.

Afraid Lydia would guess her thoughts, Tess lowered her eyes and took a quick sip of coffee, but her hand shook and she spilled some on her shirt. Cursing, she grabbed a handful of napkins from the table and blotted at the spot.

"Did you burn yourself?" Lydia asked, concerned.

"No, talk about a klutz. That's like the third cup of coffee I've spilled in three days. I should just switch to booze."

Lydia's eyes sparkled and she smiled with understanding. She really was an exceptionally beautiful woman. Why should she be so surprised that one of the Weston brothers thought so, too?

"Tess," Lydia said, her voice suddenly serious. "I wanted to—"

A noise came from somewhere in the back. Lydia froze as the distinct sound of a door opening and closing reached them.

"I must have company."

Her expression made it clear that whatever she'd been about to say would have to wait. Frustrated, Tess nodded. "I better get going anyway. I have some things to do."

Finishing what was left of her coffee, Tess pulled out her wallet to pay.

Lydia shook her head. "Be serious. The coffee's on me."

Tess thanked her and stepped outside. The instant she closed the door behind her, she felt that unmistakable familiar cold gathering within, as if it had been merely waiting for her to be alone. Instinctively she stiffened, prepared to fight the void that opened around her. But fighting didn't work, did it? Whatever *it* was, resistance did not thwart it. She hurried to her car and locked herself in. Purposefully she forced her muscles to relax. Like a wind, the sensations blew through her.

She looked through her windshield and saw the motion of the wagon superimposed over the deserted street. The effect unnerved her as totally as the awareness that she was stepping over the gulf of time. She saw Adam, turning to say something, and at the same moment, she watched the lone traffic light at the corner go from yellow to red.

Her skin tingled and the images wobbled, as if seen through a haze of intense heat. She battled the suffocating fear that rose within her and forced herself to take the step.

To cross over.

chapter twenty-three

MOLLY'S first month on the trail drew to an end on the winds of yet another fierce storm. For two weeks pelting rain changed all to marsh and sludge. Mud sucked at their shoes and sank their wheels to the hubs. Each time the wagon became mired, it had to be unloaded, forced from the cavity by either strength or ingenuity, and then loaded up again. The process was tedious and exhausting.

Dusk often brought with it frigid rains that doused their fires and chilled their bones. They grew weary of eating cold biscuits and beans while huddled in their cramped wagon. From sunrise to sunset Molly's days were filled with countless chores and wearisome tasks. She and the others were all done in by the time they made camp each evening. More than once Molly had looked up from the dinner dishes to find everyone else asleep where they sat around the fire.

"I don't know what I would've done if you hadn't come along, Molly," Rosie told her one night.

"You would have done all that you could and the Lord would have provided the rest."

"Hmmm," Rosie said. "He ain't providing enough rest as it is."

Mr. Hastings's guidebook advised the emigrants to rest on the Sabbath. He admonished those who pushed on instead of heeding this advice, stating that they would reach California no faster and all the more worse for the wear. Molly wholeheartedly agreed, but the hostile weather had set them back considerably and Adam feared they would not reach Independence in time.

"Once we join with another group, we'll rest on Sundays. But we can't afford to miss out by getting there too late. We don't want to make this trip on our own."

No, indeed, Molly thought, shuddering at the very idea of their small party straggling behind the exodus with no one to rely upon but themselves. She kept her complaints to herself and did as the others, one step at a time.

Adam had apparently spoken to Dewey after that first day, and thankfully the revolting man had since kept his distance. At night, she prayed that once they reached Independence, Dewey would decide to travel with another party altogether. It was not exactly the most Christian of prayers, but she rationalized that at least it didn't involve broken bones or plunging falls.

She opened her eyes one morning after a particularly nasty bout of weather had ravaged them the night before and thought that it felt as if they'd been traveling for years, though the journey had barely begun. Only Arlie's happy babble and the rare promise of sunshine could induce her to leave her blankets and join the living.

It was later in the day that Brodie fell into step beside her and they walked in companionable silence. The oxen ambled beside them like well-trained pets, towing the wagon behind them. The morning sun had succumbed to dark clouds, and the threat of rain was imminent. The ground was marshy and it sucked at their boots, but when the storm broke, they would be confined once again and Molly could not pass up the opportunity to stretch her legs.

Adam had ridden ahead to scout a place to camp for the night—Lady trotting faithfully at his heels. Dewey had fallen behind to hunt, though so far his kills had consisted of tiny creatures that did not seem fit to eat. Rosie had been fighting a cold brought on by the chilly, wet weather, and at Molly's insistence, she'd lain down to rest in the wagon. Molly and Brodie were alone but for Arlie.

"You want to ride on my horse for awhile, Molly?" Brodie asked, giving her a shy smile.

"Thank you, Brodie, but I think I'd best keep my feet on the ground today. I'm afraid I will be nothing more than a dress filled with aches and discomforts before this journey is through."

"I'm thinking I won't have strength enough to dig for gold, myself," he answered.

Arlie had just awoken from his afternoon nap and now he raced beside her in the fields. He'd fought ferociously when she'd dressed him in pants and a long-sleeved shirt after his nap, but if she had not, he would have been covered in as many insect bites as he was in mud splatters by now. He tumbled frequently when his momentum exceeded his stout little legs, but the endless days filled with little else had allowed him to master the art of walking. He'd learned to run with barely a moment's pause.

"Look at him go. He's all ready for it, ain't he?" Brodie said, grinning as he watched his nephew.

"I suppose if we all took a nap in the morning and again in the afternoon, we would have equal stamina."

They watched him chase a bright yellow butterfly to a patch of daises in the green pasture. Arlie squealed with delight when he got close to it. He looked over his shoulder at Molly, checking to see if she'd observed his efforts. His smile brought with it a warm rush of emotion.

"Adam said we'd be to Indian Creek tomorrow," Brodie said.

Indian Creek sounded quite docile, but the mention of it brought Molly's thoughts to the rivers they must cross between here and California.

"I am praying for an uneventful crossing."

"Shoot, yes. And after that, we'll be home free to Independence."

"And rest on the Sabbaths."

They grinned at one another.

"I must admit that I do not look forward to the rivers we must cross. I have never learned to swim and the thought of being bereft on so much moving water . . ."

"I'm a good swimmer. I bet I could swim across the Mississippi if I had to. I can teach you how if you want."

"I appreciate the offer, Brodie, but I'm not so bright a pupil that I could master it before then."

"I bet you could. I've never met no one as smart as you. No one as pretty either."

He gazed at her with limpid blue eyes until she felt her own face grow hot. "Oak Tree is a very small town," she said, "or you surely would have met many others far more intelligent and pretty. I couldn't hold a candle to my sister, you know."

He scowled and looked away. "You're a lot prettier than *her.*"

She didn't like his tone but it seemed ridiculous to argue with him. Vanessa had been an uncommon beauty and they both knew it.

"Anyhow, you won't have to worry about swimming across any rivers tomorrow. Indian Creek won't hardly get your feet wet. You'll be on the wagon and the ox will make it across fast. And when we get to the big ones, I'll be there to save you if you need me to."

He smiled at her with childish earnestness, but the gleam in his eyes made her uncomfortably aware that Brodie Weston wasn't nearly so young as he might appear.

Blushing, she said, "I am much reassured. Thank you."

"You know what else?" he said suddenly. "You know what I'm going to do? I'm going to put a swimming pool in that mansion I'm building for you so you can practice."

"A swimming pool?" Molly laughed. "Oh my, Brodie, I will need a title to go with my grand palace."

"We could get married and then you'd be my wife."

Feeling as awkward as an adolescent herself, she said, "I am much too old for you, Brodie. You should be thinking of the young girls you'll meet in California. I'm sure they will be all too eager to make your acquaintance."

He shook his head. "I don't want any stupid young girls who ain't interested in anything but my money."

Money he had yet to make, Molly thought with a smile. Prudently, she kept it to herself.

"I know you don't think of me as a man yet, but I am. I've got two strong hands and a good head on my shoulders. I'm a hard worker and I aim to prove myself to you."

"Brodie, I don't doubt for a moment that you will be—that you are a wonderful young man. But my feelings for you are of friendship only. There can be no other bond between us."

The look he gave her then made her realize that he must have had this conversation in his mind many times before and that her response contradicted his imagined replies. Brodie stared at her silently, mired by his bewilderment.

"I am sorry, Brodie, but I would do you a disservice were I not honest with you now."

Arlie chose that moment to voice a complaint. He'd conquered the daisies and moved closer to pillage the tall grasses that bordered their path. Realizing that no one was paying attention to him, he'd tried to eat the waving stalks and now he stood crying with green globs sprouting from his open mouth. She took the opportunity to step away from Brodie.

"Arlie, what have you been up to," she said, using her handkerchief to wipe the mess from his tongue. After she'd rinsed his mouth with water, he raised his arms and opened and closed his small, pudgy hands. "Holju."

She reached her own arms out to him. "You want to hold me or do you want me to hold you?"

"Holju," he agreed.

Molly scooped him up and settled him on her hip. Immediately he laid his little head on her chest. Small though he was, his weight would multiply with each step until her arms felt wrenched from their sockets. She could not carry him across the country. She was not strong enough. However, if the beginning of the journey was anything to measure by, she understood that she would most likely do it all the same.

Brodie had recovered his equilibrium and fallen in step with her again. "You'll change your mind about me after I teach you to swim," he said with an irresistible grin.

She had to laugh. Arguing the point appeared to be futile, anyway. "You are most certainly as obstinate as any man I've ever met."

And almost as charming as your brother, she thought with a sigh. She couldn't help imagining how different the outcome would have been had this conversation taken place with Adam instead. Each day she spent in Adam's company made her long for another.

"Hey, Arlie. Want to ride my horse?" Brodie asked.

Arlie popped his head up immediately and nodded. Arlie's fascination with the horses and his love of riding had been the only savior of Molly's arms thus far. She hoped his fascination would not wane before they reached California. Brodie fetched his mount from where it was tethered to the back of the wagon and placed the boy up on the saddle. Happiness restored, Arlie held on to the saddle horn while Brodie kept hold of the reins.

"I believe he looks more like Vanessa each day," she murmured. "Not much like his father, though."

Brodie gave a wry snort at that. "At least he don't act like her. Your sister wasn't anywhere near as nice as you."

"I'm sorry."

Brodie shrugged, deliberately casting his gaze out to the fields. Thunder rumbled in the distance, and a sprinkling of rain touched her face.

Ignoring it, she said, "May I ask you something about my sister, Brodie?"

He hunched his shoulders, looking wary. "If you want."

"It's just that . . . well, since the day I arrived, it's been painfully obvious that Vanessa endeared herself to no one. At times I've wondered if even her husband cherished her. I've been disinclined to speak of her after my shameful outburst on my first night . . . but I long to know how . . . it was with her."

"I guess you have that right," he said solemnly.

Molly let a few moments pass, waiting for Brodie to continue. Their footfalls made soft thumps against the damp earth. He waited so long that she feared he'd changed his mind about confiding in her. Then at last, he spoke.

"When Adam brought Vanessa home, I thought he'd gone and married an angel," he said. "She was so pretty. I'd never seen anyone so pretty. And at first she was real nice, too. The way she talked and the way she looked . . ." His lips curled into a small smile. "Ma fussed around her like she was royalty and Vanessa just ate it up. Course, after a while, it wasn't so great no more."

No, Molly imagined that it hadn't taken long for them

all to grow weary of having the queen to visit. She'd been Vanessa's lady-in-waiting many more times than she cared to admit.

"Adam, he don't have no patience for laziness and I kept waiting for him to lay into Vanessa about it, but he never did. Sometimes it takes me a while to figure things out." He gave a rueful shake of his head. "I didn't know she was going to have a baby until Ma told me. Then it made sense."

So Adam had been a doting husband to his expecting wife. Having seen him as a father, Molly did not have trouble picturing him nurturing his son's mother.

"I imagine Vanessa was a beautiful mother-to-be," she said, picturing her sister, glowing with the love of her husband and the excitement of carrying his child.

"Oh, she was."

Something in Brodie's voice contradicted his words. "But?"

He looked down at his feet. "I don't think I'm supposed to talk about this. I don't want Adam to be mad at me about it."

She took a deep breath, feeling underhanded for pressing him but needing to know all the same. "Your confidence is well placed in me, Brodie. I will not betray it. Vanessa was my sister, and as you said, I have a right to know what her life was like before it ended."

Perplexed by his decision, he scratched his head and continued to look at his feet. Behind him Arlie rode with a contentment that wouldn't last long. She feared if she let Brodie delay any more, she might never know the truth. A few more scattered raindrops fell around them, but the storm held off. As if on cue, however, Arlie began to fuss. Quickly she reached for him and settled him once again against her body.

"What happened once the newness faded from Vanessa's arrival?" she asked.

"Well, there ain't a lot to do in a working man's house but work. She didn't want none of that."

His pause said nearly as much as his words. Vanessa had grown bored yet had refused to contribute to the household, and the Weston family had become tired of her idleness. Molly glanced up at Brodie. There was more.

"What did she do all day?" Molly asked.

"Not much at first. And then later she was getting big and she slept a lot. And after Arlie came . . ." He looked at Arlie with a pained expression. "Well, look at him, Molly."

Frowning, Molly followed Brodie's pointed stare down to the child, his head nestled beneath her chin, his face angelic and peaceful.

Look at him. He doesn't look anything like Adam.

She shook her head, but denial was not an option because at that moment Arlie turned his face to look back and the shadows played on his features. Suddenly she saw what she'd been previously blind to.

No . . . oh dear Lord, no. How had she missed it before?

Brodie remained quiet while the revelation rolled over her.

"Things just kept getting worse after that. Vanessa, she didn't want nothing to do with the little guy. She'd let him cry all the time and . . . I don't really remember what all happened after that."

Molly peered into Brodie's face, knowing that he was lying but confounded as to how to make him tell her the truth. "Did she never take interest in her new family?"

Glumly, he shook his head. "Then one day Adam came home early and he caught her doing what she shouldn't have been."

"What was she doing?"

Brodie inhaled deeply and slowly let the breath out. "She wasn't alone."

Molly was glad they were walking. Walking kept her from fainting.

"She got all crazy then, I guess. She was hitting and scratching and using language that had no place in a woman's mouth. Then she told Adam that Arlie ain't his son."

Molly looked down at Arlie's face pressed against her. It was as if a veil had been lifted and now she could see clearly. The child she held so dear not only resembled her sister. He also bore a striking resemblance to someone else she knew, someone who had stood at her father's side each and every Sunday assisting with the rituals of the church. His wife and six children invariably took up the first pew. His youngest son would be just a few weeks older than Arlie. The two could be twins.

"Adam knows that he is not . . ."

Miserable, Brodie nodded.

"How did he . . . what was his reaction?"

Brodie simply shrugged. The magnitude of his understated gesture implied an outcome so fierce that Molly shuddered to imagine it. She waited for Brodie's next words, wishing with all her heart that she didn't have to hear them. But of course, she did.

When he spoke, his voice was low and charged with emotion. The timbre resonated through Molly's heart. She clutched the baby tight to her bosom as she listened.

"It wasn't more than a few days later Vanessa had her accident," Brodie said.

chapter twenty-four

THE next day emerged reluctantly. Cold and gray, the low-hanging clouds inched down on them and blocked out the feeble sun. Like torchlight piercing the darkest of dungeons, lightning flashed deep within the solid bank of clouds above, stealthily traveling from one black chamber to the next. Deep, guttural thunder followed close on its heels like the echo of slamming doors.

The small Weston party trudged below. They would reach Indian Creek by midmorning if the rain held off, but with each passing minute, that seemed less likely. Molly dreaded the thought of spending another day trapped by fierce weather more than she did traipsing into the cold creek water, and she dreaded that more than she cared to admit.

Adam walked ahead of the rest, his worry as evident as the rumbling sky. He had seen the creek yesterday and returned from it tight lipped and silent. Arlie, ever the barometer of his father's emotions, had become fractious until sundown when exhaustion quieted him. The first morning's light, however, began with his whining and fussing until Molly finally capitulated and carried him as they began the day's endless walk. Now her shoulders, arms, and back felt as wretched as the growing trepidation inside her.

Thoughts of her conversation with Brodie only added weight to the burden of worry she carried. Could she trust his explanation of the events leading to Vanessa's death? And if so, what did it mean? Was it a tragic coincidence that Adam had found his wife with another man only days before she would die an accidental death? How could it be anything but that? It was ridiculous even to imagine a different conclusion, one where Adam had forced fate's hand against his cheating wife. Wasn't it?

The questions buzzed painfully through her head until she wanted to shout out loud. None of it made sense. Adam did not treat Arlie as anything but his son and she could not, would not, believe that he was capable of wrongdoing where Vanessa was concerned.

So what, then, was the truth?

Thunder rumbled in ominous response and Molly looked up with a knot of anxiety wedged somewhere near her heart. She should be more concerned about what was happening now, today, than about Brodie's vague allusions to what might have been.

Dewey caught her eye as she looked away from the turbid sky and he grinned with a malicious gleam in his eyes that she liked not at all. Before breakfast he'd taken delight in teasing Arlie by snatching away the carved horse his father had made and holding it just out of reach. From there he'd progressed to taunting Brodie about his skill as a craftsman. He'd revisited the subject of the now-infamous rocking chair that had collapsed so long ago.

Today Brodie was disinclined to take Dewey's ribbing with silence, and by midmorning, the hostility between them had become a friction that sparked like static from one to the other. She feared they would come to blows before the day was through.

Feeling like there was nothing about which she was not worried, Molly trudged on beside the wagon. But when they finally reached the flooded, swollen banks of Indian Creek, every other concern was wiped clean from her mind.

"That's not a creek," she said, but the thunder drowned out her voice.

The water churned in a turbulent froth as it raced through the valley, spewing out of its banks in an angry roar. This was no creek. This was a wild, rampant river. Arlie lifted his head and stared at the rapids with round eyes. He looked from the rushing water to Molly, as if to question these adults who contemplated its crossing.

"How we going to cross that sum'bitch?" Dewey asked, raising his voice to be heard over the roar of water.

Branches and leaves, ripped from trees during recent storms, rushed by in the white-capped water. Molly seized on the thought of their wagon and precious supplies smashed against the rocks.

Adam stood beside Brodie and looked at churning waters with grim resignation. "It's worse than yesterday," he shouted over the rumbling din.

"What are we going to do about it, Adam?" Brodie yelled back.

"We can try farther up. There's got to be an easier place to cross."

"You didn't scout for one yesterday?" Dewey hollered.

Adam nodded once and looked away. With sinking spirits, Molly gathered that he had looked but found no better passage.

"Up was just as bad and down was even worse yesterday. But the way this water is moving, it might have cut through the banks and chopped out a new way across."

"A new way to die, maybe," Dewey yelled.

Brodie turned on the filthy man and shouted, "You just shut your mouth, Dewey. Adam knows what he's doin'."

"That's good, cuz I sure ain't following no *boy* anywhere."

The steely tone of Adam's voice rose above the thundering water. "You can go on alone if you want, Dewey."

Molly and Rosie exchanged silent glances. Beside them the flooded creek roared like a caged beast bent on revenge. Adam took off his hat and slapped it against his thigh.

"It looks bad, but we can do it," Brodie said with unwarranted optimism. "Shoot, it's Indian Creek, not the Mississippi we're fixing to cross."

Adam nodded and gave Brodie a reassuring pat on his back. But he paced away, wearing the grim and troubled expression of a man faced with too much responsibility and few options. He looked up at the festering storm clouds and back at the racing water. "We should wait," he shouted back at last.

"What for?" Dewey demanded with a guffaw. "For the next storm to come and make it worse? You said yourself it's even higher than it was yesterday. We're running out of time."

"Nobody's asking you," Brodie hollered.

"It may get worse," Adam said, his voice hoarse from yelling. "It may get better. But getting ourselves killed isn't going to get us there any faster." He put his hat back on and gave a nod of conviction. "I'm going to ride up a ways, see if there's a better place to cross."

"You're wasting our time," Dewey sneered.

It was the last straw. Brodie spun around so quickly that Dewey took a stumbling step back. "You're not in charge, are you, Dewey?"

"You ain't neither," Dewey shouted back. "You ain't got enough brains to be in charge of your own pecker."

Molly gasped at his language. Dewey's loathsome face split into a rotten smile and he laughed at Brodie.

"You don't even know what yer pecker's for yet, do ya, *boy*," he exclaimed.

Brodie launched himself at Dewey and knocked the fat man off his feet into the mud of the riverbank. They rolled one over another, punching and grunting, shouting curses, grinding silt and sludge into their clothes and hair until Molly couldn't tell who was striking whom. Brodie was stronger and more agile, but Dewey was heavier and more cunning. He wiggled and squirmed and tried to poke at Brodie's eyes.

Adam waded into their midst and tried to break them up but managed only to catch a glancing blow that bloodied his lip and fanned his temper. Cursing as well, he at last captured Brodie by his shirt collar and hauled him up and away. Blood streamed down Brodie's face, making red rivers in the caked mud. Dewey lumbered to his feet and glared at Brodie. He spat a mouthful of silty blood onto the bank.

"What the hell is wrong with you?" Adam demanded. "Isn't there enough to worry about without you two killing each other?"

The three men stood like points of a triangle, all at opposite sides and of opposite minds. Molly tried to keep Arlie from watching, but the boy wriggled this way and that, craning his neck and twisting his body until she gave up her effort to shield him.

"He started it," Dewey hollered, pointing a finger at Brodie.

With a shout, Brodie slammed into Dewey again and hurled the bigger man back into the side of the wagon. The wood creaked loudly, popping like gunfire, and the oxen shuffled in alarm. The two bounced back and hit the ground once more, rolling between the agitated team's shifting hooves and out again.

"Goddamn it!" Adam yelled.

He kicked at their writhing bodies, herding them away from the wagon and oxen until the two at last separated. Brodie staggered to his feet and wiped his face with a muddy sleeve, succeeding only in smearing the muck across his cheek. Dewey swayed as he struggled to stand.

Above, lightning exploded from the sky and touched down so close they heard it hiss. Thunder boomed behind it and half a second later came the rain. Fat, cold drops plunged down on them, splashing the mud onto their clothes and drenching them in the reality of their situation. Any fool could see that the rain was just the beginning. Dewey was right. It would only get worse.

Another bolt of lightning snaked out of the sky and fierce thunder rocked the ground.

Adam paced to the water's edge and finally stepped in.

Molly asked, "Adam, what are you doing?"

"It's going to rain like the end of the world and we're going to be stuck on this side until June," he said. His voice was hard and cold, but in it was a thread of desperation. He took another step and then another. The water rushed over his boots.

"It's not going to be easy, but we've got to get across." He turned and faced the women. "We don't have a choice."

Molly shook her head, more in denial than disagreement. She was frightened and there was no hiding it. Adam waded back to shore and took her icy hands in his.

"This is only going to get worse. The rain's going to bring the water up and our chance will be gone. We'll have to turn back."

"I know, but—"

"This trip's going to be filled with rivers. I wish it weren't, but there you have it. If we're going to run scared at the first one, we may as well go back to Oak Tree."

Molly stared at him helplessly while fear and cold chattered her teeth. More lightning cracked from the bottom of the black clouds and sparked across the sky. The clap of thunder that followed spooked the horses and made the oxen pull at their yokes. As if to prove it wouldn't be outdone, the rain became a downpour.

"Molly, I'm scared, too. But this isn't even a real river and I don't think it's as deep as it looks." He glanced back and forth between Molly and his mother. "Will you try?"

She had to bite her lip to keep from crying out, "No," but she managed to nod. His answering smile rewarded her courage and sparked a warmth deep inside her. Maybe they *could* cross it. They could do anything Adam told them they could do.

"Ma, how about you?"

"Well, I didn't come all this way just to turn around."

"Brodie?"

"Shoot, yes, Adam. I ain't scared. I could swim across it if I had to. You know that."

"Why don't you go ahead and do that, dummy?" Dewey snarled.

"Why don't you just go on home, you yellow-bellied coward," Brodie shouted back. "I didn't want you along in the first place. We don't need the likes of you on this trip."

Adam calmly crossed to Dewey's side and said something to him that the rest of them could not hear. Molly could guess what it was, though, by the stiff nod Dewey gave in response. They were in for all or for none. There was no room for discourse in this game of life and death.

When Adam swung into his saddle, he looked questioningly at the women. Rosie gave Molly's hand a squeeze and then climbed up on the wagon. Molly's hands were shaking so badly she nearly dropped Arlie as she passed him up.

"Can you swim?" she asked when she'd taken her seat on the bench.

Rosie nodded. "But if we hit that river, swimming ain't gonna save us."

Rosie clutched Arlie so tightly that he whimpered and Molly prayed for guidance . . . or shallow water, whichever was most readily available. She held tight to the reins, cringing as the oxen stepped forward and vocalized their opinions on what the foolish humans compelled them to do. The wagon bumped and rocked to the edge and then she felt the current hit the wheels and shake the wagon like a twig.

Please be shallow, please be shallow.

The oxen tossed their massive heads, nostrils flaring and ears swiveling with fright. Terrified, she held on, gripping the seat's edge with one white-knuckled hand and the reins with the other. Sounds of fear reached her as the animals called to one another and tried to shake off the insistent tug of the yoke.

Lord help us and protect us in this time of need. And please make the water shallow.

Adam cracked his whip over their heads, driving the team forward into the fast, icy flow. The powerful current splashed against the wagon and washed over Molly's feet. Arlie's terrified cries joined the melee.

"Hold on to him, Rosie. Hold on."

From the corner of her eye she saw a flash of color. Dewey, fighting with his mount as the frightened horse reared up and whinnied with alarm. Terror spread like fire from one beast to the next. The team rebelled and tried to turn against the surging flow, tried to go back.

"Adam!" Molly cried as the powerful animals pushed against his horse. "Adam, stop them!"

Adam fought the oxen as they tried to drag him backward. Brodie scrambled to help but the current was too powerfully set against him. The wagon rocked, slamming her and Rosie to the wood floor. Frantically she caught hold of Rosie and

Arlie while gripping the railing. She managed to keep them all inside while the rushing water tried to suck them out.

The river roiled but Adam somehow righted the team and aimed them to the west. Brodie's mare swung around and Dewey's horse reared again. Before Molly and Rosie could regain their seats, great torrents of water rushed over them, blinding Molly to anything else. And then she was screaming as the wagon jolted to the side and slammed back to its wheels. In an instant, the raging rapids scooped her out of the wagon.

Water choked her screams as she frantically fought for something to hold on to. Fear for Rosie and Arlie magnified her terror, but she could see nothing. The freezing water hurled her crazily until she couldn't tell what direction was up or down. What it lacked in depth it made up for with power, pulling her under to slam her against hidden rocks and deadwood. She surfaced, gasping hysterically. Dewey floundered beside her, crying out as the current thrashed him about. He reached a hand out to her and she struggled to grasp it, missed, and then tried again.

"Come on," he shouted. "Come on!"

Her fingers found his and he pulled her hard against him. Immediately she felt the strength of his mass fighting the water and shielding her from the debris. He seemed to gain control, to slow them down and move them toward the shore though how he managed it was inconceivable. Then suddenly Dewey's arms opened and the rushing water sucked at her heavy skirts and towed her under. She couldn't see, couldn't catch her breath or keep her head above water. She was drowning, she was drowning . . .

Her flailing arms grew weak and blackness began to force its way through her panic. Then something slipped over her head and down to her shoulders and jerked tight, yanking her backward. It had her, whatever it was, and her fear blossomed into crushing terror. She kicked and spun like a fish on a line until she heard her name through the frenzy and then Adam's arms were reaching down and hauling her up and she was beside him on his horse. She held on with all her strength as the horse labored toward the shore.

She gasped, coughing up the water in her lungs, retching into the river that sped beneath them until, at last, she sucked in a breath of air. Short, hysterical bursts of sound broke from her lips. Where was Arlie? Rosie? Were they still in the water? She twisted around to search for the wagon.

"Hold still," Adam yelled.

"The wagon?" she cried.

"They're okay. They made it."

The horse hauled them up the bank. Still holding her tight, Adam spurred the exhausted animal parallel to the vicious rapids. She tried not to think of the long way the current had taken her. She tried not to think at all. Adam brought the horse to a stop, swung from the saddle, and reached up for her. His rope hung slack from around her waist as she slid to the ground. She was crying, silent wracking sobs that came from deep within. Adam cupped her face in his hands. "Are you all right?" he asked, his voice throbbing with emotion that betrayed his steady touch.

She nodded and he gathered her close to him, rocking her frozen body in his arms. Her teeth chattered and shock quaked through her limbs. Over Adam's shoulder she saw Rosie and Arlie locked together with the same stunned agony. Brodie lay just to their side, his chest heaving with the breaths he took.

Finally she was able to pull back, but she still kept hold of Adam's arms, as if the river could pounce from its banks and seize her from safety. She lifted her shaking hand and smoothed it over his forehead and cheeks. Adam pressed a fierce kiss into her palm.

"You're hurt?" he said, gently touching her face. His fingers came away with blood.

She shook her head, but she didn't know if she was hurt or not. She was numb and tears still streamed uncontrollably from her eyes, but as she stared around her, she realized where they were. "We're on the other side?" she breathed.

Adam made a sound low in his throat and leaned his forehead against hers. "Yeah, city girl. We made it."

Dewey, however, had not. As soon as they caught their breath, Adam and Brodie mounted up to search for him. In tandem they disappeared into the thicket that framed the long shores of Indian Creek.

Molly's rubbery legs would hardly support her as she stumbled to the place where Rosie and Arlie huddled. She sank down next to them and Arlie crawled into her lap.

Rosie dabbed at a gash on Molly's forehead, making a hissing sound as she worked, but she mumbled that it would mend and set about binding the wounds on Molly's arms and legs. Molly didn't feel any pain; she was too numb yet for that. But tomorrow she would be black and blue.

As if in reprieve, the rain slackened, and after a time the women moved camp away from the banks where the ground was firmer and more open. It was sometime later that the men returned. Dewey had not been found.

Molly was torn by her guilt for the uncharitable thoughts she'd had about him and his heroic attempt to save her from drowning. Over and over she replayed the events of the crossing, trying to remember just how it had all happened.

Rosie set to frying some of their potted pork and the warm, homey smells conflicted with the wild, open kitchen in which she cooked. Arlie would not release Molly, so she held him beside the fire, rocking them both as she hummed lullabies and hymns. Adam and Brodie dismounted and unsaddled their horses in silence.

"He probably ran off on his own," Brodie burst out suddenly. "I knew he was a coward. We'd have probably crossed a lot easier if he hadn't been there. It was his horse that spooked the team. That's what caused all the problems."

Adam's eyes reflected the turbulent sky. Doubt, disillusionment, fatigue—all flashed like lightning through their bleak gray depths. He stared at his brother until Brodie looked away. "I guess we're lucky we're not looking for more than one body washed up," Adam said wearily.

"It's not my fault," Brodie muttered.

Molly looked up in surprise. Of course it wasn't his fault. How could it have been?

"I know," Adam said, sounding tired and aged. "I know. I'm going to gather some more firewood." He trudged off, his shoulders hunched and his steps heavy.

Above them, the sky rumbled and in moments fat raindrops began to fall again.

chapter twenty-five

AFTER more than a month of unbroken travel, Molly was not prepared for the noise and excitement of Independence. Since crossing Indian Creek, the violent storms had diminished and then ceased altogether and the weather had made a miraculous turn into a gentle spring. The quiet of the following days spent forging miles of untamed terrain had lulled her into a sense of predictable solitude, where each day could be counted on to unravel much as the one before it.

But beneath a bright blue sky, Independence exploded with sights and sounds and excitement. Emigrants packed the stores, restaurants, and walkways, overflowing in a throng of foreign languages and apparel. Wagons and livestock swarmed the muddy streets, crowding the narrow passageways down the middle. And everywhere, talk of gold ignited already combustible conversations.

Entering town, Brodie drove their oxen team cautiously into the masses, tipping his hat and apologizing when necessity demanded he force his way forward.

"I ain't never, ever, *ever* seen so many people," Brodie exclaimed for the tenth time. "If they all make it to California, there won't be enough gold to go around."

Even New York City had never seemed like this. The throng made Molly unreasonably apprehensive. Adam had ridden ahead early that morning to explore the town, and Molly was anxious for him to rejoin them. She'd grown dependent on the sight of his straight back and broad shoulders riding ahead, but she sensed that something had changed in him since the river crossing. Something she couldn't put into words, but felt acutely.

He'd become withdrawn, his smile came less frequently, and his guard never lowered. At times she'd find the weight of his stare resting on her or Arlie and she knew that his confidence had been shaken. They'd never found Dewey Yokum's body and they'd no choice but to presume him dead. When Adam looked at them, she knew he was thinking how easily it could have been one of his own.

"There he is," Brodie said, pointing. Molly followed with her eyes, peering through the surging masses until at last she saw Adam riding toward them.

She watched as he navigated the crowds before he reined in beside them, looking tired and road weary but obviously relieved to have found them. His clothes were dust covered, his face drawn. His horse, which Molly had named Storm after his courageous rescue in the thunder and lightning, pawed the ground impatiently.

"Thought I'd lost you," he said, taking off his hat to wipe his brow.

"With all these people, it wouldn't have been hard to do," Molly answered, smiling at him.

Beside her, Brodie shifted closer. Adam was not the only one to have undergone change since crossing the river. Brodie had become unbearably protective of Molly. She knew that his youth made him emotional, and having seen death at Molly's feet, he felt strongly about her well-being. But his attentions went beyond that and they both knew it. Yet no amount of discouragement on her part could deter him.

"Adam, have you ever seen so many people in all your life?" Brodie asked.

Adam glanced at his brother with indulgence. "Never in all my life, Brodie. They're here from just about everywhere, too. I heard one fellow say he was from Iceland." Adam clicked his tongue at Storm and backed the gelding up a step. "I've spent the morning getting tramped on by half of them. There's a line a mile long to sign up for the ferry. Look over there." He pointed to a city of wagons that crouched at the edge of town.

The canvased tops, milling cattle, and people seemed to stretch forever. "You see those wagons? Most of them have been waiting for days to get across the river."

"Days?" Molly exclaimed. She turned and exchanged a wide-eyed look with Rosie.

"From what I hear, could take as long as a week before the last of us get across." Adam eased back in his saddle. The exhaustion in his voice was echoed by the slump of his shoulders. The weight of responsibility seemed to ride heavy these days. "Follow me over there where that white tarp is. Someone is holding my spot."

They followed him through the crowded streets and found a spot to wait off to the side. The crush of people had left an unpleasant odor in the air, and Molly found herself wishing for the wide-open land again. The past month had done much to wear her down to bare threads, stripping her like lace and beading from a gown. How would she fare in this makeshift civilization?

A part of her didn't care. It would be heavenly to stay put for a few days.

Adam worked his way up in line, signed a registry, and then moved to another line. Nearly an hour had passed while they waited until at last, one of the men behind the table called, "Francis A. Weston?"

Adam raised a hand and said, "Here."

Surprised, Molly looked at Rosie. "Why did that man call Adam 'Francis'?"

Rosie smiled and Molly acknowledged yet another transformation since the river. Rosie seemed to have aged a lifetime and now she looked frail and very old. So different from the woman who had left Ohio just a month ago. Molly worried about her constantly.

"Francis is Adam's Christian name," Rosie said. "My husband's family started the tradition after they lost six boys in one winter. Think it was Frank's great-great-grandfather that decided after that all the Weston boys should carry the family name." She nodded at Arlie, "Francis Arlington," then at her eldest son. "Francis Adam," and then at Brodie, "Francis Ambrose."

"Ambrose?"

Rosie's smile took on a reminiscent air. "I picked that one. It was my Daddy's name."

Adam worked his way up to the man who'd called him and bent over the table. A paper of some sort passed between them, followed by money. He returned and gave them all a tired smile.

"We'll be crossing end of the week. Until then we get to take a rest. I found out there's a party looking for others to join up. See that man over there?" Adam pointed to a stern-looking man standing to the side of the tables. "His name's George Hanson and he's in charge of it. It'll cost us forty dollars, but they've got a guide who's made the trip once already. We'll be joining with them."

Molly let out a deep breath. So they'd made it in time. Soon they would be "joined up" and on their way west. Wishing she didn't feel as if they should turn back, Molly said a prayer of thanks.

chapter twenty-six

COMING back to the present, Tess thought, was never as difficult as launching herself into the past. The return came with a blink and the realization that it was over. The initial vault through history was always gritty with motion and fear.

She should be used to the fact that the weeks spent traipsing across the country as Molly Marshall equaled moments of oblivion for Tess Carson. But she wasn't, and each nuance of what she'd done, where she'd been, how none of it could have really happened, pricked her like a hypodermic filled with speed.

She was still in her car, parked curbside in front of the library, but she was breathing as if she'd run a marathon and her heart pounded hard and fast in her chest. Minutes ago she'd been talking to Lydia and drinking coffee. Before that, she'd been standing on Grant's porch as the sheriff picked him up. Yet in her mind she'd crossed a river and straggled into Independence with a part of the Weston family that had been dead for over a hundred years . . .

Tess covered her face with her hands and took a deep breath. Then and now. Both realities tugged at her, demanding she acknowledge them as real. But each time she went back, the line blurred until both the past and present felt equally conjured. She stared out the windshield, torn between the defensive desire to go home, shut the door, and seal herself in, and the paralyzing fear of doing just that.

With a deep breath, she forced herself out of the cocoon of her car. As she locked the doors and faced the library, the hairs at the back of her neck rose and a chill whispered through her.

She turned slowly, giving the street a three-sixty that revealed nothing. But, she was sure someone was watching her.

She hurried inside the library, breathing heavily as the door closed behind her. Was she being followed? Yesterday the thought would have struck her as ridiculous. But now everything had changed. She stood in the shadows and looked out of the window in the door. No movements. No cars suddenly starting and driving away. Nothing but the certainty that eyes watched her, even now.

She moved deeper into the old stone library, where silence and the smell of must hung thick as dust. Burgundy carpet worn pink by years of traffic laid a trail through the entryway and into the main chamber. To the left of the front door a battered table offered voter registration applications, income tax forms, and brochures from the Chamber of Commerce. Pictures of a historical Mountain Bend hung throughout the lobby and beyond.

Feeling better away from the windows, Tess looked from one picture to another, reading the small gold plaques mounted beneath. The earliest photo had been taken at the opening of the Weston Mill, circa 1870. It showed a paddle wheel as it dipped into the river and turned through the wooden structure that housed it. A tiny shadow stood in the doorway.

A church was built in 1877. Tess recognized the building as the same one she'd seen in the school counselor's office. In later years it would become the first schoolhouse. A bank opened in 1878, and by 1880 a full-fledged town had blossomed.

She moved down the ramp into the main room, past an entrance closed off by a sheet of plastic. A sign hung in front of it announcing, RENOVATIONS ON HOLD. A giant handmade card from the students of Mountain Bend implored the citizens to donate to their cause. In the center of the card a photograph showed Craig Weston surrounded by a hundred or so children, all with books clasped in their hands and bright shiny smiles on their faces. Their signatures made a color framework around the photo.

Did Craig know that less than an hour ago his brother had

ridden off in the backseat of the sheriff's cruiser? Did he know about Tori and his father? Did he harbor the same burning resentment as Grant that she'd insinuated herself into Frank Weston's life and finances? And why had Craig claimed to know Tori only as well as he knew any other parent, when Caitlin said her mother had dined with all three Weston men?

And could he be the man Lydia was unofficially engaged to? If he was, there'd been ample opportunity for him to mention it last night at dinner, but he hadn't said a word. Nor had he acted like an engaged man. There'd been nothing inappropriate said or done, but the way he'd looked at her had definitely given her the impression that he was available. Her mistake or his?

The books were kept in a large room that was divided into aisles by shelves, which in turn were divided into sections that fanned out from an apex. In the center, the card catalog and an assortment of tables and chairs waited in view of the information desk and checkout counter. Not surprisingly, online systems hadn't ventured as far as Mountain Bend.

The middle-aged librarian gave her a suspicious look, making her feel like a teenager caught smuggling chocolate into the reference section. At least the feeling of being watched had subsided. She felt safe, if only for the time being. Tess walked purposefully to the card catalog and fingered down to the M–N drawer. The librarian watched as she pulled it out and took it to a table before stepping from behind her counter.

"May I help you?" she asked.

She spoke in a loud whisper, though as far as Tess could tell, they were the only people in the library. The woman had a short upper lip that didn't quite cover her teeth. When she spoke, her nose wiggled, as if tugged down by the effort to overcome the deficiency.

What would the woman say if Tess actually told her what kind of help she needed?

"Thanks, I'm just looking."

The librarian watched her for another minute and then said, "You're not from Mountain Bend."

"No." Tess paused, trying to find the least descriptive way to say who she was. "I'm visiting my sister."

"Caitlin's mother," the librarian said with a satisfied smile. "You look like her."

"That's a first. Tori and I don't really—"

"I meant Caitlin. You look like her. She's a sweetie, that one. And so bright. Her class was just here on Monday. Terrible business with her mother, though," she said, frowning. "Has there been any word?"

Tess shook her head.

"I'm sorry. I'll keep her in my prayers tonight."

"Thank you." Tess smiled politely, and went back to the card catalog. She didn't want to talk about Tori, not with a stranger who'd no doubt heard only gossip about her sister.

"Are you sure I can't help you find something?"

"Well, actually, I'm interested in the history of Mountain Bend."

The librarian's brows shot up at that. "Are you writing an article or something?"

"No, I'm just a history buff."

"A writer?" There was a distrustful lilt to the question.

"Lord, no. Not a writer."

Apparently, those were the magic words. "I don't mean to sound so suspicious," she said with an embarrassed titter. "You see, *I* am a writer. Not a real one, of course. I mean, of course I'm a *real* one. I haven't published, though. You won't find my name on any of the spines on these shelves."

The last was said with a defensive shrillness. Tess felt a little like a voyeur, peeking in on this woman's therapy session. "I think writers are amazing," she said cautiously. "I have difficulty writing a to-do list. A book is something I can't even imagine."

The librarian stared at her for a moment, her nose wiggling a bit, as if she were sniffing out falseness in Tess's statement. Evidently Tess passed the truth test because the other woman beamed suddenly and said in a confidential tone, "My book is an anthology of sorts. On California settlements. My husband's family has lived here for generations."

"Really?"

"I can't help but be fascinated by that. I was an Army brat so I never lived anywhere very long."

"Me, too. Air Force, though."

The woman introduced herself as Karen Post and sat down at the table.

"What is it you want to know?" Karen asked.

"I'm most interested in the town founders, the Weston family."

Karen gave her a hard look, obviously trying to make a connection between Frank's death, Tori's disappearance, and Tess's curiosity about the founders of Mountain Bend. Tess waited, knowing the librarian would never figure out the real reason Tess wanted to know.

"I'll tell you what I know, but I'm afraid it's not much."

With an enthusiasm that made Tess suspect she was starved for interested listeners, Karen launched into details of the early settlement that had become Mountain Bend. Despite her claim that she didn't know much, Karen relayed an astonishing amount of facts. She never mentioned Adam and his family, though. Because they weren't real? The thought formed with conflicting feelings of relief and disappointment. Karen's next words replaced both with shock.

"November 1870 was when Francis A. Weston filed the first claim."

"Francis A. Weston?" Tess repeated hoarsely.

"That's right."

"What does the 'A' stand for?"

"I honestly don't know. All of the records used to be stored in the church basement. It burned down twenty-five years ago and everything in it went as well. A Weston died in that fire, as a matter of fact. Grant and Craig's mother. A lot of people died." She paused reflectively before taking a deep breath and continuing. "As I understand it, there used to be a wealth of information on the history of the town."

Oblivious to the reactions her words caused, Karen went on. Very little was known about Francis A. Weston himself. She speculated that his journey began in Ohio in the spring of

1849 and that he "jumped off" from Independence, Missouri. The Weston name appeared on the register of a large company led by George Hanson, who had left Independence in May of that same year.

George Hanson. With a queer sense of horror, Tess put a face to the name.

"After that, the details are sketchy about what happened to the Westons," Karen was saying. "Now I've read in several places that there seemed to be two of them. Brothers. But I only ever find the one name so I can't figure that out."

Tess could. They both shared the family name so it could be carried on by either of them. She forced her clenched hands open and laid them flat on the table. Her palms were damp. Karen went on.

"The rest of the original Hanson party arrived in Sacramento five months after leaving Independence. Generally it was considered a four-month journey, so it took them some time to get there."

"Was he alone when he settled here?"

"Well, according to the Hanson registry, there were five Westons when they started out, but close to twenty years passed before he made it to Mountain Bend, so I don't know."

"There's nothing on the years in between?"

"Nothing that I've found."

Tess exhaled, frustrated. "Don't the Westons have a family history archive? Wouldn't they keep information on their family and the town?"

"They did. They donated it to the historical society in the fifties."

Her tone answered Tess's next question, but she asked it anyway. "And it was stored in the church?"

"Just makes me sick to think of all that history burning up."

A phone began to ring and Karen excused herself to answer. Sighing, Tess pushed her hair back and stared past Karen at the framed pictures that hung in the lobby. She'd hoped to find some solid proof that the Westons who had settled Mountain Bend were unrelated to the Westons of her "hallucinations." She'd found just the opposite. So what did

she make of that? Did she now accept that the visions were
not delusions, but rather latent memories from a . . . from a
past life, for heaven's sake? It sounded no less whacko, but
she had to acknowledge there were too many coincidences to
pretend otherwise.

Not only was there the Weston name itself, which had actually been the key point in convincing her that the "happen-
ings" were hallucinations brought on by extreme stress, there
was Vanessa, who had a child conceived out of wedlock, and
Tori, who was pregnant and unmarried. Vanessa had trapped
the first available bachelor she could find into marriage. Tori
had designs on a man old enough to be her father. Was she
motivated by the same need to cover up the illegitimacy of the
baby? But why? Tori never conformed to anything. Caitlin
said the relationship her mother had in Los Angeles was a secret. If the man was married with no plans to leave his wife,
why wouldn't Tori have just moved on with her life? Unless
Frank Weston was the baby's father and her relationship with
him was born of love? If that was the case, had it made someone angry enough to forcibly put an end to it?

And what about the parallels between Molly and Tess?
Tess's house on West Eightieth Street was very near to where
Molly had lived on Columbus Avenue. In fact, Tess had cho-
sen the neighborhood because she loved to walk past the his-
torical homes there. Coincidence? Not likely. Both Tess and
Molly had traveled west to take care of their sister's child.
Both women had been raised by a cold, dictating man—a man
of God, no less. Neither woman had had a life of her own.
Molly's sister was dead when she arrived . . . Tess's sister . . .
She stopped herself from finishing the thought.

The same comparisons couldn't be made about the Weston
men, though. Adam was a pioneer who cared about his brother.
Grant was a washed-up actor who'd last been in the public eye
when he checked into a rehab for alcoholism. Flesh and blood,
complete with tawdry past and human error, not to mention an
intense dislike of his brother . . . and a grudge against her sister. How could she possibly draw a parallel there? Unless she
was comparing the wrong men. Hadn't Craig struck her as the

kind of man someone could depend on? Didn't he seem grounded? A person who cared about others and had a gentle way with children? Didn't that sound like Adam?

She clenched her fists. For the love of God, this was insane.

At least now she knew one thing for certain—the past was real. More to the point, *Molly's* past was real. In her mind she heard the echo of Rosie's voice, *". . . all the Weston boys carry the family name . . . Francis Arlington . . . Francis Adam . . . Francis Ambrose . . ."*

Tess's argument that the episodes were fabricated from bits and pieces of forgotten books, movies, and conversations then compounded by stress would not stand up to the plain and simple fact that she could not have dreamed up multiple Francis "A." Westons. She could not have dreamed up George Hanson. And since they were actual people who could be traced through history—*real* people—then Molly was real, too.

They were real and they'd lived over a hundred and fifty years ago. So why had they decided to replay their lives in Tess's head now? Why had she seen Adam on horseback that first day? He'd been calling Molly's name. What was the connection between Tess Carson and Molly Marshall? Was it Mountain Bend? Was it the Weston brothers themselves? Or was it Vanessa and Tori? Was it possible that Molly had come "back" to help Tess find her sister?

She sighed, shaking her head in frustration. It could be any of those reasons. It could be all. It could be none.

She thanked Karen for her help and left the library feeling more confused than she had when she'd arrived. Outside, the sun made one last valiant effort to redeem itself. The air held the softness of coming spring. She stood on the sidewalk like an animal sniffing for predators. The feeling of being watched was gone.

Overwhelmed with relief, she looked around, letting her eyes adjust to the sunshine. In the distance, brilliant orange poppies grew wild on the mountainside, joined by a riot of sage that clustered about the boulders and scented the air. Around her, old buildings stood solid and proud, looking as if they'd guarded the sidewalks for over a hundred years. Through the peaked rooftops she caught sight of a white cross, perched atop a spire. As she climbed into her car, it occurred to her that churches burned down, but cemeteries generally did not.

chapter twenty-seven

USING the steeple as a guide, Tess drove up a winding road to the church grounds. She parked in a lot next to the quaint chapel and climbed the grassy hill to the side of it. Wearily, she made her way to a bench under an enormous, gnarled maple tree and, with a wince, sat down in the cool shade.

Every muscle in her body felt as if it had been jerked and torn. She knew that if she were to strip down in front of a mirror, she would find bruises and gashes on her arms and legs where the river had flung her against the hurling branches and hidden rocks. Just like before. That first time—in Tori's front yard—when she'd seen Molly, Rosie, and Arlie at the banks of a swollen river. Now she knew where it was and what had happened—and why she'd had bruises afterward. Somehow the memory of the crossing had come to her out of sequence, confusing and terrifying her to the point that she'd blocked it from her consciousness. But the bruises had been there, silent testament to the experience.

She sighed, remembering her horror as she'd looked at her reflection in Tori's mirror, relieved that there were no mirrors to look in now. She was afraid of what else she might see, afraid that her eyes might have made that subtle shift from blue to green. Afraid that Molly might have followed her back to wait on the periphery for the chance to take Tess over completely.

A shudder went through her. The peacefulness of her surroundings added to the feeling of being out of sync with time and place. Around her, marble crosses, headstones, and carved statues marked off the graves of Mountain Bend's dead. The cemetery had an otherworldliness to it that transcended the calendar and defied the passage of years. Kind of like herself, she thought with a grim smile.

She stood, staring down at the granite boulder and engraved plaque that shared the maple tree's shade with her. The monument was dedicated to the seventeen women, eight men, and four children who lost their lives twenty-five years ago, in the fire that had burned ·Mountain Bend's first church to the ground. A poem followed the somber list of names, recounting the bravery of the citizens who'd died trying to save the others who were trapped inside. Most of the children had been rescued, but only a few of the women and men present at the Sunday service had made it out alive. The community would have been devastated by such a loss.

The name "Ellen Weston" was on the list of victims from the fire. Was her death the tragedy that drove the family apart? Or was there something else?

Tess's cell phone rang as she sorted through the possible answers. She looked at her purse, momentarily confused. As both Lydia and Craig had pointed out, signals were few and far between in Mountain Bend. Up here on the hilltop must be the exception. She fumbled the phone from her purse and answered.

"Tess? You never answer your phone."

"Sara." It felt so strange to hear her voice.

"What's going on? Is your sister back?"

"No, she's not."

Taking a deep breath, Tess told Sara what had been happening since she'd arrived, beginning with Caitlin pulling the key from her pocket and ending with the visit from the sheriff that morning. Sara's exclamations, curses, and noises of disbelief would have been comical had the subject matter not been so serious.

"Sheriff Smith said they'd found her car parked at the bus station," Tess concluded. "One of the ticket sellers recognized her. And a woman here remembered Tori had used the phone outside her coffee shop and was upset the morning before she disappeared."

Tess had been bothered when the sheriff told her Lydia saw Tori and then forgot. As she told Sara about it, she was even more disturbed. Too many things didn't make sense. First, Lydia's claim that she was so busy at the time contradicted the many comments Tess had heard about how the town was drying up. She'd hardly seen another soul when she was "downtown." So where had all that business come from? And then there was the news that Tori had been a regular customer. House Blend, every morning. And yet Tori didn't have a single genuine coffee bean in her house?

"None of it makes sense," Tess finished.

"No shit," Sara answered. "I mean, holy hell, what do you think is going on? Who could Tori have been calling?"

"Anyone. Me, even. I just don't know."

"Could have been the baby's father."

"Unless he's Frank Weston. Why would she phone him? She saw him every day and presumably she was on her way to the ranch that morning."

"My money's on the L.A. secret. Who did she work for there?"

"I don't know. Sara, I have a hard enough time keeping track of where she lives. I gave up on the other details years ago." Tess paused as something occurred to her. "Last night when Grant was at the house, he said she'd been referred by a friend. Today he mentioned that he only had a few friends left in the business. One is a producer . . ." Tess searched for the name. "Forsythe. Brandon Forsythe."

Sara whistled. "He knows how to pick his friends. So what do you think the chances are of you getting to talk to Mr. Forsythe?"

"Probably less than zero."

"You're going to try, though."

"It's a good idea." Tess felt better for the plan, even if it led to nothing.

"So what's going on with you and gorgeous Grant Weston?"

"What do you mean?"

Sara laughed. "Come on, Tess. This is me you're talking to. Your voice gets all husky when you talk about him."

Alone on the bench, Tess could feel herself blushing. "I don't trust him," she said.

"But . . . ?"

"It's complicated."

"Complicated good or complicated bad?"

"I don't know. I don't know how to explain it."

"You know I'm not going to hang up until you tell me."

And so she did. Everything. She began with Grant and the way he'd seen inside her. The way his touch had driven all sane thought from her head. Then suddenly she was talking about Molly and Adam. She hadn't planned to tell Sara about the strange flashbacks or the feeling of wrenching loss when she returned, but it spilled out, and with it came all her pent-up frustration and fear. Sara listened silently this time. Only the sound of her breathing let Tess know she was still on the line.

"The thing is," Tess finished, "when I was with Grant . . . I had the feeling that he was part of it all."

"Maybe you should come home, Tess."

"You don't believe me."

"Of course I believe you. God, no way would you make that up. But, Tess, you're scaring the hell out of me."

Tess half smiled. "I'm scaring the hell out of myself. When Caitlin drew that picture this morning, I nearly passed out."

"Why do you think—I mean, it's so . . . Well, there's got to be a reason for this, right? So what is it?"

Tess stared out at the rows of tombstones as icy fingers crawled up her spine. "Something happened to them, Sara. Until I know what, I'm running blind. I can't come home until I find out. I can't leave until I know where my sister is. Brodie told Molly that Adam found out he wasn't the baby's father. He said Vanessa died right after that. He made it sound . . ."

"Like Adam killed her?"

"No." The word came low and instinctive, powerful in its certainty.

"Are you in love with him?"

"He's dead."

"True, but not an answer. Are you in love with him?"

"Sara, I don't know what I am."

"How about who you are?"

Sara didn't seem to expect an answer, not that Tess had one to give. Her phone made a warning beep. "My battery is going. I haven't charged it since I got here."

"Okay. But, Tess, when are you coming back?"

"I don't know. Not until I find something out about Tori. Will you let work know? Sue left me a voice mail and told me to take as long as I needed, but I haven't called her back yet."

"Don't worry about it. I'll talk to her. Give me your sister's number in case I need it. I was nuts when you wouldn't answer your cell."

Tess gave her the number and thanked her for talking to their boss. Her phone gave another urgent low-battery warning.

"I'll call you tomorrow, Sara."

"Okay. And listen, Tess, don't you disappear, too. Do you hear me?"

"I'll be careful."

After she hung up, she remained on the bench, thinking of Sara's questions. Was she in love with Adam? And what about Grant? Where did he fit in this crazy mix of emotions?

The questions circled in her head. Finally she gave up trying to answer them and stood to make her way to the less orderly section of the cemetery at the back of the church. Unlike the brilliant white chapel and the newer gravestones that stood in its protective shadow, this part of the cemetery was obviously very old. Here the grave markers were weathered or missing altogether, burned to the ground when the roaring inferno had lashed out from the church and incinerated the ancient wooden crosses. Without the town records, a lot of the graves could not be identified and so remained unmarked, or so another commemorative plaque told her.

Tess traveled up and down the uneven rows, overgrown with a soft, fragrant blanket of grass and fresh spring flowers, before at last she came upon a headstone for Francis A. Weston. It was granite and smooth, looking far too modern for this section of the cemetery. His name stood out in stark relief and below it were the words REST IN PEACE followed by the year, 1898. His date of birth was not listed, nor was there an inscription to indicate if he was a good man, a loved man. A small metal plaque on the ground next to it explained that his original marker had been lost in the fire.

She looked for the headstones of Adam, Brodie, and Arlie but found nothing that bore their names. The same was true for Molly and Rosie. Had their markers been lost in the fire? Had they ever existed here in the first place?

Tess stood there, feeling an ache she didn't try to explain. Which Weston brother was laid to rest at the foot of the granite headstone?

"And what happened to the rest of us?" she whispered.

chapter twenty-eight

"TESS? Is that you?"

The sound of Craig's voice surprised her as she stood in front of the grave. She stared at him for a moment with the eerie sensation that he'd stepped from her thoughts. He could have been Adam, resurrected by the sheer longing she felt to see him.

"What are you doing here?" he asked as he drew closer.

Looking for ghosts, she nearly said.

"Do you know anything about him?" she asked instead.

He glanced from her to the marker for Francis A. Weston and back, looking at once perplexed and concerned. "No," he said at last. "I don't. Years ago there were quite a few branches of the family living here, but by the time I was born, they'd pretty much spread out over the country. I couldn't hazard a guess on half the Westons buried here—especially in this old part."

He watched her for a moment longer, obviously bewildered by the grief she couldn't manage to hide. She must look like a fool, standing over the grave of a man she'd never even known.

"Tess, has something happened?" he asked in an uneasy tone. "Did you hear something about Tori?"

She shook her head, turning so he couldn't see her face. From the corners of her eyes she saw him reach out to touch her and then pause, unsure, his hand poised halfway between them. She straightened her back, lifted her chin, and looked at him again.

"No," she said. "No, word on Tori."

He nodded and shoved his hands into his pockets. But he looked as if he expected her to break down at any second and his expression held such compassion that she nearly did. He seemed so strong and sturdy standing there in his conservative khaki trousers and pale green button-down shirt. Solid enough to weather the storm of her emotions.

"I keep thinking, today I'll get some answers. But there's nothing. She's simply vanished into thin air."

"Answers are usually hard to find when you don't even know the questions."

"I know one. What happened to my sister?"

Craig took a deep breath and let it out. "You should leave it to the professionals."

"Like Smith? He's already made up his mind about Tori."

"You don't know that. Hell, he was out at my house this morning poking around."

"He was at your brother's house, too. Grant left with him."

She'd blurted out the words and immediately wished she could call them back. It felt as if she'd betrayed Grant by telling Craig.

"I knew they were planning on bringing Grant in."

"You knew?" she said. Yet he hadn't bothered to give his own brother a heads-up to let him know the cops were looking for him.

"Smith told me he was going to see Grant next when he got done with me."

"You were questioned? Were you asked about Tori?"

"No. Just Dad. About the accident. Ochoa sent some evidence to Piney River, and when the report came back, they had some issues with it."

"Deputy Ochoa? Not Sheriff Smith?"

Craig shrugged. "One or the other. Smith probably told him to send it."

"So what was this evidence?"

"I'm not supposed to talk about it but . . . apparently the gas cap was blown off in the explosion. Smith found it a few feet from where Dad was." He pulled his hands out of his pockets and began fiddling with a brightly colored casino chip. He rolled it between his fingers as he spoke. "I don't really understand why that was suspicious but it has something to do with the tractor running on diesel and the burn marks on the cap. Now the coroner is questioning the accident."

It took a moment for that one to sink in. "You mean . . ."

"I don't know." He shrugged angrily. "I don't know what the hell to make of it."

"You want to know the truth, don't you, Craig?"

"Of course, but—think about it. If it wasn't an accident . . ." He stared over Tess's shoulder at the graves settled on the grassy knoll behind her. "God knows there's no love lost between me and my brother, but I don't want to think about what will come out next."

"Aren't you jumping to conclusions?"

He shook his head, his expression grim. "Maybe I am. I guess we'll all know the truth before long. Smith is being damned thorough. If something's not right, he'll find it."

"What else did they ask you?"

"They wanted to know where was I, who was I with, did I know anyone who disliked Dad or was mad at him. That kind of thing."

"Where were you?" she said, trying to sound casual.

His jaw tightened and the corners of his mouth turned down in a frown that appeared and vanished so quickly she wondered if she'd imagined it.

"I was at the coffee shop, having a late lunch with Lydia."

"Where was Grant?" She went for the casual approach again, failing more dismally than the first time.

"Your guess is as good as mine." He was looking at her through narrowed eyes and it took all her concentration not to squirm. An errant gust of wind blew her hair into her face. Craig's hand beat her own to brush it back. His warm fingers lingered a moment on her cheek. Uncomfortable, she turned her face.

"Craig . . . There's something I have to ask you. I know this is an awful time to bring it up, but I need to know. Were you aware of a relationship between your father and Tori?"

"She worked for him."

"She may have been more than just his employee. I understand they were intimate."

He made a sound of disbelief. "Who told you that?"

"Does it matter?"

"If it was true, no. But my father was almost seventy, Tess. He had trouble making it to the bathroom. The only person he might have been intimate with was his proctologist."

"What was he doing on that tractor, then?"

He shook his head and raised his brows. Good question, his expression said. "Whoever told you my dad was *intimate* with Tori didn't know what he was talking about."

Her mouth went dry and a slick dampness coated her palms. She rubbed them against her jeans. Either Craig was lying to her now or Grant had lied to her earlier. "Maybe I misunderstood."

He looked at her, skeptical. "Maybe someone is telling you lies."

She couldn't argue with that. The question was, who?

"What about you, Craig? Were you involved with Tori?"

For a moment, he looked at her with angry disbelief, but then he quickly glanced away. "I don't know who you've been talking to, but I can guess."

"Actually, it wasn't Grant. It was Caitlin who'd mentioned she'd been to dinner with you and her mother."

His expression smoothed. "Oh, that." His laugh held relief. "We met over dinner to discuss the best way to integrate Caitlin into school. Her education has been peppered with moves, to say the least."

An awkward silence followed his explanation, amplified by the serenity of the absolute quiet. His answer was pat, but it didn't sit right. Dinner meetings and small-town principals didn't mesh. Parent conferences happened in offices after school, not steak houses. Unless the parent was single and beautiful and the principal eligible and attractive . . .

He had a wounded expression on his face, as if she'd insulted his integrity. To an extent, she supposed she had. But why would he feel the need to hide his association with her sister? No one would condemn him for pursuing Tori if he'd had the inclination to do so. Single people were expected to seek one another out, weren't they? Unless Craig was the mystery man who'd put that ring on Lydia's finger . . .

Tess forced a smile. "Parent conference," she repeated. "I guess I didn't think of that. Caitlin didn't give me all the details. By the way, congratulations. Lydia told me about your engagement."

Craig blanched. His became expression stony, his body still. "What are you talking about?"

She'd plunged in before she could reconsider and now she didn't know where to go with it. "I noticed the ring on her finger and . . . Well, she didn't say that she was engaged to you, exactly. I just put two and two together and . . ."

"I'm not engaged to Lydia, Tess." He shook his head. "Never have been."

"Do you know who she's engaged to?"

"Lydia lives in a fantasy world. She has for a long time."

Tess waited for him to say more, but he just stood there, looking as if the weight of the world were on his shoulders. His hair was mussed—probably from running his fingers through it—and dark smudges underlined the exhaustion in his eyes, but his sad smile seemed warm and sincere. Was it as real as it appeared?

"She seemed lucid enough to me."

"For the most part she functions. But . . . life hasn't been very good to her." He looked at the tree and memorial where she'd sat earlier. "She was in the church the day it burned down."

"Lydia was?" Tess exclaimed.

He nodded, still staring past her. "I saw it all," he said softly.

"You were here that day?"

"I came late. I was a teenager and, well, you know how teenagers are. I couldn't be bothered to go to church more than half the time. Mom was as devout as they come and it broke her heart that we wouldn't go."

He'd said "we." Was it his father or Grant that was a part of that "we"?

"That morning she and my dad got into it with Grant and they woke me up shouting. She was in tears by the time she left. I felt bad for her so I got dressed and followed."

He swallowed and took a deep breath. "I smelled the smoke first, before I even knew that the church was on fire. By the time I made it over the hill, it was an inferno. I nearly died trying to help get people out, but it was too late."

"Lydia got out, though? I mean, obviously she got out."

He continued as if she hadn't spoken. "The fire started in the basement. They'd been refurbishing everything. Shellacking the pews, the altar, restoring the life-sized crucifix. Afterward, they blamed the spark that started it on faulty wiring. The supplies and rags went up like a torch. Smoke rose through the vents to the steeple. The people who made it out said they didn't even see the smoke until the flames were up the stairs."

"My God."

"I can't imagine what it was like in there. They couldn't get out. Things were moved around for cleaning and . . . By the time the fire department made it, the flames were everywhere. The trees all around us—everything was burning." He made a harsh sound. "Even the wooden crosses in the cemetery. All of them were on fire."

The image of grave markers lit like candles filled her head with horror. She stared at the pristine grounds, picturing it aflame.

"It looked like hell had erupted right here in Mountain Bend. I kept looking for my mother, but she didn't make it out."

"I'm so sorry."

He nodded once, and then let his head hang forward, as if the weight of it was too much to bear. "Lydia was pushed down and nearly trampled to death. Back then she was tiny—smaller than you. She didn't get big until later. Some of the pews had been knocked over in the panic and she wedged herself in a gap beneath them. She was low enough that she had a pocket of oxygen. The firefighters found her crammed between the pews, battered, bloody . . . and never quite balanced again."

Tess didn't know what to say. The silence between them

was weighted with tragedy. She placed a hand on his arm and gave a light squeeze. He covered her hand with his own.

"I didn't mean to get so morbid."

"It's understandable under the circumstances."

"What are you doing here, anyway?" he asked.

Caught off guard, she couldn't think of a reasonable excuse. Shrugging, she said, "I saw the church. I wanted to come." She looked at the white doves set in the dark blues and purples of the stained glass windows. "I haven't been to church in a long time."

"But you're a preacher's daughter."

She snapped her eyes to his face. "How do you know that?"

"Caitlin or Tori must have mentioned it."

It seemed unlikely that Caitlin, who had never even met her grandfather, would impart such obscure information. Stranger still that Tori would volunteer it. Tori usually told people she was an orphan and that she'd never known her parents. Sometimes she went so far as to give Tess an exotic yet tragic role in the story.

Craig glanced at his watch and said, "I need to get going. I'm here to finalize things for the service. Grant was supposed to meet me, but like everything else, he must have blown it off."

He was probably still with the sheriff. The fierceness of the instinct to defend him took her by surprise.

"I have to decide on the music. Like it's going to matter what they play."

"Was your father a religious man?"

Craig shook his head. "He used to be, but that was a long time ago. After Mom died, he never set foot in church again. I don't think he ever forgave God."

"I don't know that I could either. Did you?"

"Forgive God? As I recall, He never asked for my forgiveness." He took a deep breath and looked back at the church with a hard look in his eyes. "I'll see you later, okay?" He took a step away and then turned back. "Hey, thanks for listening. I guess I needed to vent a little."

Tess gave his arm another squeeze before he walked away. She watched him until he stepped through the chapel doors. As she turned to leave, a cold wind lifted her hair.

"Mooolllly!"

The sound of a child's voice shattered the quiet and cut into her thoughts.

"Arlie?" she whispered.

The scream that followed was filled with both terror and pain. It echoed around her, swelling and fading as if through a door that opened and closed. What was happening to him? She scanned the cemetery, as if the answer would be there. He cried out again and she followed the sound through the rows of graves, first slowly and then faster as the terror in his voice rose.

"Molly!"

It sounded like he was here, but she knew it wasn't possible. It wasn't. But that didn't deter the overwhelming need she felt to find him, to reassure herself he was unharmed, to protect him.

Her labored breathing plumed the air and she shook with the cold. The cries crescendoed into one continuous plea for help. Then, as suddenly as they'd begun, they stopped.

Deafening silence crowded in around her. The weight of the dead pressed closer still. Clenching her eyes, she tried to keep ahold of her sanity. But behind her eyelids black stars gave way to a brilliant blue sky with buttery sunshine and wispy clouds. Like a sigh, time whished through her. Captured moments fluttered in the draft. Here, then gone.

There was Rosie, mixing something in a bowl. Adam, reaching for his rifle. The smell of sweat, of roasting meat, of dirt and filth.

She walked beside the wagon, passing landmarks she'd anticipated for miles. There was Fort Kearny and the road, knotted with emigrants, and then the descent to Ash Hollow, where the water and grass were the best they'd had in weeks. Chimney Rock poked up like a blackened finger in the distant, desolate plains. The breeze became a wind, blowing through weeks that went on without end. Tess let it take her, as she searched for Arlie.

At last she saw him. He was there, huddled in a clearing. "Arlie!" she called, desperate. "Arlie!"

chapter twenty-nine

MOLLY awoke with a start in the thick blackness of the wagon. She sat bolt upright, eyes wide with the nightmare. The air was so tight it felt like a cocoon made of wool, but it was the fear that almost suffocated her. She turned so that she could see Arlie, nestled at the front of the wagon, inches from her own head. He slept peacefully, content and safe beside her.

Three nights now she'd dreamed that she was searching for him through a frenzy of screaming people in a night lit by fire. The smoke choked and blinded her and the feeling that she'd never find him clutched at her heart. And then, at last, she saw him in the center of the chaos, but seconds before her fingers would close on his arm, she awoke, drenched in sweat and gasping for air. She didn't believe in premonition, but the dreams haunted her and she could not escape their frightening evocations.

Knowing she would never get back to sleep, she rose. It was Sunday, but after months on the trail, she had become accustomed to waking up long before dawn. Glad to have something to do beyond thinking of her nightmare, she started the fire and set coffee to boil. The pungent scent of the buffalo chip fire she built filled the air. The smoke invariably attracted the vicious black gnats that had traveled the Platte with them and this morning was no exception. She slapped at the pests as she prepared breakfast.

By midmorning, she'd scrubbed their clothes and hung them out to dry. Still, the horrible dream kept her wrapped in its sticky threads, as prevalent as the swarming insects and unending dust. Sensing her preoccupation, Arlie had spent the morning adding to her vexation with incessant whining and mischief.

For a short time a young girl from the O'Keefe family came by to visit. She was one of their many children, so many that Molly had long ago given up trying to count them. Plump to the point of excess, Alice Ann teetered in the delicate balance between being a child and a young adult. More than once Molly had caught her staring with adulation at Brodie.

Molly thought her to be around eleven or twelve, though her pudgy face and portly body made her age hard to estimate with accuracy. Normally Alice Ann had a sweet disposition and at times she would play with Arlie, but Molly didn't trust her to watch the baby alone. There was a bit of the devil in Alice Ann and she wasn't above teasing Arlie or stealing one of his playthings.

Molly was not happy to see Alice Ann this morning, but hoped she'd keep Arlie occupied at least until she could finish hanging their clothes to dry. As if the very thought had jinxed the wish, however, the girl soon walked off, leaving Arlie frustrated and angry with something she'd done, but unable to voice his complaint.

"What happened?" Molly crooned as she bounced Arlie on her hip. Arlie pointed a slippery finger at Alice Ann's back and howled.

Unconcerned with the havoc she'd left behind, Alice Ann strolled idly away. As she drew even with Brodie, however, she paused. Molly watched uneasily as the girl affected a flirtatious pose that came across as vulgar on the young girl. She couldn't hear what was said, but Brodie's head snapped up and he stared at Alice Ann with a look of interest. He stepped closer to her, closer than propriety allowed by any stretch. Alice Ann fawned and giggled. To Molly's shock, the girl moved closer still and rubbed her plump breasts against Brodie's chest. Brodie leaned down and said something softly in her ear, then walked away.

With a whirl that showed her excitement, Alice Ann called, "I will," to his back as he disappeared.

"Alice Ann," Molly called.

The chunky girl faced Molly with a look of surprise and petulance. Reluctantly she returned to the wagon, where Molly waited.

Molly noted that she was flushed and a dew of perspiration covered her upper lip. "What were you speaking to Mr. Weston about?"

"Nothing," Alice Ann answered.

"Most certainly it was something, Alice Ann." Molly waited, but the girl remained silent. "Dear, you are far too young to be engaging in baited conversation with Mr. Weston. He is much older than you. He's nearly a man and you are a still a child."

"I'll be thirteen at Christmas."

Molly gave her a gentle smile. "Still too young. You wish to become a respectable woman, do you not?"

Alice Ann nodded, but she didn't raise her eyes to meet Molly's. Thinking of Vanessa and feeling a hypocrite for it, she said, "Of course you do, child. Respectable women have their choice of handsome men. Women who behave without discipline do not."

"Yes, ma'am."

"Now you run along home to your mother and don't dawdle on the way. Do you understand?"

Alice Ann gave a resentful nod and then headed in the direction of her family's wagon.

Molly brooded over the incident as she returned to her laundry. What had Alice Ann and Brodie been discussing? What had he said to her that she'd answered, "I will"? Whatever it was, Molly could not ignore it. Should Brodie play with the young girl's affections, only trouble would come of it. She would to speak to Adam and ask him to intervene before it was too late. Feeling better for the decision, she just managed to hang the last bit of her laundry when she caught sight of Arlie, naked as the day he was born, slipping out of the wagon where he'd played quietly for all of three minutes.

"Arlie!" Molly said sternly. "You come back here."

Barefoot and bent on trouble, Arlie let loose a shriek of pure glee and took off running in the opposite direction. The little devil! Molly lifted her skirts and chased him.

Arlie's laughter rang out as he raced away from her. Dead ahead was the roped-off area for the oxen and cows. Arlie was headed straight at them. Molly picked up her speed, but before she could close the gap, Adam appeared and scooped Arlie up into the air. He whirled him around as Arlie shrieked with delight.

"Are you up to no good again?" Adam asked him, holding him so that he could see Molly's scowl. "I think Molly's ready to twist you into a knot."

Indeed she was.

"But it just so happens, you are a *very* lucky little boy," Adam said, still talking to his son, but watching Molly. "I've got a surprise for the both of you."

"Adam, I am glad to see you," Molly said. "As it happens, I need to speak with you. I've something important to discuss."

"Fine. Grab some clean clothes and towels," he said.

Molly stared at him blankly. What on earth was he talking about? And what was his surprise? Then she noticed that *he* had on clean clothes and his hair was damp. His skin had the healthy luster of a recent washing and . . . She inhaled. He smelled as clean as the fresh laundry she'd just hung to dry.

"Soap, too?" she asked.

He winked at her. A few months ago she would have been much discomfited by a conversation that included mixed company, fresh clothing, and soap. Since then the wear and tear, the filth and grime, of the journey had greatly altered her perspective on matters of importance—or matters that lacked any importance at all. A few months ago, she'd been a different woman.

Without hesitation she hurried back to the wagon. Rosie hadn't been feeling well for several days, but this morning she had claimed to be fit enough to visit Mrs. Imogene, a "neighbor" with whom she'd discovered a distant kinship. And as for Brodie, that could wait. He was probably off milling around one of the many groups of Indians that seemed to be ever present. They came to trade and barter. More than one native had outwitted Brodie, yet he seemed incapable of resisting their lure.

She grabbed towels, soap, and a change of clothes for both her and the baby and stuffed them into a canvas bag. In moments she was following Adam away from the circle of wagons. They'd had to camp a good distance from the river, much farther than usual owing to the fact that the grass had been chewed to the dirt by the companies ahead of them, leaving nothing but mud to feed their livestock. Recently, they'd left behind Nebraska and crossed into the Wyoming territory, and each step forward seemed to bring new troubles. Food for the animals was harder and harder to come by as they progressed. In fact, *everything* was harder to acquire.

When they'd first set up camp, Molly had been disheartened by the distance to the river. All she could think of was that the dishwater would have to be hauled, as well as drinking water, as well as laundry, as well as . . .

Adam followed a narrow Indian trail that curved left from the river and came to a sandy-banked creek. A steep ravine led down to a sheltered place where two streams met. One gushed from a rocky shelf and the second bubbled up in a pool. Still holding the squirming, naked Arlie, Molly followed him down to the banks.

"It's not very deep, but it's warmer than you'd expect," Adam told her with a proud smile.

"Oh, my," she gasped, giving a little spin of excitement.

They thought of the Platte River as their guiding companion but it could also be the bitterest of enemies. Often sluggish and filled with dirt, it could be counted on only to defy any preconceived ideas of what a river *should* be. The jeering description which passed from one emigrant to another was that it was "too thick to drink and too thin to plow." Molly had been amused by the saying the first time she'd heard it, but it had long since lost its humor.

This water, clear and sparkling, noisy and gay, was as unexpected as it was delightful.

"I'll sit out there on that big boulder and make sure no one bothers you," Adam said. "When you finish with Arlie, give a shout and I'll take him so you can have some time alone."

She stared at the lovely, private bathtub and then at Adam, who looked so pleased with his surprise that she wanted to throw her arms around him.

"Go on, get in," he said as he stepped out of sight to keep watch.

Arlie wasted no time making a charge for the pool, but Molly caught his arm and stopped him short. "You wait for me, Arlie, or I'll call your father to deal with you."

Arlie harkened her warning and waited quietly by the edge of the pool, squirming with impatience. Molly stripped down to her undergarments and climbed into the cool water with the naked baby. Arlie took a gasping breath in and let it loose with a joyous squeal. Laughing, Molly held him while he splashed and kicked across the pool. After a while, Molly lathered Arlie with soap. He became a slippery fish and slid out of her grip. He plunged under the surface and she pulled him back up, sputtering with shock.

She waited for the inevitable cry but instead he shouted, "Agin, Mawee. Agin, 'gin!"

Laughing, she dunked him and pulled him up to his heart's content. From the boulder where he waited, Adam's low chuckle carried.

"I think he is a swimmer, Adam," she called. "Come see him."

The words were out before she realized what she'd said. The inappropriateness of his standing on the other side of the precipitous rocks while she bathed would have sent the Reverend into seizures. Inviting him to join her in the inner sanctum . . . There was no way around it. She'd be damned to hell. But she couldn't find the words to retract the invitation.

Adam's silence and hesitation charged the moments before the shuffle of his footsteps proceeded his appearance. A shiver ran down her chilled skin as she stared up at him. He was so tall, so powerfully built, so gentle and forgiving, so hard and unrelenting. The miles of living together had honed her attraction to him until he'd become, quite simply, the center of her world.

His eyes glittered from beneath the shadowed brim of his hat and she felt the sensation of them moving like quicksilver over her face, her neck, then down to her shoulders, covered though they were by her white chemise. Arlie shouted with happiness and arched his body backward so quickly that he slipped out of her grasp again. She scooped him back up, thankful for the distraction . . . though nothing could lessen her awareness of his father.

Adam stepped to the side of the pool and hunkered down. He skimmed the water with his fingertips and Molly instantly pictured his hands gliding over her wet skin. Good Lord, she felt giddy with the image.

Arlie splashed her. "'Gin," he urged.

Dutifully Molly held him and swam him around the circle, letting him dunk under and surface for his father. Adam smiled and praised his son, but Molly felt the intensity of his distraction every time his gray eyes met hers.

After a few moments, he said softly, "Time to get out, son. Let's go find your grandma."

Arlie complained bitterly and loudly, squirming and fighting them both. He evaded Adam's reaching hands, nearly toppling his father, clothes and all, into the shallow reservoir. Finally Molly managed to get him in a sound grip and waded out to hand him over. Adam took the drenched bundle, immediately dampening his own clothes as he held Arlie tight while Molly fetched the towel. As she wrapped it around the child, she found Adam staring at her, his eyes the color of streaming rain.

Her chemise clung to her skin. She didn't need to look down to know that the dripping material was translucent and that she might as well have been standing naked. His gaze moved from her face to her throat and she swallowed, taking a deep breath that seemed to pull that look lower to her breasts. Her nipples stood like hard pebbles, pushing out against the soaked cotton. Adam's gaze moved back to her face. He stared deeply into her eyes with a look of helpless lust that turned the heat of her embarrassment into a burn of desire.

He shifted Arlie to the side and reached out for her in one

fluid movement. His lips touched hers and turned everything inside her to a hot liquid that pulsed with her racing heartbeat. He held her face with one hand, his son with the other. She wrapped her arms around his neck and stood on tiptoe. Obviously confused by this touching of his father and his Molly, Arlie was unusually still and quiet.

The kiss lasted just a moment but it seemed to stretch through all of time while falling short of fulfillment. Adam pulled his mouth from hers with such absolute reluctance that she sighed in both pleasure and pain. Her hand slid down his neck to his chest. His heart thundered beneath her touch, letting her know that she was not alone in the wild rush of want that had taken over her senses.

Adam rested his forehead against hers for a moment. The sunshine filtered down into the chasm, creating shadows carved of darkness and light that played across his face. "Where is my mother?" he asked hoarsely.

"Mrs. Imogene's," she answered.

"I'll be back."

The statement held as much question as certainty.

"Yes."

He scooped up Arlie's things and carried him out of the ravine still wrapped in the towel. The front of his shirt and trousers were soaked through where her body had pressed against him.

The pool felt warm against her skin when she returned to it. Nervously she stripped the cotton chemise and washed her hair and body, each brush of her fingers like a memory of Adam's touch. She couldn't stop grinning.

She had just climbed out of the pool and wrapped herself in a towel when the clatter of pebbles bouncing down heralded Adam's return. Poised between excitement and embarrassment, she turned to face him as he rounded the corner into their sanctuary.

Only it wasn't Adam who met her expectant look with a big smile.

"Brodie," she gasped, clutching the towel over her nakedness. "What are you doing here? Where is Adam?"

His smile dimmed and his bright eyes lowered to the ground. "I came to see you," he said, as if that should be obvious.

"How did you know I was here?"

"I saw you come down," he said, staring at her feet and ankles in a way that made her sure he was picturing everything else above them.

Heat rushed to her face. He'd seen her coming down. What else had he seen? An image filled her head of him peeking over the rocks as she and Adam . . . Her stomach clenched.

"You got pretty little feet," he said, glancing up shyly. "Pretty ankles."

She cleared her throat and tried to look casual and unalarmed. "As you can see, you've caught me by surprise, Brodie. Would you please allow me some privacy while I dress?"

"You didn't make Adam leave. He stayed a long time."

"Were you spying on us, Brodie?" she asked in her best school teacher voice. "It is rude to spy."

Brodie flushed and returned to his examination of her feet. "I just wondered what you were doing in here, is all. I thought you'd be glad to see me."

He took a step forward and again she realized how closely he toed the line to manhood. He'd grown during the weeks on the trail. His lanky frame had filled out and he'd stretched to nearly Adam's height. His youth had somehow reduced him in Molly's perceptions until that minute. Now the surrounding walls of rock closed in on them as Brodie's imposing build seemed to force the very air from the shelter. He looked at her boldly, now with a hint of defiance that turned her unease into a deep foreboding. Where was Adam? He should have been back by now.

Molly flinched when Brodie reached out to touch her hair. He scowled, lifted a dripping strand from her shoulder, and rubbed it between his fingers.

"You were swimming," he accused. "Weren't you?"

"No. I was bathing." She pointed to the soap she had placed on the rocks next to the water.

"You said you couldn't swim."

"I wasn't swimming, Brodie. I had a bath. The water's not deep."

"How come nobody told me to have a wash?" he asked, looking from the soap to her bare shoulders with suspicion.

"I would have come to find you after I dressed," Molly said, forcing an even, calm voice. "Your mother as well."

Overhead the sun slid behind a cloud, casting a gray chill onto the pond. Brodie was breathing heavily, staring at her in an intense, feverish way that heightened her apprehension.

"Now please, Brodie. I'm getting cold and I want to put on my clothes."

He let loose the strand of her hair, but instead of moving back, he stepped closer. His hot, damp hand settled on her clean, cool skin. "You're soft," he said, stroking her shoulder. "You smell like flowers."

He smiled and his face lit up in that childish way she used to find so endearing. But where innocence once seemed to sparkle in his eyes, now deceit gleamed. He was not oblivious to the impropriety of his presence. He chose to ignore it. Her feelings of fear were inconsequential to his desire to touch her. What other inborn senses of right and wrong did he ignore at whim?

"Brodie, I must insist that you go," she said, her voice steady despite the vulnerability that made her mouth dry.

"I could've saved you," he murmured in a husky voice. "Would've, too, but Adam always sticks his nose in my business."

She grasped the towel in her white-knuckled hands and spoke sharply. "Brodie, I have asked you to leave. If you insist on ignoring me, I shall have to—" What? What could she do? Who would hear a scream? The camp was well out of earshot. And where was Adam?

"I saw you fall in and I was set on saving you," Brodie continued, as if she hadn't spoken at all. "I told you I would, now didn't I?"

Angrily she shrugged her shoulder and stepped back. Instead of releasing her, Brodie tightened his grip painfully and jerked her forward.

"I told you I could swim better than any fish." His eyes blazed. "Didn't I tell you that?"

"Y-yes," she said quickly.

He nodded. "That's right. And that stupid Dewey, he didn't think I could, but I showed him. I showed him."

Showed him? She swallowed thickly as memories of that horrible river crossing unfurled in her head, overlapping, one over another, in their fight for the surface. They tangled in her mind, revealing nothing to explain the sickening terror that lay beneath them. There was more to what had happened to Molly as she'd been catapulted down the rapids . . . but she couldn't bring it into focus . . .

"He wanted to take you from me, but I didn't let him." He shook his head, keeping one hand tight on her while the other roamed her shoulder, down her arm and up again. "That's what he wanted. He wanted to have you for himself. But you belong to me."

"Brodie, you have obviously misunderstood our friendship," she said, willing the quaver from her voice. "I do not belong to you. I belong to no man."

"I'm going to marry you and we're going to live in the mansion with the swimming pool." The roving hand hesitated an instant and then plunged down to grab her breast.

She gasped with shock as her insidious fear blossomed into flat-out terror. This was not just an unwelcome predicament; this was a dangerous one, and her isolation made it all the more so. She struggled to free herself from his grip. If she could get away, she could grab her clothes and make a dash for it. Surely there would be another shelter in which to dress. The important thing was to escape this secluded place and the frightening, possessive stranger who had her trapped there.

His gaze landed on the small circle of river water and his expression changed like lightning. "No one else is supposed to teach you to swim," he said, grabbing her face. "Adam knows you belong to me."

With a strangled cry, she wrenched free and tried to bolt. She'd managed two steps when his fist closed over her towel and he hauled her back. For one teetering moment she fought with indecision—the towel or herself? And then she released her hold on the towel and stumbled free. She paused just long enough to scoop up her clothes and she was almost to the edge of the enclosure when she plowed hard into an unyielding barrier. Panicked, she began to fight, but then a familiar voice penetrated the haze of fear. Adam.

She clung to him, her clothes a wadded bundle in her arms, exposed and vulnerable and relieved to weakness at the sight of him. An unconnected part of her noticed that he still had Arlie, another that the boy was reaching for her and crying. Adam looked ghastly pale beneath a light sheen of sweat that gleamed on his face. He was staring at Brodie with confusion and anger.

"What the hell are you doing here?" he demanded and then, in nearly the same breath and tone, said, "For God's sake, put your clothes on, Molly."

He grabbed Brodie by the shirt and hauled him away while Molly fumbled with her clothing. Humiliation and horror made the simple task an impossible challenge. She heard Brodie sputtering angry accusations and then a woman's voice, familiar and panicked, cried out to them.

"Mr. Weston! Mr. Weston!"

Molly yanked her dress over her head and at last managed the buttons as Mrs. Imogene Tate approached at a run. Molly peered around at the woman from behind the wall of rock as Mrs. Imogene stopped several yards away, out of breath, her face flushed and her eyes wide with concern.

"Thank the Lord I've found you. Come quickly. It's your mama."

chapter thirty

MOLLY sat in the hot, cramped confines of the wagon, longing to be outside where the air stirred with the night breeze. But she did not budge from her seat, wedged between two barrels and perched atop a crate.

On the mattress at her feet, Rosie lay in a twist of bedclothes and sheets. Her skin glowed with a sallow sheen and the sickly-sweet stench of death hung around her like a portent. She moaned and thrashed, drenched in perspiration and shivering uncontrollably. Molly bathed her face with cool water and pulled the sheet back over her.

"Shhh, Rosie, I'm here. I'm here."

Rosie had lapsed into unconsciousness yesterday evening and had not resurfaced to take sustenance of any kind. Occasionally she sat up and shouted, talking to people only she could see. Haints, she'd called them when she'd seen others do it. Now the haints had come for Rosie.

Molly shifted, wincing as her stiff muscles protested. The spread of sickness had begun weeks ago when an elderly man in their party took ill. He'd been traveling alone, and with no one else to care for him, the women had banded together to help as they could. Each of them took a shift at his side, bathing the fever from his brow and offering him water when he broke from the fits of convulsions that wracked his body. Still, there had been little else they could do but watch the life quite literally drain from him. He'd died within days.

Like fire, fear spread with the word of his passing, igniting imaginations and tongues alike. They all knew about cholera, and the "go-backs"—those whose journey had met ill fate and who decided to return home rather than risk more disaster—had told them that the epidemic was raging wild in other companies. It was a wonder the Hanson party had escaped it so far. Not that they needed the disheartening reports. They had all seen the graves marking the trail.

By the end of the week, three more began showing the signs of affliction, including Mr. Crawford, their guide. He and another died as quickly and painfully as the old man. The third, a young woman, made a miraculous recovery. After that, a feeling of optimism prevailed. A few days passed without any new cases of cholera and they all hoped it had taken its toll and moved on.

Until Mrs. Imogene had come running to fetch Adam. Blinking back the tears that welled up in her eyes, Molly smoothed back Rosie's damp white hair. Rosie mumbled something unintelligible and flailed her arms and legs in a sudden fit. She had survived the loss of her husband, the deaths of two children, and the settling of a new frontier, but with each moment that passed, Molly could see this battle would be lost to the devastating disease.

Throughout the night Rosie shook with wracking convulsions, losing her vital bodily fluids with a rapidity that could not be staunched or replenished. Molly stayed by her side, wishing she could stop this hellish journey long enough to care for her properly, but knowing that she could not. The pilgrimage of fifteen wagons, forty-two adults, and countless children and beasts did not halt for those entering the world with their first breath. It would not halt for those leaving it with their last. They stopped for nothing.

They were fortunate, however, that Captain Hanson had not deemed it necessary to isolate them from the rest as they'd heard was the practice of other companies both ahead and behind them. Some had gone so far as to cast out anyone who was afflicted, refusing to allow them to continue the journey until the ailing member had either died or recovered. It was barbaric, and yet everything about their westward excursion had been.

From outside she heard voices lifted in eerie incantation.

She shifted so that she could see through the opening at the back of the wagon. Not far from their encampment a small party of Indians who had been following on the fringes for several days had pitched a crude skin tent. Now they sat on the ground in front of their fire, chanting in high-pitched, despairing cries and plunging mournful wails. Their song brought gooseflesh to Molly's skin, and she crossed herself as she watched. The flames from their fire danced and flickered in the breeze, casting writhing shadows across the ghostly figures. She did not need to comprehend their words to understand their song. They sang of death.

"Molly?" Rosie's weakened voice pulled her attention back inside the wagon. She took hold of Rosie's hot, dry hand.

"I am here, Rosie. Are you thirsty? May I get you—"

"No," she whispered, her voice rasping against her dry throat.

Molly picked up a cup of water and lifted Rosie's head to dribble some down her throat anyway. The withered woman drank a small amount, but the effort seemed to sap her of what little strength she had.

"My time is come," she said softly. Molly shook her head, but Rosie raised a weak hand and said, "Yes, it is. You can't stop God's time." She coughed painfully and lay back wheezing. Her eyes held a glassy, feverish glow. "You take care of our baby when I'm gone. You promise me you'll do that?"

"Yes, Rosie, of course I will."

Another fit of coughing curled Rosie onto her side. Molly dropped to her knees at the edge of the mattress and helplessly held her as she gasped for breath. When the spell passed, Rosie lay still and drained. Molly thought she'd lapsed back into oblivion but suddenly the frail woman turned, looking around with a blind wildness.

"I know what you think of him," she shouted, pointing past Molly, as if seeing someone who was not there. A soft, whimpering sound came from her parched lips. "He didn't mean it. It wasn't his fault. Ambrose . . ." She started to cry.

"Shhh, Rosie, there is no one there." Molly held her while another wracking cough quaked through Rosie's body. It sounded as if loose rocks rattled together in her lungs. A dry heat rose from her skin. "You mustn't talk," Molly murmured gently. "It will only—"

"She *taunted* him," she said, gripping Molly's arms in a tight claw. "She was the devil, I swear it." She sputtered and coughed again, wheezing frantically to draw in a breath between the violent bursts.

"There was no good in her," she gasped when the spasm passed, "but I still can't leave this world until you know the truth. He killed her. She pushed him to it, but he killed her." She held Molly's hand painfully tight, belying the weakness that sapped her strength. "Frank . . . Frank, I hear you. I'm here."

She sat bolt upright, staring at the back of the wagon as if Frank had suddenly appeared. With a superstitious chill, Molly glanced over her shoulder. A white face hovered against the black backdrop of night for a frightening instant and then vanished like a specter.

"Don't leave me, Frank," Rose pleaded.

But it wasn't Frank whose face had peered in at them. It was Brodie.

Molly had no time to react before the next bout of coughing took control of Rosie's diminished body. The hacking shook her for so long that Molly feared it would never stop. She clutched Rosie's hand to her heart, praying silently for mercy. And then it came, so suddenly that it thundered in the quiet like doom.

"I'm sorry, child. You know I love you like my own," Rosie whispered, taking in a long, rattling breath. And then she closed her eyes and breathed no more.

DAWN glimmered like a mirage on the horizon when Molly staggered out of the wagon. Exhaustion had blunted the horror of her night, but the shock of it hovered just at the edge of her awareness where Rosie's dying confession buzzed around and around and the image of Brodie's pale face gasped with rage.

"He killed her . . ."

The early-morning air shivered down her spine. She took a

deep breath, amazed at how cool and gentle it felt after the rot of sickness and the taint of death that had filled the wagon.

Adam knelt next to the campfire, coaxing a small flame to life. He looked up when he saw her and stood. She didn't know where Brodie was. Arlie, most likely, was still asleep in the tent.

Silently Adam watched her approach. His light gaze traveled over her face to her eyes. He read the grief that she knew gleamed in them.

"She's gone?" he said.

She nodded, fresh tears spilling over her lashes. Adam covered his face with his hands, and without thought, Molly stepped forward and brushed them aside. She pulled him to her, holding him while they both cried for the loss of a woman who had always seemed unconquerable. She'd had courage and fortitude, and her tittering laughter had spurred them all from bouts of self-pity, keeping them united and brave.

But she'd kept more than their spirits afloat and their bellies full. She'd kept secrets to protect her son. Had she kept them from Adam as well, or did he know the terrible truth?

When he began to pull away, she let him go. Her troubling thoughts were too much for her overloaded emotions. She needed to escape, if only for a while.

"I need to tell Brodie," Adam said hoarsely.

She nodded and, without a word, walked away.

THEY buried Rosie on a barren hill beside the Platte River. The grave was miles from the little cemetery where her husband and other children had been laid to rest, miles from anything that she might have found familiar. Molly read from the Bible while Adam, Brodie, Mrs. Imogene and Mr. Tate, Captain and Mrs. Hanson, and plump Alice Ann O'Keefe stood by the open grave. Others gathered quietly behind. The Hansons witnessed the ceremony with stoic weariness while Alice Ann gazed woefully at Brodie.

Adam stared into Rosie's grave with a stony expression, and Arlie, who was always wont to squirm, clung to his father with uncharacteristic solemnity. He didn't understand that his beloved grandma lay before them, wrapped in a sheet, but he knew that something was very wrong that morning. Brodie cried freely and inconsolably. The vent of his grief nearly destroyed Molly's own tenuous control. She would never know how she managed to get through it.

The earth proved hard in the Wyoming territory. Adam and Brodie had toiled as long as the captain would permit and still the grave was shallow. In a vain effort, they piled stones over the heaped dirt when the grave was filled, but they knew the wolves and coyotes would get her all the same. They could do nothing but try not to think of it.

By ten that morning, the emigrants had yoked their oxen and begun their journey once more. As they moved on, Molly looked back at Rosie's grave. Brodie stood over it, staring down at the piled stones and shaking his head, as if denying her death could somehow bring her back. Not a tree was in sight and the crude wooden cross that Adam had quickly made that morning poked from the ground like a feeble growth, dwarfed by the glowering ridge of mountains in the background.

Rosie's words still hummed incessantly in her head, but for now, weariness dulled her senses until she felt as empty as the marauded graves they'd passed along the trail. Tomorrow . . . who knew what she'd feel tomorrow?

It wasn't until much later that she noticed Brodie had rejoined them. Unable to stop herself, she glanced back at him. No longer did he wear the mask of grief on his face. In his eyes she saw suspicion and fear and, underlining both, the unmistakable gleam of malice. She was not the only one remembering Rosie's last words.

chapter thirty-one

AWARENESS came to Tess with a rush. She stood in the middle of the cemetery, surrounded by Mountain Bend's dead. Why was she here? And then she remembered. Rosie. That wasn't right, though. She was Tess, and Rosie belonged in Molly's world. But the tears on her face and the sunken feeling in the pit of her stomach were testimony to the loss she felt. She moved on unsteady legs and made her way through the rows of graves.

The clouds had overwhelmed the sun and turned the sky into a sluggish shroud of shifting gray. A darker bank crouched just over the eastern mountain peaks, waiting for the perfect opportunity to advance. It was just after noon, but it had grown cold and somewhere a fire had been lit. The smell of burning pine scented the air.

A damp wind shuddered in the trees and with it came again the feeling of being watched. Tess shivered, turning in place as she scanned the deserted church grounds and gravesites, remembering how moments ago she'd done the same. Only then she'd been searching for Arlie. Had his screams been an extension of Molly's recurring nightmare? Or were they both a premonition? A sound to her left made her start, but it was only a squirrel racing down an aspen. An instant later another followed. Nothing else moved.

She headed back to her car, warily watching for the slightest shift in shadows. The lot was all but deserted. In front of the chapel were two cars. One presumably belonged to the pastor. The other was Craig's Lexus. Tess had parked on the opposite end, near the tree and bench.

She was almost on it before she recognized the only other vehicle in the lot. It was an old and battered truck. Grant's truck. The passenger door swung open as she drew near. Without question, she got in.

"Visiting anyone I know?" Grant asked.

She didn't bother to answer. He looked too tired for banter. He looked too tired for anything. His seat was pushed way back and his long legs stretched out. He wore blue jeans and a denim button-down hung open over a white T-shirt with an American flag on the chest. A cowboy hat rode low on his forehead, throwing his face into darkness.

She stared at him, longing to touch him, to smooth the lines of worry from his brow. How had he become so important to her in so short a time? If Craig was right, Grant was playing Tess for a fool. But something inside her refused to believe it. She needed Grant to be a good guy, needed it like air. But needing something to be true didn't make it so. Craig had raised more questions, more doubts, about Grant. Until she knew her belief in him was based on something more substantial than her desire, she had to stay on guard.

She forced herself to look away and focus on something other than the long length of him next to her. "I see the sheriff decided not to hold you," she said, her voice unnaturally husky.

"It's amazing who they let walk around free."

"You have a point there. This town is jam packed with creeps. Every time I turn around, someone is threatening me— or lying to me. But then you know all about that, don't you, Grant?"

His eyes narrowed, but he didn't answer.

"You told me your father and my sister had a thing. What I can't figure out is how that can be true considering the fact that your dad was practically an invalid."

"Who said he was an invalid?"

"It doesn't matter who said it."

"Does it matter that it isn't true?" His voice was low and bitter.

"You're saying it's not?" She took a deep breath and let it

out in a frustrated sigh. "Okay, Grant, set the record straight for me. Tell me, how *was* your father's health before he died? Was he a fit man?"

"Fit enough."

"Fit enough for what? A nursing home or a woman who was nearly half his age?"

He shifted in his seat, laying his arm across the back of it. His fingers were near her neck, close enough to touch, to grab . . . The lot was nearly empty and they were isolated on this side of it. What was she doing, provoking this man *again*? Why was it that she couldn't leave him alone and stay away? But she couldn't stop, not without knowing the truth, and she couldn't convince her heart that Grant Weston wasn't the man he seemed. Even as logic told her she should get out of the truck and bolt, everything inside her was keyed to the sensuality in him. She forced herself to ask the next question.

"When was the last time he rode a tractor, Grant? When was the last time he was able to do that?"

His silver eyes glittered and his jaw clenched with anger, but he spoke soft and slow. "I'd say that was about a second before he died."

It was a sucker punch, but it knocked the wind out of her all the same. He leaned closer to her, taunting her with his nearness. He moved his hand just enough that his fingers brushed the sensitive skin on the nape of her neck.

"No snappy retort, Tess?" he murmured. "No comeback zinger? Why don't you ask me what you really want to know? Go ahead, ask me."

"Stop it. Stop trying to scare me."

"Is that what I'm doing?" He touched her again and a shiver of awareness went through her. "Because that's not what I want to do to you at all."

She left that alone, knowing it was a gauntlet. Knowing she dared not pick it up.

"Come on, Blue Eyes. Let's get it out. Ask me if I killed my dad and took off with your sister. That's why you came to my house in your little apron this morning, isn't it?"

"No," she said. "That's not why I came."

"Sure it is. You don't know me. I'm just some has-been actor who fucked up the golden dream. Who knows what else I might do? Isn't that what you're thinking?"

She raised her chin. "Did you?"

He looked away, making a noise that might have passed for laughter had there been even an ounce of humor in it. "No."

Her question seemed to have stolen the fun from his game. He leaned back in his seat again, facing forward. He gripped the steering wheel with white-knuckled fists and shook his head. "Believe it or not, I loved my dad. As for Tori, I have no idea where she is."

"Where were you when it happened?"

He hesitated, his face tightening with resentment. "Piney River. I went to see a man about a horse. When I got there, no one was home. I waited for a half hour or so and then came back."

As alibis went, his sucked. "You were alone?"

Grant nodded grimly. "He called me later to apologize for standing me up. He said his wife had been in a car accident. He can vouch for the fact that he was supposed to meet me and didn't show, but he can't swear that I was at his house."

Which equaled no alibi at all. His face was in shadows, leaving only his voice, pitched low with emotion to guide her.

"I didn't even say goodbye to my dad before I left. Craig called right as I was walking out the door. It sounded like there was a fight brewing, so I got the hell out as fast as I could. When I came home, he was dead."

"Why were they fighting?"

He shrugged, but there was tension in the gesture that defied nonchalance. After a long moment, he said, "They were always fighting, always in each other's faces. Both of them convinced that the other one was wrong. When I was a kid, Dad scared the shit out of me. I never knew what might set him off. I could never understand why Craig provoked him. Me, I just tried to be invisible."

His tone, the words he conveyed without speaking, told Tess his father had been abusive in his anger. Grant shifted in his seat, looking back into his dark history. As she watched him, she realized that she was seeing the exposed truth. He'd inadvertently left the door open, making her a witness to his past. She saw the reflection of the boy who'd tried to be invisible in the man who acted to hide who he really was.

"Everywhere else, I was Mr. Bigshot. Varsity football, debate team, prettiest girl in the school for a girlfriend. But at home I was so good at being small that I could walk through a room and no one would even notice I was there. Craig couldn't do that. He had to be seen. After he got big enough to fight back, things got ugly. The two of them would go at it like they wanted to kill each other. You couldn't make them stop, you couldn't break them up. He put dad in the hospital once, banged him up so he could hardly walk. I don't know what would have happened after that, what Dad would have done when he came home." He looked at her and through the shadows she saw his smoky eyes darken. "The next morning the church burned down and everything changed."

"Oh, God," she breathed. "Your mother . . ." He frowned, no doubt wondering how she knew about his mother. "I saw the memorial. Craig told me he was there when it happened, that he tried to help the people escape, but it was no use. It must have been . . ." She trailed off, realizing any description would be inadequate.

Grant looked away, but not before she glimpsed the emotion playing across his face. She put a tentative hand on his arm. Surprised, he stared at it, unmoving. Pain glimmered in his silver eyes. Pain so deep, so raw, that it reached out to her. He must feel as if the bottom of his world had somehow come open and he was falling out. He must feel like she did, as if she were hanging on by a line far too short and much too weak.

It didn't matter that he was just what he'd said—someone she didn't know. Someone with a less than stellar track record. Someone who had gone out of his way to alienate her when she'd started asking questions about her sister. Because beneath the anger and insolence, she saw a vulnerability that echoed her own feelings of fragility. They were lost, both of them, adrift in a world they couldn't seem to control.

Not a thing had changed, and yet for Tess, everything had. In that moment, in that instant, the last barrier collapsed. Whether it was right, wrong, foolish, or impossible, it didn't matter. She was falling for this man and denying it wasn't going to make a difference.

She lifted her hand to his cheek and rested it against the warmth of his skin in a connection that traveled to her core. He inhaled softly and then released a heavy breath that was filled at once with bewilderment and understanding. Slowly, as if in stages of acceptance, he leaned across the seat, closing the distance that separated them. And then his mouth was on hers, as warm and soft, as hard and demanding, as everything else about him. Her arms wound up and around his neck, pulling him tight as she kissed him back. He tasted of sun and salt and seductive surrender. She didn't question the abandon of her response. She shut out every voice that dared to disagree with the heat that coated her skin like oil. He pulled her over, or perhaps she climbed, but somehow she was straddling his legs, pressed closer to him than skin yet needing more. The steering wheel was in the way, and without pause, he reached beneath the seat and moved it farther back. Tess felt it slide on the rails as if from a distance. It felt like falling.

"This is crazy," he muttered against her mouth. His voice was lazy and deep. It felt like honey on her senses as it taunted and teased, coating her in a warm glaze even as she was aware of the power that lay beneath it. His lips moved to her neck, to the hollow at the base of her throat, to the sensitive points beneath her collarbone.

Oh, yes. Crazy. Crazy like she couldn't breathe. Crazy like she couldn't think. Crazy like she didn't care if she ever did either again.

Her hands fumbled to pull his T-shirt free of his waistband while his skimmed up her ribs to her breasts. Her insides went hot and creamy as every part of her tuned to his touch.

Overhead thunder exploded and rain pummeled the steamy windows. Lightning lit up the inside of the truck, and was followed immediately by quaking thunder that startled them apart for an instant, an instant wrought with the reality of what she was doing. She was making out in a car like a sex-starved teenager with a man she didn't quite trust, no matter how much she wanted to. The same thought seemed to flash through him as well. She stared into his face, noting with a distant surprise that at some point he'd lost his hat. His hair gleamed dark in the muted light. He kept hold of her for a moment that was marked by the tension and tautness of his body pressing against hers. He didn't want to let her go.

She opened her mouth to tell him that she didn't want to let go either. To say that despite all the conflicting stories she'd heard, she believed in him. But somehow her voice had failed her and the withdrawal in his expression hit her deep and low. Silently, she slid off his lap and back to her side of the seat. He looked straight ahead as he turned the key and started the engine. The wipers swished and clapped across the windshield.

Disappointment left a bitter taste in her mouth as she opened the door. Without a word, she dashed through the rain to her car. Grant gunned his engine as soon as hers turned over and he was gone. Her eyes burned with unshed tears and angrily she swiped at them. What had she expected?

Reaching for her seat belt, she noticed another set of lights come on. Her spirits sank lower as she recognized Craig's Lexus. When had he come out? Had he seen her leaving Grant's truck, windows so steamed they were opaque? His car reversed, then paused before moving forward. Was he waiting for something? For her?

She shifted into drive and slowly rolled to the exit. In her rearview, she saw him follow. Of course he followed, she scolded herself. There was only one way out. Yet it felt wrong. She turned right, holding her breath to see what he did. For a long moment, his car idled at the exit and then slowly he pulled forward and turned the other way.

chapter thirty-two

TORI'S house was quiet and still, more disconcerting than the cemetery had been. Tess stepped inside feeling as if she'd been gone for days, yet unbelievably, she still had two hours before Caitlin was let out of school. She was exhausted and longed to lose herself in the oblivion of sleep, but she knew she'd never manage to shut down her thoughts. Not now.

Over and over she played the conversations she'd had with Craig and Grant, comparing their accounts of the day the church had burned to the ground. According to Craig, Grant had been arguing with their mother and she'd gone to church crying over the bitter exchange. But in Grant's version it was Craig who'd caused turmoil in the family, putting their father in the hospital, where he remained the day the church had gone up in flames. Whose version was the true one? And why would one of them feel the need to lie about it to Tess? What did it have to do with her?

Like all other answers, this one evaded her.

Filled with both resignation and determination, she went upstairs and tackled Tori's room. Although it looked bad, in reality Tori had few possessions and it didn't take long to go through them. She hadn't really expected to find anything of significance, anything that would tell her where Tori had gone, but she was disappointed all the same. Frustrated by the constant dead ends, she opened the last drawer and discovered a small address book tucked against the side. She sat on the bed and flipped through the pages.

There were few entries, most of them crossed out, but on the bottom of the "B" page, Tess found a phone number with the name "Bran" scrawled over it. Bran. Brandon Forsythe?

Tess dialed the number and waited for it to connect. She expected a secretary or a machine, but a man answered after a few rings. Wherever he was, it was noisy and she had to raise her voice to be heard.

"May I speak with Mr. Forsythe please?"

"Who is this? How did you get this number?"

"My name is Tess Carson. I'm Tori France's sister."

A long moment passed, filled with the noise of a crowded gymnasium. "Hold on," he said finally, and put a muffling hand over the receiver. A moment later the man came back. The background din was gone.

"What did you say your name was?"

"Tess. Tess Carson. This is Brandon Forsythe?"

"Yes."

"I'm calling because—have you heard from Tori?"

"Heard from her? No."

"Do you speak on a regular basis?" As she asked the question, she realized how much like the sheriff she sounded.

"Why are you asking?" he said.

"Tori is missing. She disappeared two days ago."

"She's a free spirit. She's not exactly grounded anywhere."

"That's true, but she left her daughter behind."

Now she had his undivided attention. He obviously knew Tori very well to understand how that changed the playing field. Deciding that he would be more cooperative if he knew all the details, Tess filled him in on what had happened.

"That's bullshit. Tori would never have left that man to die. And she wasn't hurting for money, either."

"How do you know?"

"I just do."

She was gun-shy about her next question, but it had to be asked. "Mr. Forsythe, Tori is pregnant. Do you know who the father is?"

The phone went silent, so silent she thought the connection had been lost. When he did finally speak, his voice was low and hesitant.

"I'm a married man."

"I'm sorry?"

"I have four kids and a perfect wife."

Glad she was sitting, Tess gripped the phone. "Whatever you tell me, I won't use it against you. I just want to find my sister."

He paused again. Did he believe her?

"Tori is like no one else in this world," he said at last. There was a waver in his voice. "I would have given my right arm to go with her. I mean that. But I couldn't. She understood."

"You are the father."

"All I could give her was money. God knows I've got enough. Short of setting it on fire, she shouldn't run out of it. She and the baby and Caitlin have enough to last them for the rest of their lives. She didn't want to take it."

"But she did?"

"To make me feel better. Money's never meant shit to her, but she knew it was all I had."

His words resonated with truth. He was the first person she'd spoken to that cared about her sister. The first person who understood that inside of Tori, there was more, there was a giving person who only wanted to be loved.

"Do you know anyone who might be . . . who might mean her harm?"

"Every woman who's ever met her, maybe." He gave a sad laugh. "My wife, if she knew."

"But she doesn't?"

"No. I'd swear to that. She has no idea."

"Did Tori talk about going away?"

"No. I hooked her up with Grant Weston. She was looking forward to a slower pace out there. She said she was hopeful about Mountain Bend."

TESS wandered downstairs after she hung up. She felt dazed, shocked to her core by Brandon's revelations. He'd answered more than her questions. He'd drawn another parallel. The married man. The sister who had an affair with him. Just like Vanessa.

She paced the living room, feeling as if the eyes in the creepy Jesus picture followed her movements. She stopped in front of it, struck again by how out of place it was in Tori's home. But for all she knew, Tori had found God again.

She shivered, suddenly realizing that she was cold. It was happening again. Anxiety crept in with the iciness, but she forced it away. She was afraid to go back, but more afraid not to. She needed to know what happened to Molly. She needed to know what happened next.

Her limbs felt like lead and she sank to the floor, letting the past have her again. The images began to form, taking shape, taking over. From a distance Tess realized the phone was ringing, but it was too late; she couldn't cross back when she was almost there.

The answering machine picked up, and a woman's voice spoke over it. "I need to see you. It's urgent. This is . . ." The woman made a small sound that carried through to Tess. Was she frustrated? Afraid? There was a click, and then a brief burst of dial tone as the caller hung up.

Still, Tess couldn't move. The feeling of both worlds layering over her cemented the certainty that the past and the present were connected. That more than Tess's own destiny hinged on the turn of Molly's fate.

A small ticking noise drew her gaze to the wall. It shimmered like oil on water, the eggshell paint fading and brightening at once. The ticking became the steady clank of pots and pans as the wagon wheels turned. Tess forced herself to focus on that sound, to race toward it, to make the leap.

chapter thirty-three

MOLLY exhaled, looking across the Wyoming landscape as she approached Independence Rock. The distinctive outcropping of earth rose like a massive round beast from the sandy banks of the riverside. It was named for the day Frémont and his men had first explored it. For Molly it underscored how far they had come and how much they had sacrificed to get there. That the Hanson party was passing it on the twenty-eighth of July rather than the fourth was a matter of much concern because Independence Rock represented only the halfway point where they would leave behind the Platte in exchange for the Sweetwater River. They still had miles and miles to go.

For the first time in days, she'd been free to walk alone. Arlie had been so needy since Rosie's death that she hadn't been able to put him down for an instant without him crying for her to hold him again. Only today had he agreed to lie down in the wagon without Molly beside him. She'd been hesitant to leave him, even in the competent and nurturing care of Mrs. Imogene Tate, but her words had convinced Molly to go.

"Miss Molly, you look like you've been carrying the worries of all the world around with you," Mrs. Imogene had said as she shooed Molly away. "That's our Lord's job, child. You go on and put some peace to your mind. I'll watch Arlie and comfort him when he wakes. Go on with you."

But each step she took toward the milestone seemed only to push it farther away. Or perhaps her perception had nothing to do with Independence Rock. She turned and searched for Adam riding far behind her, near the last of the wagons. She'd seen little of him since they'd buried Rosie. Unconsciously she wanted to put her own distance between herself and the object of her hurt and confusion.

Niether of them knew what to do next. If Mrs. Imogene hadn't stepped forward and taken charge after Rosie's death, Molly didn't know how she would have survived. With her rich auburn hair and stern beak of a nose, Mrs. Imogene could scare the scalp off an Indian, as Mr. Tate was apt to put it. But she had compassionate brown eyes set evenly beneath her smooth brow and a smile that could coax flowers from the ground. Her chin was as weak as her Louisiana-bred morals were strong and her knowledge of scripture would have humbled even the Reverend.

Gratefully, Molly acquiesced when the older woman declared, "I'd not be able to hold my head up in church if I didn't intervene on your behalf, child. Living with two unmarried men is like asking the devil to Sunday supper. Temptation is a powerful sin, and as a servant to the Lord Jesus, I must stand against it."

The devil to Sunday supper. Mrs. Imogene had had no idea just how accurate an appraisal she'd made.

Molly had not spoken of Rosie's dying words, not to Adam and certainly not to Brodie, who had no doubt heard them himself. At first, it was the sheer grief of her loss that had kept Molly silent. She couldn't bring herself to bear accusations against Brodie based on Rosie's dying confession. To do so would have been a betrayal of the beloved woman. But there were many times in the dark days that followed when Molly had been overcome with the need to point at Brodie and condemn him for what he was. The only thing holding her back was the realization that if she did so, Adam would be the one to pay the price.

Rosie had not kept her secret from Adam on a whim. She had known that it would destroy him to learn what his brother had done. In her heart, Molly believed that Rosie felt Brodie's crime a mishap. An unfortunate accident that would never be repeated. She'd blamed Vanessa for pushing him to it, not Brodie for carrying out the unforgivable deed. If she'd told Adam, it would have ripped her family in two. So she'd carried her dark secret across all the miles, but she couldn't take the burden with her to the beyond.

Now it was Molly who bore the burden. She cared not what happened to Brodie. He deserved every punishment that might be his. But Adam . . . What would he do if she told him? Cast out his brother? Relinquish him to whatever fate awaited him, when it was Adam who had brought him here, who'd brought Vanessa home in the first place?

And that left her with the most painful thought of all. What about Vanessa, who had been murdered by Brodie Weston and then buried under the guise of an accident? What justice was there for Molly's sister? Who, but Molly, could avenge her death?

Lost in her troubled thoughts, Molly at last reached the enormous rock formation. When she turned to look back at the wagons lumbering behind, she was surprised to find how much distance she'd put between herself and the rest of them. Placing a hand on the rough stone, she took a deep breath and stared at the hundreds of names carved and painted on its sides. She read the messages left by those who had come before her for those who would come after and for the go-backs who might tell those at home that VD Moody or Miss Mary Zachary had been there.

She let her fingers trail over the carvings as she made her way around the rock, losing herself in the brief messages and tidings. So many people had passed this way; so many had not been fortunate enough to survive thus far. The brief passages inscribed here struck her with the sheer impossibility of their quest. Why had they all felt the need to make this journey? How many more would follow? Could they actually achieve their destination, or would it all be in vain? All the suffering, the loss of loved ones, the sacrifices . . .

Feeling like another step might be too much to take, she leaned against the stone and stared heavenward. She'd thought herself alone, but the sound of boots on the loose gravel forewarned the appearance of a shadow from the other side of the rock. An instant later, Adam materialized like a mirage in the hot sun.

The anguish of Rosie's death had drawn haggard shadows beneath his eyes and etched lines of strain on the strong plains of his face. He shaved every Sunday, but the weekly grooming could not combat the stubble that darkened his cheeks and made him look as rough and savage as the rugged wilderness surrounding them. His hat was pulled down, but his eyes glimmered with a translucent light from below the brim.

She stood motionless as his quicksilver gaze traveled over her face, no doubt making the same assessments as she had. The time they'd spent apart had not been kind to either of them.

"I left Brodie in charge of the wagon," he said, as if in answer to a query. "I'm thinking I'll probably find them both in Mexico, but I needed the break." He gave her a halfhearted grin that looked as tired and forced as the one she tried to muster in return. "Arlie's with Mrs. Imogene?" he asked.

Molly nodded.

"Looks like we're the first ones here," he said, taking off his hat to run his fingers through his hair.

She was struck anew by how tall and broad shouldered he was. The buttons on his shirt strained with the movement of his arms, and the muscles beneath his skin bunched with strength. The sun had browned his forearms, and the soft springy hairs glittered in tawny shades of ochre and auburn lightened by exposure. Molly watched each flexing movement with fascination.

He wore the ordinary dress of the emigrants, but on Adam nothing appeared common. Was it the breadth of him or the person within that made him stand out like a vein of gold in the depths of granite? There was a small, triangular tear in his shirt just at his ribs and she felt a pang of guilt at the sight of it. When Rosie had been alive, the two had managed to keep them all in clean and mended clothes. Without her, Molly was lucky to keep up with the washing alone. There wasn't time or energy to tend to the stitching as well.

Seeing the direction of her stare, Adam poked a rueful finger at the hole. "Caught it on a corner."

She looked down, hiding her face beneath the brim of her bonnet. She wanted to say something to him, but her emotions had somehow caught up in her throat and she couldn't manage a sound.

"I heard someone say you can climb to the top of it," Adam said, looking up.

Molly followed his gaze. Independence Rock looked much like a giant buffalo crouched down to slumber. One side was relatively smooth and rounded, but the other had irregular ledges that jutted out.

"Why would one care to climb after so much walking?" she said, her voice shaky but clear.

He shrugged. "Must feel like being on the top of the world once you make it up."

They stared at one another again as everything else fell away. This time her smile felt whole and right and the glimmer in Adam's eyes burned like a flame beneath the iceberg that had become her heart. He reached out and touched her face with his work-worn hands. She knew they were rough, but against her skin his fingers felt like warmed silk.

"What do you say, city girl?"

The ascent was not so difficult as she'd first thought, but she'd had to hike up her skirts and knot them at the side to give her freedom to move. The knowledge that Adam was just below her, settling his large hands in the places where hers had just been, brought a sense of uncanny connection, as if she were leaving pieces of herself behind for him to gather and carry up.

When she reached the top, she was out of breath and the muscles in her arms and shoulders were pulled and sore, but the agony in her soul took flight as she stepped onto the plateau. Adam followed, winded. There was a fine sheen of sweat on his face. This high, the breeze was cool and it blew like heaven's breath over their heated skin.

"It *is* like being on top of the world," she said.

For miles in any direction they could see the unbroken terrain stretching out like a quilt of dirt and rock, seamed by a river down the center. To the east, the winding snake of the Hanson wagons forged on. Far off in the west, the tail end of another party of emigrants curled into the distance. They looked like toys, moved by the invisible hands of God.

Adam unscrewed the lid to his canteen and offered Molly a drink. The water was tepid and brackish, but her throat was dry and its moisture was as welcome as a fresh stream.

"Thank you," she murmured, handing it back. She watched him place his mouth where hers had been and drink. He tipped his head back, as if in worship to the sun, and the muscles of his throat moved with sinewy grace as he swallowed.

They sat quietly for a moment, looking out over the land like a king and queen surveying their kingdom. Molly thought longingly of all the times they'd made conversation without awkward pauses or stumbling words. Now the space between them was as filled with the unspoken as it was with the tiny dust particles that danced in the air.

He shook his head and turned to watch the wagons lumbering closer. "Sometimes it doesn't feel like we're ever going to get through this. I keep thinking what a fool I was to drag everyone out here. Now Ma's dead. You're living with strangers. I don't hardly see my son and I want to wring my brother's neck every time I look at him."

What could she say to that? They'd all made their own decisions to come, but who could have foreseen what would happen?

"I've missed you, Molly." He looked at her then, his eyes like thunder, swirling and clashing with feelings he didn't try to conceal. He opened his hand and held it out to her. She placed her own inside, watching with bemusement as his fingers closed and her hand was engulfed by the gentle strength of him.

She had imagined moments like this so many times that now she doubted it was real. Had she conjured it from her shattered desires? The breeze teased between them, like a kindly spirit urging them closer. It was all the invitation Molly needed. She leaned toward him and Adam met her halfway, gathering her up against the hard muscles of his chest and kissing her with a hunger that echoed in her heart. It seemed that here, on top of the world, they were at last free to explore the shape and taste of one another.

The trail had worn them both to leanness, but it had not diminished the solid feel of him. Her hands roamed the thick muscles of his shoulders and back, moving restlessly to the rough beard on his cheeks and silky strands of hair that brushed his collar.

His skin smelled warm and faintly of soap and sweat and he tasted of the honey mint drops that Mrs. Imogene seemed to have in endless supply. They kissed for all the days of separation. They kissed for the promise of the future. For past, for present, for the aching losses they had shared.

"It's been hell with you gone," he muttered against the sensitive skin of her throat.

His beard rubbed her chin and made her lips feel tender as windblown petals, but she didn't pull away. He pressed his mouth to her forehead. "I want to marry you," he said, his voice low and hoarse. "As soon as we get to California, I want to marry you."

His words swelled through her heart but with them came the beat of reality. Right now, here in his arms, she felt like the princess in a bedtime story. But every fairy tale had a villain and this one was no exception. She'd managed to banish Brodie from her daily life, though she'd not been able to keep him from her thoughts. But she couldn't avoid him forever and she knew it.

Adam pulled back to look into her face. "That's not the reaction a man usually gets when he tells a woman he wants to marry her."

No, it wasn't. But she wasn't any woman and he, most certainly, wasn't any man.

When she didn't say anything, he asked, "What is it, Molly?" Uncertainty flickered in his eyes. He dropped his hands and moved back. "Have I misunderstood—"

"No," she said quickly. "It's not that. It's— There are things we must discuss before we can talk of our future, Adam."

Silently he nodded. Molly gathered up her thoughts and tried to order them. She could not begin by asking if Brodie had murdered Vanessa, though she knew without a doubt that it must be the place to end.

"I want to know about Arlie," she said at last.

Her words cooled the warmth in Adam's eyes. Fearing a complete withdrawal, she rushed on, "I have guessed who his— He bears a strong resemblance to a trusted friend of my father's, but Vanessa never confided in me about . . . about anything."

He dropped his hands back to his sides and said, "Well, I guess that makes two of us that she kept in the dark. It wasn't until after Arlie was born that I figured things out."

"When you realized—did you feel betrayed?"

"There aren't words for how I felt," he said bitterly.

"Brodie told me there was an awful scene between you two."

Adam paused, frowning. "When did he tell you that?"

"Months ago, when we first began the journey. He said you had a terrible row and then a few days later she died."

He made a sound of disbelief. "I don't know why he'd tell you something like that. Vanessa never did tell me the truth. She didn't have to tell me."

Molly stared at him, trying to see through his words to the truth. She had to speak of Rosie's confession, or forever question what had really happened to her sister.

Adam scooped up a handful of pebbles and began lobbing them over the edge of the plateau. Silently, Molly looked down at the rocky surface on which they sat. Off to the side, industrious ants were hard at work dragging the remains of an unlucky insect back to their colony. Next to her, a sprig of green defied all odds by sprouting from a crevice in the stone.

"Adam, before your mother passed on, she spoke to me about Vanessa. She told me that she couldn't leave this world without telling me the truth about my sister's death. She told me Vanessa was killed."

Adam shook his head, whether in denial or disbelief, she wasn't certain.

"She said, 'He pushed her to it, but he killed her all the same.'"

"Who?" Adam demanded.

"I am convinced she was speaking of your brother."

With a muffled curse, Adam pushed to his feet. Anger

knotted the muscles beneath his shirt and drew tension to his jaw. "No one killed Vanessa, Molly. How many times do I have to say it? She died in an accident. She fell. Every one of us warned her to be careful going up and down the ladder to the loft, but she wouldn't listen. She wouldn't hear of having her things moved down. She didn't want to be too close to the rest of us."

What he said sounded conceivable, likely even. And yet an accidental fall could be contrived, could it not?

"Molly, think about it. Why in the hell would Brodie want to hurt my wife?"

This brought her eyes up and round. In that instant, the answer leaped between them. Memory of the day by the river flashed though her mind as quickly as it did his.

Adam shook his head. "No. He's a boy, Molly. He may look like a man, but inside he's a boy. He was afraid to even talk to her."

"Your mother said she taunted him. She did, didn't she, Adam?"

"Oh, yes. That she did. She made him cry a time or two. She made him cry like a baby, like a child." He came back to her and squatted down. "Molly, Ma was out of her mind with fever before she died. I could hear her crying and babbling to people that have been dead for years. She didn't know what she was saying."

It was true. Rosie had been delirious, hallucinating, talking to the haints . . .

"I found Vanessa. I swear to you, nobody killed her."

They stared at one another, on top of the world and completely isolated. The sense that the rest of her life would hinge on this moment felt as overwhelming as the dust and heat of the trail.

"What about me, Adam?" she whispered.

"I'll talk to him."

"And tell him what? That day by the river Brodie was not the person you think him to be. I know that it must be very painful to consider that he might—that he could . . . But,

Adam, I beg you to open your eyes before someone else pays the price."

"You're wrong, Molly."

She shoved up her sleeves so that he could see the bruises Brodie had left on her arms. "For a boy, he has a strong grip," she said.

He winced, reaching a gentle finger to touch the green-and-purple skin. "There's no excuse for what he did," Adam began. A tremor rumbled in his voice. "All I can say is that I promise you it will never happen again."

"He imagines there is an infatuation that we share. He will not be discouraged from his fantasy. Lord knows I have tried to dissuade him."

"Oh, he'll be plenty discouraged when I get through with him," Adam said. "Don't doubt that for a minute. Before, he didn't know how things were between you and me, Molly. He does now. He'll respect it."

"How can you be sure?"

"I'm his big brother," he said simply. "You've got to trust me on this. You have to. Please, trust me."

Though deep inside a frightened voice warned her against it, Molly nodded and let him pull her into his arms.

chapter thirty-four

A knock on the door joined in Tess's mind with the desperate thud of her footfalls on the packed and dusty trail. The sound had a menace that she couldn't ignore, and it grew louder and louder until she jerked into the present with a gasp. She looked around, fighting disorientation. She was sitting on the floor, still in Tori's house. Not in Adam's arms. Not walking the endless miles. Not Molly.

She glanced at her watch. The hands on it had barely moved, yet it felt like so much time had passed. The knock came again, insistent now. She rose and shuffled toward the front window, cautiously pulling back the thin curtains to see outside. Grant's truck was parked in the drive. Grant stood on the porch.

He was watching the window and lifted a hand when he saw her. They stared at one another for a charged moment before Tess let the curtain fall back into place. Thoughts of her behavior in his car made her blush as he stepped inside. She'd given herself to him like an idolizing fan. What had possessed her? But really, she knew the answer to that question all too well. Grant had.

"I just heard about finding Tori's car at the bus station," he said. "I'm sorry."

"She didn't drive it there."

"How do you know?"

"I just do."

Wisely, he didn't argue. Shifting his weight, he glanced around, as if for inspiration. He looked as uncomfortable as she felt and she steeled herself against the impulse to put him at ease.

"What do you want, Grant?" she finally asked.

A flush crept up his cheeks at her sharp tone. For a moment she glimpsed something like torment in his eyes.

Letting out a pent-up breath, he said, "I was abrupt earlier. I didn't want to leave it like that." He hesitated before going on. "It's an old habit—a bad habit, leaving when I don't know what else to do."

"What else was there to do?"

A smile flitted over his lips and vanished, but not before it filled her head with images of the two of them, locked together in the heat of their need. He looked away, as if the contact he'd initiated had become too intense for him to manage.

"Do you ever stop?" she asked.

"Stop what?"

"Acting."

He looked stunned by the accusation and again she glimpsed something raw in the quicksilver of his eyes. Something vulnerable and hurt. She sensed emotion building in him, looking for a vent. He ran fingers through his hair and shook his head.

"I don't know anymore," he said finally. "You tell me."

"That's why you don't like Tori, isn't it? Because she could see through your bullshit."

"I don't like Tori because she used my old man. She landed on my doorstep with her problems and her—"

"Wait a minute—what do you mean, landed on your doorstep? You hired her."

"I need a bookkeeper like I need a dead horse."

Tess stared at him, uncomprehending. "But—"

"There are no books. There's no money to tally. There's just bills and back taxes." He turned away and lowered his voice. "I was doing my buddy a favor. Take in his girlfriend and he'd throw some work my way. He's paying her salary, not me."

"Brandon Forsythe."

Grant looked up at her.

"He told me he gave Tori money," she went on, "because he couldn't give her anything else. He had to let her go."

"I'm sure he did. But obviously he didn't want her to go too far."

"Just far enough that his wife wouldn't know."

"I told you that you wouldn't like what you found here."

Yes, he had. And with each answer came another question. Like where was all this money Brandon had given Tori? And what other favors was Grant willing to do for his friend? Get rid of Tori all together? She lowered her gaze and noticed the white bandage covering his left hand. "What happened?" she asked, pointing at it.

He gave the bandage a glance. "Hurt it."

They stood like opponents, facing each other across the small expanse of the living room, but between them was a sense of seeking, of needing to find a way to breach that gulf. He hadn't come to fight with her. He'd come to offer solace when he'd heard about Tori's car. He'd come to hold her, and no matter what doubts she still harbored, Tess desperately wished he would.

He lifted his hands, palms up. "So what now?"

She looked helplessly into his eyes, captivated by the gold-flecked gray swirling within them. "I don't know."

"Do you want me to go?"

"I don't know what I want anymore. I mean—well, you were right. I don't know you from . . ." Adam, she'd been about to say. *I don't know you from Adam.* "I don't know you at all."

His pause felt baited, alluring in its very existence. When he spoke, his voice was strong and low. She found herself wanting to lean closer, to catch the breath of it. "Yes," he said. "You do. You know me."

Dry mouthed, she shook her head.

"Then why do I feel like you should?" he said, at last closing the distance between them. "Why is it that something about you keeps at me? Every instinct I have is telling me you're as much trouble as your sister. Trouble I don't need. But then I look into your eyes and I feel like . . ." He shook his head slowly, not looking away. "Like I've been waiting for you." He let loose a short laugh. "Sounds like a crappy pickup line, doesn't it?"

It should have, but of course it didn't. Hadn't she felt it from the moment she'd met him? That undeniable pull that was stronger than reason?

She stared at him, standing there in his faded blue jeans, scuffed boots, and denim button-down. He looked like any honest, hardworking Joe that Hollywood had ever dressed down and passed off as the real thing. And that's what worried her. Images were deceiving. Still, he mesmerized her, convincing her with one look that he was what she needed him to be.

She gave herself a mental shake, trying to focus on the moment. The here. The now. But she couldn't. It felt as if the hue of that other life had cast a glow on him and she was incapable of looking away.

"Don't be afraid of me, Blue Eyes," he murmured, reaching out to cup her face in his hands. His bandage was rough against her skin, his fingers warm. The look in his eyes sucked Tess into a world of swirling colors and unlikely truth. And she felt her last ounce of willpower give way.

"I'm not," she whispered. "I'm not."

His mouth settled over hers with undeniable possession. It was as if the doubt didn't exist. As if the kisses in his truck had never stopped. Her arms went to his neck; her fingers curled in his hair. In her mind, past and present melded into one, and she was Molly, kissing Grant; she was Tess, holding Adam.

She felt weightless and realized he'd lifted her. She wrapped herself around him and deepened their kiss as his hands slipped low to her hips. He crossed to the couch without taking his mouth from hers and followed her down to the soft, cushioned length of it.

His hands slid beneath her shirt to cup her breasts while hers fought their way under his clothes. Her fingers hesitated at the button fly of his jeans and then they were each shedding the last barriers until the only thing separating them was the heat of their skin. Each touch, each movement, overcame her as past and present were woven together. She was overwhelmed by feelings of displacement and intense belonging. He stared at her, his eyes glowing like pewter, so like Adam's.

Why hadn't she noticed it before? Her two worlds slammed together into that one moment. Then the soft hair that veed from his chest to his belly pressed against the sensitive skin of her ribs and stomach and it no longer mattered who or when or where they were.

The hard muscles of his biceps flexed as he shifted over her. His lips found hers again and in his kisses were whispered words that seemed to answer every pulsing question that raced through her body. She heard her groan of pleasure echoed as the contact between them became a connection and she was lost in sensation. Her arms moved to his back and swept down the dip of his spine to the rise of his buttocks. She pulled him closer and deeper, and she heard him whisper her name as he drew in his breath and released it.

They began to move together in rhythm with their clamoring hearts and frantic breath. She was caught in a hot spiral that coiled tighter and tighter until every inch of her was taut with the tension. And then he thrust deep with a growl low in his throat. Whatever it was between them, he could control it no more than she could. The realization released the tightness inside her in a wash of dark, liquid waves.

For a long time, they lay locked together, slick with sweat and rubber-limbed.

"Tell me you don't know me," he challenged, his voice low and hoarse.

She didn't need to speak the words because he saw the answer on her face. Yes, she knew him. She always had.

chapter thirty-five

THE day had ticked by slowly, but when she was in Grant's arms, the minutes seemed to speed past in a blur. Before she was ready to release him, it was time to go.

"I have to pick up Caitlin. I don't want to be late. She'll worry."

He kissed her again and helped her to her feet. They watched each other as they pulled on their clothes. She buttoned his shirt, letting her fingers linger on his chest. The steady beat of his heart matched her own. The moment felt solid, enduring. She felt as if her entire life had been spent searching and at last she'd found what she needed.

"I don't want you to stay here tonight," he said, his lips teasing the sensitive flesh behind her ears. "Not after last night."

She went suddenly still. "How do you know what happened last night?"

"Ochoa told me."

Of course. Together they stepped outside. As she reached back to close the front door, a flashing light caught her eye. Frowning, she stared at the telephone with its attached answering machine. The number one was blinking. Like an ancient memory, the sound of a woman's voice telling Tess to call her surfaced. Grant turned as she hurried back inside and played the message. He frowned at the cryptic words. "Is that Lydia?" he asked.

Tess nodded. "I think so . . . she sounds strange, though, doesn't she?" The message was hasty and whispered,

as if Lydia was afraid she would be overheard by someone. The message beeped off and Tess glanced at her watch.
If she didn't leave now, she'd be late. "I'll have to talk to her
later. Right now, Caitlin's waiting."

chapter thirty-six

IRONICALLY, it wasn't the smell that brought them to Lydia's bed-and-breakfast. It was the lack of it.

As Walter McKinnley told Deputy Ochoa when the cruiser pulled to a stop, "I saw that her 'open' sign wasn't flipped and I knew something was wrong. I've been having my afternoon coffee and muffin here ever since she opened shop. She's got me so I'm addicted to her coffee and it just wasn't like her to take off without notice."

He glanced at the "closed" sign forlornly. "I know something has to be wrong. And with her being . . . well, I was afraid she'd slipped and broken her leg or something. I looked in back for her car and it's still parked right where it always is."

"It was good you called us, Walter," Hector said, patting the old man on his shoulder.

Hector followed Smith to the front door, wondering at the sheriff's tight-lipped silence. He hadn't said a word since the dispatch came through.

"Lydia?" Smith called and pounded loudly on the door. "It's Sheriff Smith. Are you in there? Are you hurt?"

They waited in the silence for an answer that didn't come.

"I tried that," Walter said. "I knocked and rang already."

"That's good, Walter," Hector told him. "Why don't you go on home now? We'll call you if we need you for anything."

Walter looked less than happy with the suggestion, but a glance at his watch seemed to confirm that he did, indeed, need to be on his way. Reluctantly, he climbed behind the wheel of his Malibu and drove off.

Hector trailed Smith around the renovated house to the

back door, which led into Lydia's kitchen. Smith pounded on the sliding door, trying to peer through the sheer curtain that covered the glass. Hector noticed another window with a view of the backyard and no curtain, but the ground beneath it sloped down sharply. He had to jump and grab the ledge to look in. He only got a glimpse, but that was all it took to justify Walter's concern. Lydia hadn't simply gone away or decided to close down early that day.

"Looks like a tornado went through there," he said, jumping up for a second time. "Looks like it went through twice."

By silent agreement they circled back to the front. Smith pulled his club from his belt, smacked it firmly against a pane of glass, and then reached in to unlock the door.

"Lydia? It's Sheriff Smith. You in there, Lydia?"

Broken glass crunched beneath their shoes as they stepped inside the foyer. The drawn curtains gave the house a cave-like atmosphere. The quiet made it feel like a tomb. Mixed in with the window glass large chunks of porcelain littered the floor.

"What's that smell?" Hector asked, not really wanting to know the answer.

They rounded the corner to the kitchen braced for the worst, but what they saw was so chaotic that at first they couldn't tell if they'd found it. Opened cupboards lined two walls and their contents spilled out everywhere. A bag of flour had crashed to the counter and then the floor, spewing white dust all over the kitchen. Fat, sluggish flies buzzed in and out of the sticky batter in a large blue mixing bowl. On a tiny round table, a half-eaten pie oozed gooey apple filling, as if the pie pan had been tossed from across the room and landed with a plop on the table.

"We should get someone in here," Hector said.

Smith made a sound of disgust. "Like the health inspector?"

Alarm bells were ringing in Hector's head as he followed Smith through the disaster zone and into the parlor. Every one of his instincts protested as Smith went around the room, touching things at random, making no effort to preserve the scene.

"Looks like there's been a struggle in the kitchen," Hector said.

"With the cleaning lady, maybe. Looks like she lost."

In the nook where Lydia set out her coffee and pastries, this morning's offerings still waited to be cleared. The coffee had simmered down to a blackened crust at the bottom of the pots. Smith stepped carefully through the broken cups on the floor and switched off the burners.

Lydia's private rooms were in the back of the first floor. The bed was made, the bedroom tidy. In the bathroom, the towels all hung at perfect angles, cosmetic bottles made a precise line on the sink, and her toothpaste and brush were neatly placed in the holder.

"If she went somewhere, she forgot her toothbrush," Hector said.

Smith made a noncommittal sound and gave him a look of indulgence that was insulting. If Hector wasn't playing cops and robbers, he was assessing a potential crime scene.

They moved upstairs, looking at the empty rooms. Up here, everything was in order. In one of the rooms the beds had been turned down and mints set on the pillows.

"She was expecting someone," Hector said.

"Looks that way."

"That doesn't seem weird to you?"

"This is a bed-and-breakfast. She's supposed to have guests."

"Then why isn't she here?"

"Maybe she ate herself into a coma."

"That's bullshit," Hector said. "This isn't rocket science, Sheriff."

"It's not a crime scene either."

Angry, Hector followed Smith back to the kitchen. The place had a sweet, faintly rotten smell. Not surprising with all the half-eaten food sitting out. He stepped inside the walk-in pantry at the far corner, looking for what, he didn't know. All he found was shelf after shelf of canned, bagged, dried foods and, against one side, a freezer chest big enough to keep a side of beef frozen solid. The busiest of restaurants would consider itself well stocked with a pantry like that.

"Maybe she took a walk," Smith was saying.

Hector stepped out of the pantry, and scanned the kitchen. To his right was a walk-in refrigerator. In front of it there were footprints in the spilled flour. Had he and Smith made them or— Before he could speak up, Smith tromped through them.

"Maybe she rolled down the hill and can't get up," Smith said, laughing.

Hector glared from the destroyed prints to Smith to the oversized refrigerator. Suddenly a wave of horror washed over him.

"Shit," he said, striding forward.

"What?"

The smile vanished from Smith's face when Hector pulled the handle and the door swung open with a gust of chilled air. What he saw within made him stumble back with a gasp. He heard Smith rush up from behind, but he couldn't take his eyes off the refrigerator floor.

"Jesus Christ," Smith said as he drew level. "God dammit to hell."

chapter thirty-seven

TESS pulled into the parking lot and sat, waiting for the bell to go off. Raindrops plunked down on the windshield sporadically. In the distance, lightning snaked over the mountain peaks and low thunder rumbled. She couldn't tell if another big storm was brewing or if this one was blowing away.

She still felt warm from the touch of Grant's hands on her skin, but it was chilly in the car. Chilly in her thoughts. She didn't know what was right anymore. A part of her, the rational part of her, urged her to take Caitlin and get the hell out of Mountain Bend. But on the heels of that, came too many questions. What about Tori? What about the life she'd lived before? What about figuring out why all this was happening? What about Grant and the certainty that she would die if she couldn't be with him again?

A Lexus pulled into the space by hers, driver's side to driver's side. Craig rolled down his window. She did the same.

"We've got to stop meeting like this," he said, but his smile didn't reach his eyes.

"Did you make all the arrangements for your father?"

He nodded. "You stayed at the church grounds for a while today."

His expression held a hint of accusation. She ignored it.

"The service will be tomorrow?"

"Yes. And then everyone in town will end up at my house. There's no avoiding it, but it's the last thing I want."

"Why will everyone go there? Surely if you said something . . ."

"My dad was the kind of man who took care of people.

They'll want to come by and tell me personally how he helped them."

That description didn't fit with the one Grant had given of a violent, abusive father. She wasn't surprised. It was just one more inconsistency in this house of mirrors.

"He sounds like he was a special man," she said.

"Special? Yeah, I guess he was. He was never too busy for a friend. He worked his land and then went to his neighbor's and helped them work theirs."

"But that was years ago."

"People don't forget." He wiped his eyes and looked away. "How is Caitlin?"

"She's okay. As well as can be expected."

"Have you decided what you'll do next?"

"I was just thinking about that. I don't know."

He shifted so he could look deeply into her eyes, refusing to let her look away. "I can't stand you being in danger. It keeps me up at night, you know that?"

"I can take care of myself."

"But sometimes people aren't what they seem, Tess. I know I'm just a simple elementary school principal. There's nothing glamorous about what I do. There's nothing glamorous about me at all. But I'm a good man. The kind that comes home after work. The kind that pays my bills and helps my neighbor when he needs it."

"Like your father."

"I'm the kind of man you can depend on to be there," he said. "I know that's not exactly the stuff that sweeps a girl off her feet, but maybe it should be."

What he said went deeper than the words. He was speaking to her fears, and he knew their language.

"Things have never come easy to me, not like they have for Grant. Maybe that's why I appreciate a good thing when I see it much more than he'll ever be able to."

"Is that what bothers you about him? Everything is easy for him?"

"Maybe. Maybe it's just jealousy, and thinking it's anything more is my way of justifying it. But I hope not. I think the real problem isn't that it comes easy. It's that it goes the same way."

"What do you mean?"

"We've been trying to steal each other's thunder since we were in diapers. We fought over our mother's love, we fought over our father's love, we fought over girls. We fought over women."

Women. Plural. Tess couldn't help the sinking feeling the word brought.

"Back in high school, Lydia and I used to be an item. She was tiny and she was a beauty and I loved her. Every boy wanted to date her, but she chose me. Grant couldn't live with that."

"High school was a long time ago, Craig."

He shook his head. "Don't misunderstand me. I'm not holding a grudge over a lost girlfriend. It's not that. I can live with him trying to take her away. Hell, I can even live with him succeeding. But once he had her, he used her and then he threw her away like trash. She was the American sweetheart and he destroyed her."

"That's a pretty heavy sentence, Craig. We all did stupid things when we were young."

"I know. But Grant never stopped. He still strings her along and she still thinks he loves her. The more I thought about what you said today—about Lydia being engaged—the more I wondered if it was Grant. Grant, still playing her."

Tess swallowed, feeling as if she couldn't catch her breath.

"Don't tell me you never heard about him and his ex-wife?" Craig continued.

Of course she had. Anyone who watched TV or read a newspaper had heard about it. He'd married a starlet who was as breathtaking as he. They'd been the shimmer on every party. The movie magazines had loved them. The paparazzi had caught them in every act imaginable. Still, they'd managed to escape censor until the spiral of alcoholism had become a corkscrew roller coaster. They began fighting in public, making scenes anywhere, anytime. And then the affairs began for both of them. Tess remembered how, for a solid week, even the legitimate news shows had covered the gossip. But again, that was years ago.

"When he drove their car through their garage and out the back, he could have killed them both," Craig said. "If it had been you or me driving, we'd have done time. Grant walked away and the only casualty was his marriage. He didn't stop making movies. He didn't stop making money. He certainly didn't *start* sending any of that money home, even though Dad was barely keeping his head above water paying his mortgage."

"Grant said he did send money."

The look Craig gave her was filled with sympathy. "Grant says a lot of things."

She didn't know how to respond to that, how to express what she felt at that moment.

"I know he has your head spinning right now, but all that leaves you in the end is dizzy. I promise you, when the going gets tough, Grant won't be there for you. But Tess . . . I will. I'll be there. I just want you to know that."

Keeping her eyes on her white-knuckled hands, she nodded.

The bell rang and Craig sighed. "If you need anything, I'm here," he said before rolling up his window and stepping out of his car. She watched him walk away in the spitting rain. A moment later the school's doors burst open to release a flood of ponytails and backpacks. Taking a deep breath, Tess got out of the car and looked for her niece.

chapter thirty-eight

TESS stepped through Tori's front door completely exhausted. The scent of the sausage casserole she'd made for Grant that morning lingered in the air, mocking the optimism with which she'd made it. Caitlin dropped her backpack and headed upstairs to her room. Tess followed the slanted sunrays to the kitchen, where she leaned against the counter and tried to get a grip.

The dishes she'd washed earlier sat in the strainer where she'd left them to dry. The cupboards were all closed, the counters clean and shining, but a wad of white fluff perched at the edge of the sink. Frowning, she moved forward. More of the damp and matted stuff filled the sink and clung to the sides, but she had no idea what it was or how it got there. Wrinkling her nose, she picked up a clump of it and rubbed it between her fingers. It felt like the fiber that filled pillows and—

"Jesus Lord," she whispered.

A piece of orange-and-yellow-patterned cloth stuck up from the dark hole of the garbage disposal. It bore a peculiar resemblance to the ear of—

"Aunt Tess? Have you seen Purcy?" Caitlin called from upstairs.

No . . . Tess reached into the sink and pulled on the soggy triangular shape. Up popped what was left of Purcy's head.

"Aunt Tess?"

Stifling a scream, Tess pushed it back down and turned to face Caitlin as the child stepped into the kitchen with a worried frown and said, "I always leave him on my bed when I go to school, but he's not there."

"I haven't seen him," Tess managed, but the lie felt chalky on her tongue. She turned her back to the sink and Purcy's mangled remains.

"Maybe I left him in Mommy's room," Caitlin said. "I'll look some more."

Tess waited until her footsteps made it up the stairs before she faced the sink again. The chewed-up remains immobilized her with fear that went deeper than any she'd felt so far. This threat could not be misinterpreted. Whoever had made it played without rules.

She didn't know how they'd gotten in. Deputy Ochoa had sent someone out to put a new lock on the back door and the bolt was thrown, the door secure. The same for the front door— she'd had to unlock it when she'd come home with Caitlin. The windows were closed. Yet someone had been inside the house. Someone who didn't think their first threat had been received.

She spun around, scanning the rooms behind her. Quietly she went upstairs, peeking in at Caitlin in her room before checking Tori's room. She looked under the bed and in the closets and bathroom. No one was there.

A shudder of relief went through her, though she hadn't re-ally expected to find the culprit. So far the threats had been delivered in a cowardly manner. Whoever was behind them wanted to scare her off, but not engage her.

Their tactics were working. She was frightened.

She reached for the phone to call the sheriff and had an-other realization. The answering machine read zero. She hadn't deleted Lydia's message before she left, but it was gone now.

She lifted the receiver and called Information. While the operator connected her to Lydia's number, she scanned the kitchen, looking for anything else out of place. On the other end, the phone rang. No one answered.

She hung up as Caitlin came downstairs. "I still can't find Purcy."

Tess stared at Caitlin, her heart breaking at the desolation she saw in her eyes. But what could she say? Keep looking? He'll show up?

"I'm sorry, honey," she managed as she crossed the room to comfort her. The eyes in the Jesus picture followed her with censure, seeming to condemn her. How had Tori managed to live day to day with those judging eyes watching her? How had the image managed to retain its position on her irreverent sister's wall in the first place? It was tacky and creepy and absolutely out of place.

"Did your mom like that picture?" Tess asked Caitlin, looking at it over her head.

Caitlin shrugged. "She said it was perfect when she brought it home."

"You mean *she* bought it?"

Caitlin nodded.

"When? Recently or right after you got here?"

"I guess it wasn't that long ago. We'd lived here awhile."

Frowning, Tess stared at the eerie print. Why on earth would Tori—

And then it came to her. "Jesus," she murmured.

chapter thirty-nine

HECTOR'S insides felt like beef jerky after he and Smith found Lydia Hughes dead in her walk-in refrigerator. Her body was battered and bloated, gruesome even with the preservation of the refrigerator in play. That she'd been murdered was brutally obvious. That he and Smith had trampled the crime scene like a pair of cartoon cops made it all the worse. What had they taught him at the academy? What did they pound into his thick head over and over again? Always preserve and protect the crime scene, no matter what. Hector was glad his old sergeant wasn't here to see his performance today.

After he'd found her, Hector had gone outside and thrown up like the rookie he was. He'd heaved until he was empty. Then he kicked dirt over his mess and vowed that he would never again be sick because of his incompetence. He'd known that Lydia's disappearance was more than a Saturday stroll and he'd ignored his instinct. He would not make that mistake again.

Shaken but determined, he went back inside Lydia's kitchen. The smell of the place had fermented into the reek of blunder and the stench of violent death. It took all his resolve to face it again. Smith was standing just outside the refrigerator and he put a hand up to block Hector's entrance. He looked a little worried himself about the mistakes they'd made.

"We should call this in," Hector said.

"Already did."

Cool air wafted from the open refrigerator and on it the sharp scent of ground coffee overrrode the pervasive smell of death.

Frowning, Hector leaned in and identified the source. One section of the refrigerator was dominated by twenty or so bags of coffee beans. Below them, labeled and dated plastic containers filled with ground coffee waited to be brewed. One of the containers had been knocked down and spilled over the floor.

"Do you see what I see?" Smith asked, pointing.

Lydia lay on her back with her right arm draped across her chest, as if she'd tried to roll onto her side but had flopped back before she'd made it. Her right hand was clenched and it looked like a colorful strip of paper or plastic was clasped inside.

Mouth dry, Hector looked at the pile of spilled coffee beside her and back to her hand. He felt sick thinking of how he and Smith had barged in, checked for a pulse, almost tried to move her. He'd been so focused on Lydia, he hadn't even noticed the coffee. But for the grace of God, they both might have walked right through it.

Smith squatted down. "Look there, wedged up under her arm."

Hector crouched down beside him and looked. Hidden between Lydia's arm and breast was a half-roll of LifeSavers candy. The bright scrap in her fist was a piece of the wrapper.

They exchanged glances and stood.

"Christ," Smith said. "This is one hell of a mess."

Hector stared at Lydia and the bit of striped candy wrapper in her hand. He'd seen Grant Weston pull out his roll of LifeSavers a dozen times, but that didn't mean he was the only one in town who ate them.

"I want to search Weston's place," Smith said, as if to himself.

"The judge isn't going to issue a warrant based on a candy wrapper."

"You're right, but that isn't all I plan to base it on. Craig Weston said he came here for some coffee yesterday and found his brother knocking Lydia around. Apparently he's had a closet relationship with her since he moved back from L.A."

"What do you mean?"

"Men who abuse their women don't like others to know about it. I saw it all the time in Chicago. Guys who seemed too uptight to get their hair messed up could beat their wives to a bloody pulp."

Hector looked at the bruises and cuts that covered Lydia's arms.

"From where I'm standing, I'd say Grant let things get out of control."

"When did Craig tell you this?" Hector asked.

"Yesterday."

Angry that Smith hadn't shared the information earlier, Hector listened to the sheriff request the warrant to search Grant Weston's property for evidence linking him to the murder of Lydia Hughes and the disappearance of Tori France. Smith managed to make it sound as if they'd found evidence of Grant everywhere rather than a circumstantial LifeSaver wrapper clutched in her hand. As Smith ended the call, the sound of sirens in the distance heralded the arrival of help from Piney River.

"You exaggerated the circumstances quite a bit," Hector said.

Smith gave a heavy sigh and faced his deputy. "Ochoa, this is how it works. We have to prove someone is guilty or they don't go to jail—"

"I know that."

"If we don't get the evidence, we can't prove anything. The warrant just allows us to look for it. If Weston is clean, there's nothing we're going to find, right? I'm just trying to stack the deck so it's even, bad guy/good guy. Sometimes you got to bend the rules a little to do that. Understand?"

Red-faced, Hector nodded.

Smith met the forensics crew on the porch and produced reasonable excuses and explanations for the fiasco he and Hector had made of the crime scene. As he listened, Hector felt shamed.

"Let's go back to the station and let them do their job," Smith said when he'd finished. "They've got this covered and I want to know the minute that warrant comes through."

They didn't have to wait long. Within the hour they were on their way.

Gravel crunched beneath their tires as Smith pulled into the horseshoe drive at the Weston ranch and stopped. He had the warrant in his pocket and a look of satisfaction on his face. Hector thought he was acting like this was a game of wits, not a murder investigation, but what could he say? Maybe Smith was right—maybe Hector should straighten up and get in the game too.

Pausing as he reached for the door, he gave Hector a meaningful glance. "Let me do the talking," he said.

"We're supposed to wait for backup," Hector answered.

The sheriff paused, looking impatient. "I've served warrants to drug dealers and murderers and mothers who sell their babies, Ochoa. I don't need some puke from Piney River holding my hand now."

He slammed the car door and started up the porch. Cursing, Hector followed. Grant opened the door with an expression that changed from anticipation to surprise in a way that convinced Hector he'd been expecting someone other than the two law enforcement officers on his stoop. He made a sound of disgust and ran his fingers through his hair. There was a white bandage on his left hand.

Smith didn't waste time with niceties. "Got a warrant to search your house, Grant."

"For what?"

"The body of Tori France," Smith replied, stretching the truth beyond recognition.

"That's bullshit," Grant answered.

"Could be, but we've got a warrant all the same."

Smith pulled it out and handed it over. With barely a glance, Grant threw open the door and gave them a sweep of his hand that both invited them to enter and dared them to cross the threshold. Despite his vows not to go against his instincts, Hector followed Smith inside. He could return to the cruiser and wait for back up, but that would leave Smith on his own, which Hector suspected would be an even bigger mistake.

Before the door swung shut again, they heard a car approaching the house. Craig Weston's blue Lexus pulled to a stop in the drive.

"What's he doing here?" Hector asked.

Smith shrugged. "How the hell should I know?"

"I just heard," Craig said as he came up to the porch. His eyes were red and swollen, his face pale and streaked with tears. He shook his head and looked at Grant with a mixture of disillusionment and disgust. "Why did you have to come back?"

"Craig, you shouldn't be here," Smith said in a calm voice. "I'm going to have to ask you to leave now."

"Are you arresting him?" Craig asked.

"This isn't your business. Go home."

Craig exhaled and shook his head. A look passed between him and the sheriff. Hector frowned.

"I saw what you did to her yesterday," Craig said, looking at Grant. "I don't know who you think you are but . . ." He made a sound of frustration and grief. "She was my friend, Grant. I cared about her and you couldn't stand that, could you?"

"Craig . . ." Smith interrupted.

Hector moved forward, intending to take Craig by the arm and escort him to his car, but the sheriff put a hand out and stopped him. Grant stared at the sheriff, then at Craig, then back again. His brows were drawn together, and his face was white.

"You're not going to ride off into the sunset this time," Craig said softly. "You don't get the girl, the ranch, the happily ever after. Not this time."

Just as Smith reached out, Craig shook his head and turned away. "I know, I'm going."

He started back to his car, stumbling once, as if his pain made walking too difficult. Before Craig reached the Lexus, Grant began to clap. The sharp sound echoed loudly in the quiet. Craig spun around and glared.

"You missed your calling, Craig," Grant said. "You're a hell of an actor, I'll give you that. But I don't buy it. You've never cared about anyone but yourself."

No one said a word for a moment. Then Craig got in his car, slammed the door, and drove off in a cloud of dust and gravel.

When Hector turned, he caught the sheriff staring at him, and with a flash of intuition Hector realized that Smith was

trying to gauge his reaction, trying to see what he was thinking. Something had happened just now that had nothing to do
with the actual events and Smith knew it. Hector looked down,
trying to replay everything that had occurred since Craig
pulled up to the house.

"Let's take a look around," Smith said with calm authority.

Like a small parade, the threesome made their way into the
house. A dark room to the right of the door resembled a set
from a western movie. Gleaming wooden floors, burnished
cherry tables, and thick, velvet furniture centered around a
snarling bear rug. Floor-to-ceiling bookcases flanked the massive fireplace, and heavily shaded lamps skirted the outer
reaches. In one corner stood a polished mahogany bar. Behind it
were empty glass shelves that should have held gleaming bottles of premium liquors. Centered on the wall above the bar, an
etched mirror recommended that they do their shootin' with
José Cuervo. Word had it that Grant had taken that advice more
than once.

Smith looked about with interest, like a fan on a star maps
tour. He strolled the circumference of the room with a studied
nonchalance, stopping here and there to examine an object or
touch the frame of a painting. Grant tracked the sheriff's
movements with justifiably hostile eyes. Smith was toying with
Grant and they all knew it. Finally, he started down the back
hall.

"We found Lydia Hughes this morning," he said in an off-
hand tone, glancing back over his shoulder at Grant.

"Good for you," Grant answered.

"Found her in the kitchen."

"You're one hell of a detective."

Smith stopped so suddenly that Grant almost plowed into
his back. He faced Grant with a stiff spine and a cold expression. "Found her *body*, I guess I should've said."

Hector was watching Grant, so there was no mistake about
his reaction. Grant floundered and caught himself against the
wall. His face paled to match his gray eyes, which widened
with horror.

"She's dead?"

"Either that or she's doing a mighty fine imitation of it."

Then Smith turned and continued down the hall. Hector watched Grant pull away from the wall. For just a moment, he met Hector's eyes and Hector saw something slice through Grant's shock. If pressed, he would have to say it was fear. But what struck Hector the most was that Grant didn't ask how Lydia died. He didn't ask when. He simply followed Smith down the hall without another word.

chapter forty

TESS reached for the picture of Jesus and lifted it from its hook. It was so cheap that the flimsy frame wobbled in her hands. She took it to the kitchen and set it facedown on the table.

When she saw the envelope taped to its back, a feeling of irritation made her want to shout. From the moment she'd walked into Tori's house, she'd known that something was wrong with the picture being there. Why hadn't she thought to take it down and look at it before? Caitlin hovered at her elbow watching as Tess pulled the envelope free and opened it.

"What's that?" she asked.

Tess had half expected her niece to make another casual confession about knowing the envelope was taped to the back of the frame, but Caitlin peered at it with open curiosity.

"Let's see," Tess said, opening it up. Inside was a key, a sheet of notebook paper, several photocopied documents as well as a newspaper article, and a hand-drawn map. She set them all on the table.

She looked at the copied documents first. The words "Pine County" were on the top of each one, followed by line after line of numbers. They appeared to be tax records of some sort. She scanned through several pages before setting them down and picking up the piece of paper that had been torn from a notebook. It was covered in Tori's loping scrawl. Tess scanned the page. Grant's name jumped out at her and, next to it, the word "MONEY" in all capital letters. Tori had listed dates. There were question marks next to every third one, then every other. What did that mean? And then at the bottom of the page she had written the words "church fire," and circled them.

Her mouth was dry as she reached for the photocopied article. It was from the *Piney River Daily,* dated December 20, 1978. Tess skimmed the clipping that detailed the fire and tragedy. The words furthered the images that Craig's telling had evoked.

"I know where the key goes," Caitlin said.

Startled, Tess faced her. "You do?"

Nodding, Caitlin led her upstairs to the rug in the hallway. She got on her knees and pulled it back. Under it was a hatch. Tess tugged it open to reveal a lockbox inside a small cubbyhole. She pulled it out and took it downstairs to the table.

The box required both a key and a combination. She stuck the key in the lock and dialed the date of Tori's birthday, then Caitlin's, then her own. None of them worked.

"You don't know the combination, do you?" she asked Caitlin.

Caitlin shook her head. Tess closed her eyes and thought again. She tried the Colonel's birthday and then their mother's. Frustrated, she sat back. And then she had an idea. Carefully she turned the dial to eighteen, then four, and nine. 1849, the year Vanessa died. The lock made a small clicking sound and the lid popped open.

Inside were stacks of neatly bound bills, each bundled with a ten-thousand-dollar band. There must have been over a half-million dollars in there. Brandon Forsythe's money. If Tori had left on her own, why hadn't she taken it with her?

"Wow. We're rich," Caitlin said.

"Did you know about this?"

"Mommy showed me the box, but I didn't know what was in it."

Tess pushed the safe back a bit and reached for the last item that had been taped onto the back of Jesus. The map was crudely drawn, with little triangle shapes representing mountains and squares grouped to represent towns. Pine County and its borders were identified with a thick dashed line. Mountain Bend and Piney River perched like twin jewels in the midst of the mountainous setting. A large red circle enclosed the expanse between the two towns. Tori had written "Winter Haven" in its center. In a lighter hand, she'd outlined sections of property that butted up to "Winter Haven." She'd labeled the first section "Weston Ranch/to G." The ranch spread like a stain over the majority of the space. Off to the side was a substantial piece of property labeled "L. Hughes." Beside that a larger oblong area was labeled "E. Smith." And finally a tiny parcel that only just touched the Winter Haven area was labeled "C. W." Tori had used the side of a pencil to shade in the pie-shaped plot where this house stood.

With a feeling that was part disbelief and part certainty, Tess went back to the notebook paper and scanned it again. There was a note scrunched in the corner. It said, "Lydia, mortgaged out." Beneath it, she read, "Eugene Smith—where'd he get the money?" Tess frowned. She knew who Lydia was, of course, but who was Eugene Smith?

She thought for a moment. *Sheriff* Smith?

She knew the number by heart now and without hesitation she dialed the sheriff's station. A woman answered and Tess asked for Eugene.

"You mean Sheriff Smith?" the woman asked with a wicked cackle. "You better not call him Eugene or he's likely to shoot you. Hold on, I'll see if he's back."

Tess hung up as soon as she heard the line click to hold. Caitlin had seated herself at the table and waited patiently while Tess sorted through the papers again.

"Did you figure it out yet?" she asked after a moment.

"No, but . . . Have you ever heard of Winter Haven?"

"Uh-huh. It's a place."

"What kind of place?"

"There's nothing there yet. Mommy and me went there to see it once. We had a picnic and Mommy said they were going to make it a place to go skiing right where we were sitting."

Tess nodded. A proposed ski resort between Mountain Bend and Piney River. With resorts came tourists who needed hotels and restaurants. And, of course, that meant land to put them on.

She let out a deep breath and looked back at the papers on the table. From the tax records she learned that last year Lydia and Smith had both bought up the parcels of land between the two towns like it was beach front property on a golden coast. But the miles that divided Winter Haven from everything Smith and Lydia now owned had belonged to Frank Weston. Up until his death, that is. Now they belonged to Grant.

Not liking where that took her, Tess studied the map some more. *If* Winter Haven became a resort, the property around it would be valuable. However, without the Weston ranch in the loop, the land belonging to Lydia and Smith would be outreaches, accessible only by roundabout routes that would make them seem more distant than they actually were. The Weston ranch was the key.

The records of sale for both Smith's and Lydia's purchases were not top-secret information. County records could be accessed over the Internet. So why had Tori felt the information needed to be guarded, hidden behind the picture? Had she discovered that the sheriff and Lydia were involved in some kind of swindle? Perhaps Frank Weston hadn't been in favor of turning his ranch into a tourist trap and the two had—what? And where did Grant and Craig fit into the puzzle? She looked down at Tori's writing. "Weston Ranch/to G."

Craig had told her that Grant didn't want the ranch tied up in probate by a lengthy investigation. And then he'd said maybe Grant didn't want the investigation for other reasons.

What other reasons? Could Grant have been in partnership with Smith and Lydia to pull the ranch into their business venture regardless of his father's wishes? If so, to what lengths had he been willing to go to secure his investment?

Tess's mouth felt dry. Surely not as far as murder? God, no. No. Everything inside her rebelled at the very idea of it. He wasn't capable of murder. He couldn't be.

But that wasn't true. He could be involved, whether or not she wanted him to be. Tori had a reason for hiding these documents. It wasn't a leap to connect them with her disappearance. The question was, which of the cohorts had suspected her of gathering this information about them? And what had they done about it?

And what about Tori's money? Did Grant know that in addition to funding her job at the ranch, Brandon Forsythe had paid Tori a large chunk of change? Could Grant be that desperate for money?

She looked out the window, seeing nothing but her own confusion. A rush of images came at her, mixing past with present. Tori, Vanessa, the Reverend, the Colonel, Adam, Brodie— And then the images honed down to only the past, only Molly and her group of travelers as they straggled across the miles of open country. In snapshots she saw them reach the South Pass, cross the Continental Divide, spend day after day futilely hoping for better water, better feed for their animals, less sickness, less death. Each day was filled with filth and stench. Tess could smell the alkali-poisoned waters, so deadly that even the grass at its banks could kill, as Molly trudged by them.

In a blink of Tess's eyes, Molly and the rest reached the Great Salt Lake Valley, where the mountains coddled the enormous lake, keeping it hidden like a magical place. Steep canyon walls and tight, rough turns marked every step. The dust was thick yet light as powder. It coated them all from head to toe, making them look like they'd been floured for the frying pan.

"We're there," Caitlin whispered.

Her voice came through the onslaught of imagery, but it wasn't strong enough to pull Tess back. Still, she managed to turn her head, managed to meet the rounded eyes of her niece. Caitlin's expression sent a shudder through Tess even as Molly forged westward. Wherever "there" was, they'd reached it together.

"Where, Caity? Where are we?"

"Bad guy," Caitlin breathed.

A sound at the door joined the melee in Tess's head. She felt sluggish as she turned away from Caitlin's terrified face to find Craig standing just outside the screen. They must not have pulled the door closed all the way and it had blown open, giving Craig a peek at them.

Bad guy.

Here or there?

Tess managed to the gather up the papers still strewn on the table, but the overpowering sensation of being pulled back to Molly's time would not recede. In Caitlin's face, she saw the same battle waged and lost. She just managed to convey a silent, *Don't say a word . . .* as she settled the Jesus picture over the papers and gleaned an acknowledgment from Caitlin before utter blankness blanched her small face.

How she managed next, she'd never know. But somehow she banked the past long enough to guide Caitlin into the other room and give her the nudge it took to settle her on the couch.

Still Molly fought for control. Tess couldn't keep this up; she couldn't fight it off.

Craig looked weary and grim as he watched her through the door, but he seemed oblivious to her turmoil. The dark screening made his features gritty, but through it she could see that his eyes were rimmed in red. "I need to talk to you," he said in a voice that was dry and gravelly.

She nodded, but it was already too late. In a moment she'd be gone, blank like Caitlin. She let him in, hurrying to the kitchen, where she sank in a chair as the past roared and pulled at her.

Craig's voice came from far away. His words followed her down, but there was nothing she could do to stop the plummeting fall. Nothing she could do until it was over.

"Tess, I've got bad news."

chapter forty-one

ON Sunday, the women did their washing. It was a back-breaking, tedious, and necessary chore. The fact that they all had to do it hardly made the task more bearable. Sunday was, after all, supposed to be a day of rest. But the very notion was laughable. There was no rest on the trail.

Molly had been determined to conquer the mending as well as the wash this Sunday, but there were only so many hours in the day and the sun was beginning to set earlier and earlier. Her nightmares had become more frequent and disturbing until they leached into the mornings and hung over her throughout the afternoon. She couldn't focus on anything beyond Arlie's whereabouts and safety. Even having him at her side was not enough. She worried constantly and carried dread like a stone in her heart. A storm was on the horizon and she knew when it struck the outcome would be terrible.

Dusk had glazed the sky to a silver gray by the time she removed the last of her clean clothes from the line and folded them. Armed with soap and towel, she took Arlie to the river as twilight deepened, turning the world into a mysterious place of shifting shadows and night sounds that heightened her tension and dogged her steps.

It was not possible to bathe completely, but she did her best each night to maintain some sense of cleanliness. After waters so bad that even boiling did not help, this bend of the Humboldt smelled fresh, and for once it wasn't gritty as the dusty air. She longed to wash away her uneasiness with the grime of the day.

Usually they were not alone in their nightly ablutions, for

there was but one river and many of the same mind to use it. But when she and Arlie reached the muddy bank, she found it surprisingly deserted. Under other circumstances Molly would have reveled in the thought of washing without an audience. Tonight, however, the seclusion felt like a foreboding. The hairs rose on the back of her neck, and a knot of anxiety tightened deep within her. Wishing she'd asked Adam to accompany them, she undressed Arlie and let him splash happily in the shallows.

The chirping crickets grated against her nerves and she found herself peering into the darkness. Every rustle of the breeze and each gurgle from the river held a menace that intensified her disquiet. A soft, furtive sound spun her around with the certainty that someone was there, watching her. She stared out until her vision blurred, knowing she was right. Directly to the left was an embankment that rose above her head and dipped down sharply on the other side. Was someone there, lying in wait? But nothing moved; not even a bird disturbed the stillness. Was she imagining things now? Seeing threats where none existed?

Rubbing the gooseflesh on her arms, she turned back to the river.

Only to come face to face with Brodie.

A startled shriek caught in her throat. He stood in front of her, holding Arlie by the hand. She lurched forward, reaching for the little boy as she demanded, "What do you want?"

Brodie sidestepped her easily, pulling Arlie out of reach. Even by moonlight she could see the wild look in his eyes. His jaw was clenched tight, his shoulders hunched, his stance hostile. Arlie squirmed like a hooked fish at the end of his arm.

"Go!" Arlie cried.

Brodie kept hold of Arlie's hand as he stared at Molly. His light eyes seemed to glow in the murk. "Why'd you have to do it?" he asked in a shaky voice. "Why'd you have to tell him those lies?"

Molly didn't attempt to argue, didn't endeavor to point out that it was truth, not lies, that she'd told. Instead she said simply, "She was my sister."

"She was a whore. She came here thinking she could pass her bastard kid off as Adam's, but she was wrong." He jerked Arlie's hand and the little boy stumbled into him.

"Let Arlie go," she said, amazed at the calm and commanding tone of her voice. Inside she was quaking.

"You'll be sorry if you tell him any more lies. I'll make you real sorry."

"I'm not afraid of you, Brodie. You're out of luck this time. Unless, of course, you plan to kill me as well? But you won't get away with it again, not now that Adam knows what you are."

This made him recoil but he recovered quickly. Her mouth was dry, her heart hammered painfully, and her skin felt like it had thinned to translucence with the exacting alarm that gripped her. Brodie watched her through hooded eyes that made her think of a hawk ready to swoop on its prey. He was assessing and she was powerless to deflect the knowing probe.

"You're not afraid of me?" he murmured, his words dripping like melted butter, clogging her pores with the fear of what he'd say next. "You don't wake up at night and think I might be watching you? Touching you?"

Her head was shaking in denial even as a voice inside her shouted with revulsion. Her skin took on a clammy chill while the blood beneath burned hot as coal.

"I know everything about you. What you do, who you talk to, where you go." Slowly, deliberately, he lifted Arlie into his arms. "I know what you like, what you hate. I know what's got meaning to you."

Angry at being manhandled, Arlie tried to push away but Brodie held him tight enough to make him whimper.

"Let him go," Molly said again, taking a step forward.

"No one knew about your sister. No one even thought twice about it. Why would they? Lord knows, I ain't got a mean bone in my body. Ask anyone and they'll tell you it's true." He nodded in agreement with himself. "Me and Adam had plans. Big plans to strike it rich and live like kings. You think I'm just going to let you ruin that?"

"Is that why you killed Vanessa? Because she meant

changing your stupid plan? Do you honestly think you can do it again and no one will be the wiser?"

Fed up with being ignored and trapped, Arlie smacked Brodie's face with his small hand. Without looking away from her, Brodie grabbed Arlie's face and turned it to his. The boy hiccupped and stilled, staring into the malevolent eyes of his uncle.

With measured movements, Brodie leaned in and planted a rough kiss on Arlie's forehead. The gesture held as much threat as a loaded gun, and the meaning ripped through Molly like a bullet. She understood his ominous message completely. Blood rushed to the white indents on Arlie's cheeks where Brodie's fingers had been and he let loose a cry of confusion and pain.

"Please put him down, Brodie."

"Please is it now?"

Her stomach plunged at his mocking tone. She licked her dry lips, staring helplessly at Arlie trapped in Brodie's arms. He was howling, his face red and frightened as he reached for her with outstretched hands.

"Don't do this. Brodie, please, let him go. He's just a baby. He never hurt anyone. Oh God, Brodie let him go—" Hot tears stung her eyes. She was begging, but what else could she do?

A sound came from the embankment beside them, catching them all unaware. Brodie snapped his head around and looked fiercely into the darkness.

Without missing a beat, Molly cried out, "Adam?"

It was a bluff, but a good one. Brodie jerked, squeezing another howl from Arlie. Molly prayed that someone at camp would hear the boy's cries, but she knew that the distance, the lowing animals, and the animated activity of the campers would no doubt hide any sounds made from so far away.

Brodie clamped a hand down over Arlie's mouth. His eyes shifted from Molly to the embankment to the shadows beyond and back. The moment stretched as the tension rose notch by notch. Then the sound came again, this time distinctive. Footsteps. Coming toward them or retreating, they couldn't tell.

Arlie squirmed and fought against the vicious embrace, but Brodie held tight.

Suddenly Arlie shouted, "Ay Ay!" There was a yelp and a black shape lunged over the rise straight at Molly. The scream in her throat exploded before she recognized Lady hurdling to a stop at her feet.

The dog stood poised before her, trembling and whining with distress, her loyalties clearly divided between the three. She knew that someone was in trouble, but she didn't know who. On the other side of the embankment, footsteps pummeled the ground and faded away.

"They're going back for help," Molly said triumphantly, praying to God she was right.

Brodie made a sound deep in his throat and swung Arlie roughly to the ground. Molly swooped, reaching for the boy with dizzying relief. But Brodie grabbed her arms in a grip tight enough to crack the bones and shook her so hard her neck snapped back and her teeth chattered together. Then he shoved her backward and she careened into the dirt.

Brodie was climbing the embankment before she realized what had happened. He paused at the top and looked back at her in warning. Molly knew without being told that their encounter was far from finished, but his words sliced her to her soul.

"Better watch over him," he said. "Bad things happen all the time on the trail."

chapter forty-two

MOLLY wasted no time scooping up Arlie and racing back to camp with Lady dashing at her side. Arlie sobbed in her arms, but only when she'd reached the safety of the wagons did she pause to comfort him.

"Are you hurt?" she asked. Eyes round and damp, Arlie shook his head. Tears burned her eyes as she hugged him to her. His clothes were still beside the river with their towels and soap, but she would not go back for either. Brodie might have returned. He might be waiting to . . . to . . . She dropped into Mrs. Imogene's rocking chair and held Arlie in her lap. If it hadn't been for Lady appearing from the dark and the mysterious footsteps, who knew what Brodie might have done?

"What were you doing by the river?" Molly asked the dog. "Who were you with?"

Lady looked as if she'd dearly love to explain what she'd been doing, but settled for licking Molly's hand instead.

She felt numb as she readied Arlie for bed. She needed to find Adam and tell him what had happened. But what if she found Brodie with him? What if Brodie saw her talking to Adam?

I'll make you real sorry . . .

He would. No matter what the consequences, he would exact his revenge. She'd have to be careful. She needed to be certain Brodie was elsewhere and then she'd find Adam. She'd tell him about his threats, show him the bruises on her arms. She'd make sure Adam understood that they could not be taken lightly. She had to convince him that Brodie had proven himself to be capable of seeing his threats through. It took more will than she ever thought she possessed to keep herself from going to Adam now. But in her mind's eye, she could see Brodie sitting with Adam at their campfire, just waiting for her to make the fatal error. She would have to wait until everyone else was asleep.

By the time she climbed into the wagon, Arlie was already deep in slumber, sprawled on his pallet between Molly's and Mrs. Imogene's. Weary beyond words, she lay down to wait while the sick feeling of dread pounded at her temples. Even Mrs. Imogene's ferocious snoring could not chase away her fear.

In the center of the corralled wagons, the cattle lowed and shifted. The horses roped off to the side nickered in response, in harmony with the orchestrated rasping and chirping of insects in the night. Fires had been banked, and campsites set ready for the morning. She sat up and peered out the opening in the back of the wagon, trying to gauge if she should go now or wait a few more minutes.

Suddenly, an inhuman scream came from the mass of milling cattle and then they were moving like a tide crashing toward shore. Molly scrambled back as the throng surged forward and the wild-eyed beasts stampeded into the wagons.

The Tates' schooner shook with the force of the massive animals slamming against it as they all tried at once to escape through the narrow openings in between the wagons. The sound of splintering wood cracked the night and shouts of panic and cries of terror rose from the waking campers. Horses screamed and reared, breaking their tethers to race away from the frantic herd.

Arlie scrambled into Molly's arms and Mrs. Imogene jerked out of sleep with a "Lord save us!" Molly watched in horror as two oxen careened broadside into the Swansons' wagon and sent it crashing to its side. The shrieks that came from within ricocheted through her head. Frenzied, the beasts collided with another wagon and rocked it crazily on its wheels before it smashed to its side amid more screams.

The destruction and terrifying pandemonium seemed to last forever. Molly and Mrs. Imogene held hands and prayed while Arlie clung to them, sobbing with fear. When at last the rumbling din subsided and the stampede made it free of the wagons, three had been overturned and many more damaged. The quiet rang in Molly's ears, pierced only by the disbelieving gasps of the survivors.

With Arlie clutched in her arms, Molly and Mrs. Imogene joined the other emigrants that staggered toward the center of camp, staring at the damage with shocked eyes and open mouths. Those that had endured the worst of it huddled together, looking as lost as abandoned children.

Molly saw Adam hastily pulling on his suspenders as he pushed his way through the crowd to her side. Wordlessly he stopped before her. Oblivious to the chaos around them, Adam and Molly faced one another in silence. Before either could speak, Captain Hanson began calling to the men. Adam exhaled, looking as if he meant to say something, but settled for a gentle touch to her cheek. Reluctantly, he turned to join the others.

chapter forty-three

"DID you hear me?" Craig demanded. "I've got bad news."

His voice yanked Tess out of Molly's world as violently and as suddenly as she'd been thrust into it. The effect made her reel. She was in Tori's house. Craig Weston sat across from her at the kitchen table. But she was pinioned by the duplicity of the moment and she couldn't separate, couldn't staunch the aches in her body or the burn of her lungs. She stood suddenly and knocked her chair on to the floor.

"Tess? What is it? You look—" Craig jumped up and steadied her as she swayed on her feet.

"I need to use the bathroom."

She fled up the stairs, closed herself in the small tiled room, and leaned back against the door. Her breath came in ragged gulps and her stomach churned with fear and confusion and the certainty that what came next would be much, much worse.

She flinched at the sight of herself in the mirror. Had she expected to see Molly in the reflection? Or was it the terrified eyes staring from her pale, drawn face that made her heart freeze in her chest? She splashed cold water on her cheeks, wincing as she reached for a towel. She didn't need to push her sleeves up to identify the cause of the pain. Brodie's hands had nearly crushed her bones, hadn't they? Still the sight of the dark, ugly imprints on her skin made her groan. She sank on to the closed lid of the toilet, holding herself as her worlds collided with force enough to stop her breath, to squeeze the very life out of her. It was too much. She couldn't take it anymore.

A knock on the door jerked her to her feet.

"Tess?"

"Yes. I'll be right out."

"No rush. I was just checking to see if you were okay."

"Of course. I'm fine." How long had she been in here? Time ceased to have meaning. In Tess's world, it was marked by a deviant standard.

She fumbled to push down the sleeves of her blouse and comb her fingers through her hair. But nothing could smooth the raw terror from her face. Brodie meant to kill Molly. She knew it with a certainty that denied reason. Equally terrifying, he'd used Arlie without qualm, without remorse. He wouldn't hesitate to kill the child as well. Tess thought of Purcy and the threat in his mutilation.

"God, no."

She hurried back to the kitchen, giving Caitlin a reassuring glance as she passed through the living room. But Caitlin wasn't fooled. The pools of her eyes glowed with knowledge that Tess couldn't deny.

We're there. Bad guy.

When she reached the table, she found Craig with the Jesus picture in his hands, staring at the papers she'd so hastily hidden beneath it. The map lay face up. The safe was open. Craig shook his head, confused.

"What is this?"

"You don't know?"

He put down the picture and picked up the map. "I'd heard rumors, but I didn't . . . They're building it on the other side of the ranch? Is that it? Is that why—?" He gripped the page hard, crumpling the edges as anger flooded red into his face.

"Where did you get these, Tess?"

"I found them."

"Who have you told about them?"

"Why?"

"Don't you get it? God, how could I have missed this?" He turned away, running a hand through his hair. The breath he released was burdened with disbelief. "Grant was so convinced that Dad's accident was just that. Smith, he kept insisting that it was unfortunate, but nothing more. Ochoa was the only one who believed me, but even he couldn't prove anything."

"What are you talking about, Craig?"

"Grant had been fighting with Dad almost since the day he came back. I kept asking myself, why? Why would he come back here when no one wanted him to? He carted out that bullshit story about the horses. Grant's not a rancher any more than I am. But now I get it. He knew. He knew about this resort and he wanted in. Dad told me he was going to change his will. But he never had the chance."

"Craig, slow down. Listen to yourself. Listen to what—"

"Grant didn't give him the chance to change it. Grant wasn't going to take the chance of losing the ranch."

"You're accusing Grant of killing your dad over property?"

"Money. Grant's used to living the high life, but now he's broke. What he didn't piss away he used on lawyers to keep him out of jail. He can't afford a cup of coffee at Lydia's— Oh, God."

Craig slumped into his chair. He covered his face with his hands and made a sound of despair.

"Lydia. Tess, I came here to tell you. I didn't want you to hear about it from a stranger. They found Lydia today, dead. Killed. Her body was left in the refrigerator."

"Lydia was murdered?"

Craig picked up the map and looked at it. "She called me earlier, when I was leaving for the cemetery. I was short with her. I was late and I didn't have time. But she was upset. She said she needed to tell me something, but not on the phone."

"She called me, too. It was on the answering machine. And then when I came home from getting Caitlin, the message was erased and . . ." She paused, looking in the living room where Caitlin sat, absorbing every word. "There was another threat."

Craig stared at something beyond Tess's shoulders, as if seeking words in the distance. "She knew something, and Grant killed her before she could tell."

Tess's mouth went dry and her heart seemed to seize up inside her. "Where is he now, Craig?"

"With Smith and Ochoa. They went to the ranch to search

it. Tess, they think they're going to find Tori's body there."

The words seemed to echo up from a tunnel. Tori's body? They thought they'd find her body at Grant's place? Lydia dead? She couldn't believe it. It was as if she'd gotten to the last two pieces of a puzzle only to discover they were from another pattern and would never fit. And yet, hadn't Craig been warning her about Grant all along?

She shook her head, sick with the feeling of betrayal— sickened by the voice in her head that still refused to believe it. Even faced with this evidence, she couldn't accept it. Grant was not a murderer. No matter what the evidence was, Grant could not have done what they said. He was a good man. A man she loved.

The assertion seemed to center her. Grant was innocent. She took a deep breath, holding firm to her belief. And she loved him.

She looked at Craig, intending to tell him this. To convince him that he was wrong. But without warning another feeling swept over her, one that came with the familiar cold. This time there was no chance to brace for it. The echo was on her in an instant.

chapter forty-four

AS far as Molly could tell, it appeared no one had been seriously injured in the stampede, but she didn't need to see the troubled and discouraged face of Captain Hanson to know the damage to equipment and supplies was considerable. By dawn he had reluctantly agreed that there must be a halt to their travel until repairs could be made and the rest of the animals found. They might be stopped for as many as three days. Three days when they were already so far behind.

She spent the morning helping her neighbors sort through the chaos and it wasn't until after she had put Arlie down for his nap that she could go in search of Adam. Brodie's threats had not paled in the aftermath of the stampede. If anything, those terrifying moments of hell had only solidified her feelings of desperation. The journey itself presented too many opportunities for catastrophe without the added danger from one of their own.

As she drew near the Weston wagon, she heard voices and slowed down. Brodie was there. Every instinct shouted for her to bolt, but cautiously she sidled up just out of sight.

"Are you mad at me, Adam?" Brodie was asking.

His question sounded childlike; his voice was timid and needy. She could easily picture his forlorn expression as he made his appeal for reassurance. Her stomach knotted with a twist of anger and deep, undeniable fear. He played the part so well—had been mastering it his entire life. How could she begin to convince Adam that beneath the angelic face lurked the soul of the devil?

"I'm not mad," Adam was saying. Footsteps and sounds of harnesses jangling followed.

"You sure seem like you are. It's because of the lies she told you, isn't it?"

"I'm not mad at you. I'm just checking our gear. I want to make sure nothing was damaged in the stampede."

"That sure was scary, wasn't it? Wonder what made them take off like they did," Brodie said.

"Do you?" Adam asked sharply.

"Well, sure. Don't you?"

"Where were you last night, Brodie?"

"What do you mean? I was here with you. Don't you remember? We drunk coffee and—"

"I woke up just before the stampede and you were gone."

"Why, that must've been when I went out in the bushes to relieve myself."

The wagon concealed Molly from the two men, but at the same time prevented her from observing what *they* were doing. The pause that followed Brodie's statement felt weighted and Molly wished she could see Adam's face.

"What happened to your hand?" Adam asked.

"Burned it in the fire last night."

"I didn't see it happen. Why didn't you tell me about it?"

"Didn't think I'd hurt it too bad, but later it started troubling me so I just got me some of Molly's bandage strips and wrapped it. It's fine now."

"When did you do that? When you got up last night?"

Adam's voice was taut with impatience but Brodie didn't seem to notice.

"Yeah, when I got up," he answered brightly.

"God dammit, Brodie, don't lie to me," Adam snapped. "Where the hell were you?"

"I wasn't nowhere, honest, Adam. I wasn't doing nothing. I just . . . I just . . . I went to check on Molly and Arlie, that's all. I wanted to see that they were all right."

Through a tight ringing in her ears, she heard the reins being tossed angrily to the ground. Molly shuddered, picturing Brodie skulking outside their wagon.

"You stay away from them," Adam said in a tight, hoarse voice. "You hear me? You stay away from them."

"I wasn't hurting them or nothing. Just looking to see that they was okay."

"The Tates are looking after them. They don't need you stumbling around scaring the cattle."

"I didn't scare anyone, Adam."

"How do you know?" Adam demanded.

Molly bit her lip and looked back at the damaged wagons and the men working on the repairs. Adam thought Brodie had something to do with what happened last night. Every time she thought she was beginning to understand the depths of Brodie's evil and obsession, she learned something that froze her blood even more. She trusted Adam's instincts. As much as he loved his brother, he would not make such claims mildly. *Brodie, what have you done?* People could have been trampled, killed . . . Holding her breath, she chanced a peek around to see Adam towering over Brodie, his face tight with suppressed anger.

"I don't want to tell you again. You keep away from them. Both of them."

"She's turned you against me, hasn't she? Just like Vanessa tried to do. You wouldn't never talk to me like this before she came."

"No one's turned me against you—"

"Yes, she has. She tells lies about me and you believe her. You take her side just like you did her whore of a sis—"

Adam had started to turn away, but now he spun around and grabbed Brodie by the front of his shirt. He hauled Brodie up, the fury on his face enough to finally strike Brodie mute. "God damn you," Adam said through clenched teeth. "God damn you—"

Brodie struggled free and staggered a few steps away, staring at Adam with open fear and bewildered hurt. Adam's chest heaved with the gulping breaths he took. He glared at his brother with such a mixture of rage and pain, confusion and conviction, that Brodie cowered beneath the complexity of it.

"You never would have hurt me before," Brodie whispered.

Molly couldn't catch her breath as the resentment in his voice pulled the very air from her lungs. Carefully she took a step back, and another, and then she turned and flat-out ran to the safety of the Tates' camp.

She was out of breath and perspiring when she reached it, Adam's confrontation with Brodie still echoing in her ears.

"Lord, child," Mrs. Imogene said, looking up from a big black pot over the fire where she was stirring the filling for her buttermilk pie. "You look like a ghost is chasing you."

Molly brushed back the hair from her face with a shaking hand and tried to quell her fear. "I thought I heard Arlie crying."

"No, he's still sound asleep after last night, poor baby. I could use a nap myself."

Mrs. Imogene grinned at that ridiculous wish. Just because they would be settled for the next few days didn't mean there weren't a million things to be done.

"Did you hear about that plump Irish girl, Miss Molly?" she said, glancing up. "I do believe she's one who belongs to the O'Keefe family."

Molly let out a heavy breath and tried to focus on Mrs. Imogene's words, but her thoughts were still with Adam and Brodie. Her skin felt clammy and her heart was racing, but Mrs. Imogene was too intent on her pie filling to notice.

"You know the one," she was saying as she gave the mixture a steady churn. "She's quite large for her age and covered in freckles, poor dear. She's always following young Mr. Weston and begging to play with that little dog that belongs to Arlie's father."

"It's Brodie's dog," she corrected automatically.

Mrs. Imogene frowned with disapproval at Molly's casual use of Brodie's Christian name. "Well, however it is, she hasn't been seen since the stampede."

"What?"

"Her mother said she came up missing in the night."

Molly sat down on the bench beside the fire before her legs gave out and pitched her into it.

"Only thing that makes sense is she got caught up in it. No one knows much more than that. However, I do believe that the way her folks let her run wild, it isn't any wonder they can't find her. I'm surprised the Indians haven't found opportunity to be off with her." She dipped a small spoonful of the thickening filling out to taste and then tapped the spoon against the side of the pot. "I am praying to the Almighty that she's just wandered a bit and will be found. I suggest others do the same."

chapter forty-five

AS if beckoned by some unseen signal, a band of Indians appeared on the outskirts of camp that afternoon. Perhaps they'd seen the stampeding animals or the men out searching for them and instinctively known that the party would be staying put for a day or two. Perhaps it was luck that they arrived heavily stocked with goods to trade. Perhaps it was fate.

Most of the cattle had been recovered early in the morning. By suppertime, the remaining stragglers were shepherded back inside their makeshift corral. Only two beasts remained missing.

The body of Alice Ann O'Keefe was found not far beyond the outskirts of camp. She'd been trampled by the oxen and come to rest beneath the low scrub. Her mother, heavy with child, huddled within their wagon, weeping and wailing her daughter's name for the rest of the day and long into the night. Mr. O'Keefe and his four oldest sons dug a grave for her and Adam carved a cherub to mount atop her wooden cross. Though more times than not Alice Ann had brought mischief where she went, they all felt the loss of her youth and vitality.

Each of the many times Molly went in search of Adam, she found Brodie by his side. So far, she'd managed to leave without being seen by either. Brodie had known exactly what he was doing when he'd threatened her with Arlie. While she would have faced him one on one no matter what the danger to herself, she could not do the same with Arlie's life at risk.

Just before supper, Molly unexpectedly came upon the captain engaged in deep conversation with Mr. Tate and Mrs. Imogene. She hesitated, not wishing to interrupt, but their words drifted with the smoke from the campfire and froze her in place.

"She was trampled, Captain," Mr. Tate was saying. "How could he tell what else had happened to her before that?"

Captain Hanson glanced at Mrs. Imogene and then quickly away. "Mr. O'Keefe said things were done. I believe him to be speaking the truth."

Molly's gasp drew Hanson's attention. Taking Mr. Tate by the arm, he lowered his voice and guided the other man away.

Mrs. Imogene looked pale and shaken as she made her way back to the wagon and began her supper preparations. Molly followed, wanting to question her about the men's conversation. But Mrs. Imogene's silence felt thick and sullied, coating them both in an impenetrable residue until at last Molly could stand it no longer.

"Were they talking about Alice Ann?" she finally asked.

Mrs. Imogene bit her lip. "I'm afraid so, child."

"But what happened? I thought—"

Arlie cried out from the wagon where he'd been napping, interrupting her. Frustrated, she considered letting him cry for a few minutes but Mrs. Imogene jumped up and hurried off, calling over her shoulder, "I'll get him," before Molly had the chance to argue or delay her.

The captain had said things were done. The horrifying images conjured by that ill-defined statement filled her head and made her sick to her stomach. But what followed on the heels of it was worse still. In her mind, she replayed the moments before Lady had jumped from the embankment. Arlie had cried out, "Ay Ay," and Molly had assumed it was Lady that he'd yelled for. But now . . . She pictured Alice Ann pressing against Brodie, saying "I will," to his retreating back.

Numb, she moved away from camp, needing to find a place to be alone. Overhead a black arrow of geese glided through the turbid sky, honking to one another as they flew in formation. She found a rock close enough to the wagons to be safe, yet far enough away that she could think.

She stared at the settlement of wagons, but what she saw was Alice Ann's chubby face, eyes gleaming with longing as she stared at Brodie during Rosie's funeral. Alice Ann, coarsely suggestive as she rubbed her body against Brodie's in an open invitation for trouble. And then Alice Ann, forever still beneath a crude cross and a carved cherub.

She didn't know how long she'd sat there before footsteps drew her from the horrible thoughts. Before she could turn to see who approached, an all-too-familiar voice said, "Evening, Molly."

She jumped to her feet, and faced Brodie while the urge to run slammed against her numbing fear and pinned her in place. What did he want? How long had he been watching her? He came closer, his footsteps shuffling furtively over the dust-packed ground.

Things were done to Alice Ann. What things? What terrible things was Brodie capable of?

"Why are you out here all by yourself?" he asked.

"I was praying and you've interrupted me."

"What are you praying for?"

"For the soul of young Alice Ann," she said.

He nodded. "Sure is sad what happened to her."

His pale eyes shone like granite and the dark spikes of his lashes framed his false sincerity, his feigned bafflement over the twists of fate that could snatch a young girl from her family and leave her for dead beneath a stampeding herd of oxen.

"Sad is a rather mild euphemism for what happened to her, wouldn't you say?"

Brodie eyed her warily. "I guess."

"Bad enough to have her body thrashed by the hooves of stampeding oxen, but the other was even worse . . ."

"What are you talking about?"

Molly shrugged and let her silence and shrewd look speak for her. Emotion played across Brodie's face. Suspicion, surprise, fear, confusion, cunning, anger . . .

"Well, she got trampled," he repeated. "They can't blame anyone but her for getting run down by a bunch of dumb ox."

"Oh, I think they can. The captain said things were done to Alice Ann," Molly said. "Apparently whoever hurt her wasn't very smart."

"She was trampled."

"Oxen don't have hands or fingers, though it is true that they aren't very smart either."

"You can't prove anything."

"Maybe not. I don't know exactly what *things* were done to her. But you do, don't you, Brodie? Do you think Adam would lie to the captain if asked your whereabouts during the stampede?"

Brodie closed the distance between them with such sudden ferocity that she had no time to step back. She braced for his violence, fearing in that split second that she'd gone too far, but he stopped inches from her and leaned in. He'd grown so much over the months of travel that she had to tip her head back to look into the coldness of his eyes.

He still had the baby-smooth skin and the downy soft facial hair of a young boy. It would be months before he would shave for the first time. Longer still before he would fully mature into a man. But there was nothing innocent in the expression that distorted his features. Nothing childlike in the gleam of malice that shone from within.

In his face she saw everything he could and would do. She saw cruelty without conscience. She saw jealousy that had festered into something so twisted, so perverse, that it struck her mute with fear. How had this monster come from the same woman as Adam? How could the goodness of Rosie be any part of Brodie?

"Are you scared?" he whispered in her ear. He trailed his fingers up her arms like a lover, pausing as they drew level with her breasts to brush the sides in an intimate caress. Her shudder brought a hateful stillness in him that reeked of satisfaction.

"No one's going to believe I touched that fat girl," he murmured, his breath a flutter against her ear. "I'm just a boy, myself. Isn't that what Adam says?"

She was afraid to move. Afraid to stand still. The violence beneath his soft words and gentle touch terrified her more than wild ranting and vicious blows. This Brodie was more dangerous than any she'd seen so far.

"I see the little wheels going round and round in your head, Molly," he said, moving closer, still holding her in that deceptively light grip. Now his thighs pressed against hers, the slope of his belly fitted at the base of her ribs. His breathing was a little ragged now, his touch greedy and insidious. "You don't want to speak against me, Molly. I know you don't want to tell anyone stories about what I might have done when you know I'll have to prove you wrong. You'd be a fool to do that." He pressed his damp mouth to the hot skin below her ear and nibbled.

Her voice felt like sandpaper against her dry throat. That she managed to push it past her trembling lips was unbelievable. "I've already talked to Adam and he does believe me. He's probably looking for you right now."

Brodie's fingers tightened on her arms and slowly he raised his head and looked into her face. She tried to meet his eyes, she tried to boldly stare back, but he was like a wild animal feigning tameness to lure his prey closer. He would hurt her without qualm. He could kill her without conscience. He'd all but promised to do the same to Arlie. The sour smell of his breath and pungent odor of his body rushed at her in a wave.

"Did I ever tell you how Vanessa liked to call me up to her little room when no one was around? She liked to show me things. She showed me lots of things, things I wanted. She thought she'd use me against Adam. But I couldn't let her do that. Adam, he's all I got."

She lifted her chin higher and forced herself to look at him. "The captain knows everything, Brodie. He knows about Dewey and Alice Ann. And if you hurt me, he'll know it was you who did it. He's not Adam. He has no love for you and he owes you no loyalty."

Brodie's stare was deep and probing, his face inches from hers, his eyes opaque with suspicion. But within she saw something that gave her strength and courage. She raised her brows, curling her lips with all the arrogance she could muster. "I told you all on my first night in Ohio. I am not Vanessa. Don't imagine you can play me like you did her."

She wrenched herself free of his grasp and purposefully turned her back on him. Beneath her skirts her legs shook, but they held her up and carried her away without failing. Her ears rang with the effort of listening for his footsteps, but she heard nothing behind her, nothing but the sound of her own tortured breathing as she forced one foot in front of the other. She didn't dare look back until she was safely within the circle of wagons.

WITH the last of their hours of leisure dwindling away, lively trading went on between the emigrants and the band of Indians. While Molly worried over what to do, the other campers seemed to be unanimously caught up in festive gaming. Molly wished she, too, could lose herself like the others, but she was trapped in an agony of indecision. She knew that Brodie would never permit her to betray him. How he would stop her seemed equally clear. But guilt over poor Alice Ann rode heavily on Molly's shoulders. If she'd spoken out against Brodie earlier, perhaps the girl would still be alive. Molly could not risk delaying again.

After circling the camp several times without finding Adam or the captain, Molly returned to the Tates' wagon. Mrs. Imogene was there, sitting in her chair stroking Lady's silky head and watching Arlie play at her feet. True to his word, Adam had carved the boy a herd of horses, which Arlie galloped happily over the dirt. When he saw her, he let loose a gleeful squeal. He grasped a horse in each chubby fist and lifted them for her to see.

"No, no!" he shouted.

Despite the worries that made her feel ancient and exhausted, Molly smiled. "Horse," she told him. "Horse."

"No, no!" he agreed, waving them in the air.

"Have you seen Adam, Mrs. Imogene?" she asked as she knelt down beside Arlie.

"He's with the men over yonder." She nodded in the direction of the teepees set up on the outskirts of camp. "Everyone's been talking about the things those Indians brought with them. About an hour ago talk started about some game they were planning for later. Mr. Tate says there's going to be a competition of shooting and riding between us and the Indians."

Molly had heard the rumors herself that the Indians had

everything, from baskets—beautifully woven and tight enough
to hold water—to skins so soft and warm that they were fit for
a baby's swaddling. They even had rifles and ammunition.
Some of the campers said they were of the Washoe tribes,
renowned for their basket weaving. Some thought them Utes,
and still others suspected they were Snake Indians. Molly even
heard talk that they were Apaches and must be watched around
the clock lest they all wake to find their children's throats
slashed and their women violated, though so far none of the
Indians they'd encountered had shown the slightest tendency
to violence. On the contrary, they'd been friendly and helpful,
very different from what she had imagined in Ohio.

No one knew for certain from which tribe these Indians
came, but what was clear was that they had amassed an amazing store of goods to trade and barter. With time on their
hands, the emigrants cared less about who they were and more
about what they had.

"I heard that the oldest O'Keefe boy is going to race," she
continued. "Captain Hanson and your Mr. Weston are known
for their aim, so I imagine they'll be chosen to shoot. Everyone is running around like the second coming is about. Guess
they're planning a victory party already." She shook her head.
"Even Mrs. O'Keefe has come out to watch."

Surprised, Molly looked across the camp. Mrs. O'Keefe
sat in front of their wagon, a shawl wrapped around her thin
shoulders, the ends resting on her swollen belly. Molly knew
that it was common for furious celebration to follow the sinking misery of death. She understood that survivors must at
times rejoice in life to prevent themselves from lying down
with the deceased, but it seemed wrong that the mourning of
Alice Ann should be so short.

Later, Molly and Mrs. Imogene watched the proceedings
from a distance. At the inner circle stood Adam and Captain
Hanson. Adam had been inaccessible the entire afternoon and
Molly's anxiety had worn a pain in her head that felt crippling.
There was nothing she could do short of charging into the
midst of things, demanding that Adam give her his attention.

While the idea crossed her mind, she knew she had to approach Adam carefully. She had no doubt that Brodie had planted seeds of deception in his brother. She must be careful not to become entwined in the thorny sprouts of their growth.

Late afternoon found the wagons circled in their customary corral and the livestock milling around inside. Their lowing mingled with the snatches of conversations that filtered through the slanted rays of sunshine. Word of the wealth that the band of Indians brought had spread as far as the company that followed them. With the day's end came three young men from that party to join the wagering.

The women had gathered at a vantage point on the outskirts of camp. Mrs. Imogene sent Molly to join them. "I'm done in, Miss Molly, but you go on without me. I'd rather stay here with our little man than watch the big ones act foolish."

From where Molly stood with the other women, she had a clear vision of Adam and the men on one side of the fire. On the other side were an ancient Indian and half a dozen young warriors who squatted, listening intently to the rise and fall of the elder's voice. In the background, two squaws in pale buckskin dresses spoke quietly while they made their meal preparations. A naked little boy of Arlie's age played nearby.

Whiskey jugs were passed freely between the surrounding men, Indian and white alike, and the spicy scent of excitement mingled with the aroma of burning buffalo chips and roasting meat.

Buffalo skins towered behind the Indians alongside other soft furs, rugs, cradleboards, baskets, hatchets, and saddles. Molly heard much speculation on how many of the saddles and firearms were contraband, pilfered from other emigrants they'd met along the way. They'd all heard stories of Indians trading horses for goods, and the unlucky emigrant who thought he'd made a good deal only to find out that the horses were stolen from a company either ahead or behind him. Molly had to admire their audacity if not their morals.

The emigrants had amassed their own stores of fortune to be wagered. Copper cooking pots and heavy skillets, hammers, bright bolts of fabric that had been wrangled away from their women, whiskey, and sugar waited in neat segregation for the contest.

Molly stood beside Mrs. Carlisle, who told her that she'd already missed much of the competition. Adam had won his round against a stern-faced Indian who had eyes of coal and skin that glowed like bronze. The captain had not been so lucky and had lost to a brash young man who, according to Mrs. Carlisle, had been a poor sport about it. A few items of the wagered goods had exchanged hands, but the majority was left to ride on the race. The next competitors were about to take their places and all eyes were on them.

The last glow of sunset slipped beneath the desert landscape and the campfires lit the night. The women huddled together, watching as the tension became thick as the hissing smoke from the campfires. Molly looked for Adam, but couldn't find him in the tight cluster of men. Quietly, she slipped away from Mrs. Carlisle's side and went to where Storm waited beside the Indians' horses, hoping to find him there. The darkness cloaked her and the ground muffled her footsteps as she moved behind the spectators. Everyone was focused on the competition and no one even noticed her.

As she drew near the tethered horses, she saw a shadow moving between them. Adam, she thought, with mixed emotions. The very thought of him filled her with happiness, but the burden of Brodie's treachery overwhelmed her. The horses whinnied nervously as he went about his business.

"Adam?" she said softly.

He was bent low between Storm and another horse, so intent on whatever he was doing that he didn't hear her. She moved closer and tried again.

"Adam?"

He jumped straight up with a low shout that spooked both horses. His gelding danced to the side and the other horse let loose a snort of alarm and pulled away.

"Whoa," he said. "Settle down, you stupid horses."

It wasn't Adam. No sooner had the realization dawned than

another shape parted the cluster of applauding men and crossed over to join the first.

"Everything all right, Brodie?" Adam asked. "The race is next."

"Damn Indian horses are scaring Storm. Had to calm him down."

The shouting crescendoed into deafening cries as, in the distance, the victor triumphed over his contender. Brodie took Storm by the halter and led him forward. Molly held her breath, watching as he passed unknowingly in front of her. She moved not a muscle, but as he drew even with her, he paused. Slowly he turned his head and looked right into her face.

There was promise in his eyes, hatred in the hard set of his jaw, violence in the thin line of his lips.

"Come on, Brodie," Adam said sharply. "They're ready to start."

As if to confirm his statement, one of the Indian men materialized beside them, took his own horse by the halter, and led it into the circle.

Knowing that whatever advantage she might have gained by waiting to find Adam alone had been destroyed by her slip, Molly quickly moved from the shadows. "Adam, I must speak with you," she said.

Brodie's pale features flickered like bone in the moonlight as Adam turned with surprise. He frowned at her, obviously wondering where she'd come from before he noticed the anxiety that must surely have been written in bold lines across her face. "What's wrong?" he asked with deep concern. He handed Storm's reins to Brodie and stepped to her side.

"They're waiting on us," Brodie snapped.

Lowering his head closer to Molly, Adam looked deeply in her eyes. "What is it, Molly?"

"Weston, you coming?" Hanson demanded from the edge of the clearing.

Adam glanced over his shoulder with impatience. "Go on," he said to Brodie.

"The captain wants you out there," Brodie said.

"Weston!" the captain shouted again.

"Molly, I—"

Panic swelled up inside her. She'd shown her cards before she could play her hand. "I know. You must go. But Adam, as soon as the race is over, we must talk. It's urgent."

He nodded, looking as if he might say to hell with the race. For a moment, she thought he would. But then one of the men in their party appeared. "Captain's shoutin' for you, Adam."

"I'll find you when it's over," he told her.

She nodded and let him go. Dry mouthed, she watched the circle part and then close again as he and Brodie made their way to the center. Just before he moved out of sight, Brodie looked back at her.

Vanessa thought she'd use me against Adam. But I couldn't let her do that.

He wouldn't let Molly do it either. In that look she'd seen determination. She'd seen desperation. She'd seen vengeance.

She felt sick when she rejoined the women. She tried to re-assure herself that Adam would find her and she would make things right. What could Brodie do in the meantime? Nothing. But a part of her didn't believe it. She watched Brodie as he stood at Adam's side, the harnessed gelding still in his grasp as Walter O'Keefe stepped forth to meet his opponent. The Indian he would ride against was a small, nimble man that looked quick enough to win the race on foot. By comparison, Walter seemed a giant.

The Indian took a running jump and leaped onto the horse he would ride bareback. Walter swung into the saddle with equal grace. An expectant hush fell over the crowd.

The old Indian she'd seen earlier moved to a designated place where two poles had been hammered into the ground and a thin twine tethered between them. A weaving, erratic course had been set and marked with poles and flags. The riders would navigate the markers at top speed and the first to break the twine barrier was the winner.

She willed Adam to turn around, to see her, but his attention was riveted on Walter, who sat firm in Adam's saddle. Beside him the Indian looked like an extension of the sleek animal he sat astride. The men on both sides shouted encouragements as the horses pranced with nervous excitement. Feeding on the nervous energy that snapped with the sparks from the fire, the animals tossed their heads and pawed the ground at the start line. Molly wanted to shriek for it all to be over.

The old Indian raised a red handkerchief. A collective breath was caught and held. The handkerchief came down. The horses bolted forward, rounding bends and corners at breakneck speed before opening up to gallop the stretches. The shadows chased and taunted them across the moonlit vista. At the end of the stretch they made hairpin turns and started back to the crowd. Walter was holding his own with the Indian, and the cheers rose and echoed in the night.

Mrs. Carlisle reached out and grabbed Molly's hand in her own as she chanted, "Go, Walter, go."

As if hearing her, Storm darted forward, stretching his strides with a valiant effort. They were neck and neck. And then something went wrong.

The Indian's horse seemed to falter, her stride broken in midstep. Riding without harness or saddle, the Indian lurched to the side while urging the horse to move. The horse tossed her head back at him and reared up on her back legs, off balance and panicked. The rider launched himself off as the horse propelled herself over onto her back. Her terrified whinnies made Molly's blood run cold.

As if time had slowed to a crawl, Molly watched Walter and Storm sail across the finish line.

A deathly silence fell over the Indians as wild whoops and calls echoed through the emigrant camp. The Indian's horse struggled to her feet and limped to a stop a few feet away. Stunned, the Indians moved to the animal and the unseated rider. Peering through the dark, Molly watched as Adam shouldered his way to where they stood.

"What happened?" Molly asked Mrs. Carlisle.

"I don't quite know. Something made that horse balk."

A rumble rose from the tight circle of Indians and foreign words flew like hail.

Molly saw the old Indian who'd waved the flag push

through to the horse. Following the wild gesticulations, he bent and lifted her front hoof to inspect it. For one moment, the Indians were silent.

And then suddenly the shouts rose again, this time there was no mistaking the words for anything but accusations, hurled like rocks at the band of emigrants. Too far away to see it all, too close not to understand the consequences, the women drew together.

Adam and the captain were speaking to the elder and the enraged rider, trying to reason with them about whatever had happened. But swift as a bullet, the first Indian broke free with a cry of rage and ran into the pack of whites like a wild animal.

It happened so quickly that some of the emigrants were still parading around with furs draped on their shoulders and whiskey jugs in their hands, laughing and clowning for the others. With horror, Molly realized that weapons had been drawn. The first gunshot split the air with a resounding crack and then a war cry pierced the din.

chapter forty-six

"TESS? What's wrong with you? Tess?"

Craig's voice cut through the thundering pandemonium, hauling her back from the past even as she fought to remain. "Oh my God," she whispered, still seeing the bloodlust on the faces surrounding Molly. What was happening now? What next? Where was Arlie? What would—

"Here, drink this."

Craig thrust a glass of water into her hand and helped her back to the chair at the table. She didn't know when she'd stood up. She couldn't remember what had happened before—

Her gaze settled on the papers and memory rushed at her. Grant, Smith, Lydia all in partnership to— Lydia, murdered, and Grant . . . what had Craig said? That the sheriff was at his house right now, looking for Tori's body? But Tori was buried back in Ohio and—

No, Vanessa was buried in Ohio. Tori was still missing. Tess swiveled around to see Caitlin, who sat on the couch. The TV jabbered incessantly in front of her, but she was watching Tess with widened eyes. She was trying to sort out fact from fantasy, past from present, meaning from message.

Again and again Tess had wracked her brain, trying to understand why Molly's life was playing like a loop tape over in Tess's head. It all hinged on Tori and Vanessa . . . didn't it? Wasn't that the only reasonable explanation?

Reasonable? Ridiculous.

And yet the answer she sought was just at the edge of her thoughts, just beyond her grasp—evasive, yet there. Just out of reach.

"Tess, I'm sorry," Craig was saying. "I shouldn't have sprung that on you. I was so upset when I saw these papers. I can't let him get away with this. I don't care if he is my brother, he's gone too far. I let it go before and I've spent my life paying the price. I can't live with myself if I do it again."

"Let what go before? What are you talking about, Craig?"

He looked at her with torment. The pain she saw in his eyes was like a cavern so deep no light could ever penetrate it. "You remember at the cemetery? You remember what I told you about the church fire?"

"Of course. You lost your mother in that fire."

"I didn't lose her, Tess. She was taken away from me and from my father. That morning she'd caught Grant doing drugs behind the barn. He's been an abuser since he was a teenager. If he wasn't drunk, he was high or tripping. He'd have never made it though high school without Lydia doing all his homework for him. When Mom caught him, she threatened to send him to a camp. You know, one of those tough love places? Only back then, they didn't even pretend that love was involved. She wanted to send him to this place that a member of her church had sent her son. That kid came back a changed boy."

Craig gave her a meaningful look that left little doubt as to what kind of changes the boy had undergone.

"There was no way Grant was going to let anyone change him that way."

"You're saying . . ."

"He started the fire. He burned it down."

Tess shook her head. He was lying. But then she saw the article on the table, the scrawled words on the notebook paper. Church fire.

"How you do know it was Grant?"

For a long moment, Craig stood, his hands bracketing words he couldn't speak. When his voice finally came, it was low and broken. "I never said a word about it. I knew, and I never said a word. Not a word. He murdered our mother, destroyed our father, and I never said a word."

chapter forty-seven

SMITH hadn't found anything of significance in Grant's house. Grant wasn't surprised—he didn't have anything to hide. But he didn't trust Smith. He wouldn't put it past the man to plant something. After Craig's command performance earlier, Grant was doubly cautious. There'd been a look exchanged between his brother and the sheriff that had raised the hair at the back of Grant's neck. It was a look of alliance. A handoff in a relay only the two of them understood.

When Ochoa's radio crackled and a voice came through letting them know that backup had arrived, Smith told his deputy to go outside and meet them. Ochoa looked like he wanted to argue, but the sheriff pulled rank with little more than a warning look.

After he left, Grant watched Smith's every move. The sheriff's determination to find something struck Grant as personal. But the thing he couldn't figure out was what he'd done to arouse that kind of reaction in Smith.

His thoughts circled in his head as the sheriff concluded his search. He was so caught up in them, that he didn't look up as he followed Smith out the door, until he was on the porch. Only then did he realize how far from *over* the sheriff's search really was. The sight of the official vehicles scattered in front of his house froze him in place. His insides felt like they were squeezed in a clamp that just kept tightening. He was hot, cold. Scared.

"What the hell is this?" he demanded.

"Looks to me like it's a helluva mess, Grant," Sheriff Smith said, placing one black cowboy boot on the bottom step of the porch and looking up at him. The soles on the boots were rubber and Grant was willing to bet they'd never waded through shit. The same could not be said for their owner, however. The heels were too high and Smith probably imagined they compensated for his vertically challenged physique. In reality, they only accented it. The leather had a gloss that spoke of imitation, just like the consoling smile on Smith's wide face. "I'll bet your balls are drawn up as tight as acorns about now," he said.

He'd got that right, but Grant wasn't about to show it.

"The women in your life don't seem to have much of a chance, do they, Grant? From your mother right down the line to the temporary help, you're bad news. Bad news."

Somehow Grant managed to keep his expression impassive, but Smith's words, his tone, his meaning, detonated a hidden mine buried deep in Grant's subconscious. He felt the reverberations of the explosion rock him on his feet until he had to reach out for the back of one of the iron porch chairs to steady himself.

No, the women in his life didn't stand a chance. He'd carried the burden of guilt for his mother's death each day since she'd been gone. She was always there, in his thoughts. His father couldn't bear the mention of her name and Grant felt sometimes that he had unconsciously tried to wipe her from his memory. He'd learned over the years to dull the pain with booze and drugs. As he stood there, he wished he could do that now. But he was clean, sober, and remembering . . .

Behind Smith the detectives went to and fro, holding impromptu discussions next to an unmarked van, pointing out items of note to one another. But what Grant saw was another day, another time, when officers had swarmed the Weston ranch.

Smith said something else, but Grant wasn't listening. Instead he was hearing his dad reply to the devastating words old Sheriff Turner had uttered. He was seeing his father's face as he took in just what Turner was trying to tell him.

The church . . . the fire . . . Ellen dead . . . a boy seen running away . . .

Like a beast awakened, the latent memory raised its head and growled.

"Christ," Grant breathed, unaware he'd spoken until Smith turned back to him with a gleam of satisfaction.

"You almost killed your ex-wife is how I hear it. Drinking and driving don't mix. Big movie star like you should know that. We've been watching Tori France's house since she turned up missing. I hear you paid her sister a visit. A couple of them. I wonder if she knows what you're all about, movie star."

Grant heaved his thoughts from the past, knowing that if he didn't keep it together, he would be lost. But the memory was as powerful as the actual event. It all came back to him, breaking through to the pain he'd managed to numb for over twenty years.

"I'd say your cover is blown."

Grant answered, "You don't have a damn thing on me. Not one damn thing."

Smith's pleasant grin sent a whole new wave of horror washing over Grant. Before he could even begin to react, a shout came from the somewhere in the vicinity of the broken-down shed.

"Sheriff, they've got a DB," Hector said as he jogged to stop at the foot of the porch. He took his hat off and swiped his brow with his sleeve. The green tinge of his skin and the tremble in his hand left Grant without a doubt as to what a DB was.

"Tori France?"

Hector gulped a couple of breaths before he managed, "In a trash bag with the refuse by the shed. Looks like she was going into the incinerator with the rest of the debris."

"That's—this is crazy," Grant snarled. "I was just cleaning out the deadwood yesterday. There weren't any trash bags over there. God damn it, this is a setup."

Smith shook his head, glancing sideways at Grant. "You are one sick fuck, movie star. One sick fuck." He hiked his pants up over his sagging beer belly and patted his gun. "I guess they'll be raking this place with a toothbrush before they're through. Hector, why don't you take our movie star down and book him. I'm going to swing over to let Ms. Carson know we found her sister."

"Sheriff," Hector said, stopping Smith. "There's more. She doesn't look like she's been dead that long." Hector swallowed and took another deep breath. "There's no decomposition. Just lividity."

Smith cast Grant an assessing glance. "I hope for your sake we don't find evidence that you kept her alive somewhere on the property."

"You'll only find it if you brought it with you."

Ochoa stood on the bottom step looking from Grant to the sheriff. "It's more like she was preserved, Sheriff. Maybe in a refrigerator. Like Lydia."

The sheriff looked stunned, but all he said was, "Take him in, Hector." To Grant, he added, "I'll give my condolences to your girlfriend."

Grant's eyes narrowed in on Smith's face. The notion that this was all personal came back like a tidal wave. Why? Why was he going to see her? "Stay away from Tess," Grant said.

"I think it's you that better stay away from her," Smith replied coldly.

Grant watched the sheriff get into his car with a feeling as close to panic as anything he'd ever known. He didn't know what the hell was going on. He didn't know why anyone would murder Tori France and then leave her body on his property. He inhaled, mentally backing away from the land mine he stumbled on to. His property. That's what it was now that Dad was dead. His property.

"Why is *he* going to tell her?" Grant said quietly. "Doesn't he usually send you to do the dirty jobs like informing the family?"

Hector glanced at him and back at the sheriff. His brows pulled together over his eyes, but he didn't answer. Still, Grant knew that Hector was asking himself the same question.

"We've never had a case this big," Hector answered. "He wants to make sure things are done right."

"Sure. He's a by-the-book kind of guy, isn't he?"

"That's right."

Hector pulled his handcuffs from his belt and faced Grant to read him his rights. Time was running out and the sight of those shiny silver bands made Grant feel desperate in a way he hadn't felt since checking himself into rehab. A fine sheen of sweat broke out on his face. It was wrong, all wrong that Smith was going to deliver the sad news to Tess Carson. It wasn't natural. Smith could care less about Tess and her grief. He was going there for another reason. Grant saw again the look exchanged between Craig and Smith earlier. It had been brief, but weighted with meaning.

"Carl," Hector called to one of the deputies milling around. "I need you to drive me and Weston to the station."

"It didn't feel right to you either, did it?" Grant interrupted. "Craig, playing the injured party and Smith pretending to re-strain him. There's something going on, Hector. I know you feel it too. Smith wouldn't go to see Tess out of the goodness of his heart. Why is he going, then? Why?"

Carl had joined them now. He held the passenger door of his cruiser open, looking back and forth between Ochoa and Weston with a puzzled expression.

Grant pressed his point. "You're asking yourself why he isn't here, gloating over the arrest, aren't you? Isn't that what you'd expect? And funny how Tori France appeared from nowhere. Isn't it? You've been all over this place, Hector. You didn't miss a body."

Hector looked up and stared into Grant's eyes. Feeling as if he'd been falling and had just caught hold of something, Grant changed tactics. "If I killed her, why would I keep her around to find? Where's the reason in that? Why would I want to kill Tori France?"

"She saw what you did to your daddy," Carl offered help-fully.

"Bullshit. I was in Piney River."

"Seeing a man about a horse," Hector said. "Yeah, we got that."

Grant made a sound deep in his throat. "Dammit, Hector, this isn't right. I didn't kill her. I didn't kill anyone. You've got the wrong man."

"I'll let a judge tell me that," Hector said. "If it's true."

Moving behind him, Hector pulled Grant's resisting left arm back and locked it inside the cuff, but as he reached for the right hand, a sound in the distance caught his attention. The noise was faint, barely discernable above the voices and bustle of the investigators, but Grant heard it and so did Hector. He turned and locked eyes with Hector as the echo of it reverberated through their thoughts.

"That was a gun," Hector said, as if against his will.

chapter forty-eight

TESS felt as if she'd finally, irretrievably lost her mind. Somewhere, sometime Molly was trapped in the midst of a savage riot, Arlie was on the other side of camp, and Adam was smack in the middle. And Tess was here, trying to digest the reality that the man she'd fallen in love with was a monster capable of killing his own mother. Did that mean he'd murdered Lydia as well? Her throat constricted as she thought of her missing sister . . . of Grant in her arms. Could he be that cold, that inhuman, that he could abduct Tori and then passionately make love to Tess?

"Did you hear that?" Craig asked. "Someone is at the door."

Tess had been so ensnared in her spiraling thoughts, she hadn't heard anything. Craig stood and opened the front door. Sheriff Smith waited on the doorstep. She wanted to shout at Craig not to let him in, but the sheriff had already entered.

The small house seemed to shrink as he took off his hat and stepped into the kitchen. It stilled with his pause and darkened with his frown. Tess looked at Craig with wide eyes. Smith intercepted the silent exchange. His stare sliced between Tess and Craig.

Stifling the overwhelming desire to step back, Tess said, "Why are you here, Sheriff?"

His expression remained suspicious and somehow predatory, but he spoke gently. "I'm afraid I have some bad news, Tess."

Instinctively Tess looked past him to Caitlin, still sitting on the couch. The young girl stared at the sheriff's back as if willing him away. But the sheriff was oblivious to her, oblivious to the fact that she seemed to already know what he was going to say.

"We've found your sister's body. We're going to charge Grant Weston with her murder."

Spoken, the words became real, the fear justified, the world unhinged. The words "found" and "body" became horrifying images that crowded her mind. Dark and swirling, the visions sucked at her feet and tried to pull her down.

The sheriff shifted his weight, and fiddled with his hat, looking everywhere but at Tess.

"I know it's a shock, but at least you have closure. It would be worse to never know," Smith was saying.

He tossed his hat onto the table. It landed with a soft *whoosh* on top of Jesus's face. Craig moved closer, blocking her view of Smith, trying to turn her into his arms, but she pushed him away. The air became thick and grainy, and the sheriff, Craig, and the noise of the TV all faded out. There was a ringing in her ears and her skin felt hot as she watched everything slow down.

Smith took a step to the table. Craig reached out as if to stop him, but it was too late. Too late.

Smith cursed under his breath as he lifted the map with blunt fingers. He stared at it, looked at Craig, then back at the map. His other hand snaked out and lifted the tax records. And then he saw the safe. The lid was shut, but not locked. It popped open when he touched the latch. When his head snapped up, the expression on his face and the coldness in his flat eyes broke through her fog. The labored breath he took hissed, and his eyes became dark beads of anger.

"What's going on here?" Smith demanded.

"Nothing," Tess said, too quickly.

Craig moved toward her again and put a shielding arm around her shoulders. "It's okay, Tess. Everything is going to be all right."

Smith's attention honed in on the protective hold Craig had on her and the viciousness of his look made her want to scream. He no longer seemed to care about the answer to his question. Suddenly he slammed his fist down on the tabletop.

The picture of Jesus bounced up and clattered down. In the other room Caitlin jumped.

"You think you're going to double-cross me?" Smith said, staring at Craig. "You dumb son of a bitch. You think you can pull a fast one on *me*? Christ almighty, if it wasn't for me, one of your gambling buddies would have fed you to the bears months ago. You get that? I'm what's standing between bear food and prison."

The ringing in Tess's ears grew louder and louder, only now she realized it wasn't ringing. It was screaming, screaming from the past as it tried to punch through and yank her back. But she couldn't let it. The scene around her flickered and dimmed as she fought the power of the echo.

The sheriff was red faced with fury. He grabbed the edge of the table and flipped it over with a crash of splintering wood. In two steps he'd lunged forward, planted a beefy hand on Craig's chest, and shoved him back against the counter. Tess took the opportunity to move away.

"You stupid *goddamsonofabitch*!" he repeated, his soft voice contradicted his violent expression. "Did you think you could screw me? Are you really that stupid? I've been covering your ass from the first step and now you think you can fuck with *me*?"

Molly's screams split Tess's head as Smith reached for his gun. His fingers curved around the grip as the burning pressure of Molly's overworked lungs filled Tess's chest. She tried to run forward, to reach Caitlin before the blackness overwhelmed her, but her limbs were too heavy. She couldn't move. She heard the soft *fwush* as Smith's gun cleared the holster, and over it the terrified screams of women and children as they ran between the schooners to escape the violence surrounding them. From the kitchen, she saw Caitlin standing just inside the door. Her eyes were wide with terror. She reached out, but it was too late. Tess was already vanishing, already stepping through the threshold. But for one last second, the world snapped into focus.

Run, she mouthed to Caitlin.

Caitlin shook her head, staring with terror.

Caitlin, RUN!

She shouted with her silence, using her eyes to convey the message. Swallowing, Caitlin took a step backward, toward the door.

The past churned like a twister around her. Molly sprinted into the center of hell as Tess stared down the barrel of Smith's gun.

"You're blowing it," Craig shouted. "She doesn't know anything. She found it. For Christ's sake, what the hell are you doing?"

"What I've been doing all along. Cleaning up after you."

The cries from Molly's world exploded around her, drowning out the sound of Smith pulling the trigger, obliterating the crash of her own body slamming into the wall.

chapter forty-nine

FROM all around, gunfire blasted the night. Molly darted out from the protection of the wagons and ran blindly, thinking only of reaching Arlie and Mrs. Imogene. An arrow slammed into the wagon just behind her with an explosion of splintering wood that added to the deafening roar of violence. There were no more than thirty men, but locked in battle, they'd somehow doubled again and again until it seemed like there were hundreds of men firing thousands of shots.

Tucking her head, she ran blindly. The Tates' wagon was just ahead, but there was no sign of Mrs. Imogene or Arlie. Praying that they'd hidden and were safe, she rounded the other side and ran hard into Brodie. Stunned, she staggered back. She had one split second to realize the collision was not an accident before the flash of his long hunting knife glinted and he lunged.

Molly screamed as she stumbled backward and changed course as the tips of his fingers clawed the back of her dress. Sweat streamed down her face and the smoke stung her eyes. Gunfire cracked over her head and the hot whoosh of the burning wagons scorched her skin as she raced through camp, caught between the warring instincts of survival and the need to find Arlie and protect him.

Her indecision gave Brodie the advantage he needed. He grabbed her from behind and jabbed with his knife just as she whirled and pushed. The blade sank between her ribs but she felt only rage. She twisted, kicked, and scratched, managing to leverage his arm to her mouth and bite down as hard as she could. His shout mingled with the bitter taste of blood and the pounding urgency that thrust her away and back into the melee.

Everything became fuzzy then, as if she was looking through a fine layer of muslin.

Arlie's scream pierced her disorientation and she turned in time to see him bolt from the shelter of a wagon.

"No, go back!" she cried, but her voice was lost in the clamor. She stumbled toward him, refusing to allow her legs to buckle. She couldn't focus and her ribs felt as if they were on fire. Each step shot pain straight through her.

Arlie's face was bright red and he was sobbing hysterically as he dodged the fighting men and panicked animals. The oxen surged to the other side of their makeshift corral and broke free. Suddenly, a horse and rider loomed in front of Molly. She swerved to the side, narrowly avoiding colliding with them. Like a nightmare vision, the mounted Indian lifted a weapon, waved it at her, and spun away.

She was on her feet again in an instant, running to the last place she'd seen Arlie. But a band of fighters had come between them. As she pushed forward, unearthly cries pierced the rumble and brought it to a crescendo.

It hurt to breathe, hurt to think. She didn't dare look back. Didn't dare give in to the terror that threatened to cripple her. She heard curses flung at the Indians, violent cries hurled at the emigrants, while gunfire seemed to come from everywhere at once. The sounds of mayhem chilled her.

There seemed to be fire all around yet through the smoke she saw a small huddled shape. Arlie. He'd crouched down in the heart of the battle and wrapped his arms around his head.

She charged into the clearing, through the madness that stood in her way. But with each pounding step came snatches of terror. There was Arlie, just ahead. There on the left, the Indian on horseback. An arrow whizzed past her, someone screamed, Molly tripped, hit the ground and scrambled back to her feet, ignoring the pain and the warmth spreading from the wound Brodie had inflicted on her. She had to get to Arlie. She saw him, not far now, but the Indian loomed just a breath away from him. And then suddenly everything was closer, faster, hitting her like gunfire.

The Indian on horseback reared up, and the horse's hooves slashed the air over Arlie's head before they came down, missing him by inches. The Indian let loose a cry of rage and pain that reverberated through her. He held something up and with horror Molly realized it was the body of the naked little boy she'd seen playing by the Indians' camp earlier. Blood oozed from a ghastly hole in the boy's head. The Indian flung the body across his horse's neck. In one swift movement, he scooped Arlie up on the horse and they spun around and rode away.

Molly screamed Arlie's name and the boy answered with a cry of terror.

She ran after him, pushing her legs to move faster than the speeding horse, but it was no use.

"Arlie!" she shrieked.

Her lungs felt like they would explode and her left side had gone numb, but still she kept running. Reason told her to stop, to find Adam, but reason didn't drive her. She could still see the Indian's horse and Arlie's legs writhing with terror. If she could see him, there was still hope.

chapter fifty

GRANT didn't wait for Hector to make a decision. Though faint, it was unmistakable. A gunshot—and the report had come from the direction of Tori's house. *Tess.* Acting without thought, Grant jerked free of Hector's hold, throwing a shoulder down and into Carl's midsection as he went. Dodging away, he opened up and ran, his one hand still encased in the silver bracelet. The loose end of the cuff swung wildly, striking him with glancing blows that hurt like hell.

He heard Hector shouting to stop or he'd shoot. Grant doubted the deputy had the balls to shoot a fleeing man in the back right up until the first bullet whizzed past his ear. Still, he didn't hesitate, didn't pause as he raced to the split rail fence and launched himself over. He dropped into a fluid roll that saved him from a second bullet but earned him another hard whack, this time in the head, from the loose handcuff. He was on his feet and moving toward Midnight. A horse without brakes. She was the best chance he had. The horse danced back in surprise at the suddenness of his movements, but she'd been in as many movies as he had and was trained to ride through gunfire and mayhem. She, at least, didn't know it was for real this time.

Grant grabbed two fistfuls of mane as he swung onto her bare back and spurred her with his heels. There would be no second chance, no director to call cut and shoot the scene again. He was in it for his life and he held on.

He heard another gunshot as a bullet tore through his shoulder. He looked at the red stain on his shirt with surprise. Of course he'd been shot; he *was* an escaping murderer.

But he couldn't live with another death on his hands. The guilt of it had nearly destroyed him once. If he had to face it again, his life would not be worth living.

As he galloped past the stunned Hector, he looked down the barrel of a gun pointed right at his head. It was too late to do anything but pray.

chapter fifty-one

MOLLY had cleared the ring of wagons and now only moonlight guided her. The dark shadows absorbed everything but the sound of her footsteps and her ragged gulps of air. She was afraid to look down at the throbbing stab wound, afraid that what she saw would immobilize her.

The Indian was no longer in sight, but she could make out the prints from his horse and she followed them. Gradually her steps slowed though her mind still raced ahead with Arlie. And then she was walking, gasping with frustration as her will urged her faster than her body could go.

She had no idea how long she'd been running, how far she'd come, or where she was. When she glanced back, there was no sign of the wagons, the fires, the people.

Her mouth was parched. It hurt to breathe now and at last she looked down at her side. The beige fabric of her dress had a sheen that trapped the moonlight in glowing pleats and creases, but a seeping black stain spread from her ribs down the skirt to the hem. She touched it and her hand came away sticky and damp. Reluctantly she looked back. Midnight drops on the earth marked her weaving trail.

Her legs began to tremble with the effort of moving. She felt hot and queasy. The earth tilted and she fell.

Get up, Molly, get up . . .

The dirt ground into her cheek, mingling with the tears that streamed down her face. Memories played through her mind, mixing with the moment then fluttering away like feathers in the wind. Adam, holding her in his arms. Arlie, screaming for help. Brodie, staring at her with all his hatred.

She tried to get up, but her arms had gone numb and her legs wouldn't move. She clenched her eyes tightly, feeling the life draining out of her in a slow stream. She had to stay alive. Adam would come looking for her and he'd have a trail of blood to follow. Unless he hadn't survived the battle. For all she knew, he was laid out on his death bed, waiting for her to come back. Maybe dead already. The thought was so painful that it pushed away everything else. Alone, frightened, and filled with anguish, she wept. For Adam, for Arlie, for herself.

And then thoughts of Brodie invaded her sorrow like a summer storm, churning the heat inside her into a fierce, violent tempest. Brodie, who had killed her sister, who may have murdered Dewey Yokum and certainly Alice Ann O'Keefe, and slain how many others in the battle he'd caused today, had beaten her as well. Her rage swelled up until it filled every pulsing inch of her body. He would get away with it.

He would smile his innocent smile and he would go on to California, secure in his brother's love and devotion, forever manipulating or removing whoever might try to find a place in Adam's life. Even if Adam didn't believe him, even if Adam saw the truth this time, it would destroy him. Adam would hold himself responsible for his brother's crimes. He would punish himself forever. She clenched her eyes. It wasn't fair.

Fury did what determination could not. She forced her arms to move and pushed herself up to a sit. Slowly, laboriously she got one foot beneath her and then another. She straightened, swaying in place. A cold sweat broke out on her face. Dirt caked the bloodied fabric of her dress, and her side throbbed with each agonizing heartbeat. She looked off in the distance at the endless miles of wilderness. Her vision blurred as she turned to look back the way she'd come. Nothing, forever, there was nothing.

She was shaking, knowing that she wouldn't make it two more steps, when she saw a horse and rider. Waves of blackness washed over her, making her sway. She blinked, peering through the fog of semiconsciousness. Had she really seen someone?

The steady thud of hooves on the ground was her answer.

Yes, Adam . . . he'd come. There was still hope. Her knees threatened to give out, but she kept her balance by sheer will. A small shape running at the horse's side barked twice and then broke free to race toward her. Lady, it was Lady.

Molly began to sob and now her legs did give out, pitching her forward in a heap of twisted skirts and pain. With a soft, compassionate whine, Lady slowed to a stop and moved in to sniff and comfort her.

Molly touched the silky head and managed a smile. "I knew you'd come for me."

She looked out at the horse and rider, who were closing the distance quickly. Her smile wavered.

"No," she rasped. She tried to stand again, but it was no use. She couldn't even feel her legs now, let alone command them. Crying out from the pain, she rolled to her stomach and tried to crawl. Lady kept pace beside her, whining with confusion. The horse stopped behind her and still she kept moving, inching herself away from the evil that dismounted and approached.

"I promised Adam I'd bring you back," he said.

Molly blinked as tears streamed from her eyes. What did he say? He'd promised Adam? So Adam was alive?

"He's in a bad way himself." Brodie's voice hitched. "Thought he was dead when I found him, but Mrs. Imogene is tending him now. She thinks he'll pull through." Brodie took a deep, shaking breath. "Even all shot up, he still wanted to come after you. You're all he cares about now."

The anger and loathing in his voice cut through the pain. His boots crunched the earth as he stepped beside her. She tried to crawl away.

"Where do you think you're going, Molly?"

She shook her head, but didn't stop. Her elbows were raw and bleeding and her ribs felt like they were on fire. She was fading in and out now, but her hatred and fear of Brodie Weston kept her moving.

"You're a stubborn one," he said. "I'll give you that."

"Go. To. Hell."

He reached down and grabbed her arm, turning her with an ease that infuriated her. She willed her legs to move, to kick, to run, but they didn't even twitch in response. Her arms and hands were becoming numb as well, as if they'd already died. Colors danced behind her eyes. Brodie knelt beside her, his face filling her vision, igniting a burning fury in her failing heart.

Gently he gripped the front of her dress and drew her up. She had no choice but to let him support her. Brodie stared into her eyes with a kindness that contradicted everything she knew to be true. Her lips were dry and cracked and she struggled to wet them.

"It's all right now," Brodie whispered. "Everything is going to be all right now."

She didn't see the knife before it sliced into her, bringing new agony. He pushed it unhesitatingly deep and twisted it, all the while gazing down at her with a look of concern on his face. He held her tight as she screamed and blackness rushed in. Confident now that she could not speak out and betray him, he eased her to the dirt. He used her skirts to wipe the blood from his knife and hands.

She watched as if from above, knowing that these were the last moments of her life. Knowing that with her, the truth would die. Her rage became a heat that emanated from her core. Brodie paused, as if surprised by the gust of it against his skin. She whispered something, and with a quizzical cock of his head, Brodie leaned closer to catch the words.

Her pitifully weak fingers closed over his wrist, sliding without apparent purpose to his hand.

"What did you say?"

Molly moved with a speed that belied her dying body. She wrenched the knife from his unresisting fingers before he could comprehend what she'd done. With her last ounce of strength she brought the knife up, but she was too slow. Too slow.

The blade glanced off his chest, leaving a long angry welt that immediately oozed blood. But it wasn't a mortal wound. He touched it and rubbed the blood between his fingers.

"I will haunt you from the grave," she whispered hoarsely. "I will haunt you from the grave."

She stared into his face, her last thought reaching through the darkness to find Adam and Arlie. But her dying breath was filled with Brodie and the hatred that consumed her.

chapter fifty-two

CAITLIN ran for her life. She could hear the horse chasing her down. She could hear the screams of the people she knew. She didn't understand, but she'd always known they were coming for her. The echo of the shot the sheriff had fired at her aunt still rang in her ears. Another shot split the air above her head as she ran. But this wasn't right. She knew inside her that it wasn't right. The only way to end it was to go back.

She lurched to a halt on the road and turned around just as the thundering hooves of the charging horse reached her ears. She peered at it as time seemed to warp itself. Her pounding heart lurched with the memory of another horse, another rider who had scooped her up and taken her away from everything she'd known and loved. But it hadn't really been her. And this rider was different. This rider was Mr. Weston. The good one. She lifted her arms as he thundered toward her and, in one fluid move, scooped her up onto the horse.

"Hurry," she said. "Or you'll be too late."

chapter fifty-three

THE blaze of Molly's rage pierced Tess, burrowed deep into her heart, and then exploded in a flash that brought her bolt upright with widened eyes. The sheriff's bullet had cut through her side, making it hard to breathe, hard to stay conscious. Through a red haze of pain Tess saw the sheriff turn his gun on Craig.

"No," Craig shouted. "You got it wrong. I'm in. I'm in!"

"You fuck me and you'll wish I'd shot you here."

Craig nodded quickly.

Tess staggered to her feet and swayed in place, watching Craig with narrowed eyes, understanding at last that he'd played her. All along her heart had told her that Grant was worth touching, worth loving. She'd known he wasn't capable of the things his brother claimed he'd done.

Craig looked back at her with an expression that hinted at regret while it spoke of choices already made. It was down to the two of them, now just as it had been then. Grant wouldn't rush through the door and save the day any more than Adam had.

Craig put his hands out, palms up, and shook his head. For a moment he faltered as he searched for something to say. Like he hadn't meant for it to end this way. Or it wasn't his fault.

But it *was* his fault. It had been for a hundred years. His jealousy, his warped lust for things he couldn't have, his penchant for violence. He'd learned to hide it well and he'd nearly convinced her that he was the good brother, like Brodie had tried to convince Molly a lifetime ago. She'd played a new part this time, but the end was still the same.

"I'll haunt you from the grave."

The skin on Craig's face paled until it seemed she could see through him to the terror inside.

The ending would be the same for Tess as it was for Molly. But not for Caitlin. Molly died not knowing what became of Arlie. Perhaps she'd been fortunate. Perhaps not. All Tess knew was that *she* would not do the same. She may die on this day, but not before she knew her niece was safe.

"It wasn't supposed to be this way," Craig said. "I didn't have a choice. I've never had a fucking choice."

"Am I supposed to feel sorry for you? What about my sister? Lydia? Your own father?"

"I told you, it wasn't supposed to happen this way. All I wanted was the ranch. But he wouldn't give it to me. I told him he could live someplace better but he went crazy."

"So you killed him?"

"He attacked me."

"You said he was practically an invalid, Craig. How could he attack you?"

"I didn't mean for it—"

"For Christ's sake, get over it," Smith barked. "Quit bawling and go get the kid."

"Let her go," Tess cried. "She's just a little girl. Leave her alone."

"We're cleaning house. Everything goes."

Tess launched herself at Smith, knocking him back against the wall with a thump. Cursing, he brought the butt of his gun down hard on her head. She was bleeding badly and the unstaunched loss of blood made her weak. Blackness swirled all around her but she fought hard to stay conscious. The weight of destiny bore down heavily upon her, but in her head, Molly still shouted her fury. Somewhere outside, a little girl needed her.

As if through a haze, she saw the butcher block on the counter, the knives slotted neatly inside. She stayed down, crouched and unthreatening, gathering her strength before she lunged toward them. She fumbled, then managed to pull the largest knife free and turn it on Craig. The blade sliced into his arm and he screamed like a woman.

Insane rage darkened his face an instant before he slammed her against the counter. She swung again, but Craig chopped her arm down hard on the edge of the countertop. She heard a snap, then felt blinding pain. He grabbed the knife from her unresisting fingers and slashed at her with it.

Tess slid to the floor. Blackness crowded her vision and the familiar feeling of Molly's life slipping away settled over Tess's heart.

"Weston, get the hell outside and find that kid or you're going to burn for all of it alone. You got me? I will skin you and put you on display."

Smith's voice came to her from a distance. She couldn't hold on much longer. But there was Caitlin . . .

Suddenly the screen door slammed and at that second Caitlin raced in. Only for a moment, it wasn't Caitlin. It was a small boy looking through her eyes like a masked phantom.

"No, Caity," Tess whispered. "Run away. Run away."

Caitlin shook her head, eyes solemn and steady. "I'm not supposed to run. I come back. I'm supposed to come back."

A sound gurgled up and out Craig's opened mouth as Caitlin glared at him, her features frozen hard and cold. And then suddenly Grant was barreling into the room. Smith moved to intercept him and the two men crashed to the floor. Smith waved his gun, trying for a shot or a hit, unable to get leverage for either. Grant swung the loose handcuff at his face and it connected with a crack that sent the sheriff's head snapping back against the wooden floor. Grant followed it with his fist, pounding Smith again and again until the sheriff lay motionless.

He came . . . This time, he came . . .

Tess felt her life slipping away, relieved that Grant had come even as she accepted that he'd come too late. Slowly Grant stood and faced his brother. Caitlin waited between them.

"It's over," Grant said. "I'm ending it now."

"That sounds like a line from one of your shitty movies," Craig answered. His expression of fear blackened to cruel rage. He charged his brother, but just as Craig raised his knife and plunged it down, another shadow materialized at the door. With deadly accuracy, Hector Ochoa put a bullet through Craig's heart. The knife clattered to the floor.

chapter fifty-four

TESS didn't remember the ambulance ride to the hospital or any of the days following it. Smith's gunshot had pierced her lung, missing her heart by an inch. She regained consciousness only for brief moments that were punctuated by the sterile smell of the hospital, the blinding brightness of the room, and the feeling that death was very near. She had no concept of how long she floundered in the black world of unconsciousness, but sometime during those vacant hours she came face to face with Molly.

"You have a life to live yet," Molly told her. As Tess tried to explain that she was tired, that she felt lost, a light cut through the darkness and standing in its fringes were Vanessa, Tori, her mother, Mrs. Imogene, and Rosie. She searched for Adam, knowing that if she saw his face, she would not need to return. But Adam was not there and another voice was calling to her, its timbre deep and worn from exhaustion but familiar and loved. Tess followed it.

She opened her eyes to see Grant Weston sitting at her bedside, holding her hand, drawing her back to the living. Next to him was Caitlin, looking small and defenseless, yet resolutely whole. The three stared at one another, closing a circle that had been agape for too long. Finally Caitlin smiled and gently hugged Tess.

"I knew you'd come for me," she whispered.

"I knew I'd find you," Tess answered.

Neither offered an explanation. Neither ever spoke of it again. Whatever Grant made of the exchange, he, too, kept to himself.

Still holding her hand, he gazed at her with an expression of gratitude, as if she had saved him from death and not the other way around. When the nurses finally made him leave, he pressed a kiss to her forehead and said, "I'll never lose you again."

His words were an oath. She knew.

Later she learned that Grant had been at her side through all the dark hours. He'd had to be wrestled away to have his own wounds treated. In more ways than could be counted, he'd saved her life.

The entire town of Mountain Bend was stunned to learn that their charming elementary school principal and efficient sheriff both harbored dark secrets. Tess, of course, already knew. Faced with multiple murder charges, Smith's lawyer advised him to plea-bargain and Smith came clean about the sequence of events that led up to his attempted murder of Tess. With Craig dead, there was no one to dispute his story. At the time Smith met him, Craig's compulsive gambling had put him in debt to several unscrupulous lenders—men that would have killed him had he not been able to pay up. In short, Craig was a desperate man.

According to Smith, for years Craig had managed to keep his gambling problem concealed and debts under control by stealing from his father, but when Grant's money ran out and the checks stopped arriving, Craig was left to find a new source to supplement his paltry income. Tori, in her efforts to reconcile the Weston ranch's finances, had discovered that the money Grant sent never made it to the bank. When she revealed this to Frank Weston, he'd confronted his son and all hell broke loose. By Smith's account, Craig claimed the murder of his father was accidental, but Tori's untimely return to the Weston ranch had made her an unwanted witness whom Craig was forced to kill. He'd stashed her body in Lydia's huge freezer until he'd felt the time was right to plant the body behind Grant's shed.

Perhaps the most tragic victim of it all was Lydia Hughes. Tess learned that it was Lydia who had tried to warn her away from Mountain Bend. Lydia who had burned the pictures and mutilated Caitlin's stuffed kitty in an effort to scare Tess back to New York. When Craig found out, he'd killed her too.

Smith maintained that he was no more than an accessory to the crimes. He'd cleaned up the messes or sabotaged the crime scenes, but he had no hand in the murders. Deputy Ochoa explained to Grant and Tess how Smith's years in law enforcement had made him a pro at setting up a crime scene—but he was a little too smart for his own good and he'd taken for granted that the local yokels would be inept. He was wrong.

Tess and Grant didn't talk much about what had happened. They'd both lost loved ones and it was painful to think of it. But Tess knew that they would have to talk about it openly if they ever hoped to heal. Grant began one night by telling her about the church fire that had taken his mother. In halting tones of confession, Grant told her that it was Craig who'd been caught doing drugs the morning of the church fire. Craig was always difficult, and as he grew older, his behavior became more extreme and violent. Unable to control their aggressive son, Grant's parents had decided to seek intervention in the form of a militaristic camp for troubled boys. When he learned of their plans, Craig had gone crazy with fury, threatening them all in his rage.

"I remember the week before the fire," Grant told Tess. "Lydia had come to me for help. She was beat up. I think Craig raped her, but she denied it. She was pregnant, though, and Craig refused responsibility. I promised to help her. She wanted me to take her into Sacramento to see a doctor."

As it turned out, she didn't need the appointment she'd scheduled. The day before Grant was to take her, she'd gone to church to pray for guidance.

It was a miracle Lydia had survived the fire when so many others hadn't. Her brush with death had conveniently terminated her pregnancy—or perhaps it was no coincidence. Craig came to see her in the hospital, and she held his hand and smiled into his face. Grant always suspected that she'd known who started it. He'd had his own suspicions, but no charges were ever brought against anyone. A boy was seen running through the church grounds just before the fire began, and old Sheriff Turner had questioned all the parents in town before calling it a tragic accident and closing the case. Grant had been so desperate to believe it was just an accident that he'd let himself be convinced. Craig went off to his tough love camp and returned a changed man.

But when Grant looked at him, he saw fire. He left for Hollywood on the next bus out. Years followed in which he'd escaped the memories with alcohol and drugs.

After Grant had cleaned up his act and given up the drinking and drugs for several years, he'd returned to Mountain Bend to mend fences and reclaim his life. But during the time apart his father had become a stranger and his brother had grown to hate him. Perhaps Craig had come to look upon Grant as a jailer, a keeper of his secrets. Who knew what drove the sickness in his mind?

And Tess would never know the motivation for Tori's relationship with Grant's father. She could only hope that it had been one of love. Despite her faults, Tori had deserved to be loved.

Tess shared Grant's pain as she prepared for her sister's funeral. Caitlin was already in counseling and Tess would be spending time on the couch as well, though she would keep her focus on the present traumas and not venture too far into the past. Real or not, she knew Molly's tale would sound crazy and she didn't want to end up in the same place as her mother. Besides, the past was over now. She knew it.

Tess hadn't decided whether or not to tell Grant about the visions, about the terrifying replay of history. Each day that passed without revisiting it made Tess feel like the whole experience had been a dream. Had it really happened?

SIX months later, Grant woke her up with a cup of coffee and the morning paper. She'd moved to the ranch as soon as she was able to finalize the sale on her house in New York and quit her job. She'd said a tearful good-bye to Sara and extracted a promise to keep in touch, and then she'd left behind her life there with amazing ease. Everything she wanted waited for her in California. It always had.

Caitlin was happy here. As the weeks passed, she began to lose that haunted look in her eyes and put on weight. Grant had given her a puppy *and* a kitten the day she and Tess had moved in. She'd named the kitten Purcy and the puppy, of course, Lady. Tess and Grant were married the following weekend, though in Tess's heart, they had been joined a lifetime ago.

"Check the headlines," Grant said, pointing to the paper as he crawled into bed beside her. Tess scooted over so she could rest her head on his shoulder and lifted the newspaper.

WINTER HAVEN SCANDAL EXPOSED, the Piney River headline shouted. She quickly skimmed the article and then read it in earnest. Charges had been brought against a Chicago businessman who had allegedly leaked confidential information to potential investors about the financial proceedings of the prospective resort called Winter Haven. According to the article, the privileged information had been given to several high-powered executives who purchased properties to the north and east of the site. Mountain Bend's sheriff, recently discharged from duty pending criminal legal proceedings, learned of the resort when he was still part of the Chicago PD. According to sources, Smith had pulled over the Chicago property magnate on suspicions of DUI and then let him go. Later Smith was accused of lying about the details of the violation and rescinding the ticket he'd begun to issue. Smith had resigned before a formal investigation was launched and had managed to secure the position of Mountain Bend's sheriff without ever disclosing the details of why he'd left Chicago.

Another piece of the puzzle fell into place.

"Did you read the last part? The whole project has been dumped. Winter Haven investors are looking for a new location."

"I'm glad. I'd hate to see Mountain Bend overrun with tourists. I like it the way it is."

After spending the morning outside with Grant, repairing the shabby fence and giving it a new coat of white that sparkled in the sun, Tess made them lunch. They ate on the porch in peaceful companionship, admiring their handiwork and thinking of things to come. Tess had put Tori's money into a trust fund for Caitlin's future, but with the money she made from her place in New York and a few other investments, she and Grant were able to make some serious changes to the ranch house. Remodeling the kitchen had been first on the list.

She glanced at him, still a little surprised when she realized that this man who had made women worldwide fall in love with just a smile was her husband.

Feeling her gaze, he looked at her. "I love you."

She'd never grow tired of hearing it. "Forever," she murmured back.

As she settled down that evening, Tess flipped through the mail. Grant was upstairs in the shower. Caitlin was outside playing with Lady. At the bottom of the bundle of bills and junk mail was a small package addressed to Tess Weston. Smiling at the name, she opened the package. The brown wrapping came away easily. Inside was a book, printed poorly and bound even worse. It had taken her months to find it, but somehow she'd known it existed.

In her hand she held *One Woman's Journey,* a memoir by Mrs. Imogene Tate.

The original diary had been found by her great-great-grandchildren in 1982. Recognizing it as both an historical account of an incredible journey and a record of their own heritage, Mrs. Imogene's heirs had the diary typeset and copied for the family.

Mrs. Imogene had no children when Molly had known her, but late in life, the good Lord had seen fit to provide her with the child she so longed for. Her son had married and given her many grandchildren. She'd died the matriarch of a large, extended family living outside of Sacramento where she and Mr. Tate had finally settled. Mr. Tate had shown a flair for growing things, and Mrs. Imogene had a green thumb as well. Their orange groves still produced the sweetest of oranges.

The surviving relatives had thought it strange when Tess contacted them and asked if there was a diary, delighted when she'd told them the passages might help solve the mystery of what had happened to the Westons. They remembered the mention of the Weston family, Miss Molly, and their tragedy.

Tess thumbed through the pages, reading Mrs. Imogene's daily entries, the miles covered, the trials of bad water and sickness. She could hear the woman's voice in her head, recall completely the scent of honey lemon drops that was as much a part of her as her ability to quote Bible verse. A wave of nostalgia swamped her as she read, taking her back to days that she should not remember, but did.

Mrs. Imogene wrote about the shock and loss following the Indian attack. There'd been retaliation and ugly warfare on the trail afterward. But neither young Arlie Weston nor Miss Molly Marshall had ever been found. Though there'd been talk among the emigrants about the race and suspicions that somehow Brodie Weston had caused the horrifying events that followed, nothing was ever proven. And when Brodie had returned to camp, bleeding and weak after nearly being murdered by the Indians who'd set upon him while he tried to rescue Miss Molly, the suspicions were hushed. They all felt he was lucky to have escaped with his life, and for the sake of Adam, the matter was dropped.

"Poor Mr. Weston," Mrs. Imogene wrote. *"He never stopped looking for his son and Miss Molly."*

Tess gripped the book with white-knuckled hands.

An envelope was stuck in between the pages in the back. Tess pulled it out. A neat hand had written, "Enclosed are copies of the original newspaper clippings we found in Grandma Imogene's diary. They mention the Weston family, so we thought they might help you in your research."

The first was dated September 1852. There was a picture of a man, and though time had worn much of it away, Tess recognized Brodie Weston. He was dressed in a top hat and tails, smirking at the camera as he escorted two glittering women into a red-carpeted establishment. Beneath the picture were the words "Francis Ambrose Weston Strikes It Rich!" Tess quickly scanned the clipping before going back to read it again. She could hardly believe what it said. Brodie had struck gold, and quite a lot of it. Overnight he'd become a million-aire. There was no mention of Adam.

Poor Mr. Weston, he never stopped looking for his son and Miss Molly.

The second clipping was dated two years later. This one had a picture as well. Tess's eyes widened as she made out the grainy images. Brodie again, but this time there was no top hat, no tails, no women, and definitely no smirk. He was laid in a coffin, hands crossed over his chest. The caption read, "Gold Thief Hanged for Stealing."

The second article was as incredible as the first, yet there was a sense of justice to this one. Brodie had not struck gold after all—he'd lied, cheated, stolen, and murdered for it. Tess stared at the mask of death on Brodie's face. He'd destroyed so many lives . . . death seemed too kind. Carefully she folded the pages and put them back in the envelope.

She returned her attention to the diary. The final pages were dated April 1880—twenty-six years later. Mrs. Imogene must have been near seventy by then. As Tess read the words, she could well imagine the waver in her voice and picture Mrs. Imogene white-haired and wrinkled, but still stubborn and strong.

Last week I made my final journey to San Francisco to visit my sister, she wrote. *One fine afternoon while I was there, we ventured into town to shop and I noticed a young man standing on a street corner. The sight of him brought me to a halt, though it took many moments for me to understand why. He was so familiar that I knew I must have met him before, and yet I could not place his face.*

By some peculiarity, the young man sensed my inter-est and spoke to me. He asked if I knew him. When I said I did not, he apologized for his intrusion. He had hoped for recognition from someone because he knew no one himself. He told me he'd been raised by Indians and only recently had he rejoined the white civilization.

Had my sister not been holding onto my arm, I fear I might have fainted dead away from my shock. I knew at once who he was and in that instant I saw his resemblance to dear Miss Molly, his aunt.

I wished I had news of his father, but I knew nothing of what had happened to him. He left our party as soon as he was able and we never saw him again. In my heart, I fear he searched for Arlie and Miss Molly until his dying day.

Tess paused, thinking back to her first days in Mountain Bend, to the beginning when she'd seen the man on horseback—Adam—from Tori's bedroom window. She thought of his wasted life, of the endless days spent searching. Molly had known he'd feel responsible for Brodie's crimes. Did his shadow still darken the spaces between the trees, forever seeking a life unlived? Tess thought not—not anymore. With this realization came a profound tranquility that seemed to spring from Adam himself. Between Craig's unmasking and defeat, Grant's action to set things right, and her own happiness now with Grant, Tess felt she had helped rewrite the story, so that everyone—here and gone—could rest in peace. Smiling, Tess returned to the diary.

I thought perhaps young Arlie would be able to tell me what had happened to Miss Molly. Brodie insisted that the Indians had taken her as well, but Arlie knew nothing of her fate.

We shared tea that afternoon and he listened to this old woman with rapt attention. I told him what I knew of his father and aunt, of their dreams of owning a ranch where there would be land for miles and a place to raise a family. I confided that I'd thought one day the two would marry and have more children. Finally, with a heavy heart, I told him what I'd read of his uncle and the shame of his life.

Before we said goodbye, he asked me one final question—Did I know his full name? I was never so pleased as to say yes, indeed I did—Francis Arlington Weston! He repeated it with pride and his smile had a satisfied quality as he left me. The good Lord giveth, the good Lord taketh. I must remind myself.

Tess turned the page. There was one last entry.

A letter from Mr. Frank A. Weston arrived today. He has settled in the mountains in a place he describes as endless green meadow, banked against the bend of the mountainside. He calls his new home Mountain Bend for its picturesque setting. He has taken a wife and hopes to live there for all his days. May the good Lord bless them and watch over them.

Sighing, Tess closed the book and went to find her husband.

BERKLEY SENSATION
COMING IN JANUARY 2005

Crimson Moon
by Rebecca York
Needing a fresh start, a young werewolf changes his identity and meets a woman of many secrets—who he must protect or they'll never have a chance to explore the passion boiling up between them.

0-425-19995-9

Derik's Bane
by MaryJanice Davidson
The first novel in the new Wyndham Werwolf Tales from the author of *Undead and Unwed*.

0-425-19997-5

The Wicked Lover
by Julia Ross
Robert Sinclair never expected to catch an intruder in his bedroom—let alone one that's a woman dressed as a man. She says she needs his cravat for a wager, but Robert suspects there's more to this lady-in-disguise.

0-425-19996-7

Stay with Me
by Beverly Long
Sarah Jane Tremont is walking on the beach in L.A. when she is suddenly transported to Wyoming, 1888. Now she's been taken in by a rugged cowboy with a wounded heart that she's destined to heal.

0-425-20062-0

Jane's Warlord

by Angela Knight

The sexy debut novel from
the author of
Master of the Night

The next target of a time travelling killer,
crime reporter Jane Colby finds herself in the
hands of a warlord from the future sent to
protect her—and in his hands is just where
she wants to be.

"CHILLS, THRILLS...[A] SEXY TALE."

—EMMA HOLLY

0-425-19684-4

Available wherever books are sold or at
www.penguin.com

Penguin Group (USA) Inc. Online

What will you be reading tomorrow?

Tom Clancy, Patricia Cornwell, W.E.B. Griffin,
Nora Roberts, William Gibson, Robin Cook,
Brian Jacques, Catherine Coulter, Stephen King,
Dean Koontz, Ken Follett, Clive Cussler,
Eric Jerome Dickey, John Sandford,
Terry McMillan…

You'll find them all at
http://www.penguin.com

*Read excerpts and newsletters, find tour
schedules, and enter contest.*

Subscribe to Penguin Group (USA) Inc. Newsletters
and get an exclusive inside look
at exciting new titles and the authors you love
long before everyone else does.

PENGUIN GROUP (USA) INC. NEWS
http://www.penguin.com/news